*Having four hot husbands
is nice ... but the death threats,
not so much.*

ELEME

MISC

HIJINKS HAI

NTS OF

HIEF

BOOK ONE

ELEMENTS OF

MISCHIEF

HIJINKS HAREM BOOK ONE

TATE JAMES
&
C.M. STUNICH

1

CHAPTER ONE

The sound of shattering glass echoed through the huge, empty kitchen as my wine slipped from my fingers and I choked over what I'd just heard. Clutching my phone to my ear, I took a breath before responding.

"It's going to cost me *how much*?" I needed to clarify because surely I'd just heard him wrong.

"Seventeen thousand, ma'am. And to be honest, that's a stretch. If we ran into any *more* unexpected problems along the way, that price would go up." The man on the other end was so matter-of-fact about it. So uncaring that he was delivering such gut-wrenching news to me. "Look, I'm not going to fuck around on this. It's a seriously old house, and no one has touched that plumbing practically since the day it was installed. I just don't think I have the manpower to spare on a job like this right now."

"But what am I supposed to do?" I hated the fact that my voice had just come out in a whimpering squeak, like a pathetic little girl. I was a tough bitch normally, but not having a toilet in the house was rough. For the last few days, I'd been walking three blocks to an antique store just to pee. "I can't live here without any plumbing, and I already gave up my apartment …"

Of course this guy didn't care about my problems. He didn't care that my grandmother had just died and left me her crumbling Victorian mansion, or that I had just spent nearly every cent to my name on her funeral. Truth was, I would have had to give up my apartment regardless, because I no longer had any way to pay my rent since I was fired from my job at the local coffee shop. They simply hadn't understood why I needed so much time off to care for my grandmother in her final weeks. It was kind of lucky, in that case, that Gram had left me this house or I really would have been out on the street.

"I'd usually tell you to sell it, but no one will buy it without working plumbing so you don't really have a choice here, ma'am." The man was still speaking, oblivious to my descent into desperation, and I sucked in a shaking breath, swiping the dampness off my cheeks with the back of my hand.

"Can you recommend anyone else?" I asked politely, but my voice shook like a leaf in a blizzard. There wasn't anything quite so stressful as having toilets that didn't flush. "I'm not from around here so I don't know where else to find good plumbers."

A long sigh came down the phone.

"Yeah, look, I'll put in a good word for you with my son and his friends. They're just starting out with their own business, so they've probably got the time free to take on a job like this. He might cut you a deal or a payment plan or something, but no guarantees. At least you'll know he learned from the best."

"Oh, god that would be … fucking incredible!" Relief flooded over me. This plumbing *needed* fixing, but I was flat broke. The next door neighbor's tree roots had messed up all of the plumbing in Gram's mansion, meaning none of the taps, toilets or *anything* was working. It had been years since Gram had done any maintenance whatsoever, so who knew how bad the damage was?

"Don't thank me yet," the man grunted, "these boys are known around these parts for having a bit of a wild streak. Personally, I wouldn't hire them—even with my son involved— but you're not exactly in a position to be picky so …"

"Uh, right." *Asshole, no need to rub it in.* "So do you have a contact number for them?"

"No need. I'll let them know about the job and they can get in touch with you." He sounded a bit reluctant, like he was already regretting his suggestion. Hopefully not because of how big this job was? Or maybe he was worried about those famed wild streaks?

But please. Plumbers? How crazy could they be? I imagined them all in their late forties with big bellies and butt cracks covered in wiry hair. No, thank you. How much action could they really be getting?

"Thank you so much, sir. I really appreciate it," I gushed politely. Never hurt to have manners. More flies with honey and all that … Or wait, flies *were* actually more attracted to shit, huh? Which is what I was going to be ankle-deep in if I didn't get this plumbing fixed.

"Don't thank me yet," he muttered, then disconnected our call.

Strange man. Fuck I need more wine.

I eyed the mess of glass and liquid on the tiled floor, then shrugged to myself and grabbed the bottle. No one else was here to judge me. Swigging straight from the bottle, I headed back into the living room to watch *Pretty Little Liars*, my guilty obsession.

HIJINKS HAREM

Hey, it was better than the *Maury Show*, right?
But only by a little.

The obnoxious chiming of my grandmother's doorbell woke me, and I made a mental note to disconnect it. Or at least change the tune. My head was *pounding* and my eyelids felt like they were lined with sandpaper. Cracking one open, I spotted the empty bottle of wine on the carpet in front of my face; I must have passed out in front of the TV.

Groaning, I hauled myself off the couch when the doorbell played its cheery tune once more.

Who the fuck is at my door?

"Fuck me, I'm coming!" I yelled, not caring who I was snapping at. My hangover didn't discriminate. "What?" I slammed the front door open and was momentarily blinded by bright sunlight streaming in from behind my visitor.

"You must be Arizona," a husky voice commented, and I blinked to clear the spots from my vision.

"Ari," I corrected, "who the fuck are you?"

With my eyes adjusting to the light, I inspected my visitor, then blinked a couple more times in case my eyes were playing tricks on me.

The man on my doorstep stood well over six feet, with broad, lumberjack shoulders and rough stubble shading his jaw. His denim blue eyes, framed with lush black lashes, were laughing at me as they dragged a slow path all over my body. My skin seemed to ripple and react with the path of his gaze and I knew my nipples were standing out like headlights through the thin cotton of my tank top.

"Charlie told me you were in need of a plumber. I'm Shane, but everyone just calls me Skeeter …" He held out his hand for me to shake, and threw me a sexy wink.

I should have known, then and there, that I was in for a world of trouble.

"A plumber, right," I said slowly, trying to blink through the haze of my hangover. Were his eyes *really* that blue or did I just have too much grape juice running through my veins to see clearly? I bit my lower lip and shifted slightly, wishing I was wearing more than just an oversized tank and boyshorts … or maybe less? I wasn't sure. Too much wine. "Please, come inside."

As soon as the words left my mouth, I regretted them.

"I'd love to come inside, thank you, darlin'," he purred, his voice warm and liquid, sliding over my body and making me shiver—but not from the cool, October breeze blowing in from outside. No, this shiver was all *heat.*

Of course *he has a Southern accent,* I thought as I stepped aside to let him pass. As if it wasn't bad enough that my entire downstairs bathroom was flooded, now the space between my thighs was, too. *Keep it together, Ari,* I warned myself as Shane —or Skeeter or whatever tall, dark, and handsome wanted to call himself—set down his toolbox and crossed his arms over his massive chest.

"Something the matter, sugar?" he asked, looking me over like maybe, just maybe, he liked what he saw. "You're sweatin' like a whore in church."

"A whore in *what*?" I asked, but maybe I was still nursing a morning after drunk because I didn't push it. "Do you want me to show where the problem areas are?"

Shane's mouth split into a wide grin, this wolfish leer that made me want to pull my shirt down over my panties. Or up. Maybe I wanted to pull it up? *Why didn't I put any friggin' pants on before I let this guy in?!*

"Is the, uh, rest of your team on the way?" I asked casually, wondering if I should, like, offer him some sweet tea or something. Isn't that what Southern people always drink? I felt like I was being particularly *un*hospitable. But what the bloody hell did I know? My mum was from Australia, my dad was from the UK, and I was born in … Hoboken. But that was beside the point. I'd just realized I'd let some random dude into my house without first checking his ID, putting pants on, *or* calling to check any of his references.

I could very well be looking at the next Ted effing Bundy.

Please don't kill me, I thought as I cleared my throat and raised a questioning brow.

"So … Charlie told me that you started this business with some friends?"

"Oh, they're around," Shane said, running a hand up and down the inked perfection of his bicep. It took more effort than I had in me to look away. "Why don't you show me where I should get started, sugar, and we'll get your pipes all cleaned out."

I had no idea how to respond to that.

A few hours later, I decided my frigid Northeastern hospitality was a little *too* cold for comfort and managed to whip up a pitcher of lemonade (while drinking a glass or two or five of Merlot) for Shane. Making my way down the creepy old hallway, I tried to steel myself for yet another quote that I couldn't afford. Sure, Shane was a bit of a weirdo (a hot weirdo), but the truth was, baristas don't exactly make enough to keep savings accounts. I was down a job, had a bank account in the two figure range that needed to last me until I found a new one, and a house with toilets that didn't flush.

What else could go wrong?

I'd just turned the corner toward the downstairs bathroom when I stopped dead in my tracks.

No way.

No fucking way.

The bathroom wall had been opened up by the last plumbing crew I'd had in here to give me a quote, but the pipes were completely dismantled, and coming out of them ... was a *thing*. Yeah, I know, not very descriptive, but whatever it was defied words. I was barista, not a goddamn author.

A trail of water curled out of the pipe, clear and blue and animated, with a head like a dog and horns like a goat. It looked like a fucking dragon. As I stood there gaping, Shane coaxed it even further into the bathroom and stood back with a stupid, cocky male grin on his face.

"What's the damage in there, Reg?" he asked the water-thing as it curled its hooked claws into the wall and hung there like a goddamn lizard.

"I have no clue," it snapped at him, turning its head almost completely around on its watery neck. "I can't see a damn thing in there with George's fat ass in my way."

"Hey," another voice growled back, emanating from the darkness of the pipe, "do you want to do this yourself, Reg? There's a two hundred year old oak making its home in the plumbing of this house; it has just as much right to be here as anyone else."

"If you weren't such a tree hugger, we'd be done with this job already," the water-thing said back, its voice rife with sarcasm.

"You want to say that to my face, Reginald Bartholomew Copthorne?" the other voice continued, head sliding from the pipe to glare at the water dragon. This particular *thing* looked similar to the first, only it was made of bark. Like, tree bark. Like a second dragon coming out of a pipe in my wall.

Apparently, I had an issue with shocking news and breaking glasses because as soon as I saw … well, whatever it was that I was looking at in that bathroom … I dropped both the pitcher of lemonade and the glass full of ice cubes to the floor.

"Holy shit," I whispered, putting my hands to my lips.

They must've heard the glass break because suddenly all three sets of eyes in that bathroom were looking my way.

"Oh, hell, now look what you've done!" the wooden dragon said, staring at me with its mud colored gaze. It slithered from the pipe next, tail twitching, tiny green shoots unfurling from its skin. "She's seen us already. I *told* you this job was going to be more complicated than we thought."

"Hey there, honey doll," Shane said slowly, coming out of the bathroom with his hands raised in surrender. "It's all gonna be okay …"

I stood there for a moment, my eyes bulging out of my skull and wished with every breath I took that I'd finished off that bottle of wine.

Then my eyes rolled back in my head, and I passed out.

2

CHAPTER TWO

Blinking my eyes slowly, I frowned at the crumbling decorative ceiling of my grandmother's living room. *Did I pass out on the couch again?*

"Shhhh!" A harsh whisper came from somewhere near my head. "She's waking up!"

With a gasp, I sat up sharply, spinning to face the speaker.

"Who the fuck are you?" I exclaimed, eyeing up the gorgeous man sitting cross-legged in the middle of my coffee table. He wore only a pair of threadbare sweatpants, with no shirt or shoes. His skin seemed to be an almost unnatural shade of bronze and his eyes were a deep, woody brown.

"Is that just your standard greeting, or are we special, darlin'?" Shane, or *Skeeter*, purred as he stepped into my line of sight, holding out a glass of wine which I accepted somewhat reluctantly—but only because a stranger had given it to me, not because of the wine. I wanted the goddamn wine. "We couldn't find any other drinks in your kitchen, so I hope wine's okay at this time o' day?"

I took a *really* big gulp before responding.

"Wine's fine. Fucking Christ knows I need it right now." Arching an eyebrow at both Skeeter and the drool worthy man on my coffee table, I cleared my throat nervously. "Does one of you want to explain *what the fuck* I just saw in my bathroom?"

"What do you think you saw?" A laughing voice asked from the other end of the couch and I jumped halfway out of my skin with fright. *How the hell did I not see the third tattooed hunk sitting right next to me?*

"What ... how the ..." Words seemed to have escaped me so I took another large gulp of my wine. *Shit that's good stuff.*

"You were saying?" The cocky asshole slid closer to me on the couch, his warm thigh pressing into mine and sending tingling shivers through my body.

"I saw ... fucking *dragons* or some shit, in my bathroom. Who the hell are you two? And what are you doing in my house? Are you serial killers or something? Because I won't make this an easy kill for you." My voice was shaking (possibly more with lust than fear) and I couldn't take my eyes off this new guy as he slid his warm hand onto my knee. "Oh god, you're rapists aren't you?"

"Sounds like you've been drinking too much wine, beautiful," the overly friendly man chuckled, his hand creeping higher up my leg. Dressed as I was in tiny short-shorts, there was a whole lot of exposed leg for him to touch. I slapped at his hand, and he withdrew it with a throaty masculine laugh.

"Back off, Reg," Shane growled, propping his tattooed hands on his hips. I had mentally decided to stick with Shane, as he was *way* too damn beautiful to be called Skeeter. "She flat-out saw you two in your elemental forms; don't try and convince her she was imagining things."

"Told you to lock the door," the guy on the table muttered, rolling his eyes. "Don't worry, Arizona, we are *not* rapists."

"Wait, so I wasn't imagining those … *things* … in my bathroom? The lizard-y dragon things? They were …" I turned back to the two *sexy as fuck* men who I hadn't been introduced to yet. Coffee Table Guy had brown eyes, the color of wet earth after a rainstorm, that looked awfully familiar.

"Were what?" Perv Guy prodded, the sound of his voice sparking my memory. "Remarkably similar to me and *Earth First!* over here?" He jerked his thumb at Coffee Table Guy and then laid his hand oh-so-smoothly on my leg again. "That ain't no coincidence, doll baby—that was us."

"That was you two?" I managed to choke out, even though —let's be honest—that was kind of a ridiculous conclusion to come to. I blamed it on the wine. It was a lot easier to apologize for being ridiculous when you had wine.

Reg, the handsy one on the couch, threw me a saucy wink and crept his hand a little higher on my thigh. I pried his fingers off—squeezing them hard enough that I hoped one might break —but he didn't seem to mind.

He just smiled at me with lips carved from sex and sin, his blue eyes the color of the lake on a bright summer day. His dark blonde hair was cropped short and his gaze was full of mischievous promises and playful bullshit.

"In the flesh," he drawled, sweeping an inked finger in the air and drawing a small sigil out of *water,* like he'd collected molecules from the very air. I guess it made some sort of strange sense if he was the water dragon; it also meant the bronze god on my coffee table was the bark one.

The fact that I *wasn't* shitting my pants over this did not speak well to my sanity.

"So you're ..." I took a pause to gulp my wine again and frowned when I saw it was almost all gone. "Dragons?"

Because ... why the hell not? Either I was crazy or dragons actually existed. I'd fucking *seen* them—or at least I thought I had.

The three of them all snickered a laugh before the bronzed one responded, scooting closer and leaning forward until his face was inches from mine. "No. Those assholes just happen to share a physical likeness with us; we're elementals."

Silence weighed heavy on the room while I waited for him to continue, or someone else to pick up the explanation, but no one spoke.

"Sorry, fucking what now?" I squinted at the man in front of me, like perhaps he had just escaped from a mental facility. Then again, I was the one seeing magical creatures fixing my blocked up toilet so really, who was I to throw stones here?

"Well, technically we're nymphs ..." Bronze God continued, and Reg snorted.

"More like *nymphos*," he chuckled, and both Shane and the bronze one glared at him to shut up.

"I thought nymphs were beautiful girls who like ... hung out in forests and streams and shit?" Yes, that was the extent of my knowledge on the subject. I was a barista, damn it, not a mythology professor!

"That's how *pop culture* portrays us, sugar," Shane snarled, looking particularly pissed off at the description. Guess I couldn't blame him. Pop culture would also have you believe that actual humans liked Justin Bieber's music. "Which is why we go by elementals now. George," he nodded at the bronze god, "is an earth elemental, and Reg is a water one. Which makes plumbing a pretty easy job for us, you know?"

"Uh-huh," I murmured. "Sure, yeah, I can imagine. Was there any more wine left?"

I was gonna need it if I planned on continuing what was probably an LSD induced trip talking to three hot plumbers about elemental dragons or whatever the fuck.

Shane *thankfully* took my empty glass from my hand and went to fill it up.

"So, George?" I asked Captain Bronze, who nodded, "and Reg?"

"That's right, sugar tits," Reg purred into my ear, his lips brushing my lobe and sending *insane* spikes of arousal through my body. *How the hell is he doing that? Maybe I need more wine ...*

If there was ever a moment to guiltlessly indulge in alcohol, this was it.

"Reg, seriously, lay off. You really are a nympho." George leaned forward to smack Reg in the arm and I took the opportunity to scoot further along the couch *away* from the horny plumber in order to gather my thoughts.

"Okay, so you're … nymphs?" I was processing out loud, but George corrected me.

"Elementals would be the preferred term nowadays." He smiled, then nodded at me to continue.

"Right. Elementals. And Shane is …?" I raised an eyebrow, remembering he had said *we* when explaining what they were.

"Air," George replied, his warm, woody brown eyes watching me intently, like he thought I might faint again.

"And our buddy, Billy, is fire, but he had to teach a karate class today. Also, his element isn't really any use on these plumbing jobs until we get everything cleared and fixed, then he can solder all the pipes and shit back together." Shane finished the explanation as he came back into the room with a full glass of wine for me. It wasn't even midday yet, but I figured it was five p.m. somewhere in the world!

As I eyed my glass and wondered how fast I could down it without appearing like I had a *problem,* George cleared his throat. All that sound did was draw my eyes to the bronzed perfection of his throat, his Adam's apple bobbing with the movement. *What would it be like to trace my lips down his skin, find my way to one of his rock-hard nipples, and ...*

Wine. More wine. I needed more fucking wine.

"Don't worry about drinking too much," George said, gesturing at Shane to bring the whole bottle into the living room. He reached out and tucked it between my thighs, making me unsure as to whether I wanted to punch him ... or invite other things between my thighs. "You're going to need it."

"Am I?" I asked skeptically, fighting back a hysterical laugh. My best friend, Britt, was due over any second, and well, I didn't want to say she was a *floozy* because I don't use words like that—misogyny and slut shaming aren't really my things— but, fuck, she *was* a floozy. She'd jump these men like a starving wolf attacking its prey. "And why is that?"

"Because you're a *shimmer* now," George said, and I snorted so badly that wine came out of my nose and dribbled down the front of my shirt.

That was sexy.

"A shimmer?" I asked because nymphs and dragons and elementals weren't stupid enough. "What the hell is a s*himmer*?"

I downed the rest of my wine—a nice, tart California grape that Gram had probably kept in her wine cellar since before I was born—and then just went straight for the bottle. Why not? If there was ever a reason to drink, this was it.

"A shimmer is a human who's stumbled across the supernatural world," George continued as Reg slouched back on the couch like he thought he was all that and a bag of chips. He kind of was though, which was the frustrating part of the whole thing. He had an entire sleeve of Sailor Jerry style tattoos on his left arm and a few carefully placed finger tats on the other side.

"Okay, great. I'm a shimmer. Now, can you please get out of my house?" I paused, took a second to rephrase. "Can you please fix my plumbing and then get out of my house?"

"Arizona, was it?" Reg asked, grinning like an asshole. "You're not getting it—once a shimmer, always a shimmer."

"Yeah, cool, I didn't ask you to go all *Men In Black* on me and flash away my memories. I just want you to go." Another pause. "I want you to fix my pipes and *then* go."

The three men exchanged looks that I *really* didn't like.

"Listen, sweet thing," Shane said, kneeling down next to me and pursing his lips. "Now that you're a shimmer, you'll have a target on your back."

"Yup. Rules state that once a human stumbles into our world, they're fair game." Reg's smile twisted up at one corner, giving him this sexy, crooked little grin that I wanted to slap right off his face. "Usually, your kind would be protected under supernatural law. Not so much now that you're involved."

"Involved?!" I asked, leaning forward and pointing at the three men with the neck of the wine bottle. "How am I involved? You idiots were the ones doing ... magic or whatever the fuck it is in my *bathroom* in the middle of the day with the door open!"

I cursed myself for trying to have Southern hospitality. I should've just stayed a frigid, angry Yank and been done with it.

"Yeah, well," George started, and when he sighed, I swore I could smell the soft, damp scent of the earth, wildflowers and growing things. The heady scent of night jasmine curled around me and made me shiver. "However it happened, it's too late. Once a human becomes a shimmer, there are only two options …" He glanced over at Shane like he couldn't bear to say it.

"Sugar, you're either going to be executed …" he began, nice and slow and careful.

"More like chased, hunted, run down," Reg added as the color drained out of my face and I tried not to pass out again.

"Or the supernatural who brought you into this world has to make you their mate."

"The word is boyfriend now, I think," Reg said, looking up at the ceiling. "Or is it paramour? Concubine? Wife?"

"Those have completely different meanings," I shrieked, and then I wished I'd never moved out of Oregon and away from all those wonderful completely legal pot dispensaries. I could *really* use a special brownie right about now.

Maybe I did have a problem?

I set the wine bottle on the coffee table next to George and tried not to admire his sculpted abs. There were at least eight of them there—*eight.* Not to mention one of those yummy little 'V' shapes tracing his hips.

"I either die or marry all three of you, that's cute," I said, rising to my feet. "Real cute. I've changed my mind—I'll deal with the pipes myself. Now get the fuck out."

"Actually, you only have to mate with Reg and George," Shane continued with a sexy as hell little smile. He was a sweetie. The other two, well screw them. "You didn't see me in my elemental form." Somehow I sensed an implied *yet* dangling in the air like a fart.

"Right, mm-hmm," I said, moving past him and heading to the front door. I opened it nice and wide and stood back against the wall. "You can go now!" I shouted around the corner and into the living room, hoping to get these weirdos out of my house so that I could *then* have a nervous breakdown.

"Get out?" Britt asked, coming up the steps in fishnets and a smile. "But I brought vodka." She waved the bottle in the air and waltzed right on into the place like she owned it.

Crap.

"Britt," I started, trying to grab her by the arm, but it was already too late. She was around the corner and gawking, her mouth hanging wide, her pink lipstick this perfect little 'O' on her face.

"Ari," she said slowly, a clear note of warning in those two syllables. "Who are your friends?"

"They're plumbers," I said, gesturing at the boys and the empty wine bottle and … noticing her eyes had locked onto the fact that I was still dressed in a shirt with no bra and undies.

"You said you weren't into group stuff," she whispered, far too loudly for me to believe that the men hadn't actually heard her.

"Oh my god, Britt. They're the fucking plumbers, I swear." I rolled my eyes and gave her my very best *shut the fuck up* look, which of course she ignored, pushing past me to get a better look at the guys. Striking a sexy pose in her red leather stiletto heels, fishnets and minidress, she arched her back a bit to stick out her tits.

"Sure they are, Ari," she chuckled a throaty laugh, what I liked to call her sex-laugh, "because I see three *very* sexy men, with not many clothes on, empty wine bottles and you with a damp patch between your legs."

"What?" I squawked, reflexively bending down to check my crotch.

"Made ya look," she snickered, but I could feel three sets of supernatural eyes burning holes through my tiny shorts at her insinuation. "So, this is Gram's mansion huh? Kind of a dump, no?" She looked around at the dilapidated décor and screwed up her nose. If she wasn't my best friend in the entire world, I'd have slapped the bitch many years ago, but she meant well.

"Um, yeah. The plumbing is all fucked too, which is why these *plumbers* are here to fix it." I gave the three elementals a stern glare but the *fuckers* just grinned back at me. Reg even stepped it up a notch by reclining further into my couch and deliberately adjusting his junk before winking at me again.

"Huh, sure it is," Britt shrugged. "Well?" She looked at me with raised eyebrows, like she was waiting for me to do something really obvious. "Girl, I just drove like three days straight to be here. You could have at least had some shot glasses ready!" She waved her bottle of vodka at me and I groaned.

"I'll get them," George offered, *oh so helpfully.* "Hi, I'm George. I'm one of Arizona's new boyfriends."

"What—" The shock at his announcement had just rendered me speechless and my bestie took full advantage of it.

"Really, *one of* them, you say?" Her grin looked like she was a hungry wolf that had just been served up a big old juicy steak. Which was, essentially, what any gossip about my love life was like. It had been a *really* long time since my drain had been snaked, so to speak, and Britt was practically bouncing with glee that I appeared to be getting some.

18

"Reginald," Reg introduced himself, standing in a fluid movement and snatching up Britt's hand to kiss. "It is an absolute *honor* to meet Arizona's best friend so early in our relationship."

"We're not—" My protests were cut short by Shane, shoving Reg aside to shake Britt's hand himself.

"I'm Shane, Ari's third boyfriend," he announced, raising his eyebrow at me in a challenging sort of way.

"No. Whoa. Hold the fucking phone. You said those two!" I waved a hand at Reg and George, who had just returned from my kitchen holding shot glasses.

"Yeah, Skeeter," Reg smirked, "just *us* two."

Shane glared at his … er … magical friend, then strode over to me, snatching me by the hand and dragging me through to the kitchen.

"Shane, what the actual ever loving fuck?" I demanded, yanking my hand out of his grip and looking at him like *he* was the one who'd lost his marbles. Which made me giggle a bit, because I was still maybe half-convinced this was my inevitable liver failure messing with my brain.

Without a word of warning, Shane yanked his shirt over his head, then—*thank the lord*—dropped his pants, giving me a solid eyeful of his seriously impressive plunger before his whole body melted and rearranged into a glistening, almost see-through version of the dragons I had seen in the loo.

Pretty sure my jaw hit the fucking floor.

As quick as he had just shifted, he changed back into his human form, standing there in the middle of my Gram's kitchen in all his naked glory. A smug grin curved across his lush lips as I took a moment to appreciate the specimen before me.

"Oops," he smirked, "guess you have to marry me now, too. Sorry, sug."

"Shane!" I screeched, suddenly realizing what he had just done. "What the fuck are you *thinking*?"

"I think it's fairly obvious what I'm thinking …" he grinned, leveling some serious bedroom eyes at me while his … er … pipe started standing proudly at attention—did I mention it was *inked*. Like, all of it. Wrench, bolts and nuts alike.

With all the impeccable timing in the world, the door to the kitchen burst open and I heard my bestie suck in a gasp.

"Well, this is awfully rude of you to start the party in here without the rest of us!" She licked her bright red lips as her wide eyes trailed all over Shane's naked, chiseled flesh, and a sudden flare of jealousy spiked through me.

Whoa, where the hell did that come from? Why the fuck would I care if Britt is eye fucking this guy that I barely know?

"Oh, you asshole," Reg snapped, following Britt into the kitchen with George close behind him.

"Seriously, Skeeter?" George sighed, running his hand through his soft, nut-brown hair. "And you took the time to strip, too?"

"Bite me, dickheads," Shane replied, but the satisfied smile on his face spoke volumes to how pleased he was with his own actions.

"Jesus fucking Christ, give me that." I held my hand out to Britt and she passed me the vodka. Twisting the cap off, I took a swig straight from the bottle then coughed as it burned its way down my throat. "Britt, what the shit?" I peered at the label of the lighter fluid she had just given me to drink—there was a naked girl on a bike which was, like, almost as weird as the dragons—and she giggled.

"It's a new brand I'm trying out. Totally hipster cool, made in Portland, Oregon!" She grinned and took the bottle back from me, swigging it herself and making it look like she was drinking water, not jet fuel. *Damn that girl can drink.* "The city's famous for its yearly World Naked Bike Ride, you know —did it myself just last month."

I gave Britt a look and then decided to ignore her in favor of dealing with the naked weirdo standing in front of me. Girl could drink, but she could also talk. And talk. And talk. I had a half-erect tattooed cock to address.

"Okay, all of this insanity aside, are you all actually going to fix my plumbing before I throw you out on the street? Because I have had a lot to drink, and kind of really need to pee …" I grabbed a dish towel from the counter and tossed it over Shane's, um, well, let's just call it like it is—his hard-ass dick. "I'm off to the loo."

"The loo!" Britt chortled, not nearly as disturbed by this whole scenario as I felt she should be. "You are so cute and British, babe. It's a *bathroom*."

"First off, not every *bath*room has a bath, so I'll call it what I damn well please. And I've already explained to you about four thousand times over the last ten-or-so years of our friendship that I lived in Australia with my mom. *Australia,* bitch."

"Same difference," Britt said, totally and completely ignoring my pointed glare. *Her* attention was focused wholly on the studly Adonis standing in my Gram's kitchen. "It's like, a British penal colony or something, right?"

I just stared at her.

Britt wasn't the smartest—or most tactful—human being in the world, but she was my ride or die bitch. She had my back. She had to be loyal because otherwise, there wasn't a soul on heaven or earth that would put up with her shit.

"Excuse me," I said, gritting my teeth and taking long, deep breaths to calm my nerves. I figured there were only two options here: I was crazy or magical dragon-elemental-nymphos had fixed my plumbing. Win-win, right?

I stormed past the (deliciously decadent) naked man and down the back hall—it used to be the *servants'* hall back in the day—toward the loo/toilet/bathroom/water closet. Call it what you will—I had to piss.

"I wouldn't go in there if I were you," George said, standing at the other end of the hallway and watching me. "We're done not yet." He paused and for a second, his face softened. My steps faltered, one heel raised off the floor, my fingers brushing against the door to the downstairs bathroom.

Fuck my life.

I was going to have to put pants, boots, and a coat on and walk my ass down to the frigging antique store *again*.

So … magic dragons and still, no working toilets.

"Arizona," George said as I glanced over at him and wondered for a moment there if he might apologize for trying to ruin my life. "Which bedroom should I move my stuff into?"

I just stared at him, kicked open the door to the bathroom, and slammed it shut behind me; the shitter might not work, but at least the lock still did.

The boys wouldn't apologize for ruining my life then. Not then, not now—not fucking ever.

But who knew ruination could be such a good thing?

Certainly not this chick.

3

CHAPTER THREE

When I came downstairs after getting dressed, I found—much to my own chagrin—that the boys were still present, sitting in my living room and having shots with Britt.

"This one time," she began as I scooted across the wood floors in my socks and put a hand over her mouth. I had no idea *what* story she was about to tell them, but it wouldn't be good. Humiliation was in the cards for me when Britt got to talking; it was inevitable.

"Alright, guys, fun's over," I said, releasing my best friend and crossing my arms over my chest. "You need to leave now."

"We can't leave," Reg said, swirling a pretzel stick around in the cheese dip I'd bought myself last night. Those fuckers had raided my cabinets. "We already told you—you're a shimmer now."

"Oo, what's a shimmer?" Britt asked, leaning back into the cushions and mimicking Reg's pose. All of a sudden, it hit me.

That's why I hated the Reg guy so much. He was basically a male version of Britt. "Is this a sex thing?"

"Everything is not always about sex," I growled at her, marching around the table and extracting my snacks from the elemental's hand. "And you three have far overstayed your welcome." *Okay, so maybe I* would *like to see Shane naked again, but that's besides the point.*

While I was changing upstairs, I'd made my decision: whether or not these boys were mystical, magical creatures (doubtful—I was probably high) was unimportant. Let's just say for the sake of argument that they *were.* So what? My seeing them didn't change anything. I was a free woman; I made my own choices.

Shimmer or no shimmer, I was not dating these fuckers.

I could barely handle *one* man at a time. Three of them? I mean, I'm sure there'd be perks... My eyes drifted over to George's bare abs again, and then snapped up to his face.

No.

No, no, no.

Stop it, Ari! Get that estrogen under control, damn it. My ovaries were staging a mutiny and it was clear who was winning this fight.

"Get out of my house. I'm not sure how to say that anymore clearly."

Nostrils flaring, I lifted my chin in defiance.

"That's not a good idea, honey bun," Shane said, but I'd seen the alpha male a-hole in him, too. I was over that slow, drippy accent of his and the way it made my skin tingle and my heart pound... "The second we walk out of that door, you're fair game."

"I'll manage," I said sarcastically, staring the three men down, one after the other.

"You'll manage?" Reg said with a smirk. "Against a werewolf?"

Britt choked on her shot and lifted her head to stare at me in surprise.

"Ignore them," I told her, but there was something about the way she was looking at me… I filed it under *crap to deal with later* and pretended not to notice. "They're obviously insane."

"We're obviously just trying to protect you," George said softly, but firmly. He came over to stand in front of me, towering a good six inches above my head. Six inches… There was definitely more than *six* inches down below Shane's belt.

"I don't need protection," I told him, completely deadpan and completely serious. Sure, I wanted to get laid by three sexy plumbers (is that an oxymoron? sexy plumbers?), but I wasn't about to whore myself out for some supernatural bodyguards. "Now make like a tree and *leave.*"

The men glanced at each other for a long moment before Shane sighed.

"No means no, boys," he said in a low growl, giving me another look. "If the lady says go, we gotta respect that."

He moved past me and out the front door, George just a few steps ahead of him. They were *listening* to me, but somehow I felt like they were also still winning this war. Let's just say, I was a tad suspicious at their sudden willingness to comply.

Reg scoffed and smirked at me as he passed, tossing a business card at my chest.

I let it hit me in the tits and drift to the scuffed floor beneath my socks.

"Call us when you need us," he said, glancing down at my hardened nipples beneath my t-shirt. Hey, it was a natural reaction to three testosterone driven stud-muffins. What was I supposed to do about it? "And you *will* need us," he whispered, leaning in close and breathing warm against my ear, "in one way or another."

Stifling a whimper, I bit my lip and stared at his ass as he jogged down my front steps to join his friends. *Fuck those are some sexy cheeks; the universe doesn't make buttocks like that very often.*

"Ahem," Britt cleared her throat in a accusatory way, and I knew I wasn't getting out of this one without *some* sort of explanation, even if it wasn't the real one. If the penalty for just seeing the elementals in their magical form was death or marriage, then I hated to think what the punishment for flapping my trap would be.

"Ummm," I heaved a long sigh and rubbed at my eyes, suddenly starting to feel the effects of all my day drinking. "We had sex."

Britt squinted at me for a long moment, and I wondered if she was buying what I was selling. "All of you?" she finally asked, still squinting at me.

"Uh, yup. All four of us. All together, right there." I pointed to the couch and she raised an eyebrow at me. *Shit, I'm not selling this well. More details, Ari!* "And um, afterward they kind of got a bit clingy, thinking we were dating. Hence the scene you just witnessed."

"Really …?" she muttered, pouring another shot for both of us. "Well, girl, I'm so proud of you! What was it like? Did you take them all at once? Ew, I sat on that couch before. Hope you wiped it down when you finished!" She was gushing and beaming at me, and the tension dropped from my shoulders. It was the best explanation I could come up with on such short notice as to why those three half-naked men were claiming to all be in a relationship with me. Thankfully, Britt was a dirty bitch and *loved* the thought that I'd just had a foursome on my Gram's couch.

"Hey! Earth to Ari!" She waved her hand in front of my face. "I asked you a question."

"Sorry, babe, I was daydreaming. Repeat?" I tried desperately not to look nervous in case she saw through my lie.

"I asked, who had the biggest dick? I hope for your sake at least one of them was smaller than what old Shane was packing, or is that why you're kind of walking funny?" She cocked her head to the side in interest, like it was the most normal question in the world. Meanwhile, I was choking on the vodka I'd just taken a sip of.

"Jesus, Britt," I spluttered when I'd regained enough air to speak.

"What? Not my fault you tried to sip your drink like some sort of lightweight. Just shot it like a real woman and we could avoid these problems."

She half-heartedly slapped me on the back while I finished coughing. *Fucking naked Portland vodka ...* Oh well. Even if it tasted like shit, at least it was organic.

"Right, well. You're probably going to want to 'clean up' or something," she continued, casting another glance at the couch. "And I've been driving for *three days straight*"—she gave me a hard look, like I should be ever so grateful to her for coming all the way from Montana to see me—"so I'm going to go take a nap, then when I wake up we can go clubbing. 'kay, *sugar*?" Her fake Southern drawl on the endearment made me want to smack her around the head, but she skipped off upstairs before I had a chance.

Throwing back another shot, I gathered up the empty glasses and took them through to the kitchen. As I checked the fridge for a snack, there was a light tapping on the kitchen door, the one leading outside that the servants would have used back in Gram's glory days.

Curious—and half hoping it was one of the plumbers come back to plumb my well—I opened the door.

"Hmm," said the stranger standing on my doorstep—the *really* fucking handsome stranger. "Arizona, I presume? You're actually prettier than the boys described …"

"Who… sorry do I know you?" Maybe I shouldn't have had that last shot; the world seemed to be fuzzing a little around the edges. The stranger was tall, just like the plumbing crew, and had that sort of deliberately scruffy hair that looked to be an ashy shade of charcoal gray, without making him look old in the least. More like a bad boy biker fashion model. A shadow of stubble dusted his cheeks and I could see the edges of some serious ink happening from the collar of his t-shirt.

Plus, you know, he was ripped as *fuck*.

"Not yet," he smirked, "but I'm sure that'll change. Well, here goes nothing. Those dickwads better be right about you, Arizona Smoke."

Before I could even open my mouth to formulate an objection, his body had melted down into a smoldering fire dragon then quickly reformed into his human form, clothes perfectly in place. Which made me wonder why the hell Shane had felt the need to take all of his clothes off first … To show off his steel pipe, probably.

I did not want to admit it'd worked.

"What the fucking hell are you doing?" I shrieked, finally regaining my voice. "Don't you realize what you've just done, you … *moron*?"

"Yep. I have to say, not exactly how I pictured first meeting my mate but all for one and one for all, I guess." He shrugged at me like he had *not* just potentially fated me to become his

28

wife, or set a *fourth* target on my back for some supernatural death squad. Although, I guessed I could only die once, so there was that.

"I can't believe you just quoted *The Three Musketeers* at me," I whispered in disbelief. "There's four of you, for fuck's sake!" After the little display of his elemental form, it was becoming pretty obvious that this was Billy, the missing plumber from earlier. "Ugh, just get off my property. I need to go get a CAT scan or MRI or whatever the hell those things are that check for brain tumors." I didn't know what I needed; I was a barista, not a neurologist.

Slamming the door in the handsome devil's face, I rubbed my tired eyes.

Maybe I should drink less. In light of the day's events, that thought made me chuckle. *No, not less*—more.

Britt hadn't been kidding when she said she wanted to go clubbing. She'd woken from her nap full of fucking beans and ready to hunt herself out some fresh meat, her words not mine. We had just walked into a booming club after bypassing the line out front, when I felt the weight of someone's eyes on me.

"Do you see that guy staring right at me?" I asked, feeling this icy chill creep down my spine. Considering I was standing in the middle of a room full of a thousand sweaty, young assholes, that was quite the feat.

"Babe, *everyone* is staring at us," Britt said, like *duh.* "How do you think we skipped that line? We look hot as hell tonight?"

"Maybe we skipped that line because they were offering a senior discount?" I muttered, looking at all the seventeen year olds with fake IDs gyrating and dry humping around me. Out of the corner of my eye, I watched a tall, redheaded man in the corner as he wove his way through the crowd and came straight for me. "Fuck," I muttered, grabbing onto Britt's arm, "stage five clinger at ten o'clock."

"You want to make out or something?" she asked casually, completely ignoring me as she scoped the crowd. Once again, I had the strangest urge to describe her actions as … predatory. No more wolf references in relation to my best friend. I was cutting myself off. "Pull the lesbo card?"

"Our kisses are not for the male gaze," I said with a flutter of lashes, dragging her through the crowd and away from the man before he could get too close. In the front of my brain, I just kept repeating that the guy was just another douche-y clubbing loser that wanted to get in my pants. In the back of it, I was wondering if those weirdo plumbers were telling the truth …

Sure, as a chick, you get used to that low-grade anxiety, that feeling of being hunted (sorry, dudes are hot but also, like, seriously creepy sometimes), but this was even worse than that. I felt like a dead woman walking.

"The power of suggestion," I muttered under my breath. Clearly, I was just suffering side effects from one, seeing magical dragon creatures, and two, seeing an eight inch cock that I hadn't taken advantage of. That had to be it. "Just the power of suggestion …"

"Would you please stop talking to yourself? You're scaring off all the men."

"Girl, you've been in town for all of six hours and you're seriously trying to get laid? Can't we just spend some time together?" I tapped my fingers on the bar and tried to justify spending fifteen dollars on a drink when I had *just* enough money to buy food for the next however long until I got a new job—and I could just forget about making my car payment or my credit card payments for now.

Maybe I should've let those creepers move in and charged them rent?

"Have a drink and *relax,* Ari. For a girl who just had a foursome, you seem kind of stressed-out." Britt snapped her fingers at the bartender, making me cringe a little, and then ordered three blow job shots for us each, locking her hands together behind her back and putting on a show of drinking them using only her mouth.

It was entertaining, at the very least.

Or, it was until I felt the barrel of a gun press into my side.

"What the *fuck* is an unmarked shimmer *bitch* doing in this neighborhood?"

Jesus. Effing. Christ.

I turned and found the redheaded guy that was staring at me earlier ... making out with some random dude at the bar. Oops. Guess I had pretty shitty instincts.

The person holding a gun on me was actually a woman—a *gorgeous* fucking woman with skin the color of fresh milk and hair like fire. Her lips were painted a brilliant ruby red that only seemed to emphasize the severity of her frown.

I swallowed hard and tucked some dirty blonde hair behind one ear.

"Can I help you?" I managed to get out, my voice cracking slightly on the last syllable.

"Get your ass up and follow me outside," she said, and although the first thing I wanted to do was just start laughing hysterically, I could tell she wasn't screwing around. This bitch meant business. "*Now,* or I can kill your slutty friend while I'm at it."

"Please don't slut shame," I said as I slid off the stool, and glared at Britt's back as I left. She hadn't even *noticed* me leaving. Maybe if she had, she might've also seen the gun pressed into my spine. The woman, whoever she was, did a brilliant job of hiding it though, keeping it nice and low and bathed in the shadows of the dance floor.

I thought briefly about making a scene, but the way the woman was looking at me, like I was some sort of monstrosity marked for destruction, I didn't trust her not to start shit in the club. At least I had a trump card—under my arm was my clutch and in it, a hidden knife *and* a lipstick shaped tube of pepper spray.

My attacker might've had a gun, but I was packing a little heat of my own.

She guided me to a back exit and, with a simple nod, managed to get us right past the security guard and into the most clichéd, dark alleyway I'd ever seen in my life. It stank of rats and garbage and old, stale bum piss.

Not the most pleasant place to die, that was for sure.

The woman very dramatically pulled back the hammer on the gun and lifted it toward my face, so I could get a nice, long view down the barrel of a .38 special revolver.

"Who exposed you and left you unmarked?" she asked, but since I had no idea what she was talking about, I tried to use those conflict-resolution skills I'd learned in college.

"Listen, whatever it is that I've done, I'm sure—"

The redhead hit me across the face as hard as she could with the gun, knocking both me and my clutch to the dirty pavement. My knees hit hard enough that for a second there, I couldn't see anything but the white emptiness of pain. Pain, pain, pain, a stinging in my knees that drove all the way up my spine and made my teeth hurt.

I lifted two careful fingers to my face and felt blood draining from my left nostril.

"Fuck," I whispered, glancing up at the woman … who now had wings like a bat, stretching out a good six feet on either side of her body. As soon as I saw that, I knew.

Not only was I screwed, blued, and tattooed … but I was also an idiot.

What kind of nutter sees magical dragons and then refuses to heed their warnings?!

"What the hell are you?" I stuttered as the creature lifted the gun one more time and pointed it at my face.

"Who. The. Fuck. Exposed. You?" she asked again, her teeth gritted in anger, her eyes as red as her hair now. "You have about ten seconds to answer me."

"I don't exactly—" I started, but she was already counting down.

"Ten … nine …"

"The plumbers?" I supplied, but the woman didn't falter, didn't stop counting.

"Eight … seven …"

"Elementals," I spurted and noticed a slight widening of her eyes. "Four of them. Dudes with big packages and abs." I gestured at my midsection, but the joke wasn't really all that funny considering the pain in my knees, my face … the burning sensation in my nose from the sink of garbage.

"Six … five … four …" she continued, smiling wickedly.

"What else do you need to know?!" I asked, because no way in hell was I dying like this, jobless and penniless and boyfriend-less, living in my grandma's rundown house with a best friend who thought Australia and the U.K. were the same thing… No, I deserved some dignity, damn it.

But the winged woman was already putting pressure on the trigger, getting ready to squeeze …

A wolf the size of a fucking pony slammed into her left side, sending the shot wild and knocking her to the filthy cement.

And that wolf … it was wearing Britt's five hundred dollar Parker Black beaded cocktail minidress (in shimmering pink).

"Britt?!" I screamed, my eyes practically bursting out of my head in shock. Suddenly Reg's offhand comment about werewolves made a whole lot more sense.

Unbe-*fucking*-lievable.

My best friend was a goddamn *werewolf* and never thought to tell me!

The expensively dressed wolf ignored me as the red-haired woman rolled, narrowly avoiding Britt's snapping jaws, then threw a bitch slap across my wolf-friend's snout, raking bloody lines through Britt's fur.

Scrambling for my dropped clutch, I grabbed out my little can of pepper spray and pressed down hard on the trigger. A thick stream of the spicy stuff flew out, hitting the crazy winged chick dead in the eyes as she launched herself at me, and she *screeched* in pain.

Occupied as she was, clawing at her burning eyeballs, she didn't even see it coming when Britt pounced on her. My furred friend then proceeded to sink her massive fangs into the neck of the winged … thing. Whipping her huge furry jaws to the side, she tore the head clean off my would-be killer while somehow managing to keep the spinal column intact.

The string of bones, still held together with cartilage and pieces of muscle, slithered free of the winged woman's corpse and landed with a *splat* at my feet.

"Seriously?" I narrowed my eyes at my newly furred bestie as she licked her bloody chops and bared her teeth in what was probably meant to be a grin. "Ugh, I think I'm gonna vomit."

Closing my eyes, I took a few deep breaths to try and hold the rising bile back but all I ended up with was a nose full of coppery blood, and I bent double to empty my guts all over the recently deceased face of my almost executioner.

"What is that, just red wine and vodka? Have you actually eaten any food in the past twenty-four hours, honey doll?" Shane's Southern drawl scolded me, as his gentle hands collected up my long hair and held it out of the mess at my feet.

Where in the bloody hell had he come from?!

"Fuck you, *Skeeter*," I growled, retching up a bit more red wine-colored bile before I straightened back up and wiped my mouth on the back of my hand, like a really classy bitch.

"Now, now, that's no way to speak to your new husband, darlin'." His syrupy voice was heavy with amusement and I wanted to hit him. *So bad.* Eyeing up his chiseled jaw, dusted with dark stubble, I decided against further violence. For now.

"You're not my husband, you delusional supernatural bastard. Thanks for warning me that my best friend was a mother fucking werewolf, too!" My death glare was centered on Britt, who seemed to be watching us with interest, her long tongue lolling out of her jaws. "By the way, how long have you been standing there? A little help would've been nice."

"We weren't gonna let anything happen to you, sweets. But your girlfriend here, well she took care of the problem before we did."

"We?" I asked, feeling the blood drain from my face.

"Very stylish, Fido," Reg commented, clapping his hands as he came around the corner and joined us in the alleyway. "I always did think wolves would look great in pink sequins."

Britt shifted back into her human form with a shimmering of light, and reached into the neckline of her slightly stretched out dress to rearrange her boobs.

"I will take that as a compliment," she told Reg, flicking her dark hair over her shoulder with an eyebrow raised in challenge. "Now, have you four finished making your point to my girl? I would really prefer no one else try to kill her; I'm quite attached."

"Wait, hold the phone!" I snapped, flipping my own hair over my shoulder in similar fashion (mostly to keep it away from my mouth in case I retched again). So effing classy. "Does this mean I have to *mate* with you too, Britt?"

My stylish bestie licked her lips and winked at me.

"Only if you ask really nicely …"

A low, angry sounding growl came from Shane beside me as he glared at Britt.

"She means *no*, sugar. It's usually only the very first supernatural contact—which was Reg and George—but there are some gray areas for elemental quads. Due to the symbiotic nature of our species, we're the exception rather than the rule. These things aren't usually an issue as we generally mate … within the supernatural community."

There was a pause there that I didn't like.

I narrowed my eyes.

"But you haven't accepted us as mates yet, so you're fair game for the executioners." The smoky voice belonged to the new guy, Billy, who had just arrived with George. Billy's burning gaze raked over me in a judgmental sort of way and I shivered in response. He was *seriously* smoking hot in black distressed jeans, combat boots and a leather biker jacket.

I groaned inside my head. I bet he drove a motorbike. *So damn sexy.*

"Oh, we're all here. What are you, following me? Don't you have shit filled toilets to unclog somewhere?" It was a bit petty of me, but my head was pounding and someone had literally just tried to fucking kill me. Also, getting aggressive with these dickheads was covering up my crazy hormonal urge to strip down and let them have their way with me.

"Sweetheart, you're bleeding ..." Seeming to ignore my righteous indignation, George stepped into my personal space and cupped my cheek in one huge, soft palm. The heady scent of moss and damp earth washed over me and I sighed, leaning unintentionally into his touch. An easy smile curved his lips.

"We're taking you home. Until you accept us, you're a sitting duck," Billy snapped, his smoky voice brokering no arguments and jolting me right back into the boiling anger that George's touch had somewhat cooled.

Giving him a disgusted look, I whipped back around to face my best friend, who was watching our interaction with a wolfish grin.

"Britt, let's head back inside. I'm in the mood to get my sinkhole plumbed, and *not* by any of these four." Okay, that was an outright lie. I *really* wanted to get down and dirty with these four, possibly together, but they came with *way* too much supernatural baggage for my liking.

"Arizona! You're being ridiculous!" This from Shane, who had deliberately stripped down and *exposed* himself to me, and also showed me his elemental form, just to try and force me into bed with him?

Uh-uh. I don't think so.

Tossing my hair over my shoulder again, I threw a bit of extra sway into my step as I stalked back into the club with Britt close behind.

Once inside, I headed straight to the bar and ordered us three shots of tequila each. As the bartender poured them and Britt and I slammed them back one after another, I could sense four sets of furious eyes following my every move.

Deciding to really give them something to be mad about, I turned to the guy standing beside me at the crowded bar and tapped him on the shoulder. He turned to face me and I quickly glanced past him to be sure he wasn't with a girl—because bitches can get violent—then grabbed his face in my hands and sealed my lips to his.

The poor guy froze for a second, then shrugged and kissed me back, his tongue slithering into my mouth without warning as he took control. He was, quite possibly, the *worst* kisser I had ever met in my entire life, but hell if I was going to admit that. I was proving a point goddamn it, and if that meant letting this random dude plunder my throat like he was looking for treasure then so be it.

After way, *way* too long, and far too much excess saliva, I politely extracted my face from his tight grip and grabbed Britt's hand. Meeting her surprised gaze, I jerked my head to the sweaty, writhing dance floor.

"Come on, Furball. We're not here to fuck spiders, let's dance." I gave Britt a look once I felt we were safely out of earshot from the boys. "Why didn't you warn me when you heard I was a shimmer?"

"It took me a while to remember what a Shimmer was," she said as she gyrated and ground her shit to Cardi B's *Bodak Yellow*. I joined in, scooting close enough that I hoped it looked like we were really into each other. I just needed a minute without elementals, winged women, and stage five clinging mouth breathers.

"It took you a while to *remember*?" I asked, weighing both the pros and cons of strangling my best friend in the middle of a crowded club. "What do you mean it took you time to remember? It seems like a pretty big fucking deal to me—a winged woman just tried to *shoot* me, Britt."

"First of all," she said, pausing to mouth the words to the song, "that was a succubus. Second, werewolves don't call you guys shimmers—that's an elemental thing."

"Then what do you call us?" I asked through gritted teeth. This whole thing was not just verging on ridiculous, it had like gone full-on overboard.

"Dog chow," Britt said, and she didn't even crack a smile. Instead, she started twerking.

"You do not," I ground out, still trying to reconcile the fact that my best friend, the one in the (slightly distorted and stretched out) cocktail dress was actually a werewolf.

Maybe after I'd lost my job at the coffee shop, I'd started on a drug binge and completely lost touch with reality? That made more sense than my other options.

"We do so," she said, swishing her hair around with her fingers and closing her eyes in musically induced ecstasy. "It's in our bylaws and everything."

I stopped dancing all of a sudden, just stopped right there in the middle of the dance floor.

"Screw you, Britt," I said, and then I turned and left.

Unfortunately, all four assholes followed me outside—Britt trailing along behind them.

I walked about two blocks in heels before my feet started to crumble off my ankles. Pausing to take them off, I whirled around to glare at the guys.

"What is it going to take to get some goddamn peace?!" I asked, breathing so hard I was spitting. Definitely not my most attractive moment.

"Well, sweet thing," Shane said, stepping forward and rubbing at his ridiculously masculine chin with a tattooed hand. I wanted to trail my lips along the stubbled side of it, see if he tasted as good as he smelled. His dark hair gleamed in the light from the street lamps and his smile ... was as warm and sultry as honey.

I put both hands on my hips and tried to mentally shut my ovaries up.

"If you want us to leave you alone, we will," George inserted, his dark blue-button up open and flashing a whole hell of a lot of bronze chest and abs. "We just ..."

"Don't want to see you get ripped into teensy-weensy little pieces and shoved down a storm drain," Reg finished, his blue eyes sparkling with mischief. His short blonde hair was slicked back, tattoos oddly bright in the dusky navy light; they looked almost painted on.

"That was ... oddly specific," I said slowly, closing my eyes for a moment and taking a deep breath. As much as I wanted to deny this shit was happening to me, I could still taste the metallic tang of blood on my lips, and my knees had tiny rocks embedded in them that I was going to have to pick out later with a pair of tweezers.

Oh, and a woman had sprouted wings in front of me and tried to blow my head off. There was that, too.

"How do we get out of this then?" I asked, opening my eyes and trying not to notice the width of each man's shoulders, the way their bodies filled out their clothes ... the disturbing resemblance they bore to the *Thunder from Down Under* performers I'd seen when my mom last came to visit (and yes, it *was* creepy to attend the show with her, thanks for asking). "This mating thing? Surely, there's a way."

The men exchanged glances, and it was George who spoke up this time. His voice was like the soft dripping of dew on leaves, but with a strength behind it that promised a storm was coming, that thunder would soon boom in the distance.

Cheesy and lame, I know, but I was a barista, not a poet.

"There's really not a lot we can do," he said slowly, like he was actually putting *some* thought into this. "I mean, once we mark you, I guess you'd be safe—even if we were to ... leave."

"Mark?" I asked, raising one skeptical brow. "Is this a corny euphemism for *fuck*?"

"Sex, sure," George said, nodding like it was no big deal that he was offering to do me four ways with his friends. "But it's more than that—there's magic involved."

"Magic, great," I said, putting on a scarily enthusiastic shark smile. "And group sex. Even better. Fuck, why don't you guys just move into the house? You can fix Gram's plumbing"—*and fix my plumbing while you're at it*—"and pay me rent. It's five hundred a month." I paused, reconsidered. "Each."

I wasn't sure if I was being sarcastic or serious, and the boys didn't seem to know either.

"Look, you guys are hot, and I'm horny and that guy at the bar was a *really* bad kisser and possibly the *worst* mouth breather I've ever seen in my life. Let's go back to the house, sleep on it, and then reconvene in the morning."

I had no idea that *reconvene* was actually a euphemism for *orgy*.

How fun.

4

CHAPTER FOUR

The next morning, I had the *worst* effing hangover of my life. And I was pretty sure it was more from the influx of new knowledge and life changing facts I'd uncovered than it was about the alcohol.

"Morning, ST," Reg said when I came into the hallway and padded mindlessly toward the bathroom. He was slouched against the wall across from the door, the corner of his mouth quirked up in a wily smile, his tattooed left arm slung over the flatness of his belly.

In my disoriented state (Reg's hotness wasn't helping), I hadn't yet remembered I was going to have to walk to the antique store to pee.

"ST?" I asked with a long sigh. "Is that short for sugar tits?"

He grinned at me and I used my frontal cortex (the part of the brain that's, like, a million times bigger in women than it is in men, the one that controls aggressive urges) to not punch him right in the nuts.

"You've got me all figured out," he said as I gave him a wide berth and opened the bathroom door.

Curls of gorgeous white steam rolled out and over me, making me eyes go wide.

"You did it," I said, realizing that the shower was running and the floor was *not* flooded with gooey brown water. "You actually cleaned my pipes."

"Well, we haven't yet, but isn't that the plan?" he asked, putting his hands on my shoulders and sending lightning bolts of electricity arcing through me. He smelt like fresh rain and musk, masculine but clean.

A low groan escaped my throat as I leaned into his magical touch. The combination of near death and a wicked hangover was not making for very strong defenses against their sexual advances. *I wonder how far we can take it without activating this magic ritual crap ...?*

"Reg ..." I sighed, letting him rub the stress of the past twenty-four hours from my tense shoulders with his smooth, liquid movements. His fingers dug into my muscles, kneading all my inhibitions away.

"Yes, *sugar tits*?" he purred, his lips brushing my ear as he stepped in close behind me, his body aligning with my own and his already rock-hard dick pressing into my lower back. I was decently tall for a girl, around five eight or so, but these guys towered over me.

An intense mental image hit me, of myself climbing up on Reg, wrapping my legs around his waist and holding on for dear life while he pounded into me against the shower wall.

"What the shit was that?" I gasped, shaking my head to clear the vision and stepping out of the horny water elemental's reach. So, they used to be called nymphs, huh? *Nympho* was far more accurate than elemental. Hell, as wet as I was getting right now, maybe I was one, too?

"What was what, ST?" His smug grin said all I needed to know about the origin of that little daydream. Reg had the look of a man who was used to giving women wet dreams with a simple touch. "You look like you're thinking naughty things about me ... perhaps I can give you a hand into the shower and you can tell me all about it?" He took another step toward me, and closed the bathroom door behind himself, shutting the two of us into a confined space full of steam.

Heat flushed my lips—not just the ones on my face—as I backed up a couple more steps and my butt hit the vanity.

"Reg ..." I warned, a little breathlessly. "I'm not doing this magical mating bullshit with you right now, so get that idea out of your head."

He prowled closer to me, until there was barely an inch separating our bodies; I could smell his clean, fresh waterfall scent and feel his warm breath against the curve of my neck.

"What if I said we could just fuck, and not *mate*?" he murmured seductively, his voice pitched low, shivers of arousal rolling over me like a gentle ocean tide.

Wait, did he just say what I think he just said? Holy fucking shitballs, yes!

"How do I know you're not just saying that?" I whispered, the desire riding thick in my voice because *fuck,* all I could think about since these assholes burst into my life was exactly what Reg had offered—getting my pipes cleaned out.

"I guess you'd have to trust me, ST. And I'd say it'd be pretty obvious if I suddenly started chanting in the language of the elementals, and drawing runes on your skin while we came ..." He pulled back just far enough to look me in the eye with a challenging brow raised.

44

I was around ninety nine percent sure he was lying but, I mean, surely if we didn't go *all* the way …?

"Maybe just a little foreplay wouldn't kill me …" I was mostly thinking out loud, but the wicked smile curving across Reg's face said he was one hundred percent on board with my suggestion. "But I swear to god, Reginald, if you try any magic shit—"

"I won't," he promised quickly—a little *too* quickly.

"And we're just fooling around, not playing hide the plunger." I narrowed my eyes at him, trying to look stern but probably failing miserably. Just the idea of playing hide the plunger with Reg was making me insanely wet. Good thing it was already so steamy in the bathroom.

"I reserve the right to hide the plunger, should you change your mind at any point," he smirked, then without waiting for further rules from me, dipped his head back down and claimed my lips with his own.

Kissing Reg was, without a doubt, like nothing I had ever experienced before. His lips were soft and supple as they caressed mine, applying the perfect amount of pressure while my heart raced out of control. His tongue teased the tip of my own, flicking and then drawing away just enough to make me want more, more, *more.*

Somewhere in the back of my mind, a little voice was screaming at me that this was a *terrible* idea, but I told the frigid bitch to shut the fuck up. We were way past the point of stopping as my body pumped pure estrogen instead of blood.

The blonde elemental hooked his thumbs into the waistband of my boy shorts, sliding them down to pool at my feet, before hoisting me up to perch on the edge of the sink. My heated flesh met the cool ceramic of the vanity and I sucked a gasp against Reg's mouth before spreading my knees wide to give his roving hands access to my rising damp.

"Well, well, well, what have we here, dirty girl?" His fingers had just encountered the little bar of metal pierced through my clitoral hood, and he flicked it firmly, making me groan as my eyes rolled back in my head.

It had been on a drunken night out with Britt, *of course*, that she had convinced me to get my clit pierced. The fucking thing had hurt like an absolute *venomous tit-kicking bitch* going in but damn I loved it now.

"I think I'm going to need a closer look at this," Reg murmured, kissing his way down my neck then dropping to his knees between my legs. His warm breath feathered over my pierced flesh and I dropped my head back to rest on the mirror, sighing with pleasure and anticipation.

While I waited impatiently for him to make his move, the shower shut off and the bathroom echoed with the distinctive rattle of my shower curtain yanking open.

Ugh, Ari, you fucking moron. How did you not notice there was someone already in the shower?

My eyes snapped open and met Shane's smoldering gaze as he stood there in my shower, naked, dripping and *very* turned-on.

Reg deliberately took advantage of my distraction and seized my piercing between his teeth, lightly tugging at it while his fingers slid into my leaky faucet.

Okay, reality check—if for some strange reason I ever decided to *actually* date these guys, they were getting new professions. The puns were out of control.

"Holy shit," I groaned as I relaxed into the elemental's touch. That was when it really struck me—this guy was *not* human. All the men I'd ever been with used their fingers like

46

hammers, ramming my special place like they were in a marathon.

But Reg, the asshole? He finessed me with hooked fingertips, teasing my G-spot into a swollen frenzy, activating parts of me that had lain dormant for far, far, *far* too long.

"Well, shoot," Shane said, crossing his arms over his chest and smirking at me like watching his buddy go down on a girl was not a particularly new phenomenon. Whatever. I didn't care —having them both in the bathroom with me wasn't just twice as hot. It was like *surface of the sun* sexy. "Looks like somebody's in a much better mood than they were last night."

"Hey Skeeter," Reg said, lifting his head up briefly but continuing to work me with fingers dipped in ink. I hadn't paid much attention to them before, but the cascade of color down his arm trailed right onto those magical fingers and *inside* of me. It was hard not to notice when they were quickly and efficiently bringing me to orgasm. "How many plumbers does it take to make a shimmer climax?"

"Shit, Reg," he said, stepping out of the shower and bringing both his gloriously erect cock and dripping wet muscles close enough to touch. Like Reg, he was tattooed, too —and in all the right places. Images decorated his bare chest and shoulders, drawing my eye to all the best, most masculine parts of him. And I mean *all* the masculine parts. He even had ink on his junk. "I'd have to say *two* should suffice."

Shane stepped up close to the side of the counter and turned my face toward his with a warm, wet hand.

"No runes," I gasped out, the very idea of language quickly becoming anathema to me. What were words for again? Why did words matter? They just fucking *didn't* when I had two otherworldly studs doing their best to woo me. "No magic."

"Oh, shush up," Shane whispered, capturing my mouth with his. Later on, I was going to beat his ass for that comment, but for right now… Dear god, right now I'd have let these guys get away with murder.

Our tongues tangled in a dangerous frenzy, spurred on by the almost painfully pleasurable curve of Reg's fingers and the wicked burn of his lips against my clitoral hood piercing.

Best drunken mistake I ever made.

My gasps filled Shane's mouth the same way his tongue filled mine, and I knew without a doubt that I was close—a hell of a lot closer than I'd been in my months long dry spell. But I didn't want it to end that quick…or right there.

Crap.

Stopping at foreplay for me was like asking an alcoholic to only have one drink.

I was addicted.

And I didn't want to stop.

I can't believe I'm going to screw the plumber—how cliché, I thought, but the deed was already halfway to being done. My climax snuck up on me, curling up from my clit and gathering in my belly in an unstoppable wave. Before I knew it, I was panting and fighting back a scream as I dug my nails into Reg's head and sucked Shane's lip into my mouth, biting down hard enough that I tasted blood.

"Shit," I whispered, chest rising and falling with rapid breaths, "shit, shit, shit."

"It's okay, honey doll," Shane whispered, brushing hair back from my sweaty face. "We're not human—and we don't have human diseases."

"Like I haven't heard *that* line before," I said, wiping off my tongue with the palm of my hand and trying to ignore the violent, angry throbbing inside of me. *More, more, more* it said. *Greedy bitch,* I told my cunt.

But then Reg was rising to his feet and pushing his holey jeans down his hips, letting them fall to the floor in a pool of denim.

"Well, shimmer," he said, and there was just something about the way that word rolled off the arrogant twist of his lips that turned me on like crazy. "What'll it be next?"

I just stared at him, completely and utterly out of my comfort zone.

One, I'd never screwed the handyman before.

Two, I'd definitely never screwed *two handymen* before.

And three … well fuck three, this was happening.

"Condoms?" I asked and the two idiots looked at each other like *I* was the stupid one.

"We don't need condoms," Reg spat and Shane grinned. "Remember, runes and magic? Only way to get pregnant. Besides, you're a human, we'd have to mark you first."

"Oh, yeah, and *that* makes perfect sense." But those words came out in a breathy rush as Reg grabbed me by the hips and pulled me off the counter. Instinctively, I wrapped my legs around his muscular body and held on for dear life.

And oh, that was so not a chore at all.

Shane stepped up behind me, penning me in between the two hot, hard bodies. Thank god my Gram's house had bathrooms the size of my entire apartment (the one I'd been evicted from).

"I don't … I've never done *this* particular, um, activity before," I said, but all I got were two masculine laughs in response.

"No anal?" Reg asked, quirking a brow. "Come on, Ari, don't try to trick a trickster."

"Fuck you," I said, but then… "I threw all my shit in the drawers when I moved in. Check the one on the right."

In a New York minute, Shane had the lube in his hand and was slicking it along the length of his cock. I couldn't actually *see* anything but Reg's smirking face, but I could sure as hell hear the wet pumping of his fist.

"You ready, sugar?" he asked me in that deep Southern drawl of his.

"God, yes," I purred—purred?! since when do I ever *purr*—and felt Shane's hands on my ass. Like a boss, he helped guide the thick, hard length of Reg's cock inside of me. My gasp, that said it *all.* "Fuck me running," I whispered, but what few words I could manage to push out past lips swollen from kissing were cut right off when Shane entered me.

Slow and easy, he took me first with one finger, then two. When he got to three, I felt my body go completely limp.

Good thing I had two supernatural hotties to hold me up.

Shane moved nice and gentle inside of me, working my body up to take his cock.

"Ready, sugar?" he chuckled in my ear and I growled into Reg's neck where I was resting my face.

"Quit dicking around and fuck me already, Shane!" The words came out in more of a wanton moan than the sassy snap I'd intended but *who the fuck cared*, I was in dick heaven right now.

Reg shifted his hold on my thighs, so he was both holding me up and spreading my cheeks for his buddy. Shane didn't need to be told twice and I heard the slick slide of his hand stroking lube down his cock once more before the thick head pressed against my storm water drain.

Argh, now I couldn't stop the plumbing jokes even in my head!

Exhaling a long breath, I tried not to faint from sheer overwhelming pleasure as my body was stretched in ways it never had been before.

"Jesus Christ, Shane," I hissed when I eventually managed to suck in a breath, and he chuckled. Darting a confused look at Reg, all I got back was a broad grin that told me nothing.

"I'm not even halfway in yet, honey doll." Shane's southern drawl rolled over me and I moaned loudly as he pressed in deeper, then deeper, and then *deeper still*.

After what felt like an eternity, albeit a fucking fantastic eternity, he finally bottomed out with his rock hard abs pressed tight against my back.

"*Now* I'm in," he panted, wrapping his own hands under my thighs to assist Reg in holding me aloft. They began to move in and out, their synchronization nearly flawless, their cocks compressing that thin layer of flesh between my pussy and my ass. It was a massage of the best kind, two thick hard shafts stimulating a bundle of raw nerves.

Biting my lip *hard,* I held back porn worthy whimpers of pleasure, all coherent thoughts abandoning my brain for greener, sexier pastures. Waves of ecstasy rolled over me, dragging me under as I dropped my head back to rest on Shane's broad, wet chest. I could feel his breath stirring my hair, the faint scents of mint toothpaste and floral shampoo mixing in the steamy air.

Far too quickly I felt another earth-shattering orgasm building and I knew that trying to hold it off would be like trying to sandbag a tsunami. Muscles clenching hard, I shifted my weight forward to rest on Reg, and as my climax thundered through me, I sank my teeth into his shoulder in order to stifle my scream.

"Oh fuck," Shane hissed, at the same time as Reg cursed something unintelligible and their thrusting picked up pace, never once losing the rhythm as they reached their own orgasms. *Definitely not human—they had far too much skill* and *stamina.*

For a moment, we were all frozen on the spot, hearts racing, trying to catch our breath until the bathroom door flew open so hard it practically fell off its hinges.

"Ah hah! I knew it!" Britt crowed, with the biggest grin I think I'd ever seen on her face. "I told you I could smell sex! Damn girl, look at you just taking it like a pro or some shit."

"Fucking werewolves," Shane muttered, still lodged firmly inside my ass. "Furball darlin', do you mind? You're letting a draft in."

"Well isn't this an interesting turn of events?" Billy leered as he appeared in the doorway behind my best friend. It ought to be a crime how good looking that man managed to look at this hour of the morning. His charcoal gray hair was artfully disheveled and his eyes were like hot coals as they seared a path all over my skin where he inspected me.

"Come on guys, give them some privacy—*this* time." George, ever the voice of reason, coaxed. He dragged a very reluctant Britt out of the doorway then returned to pull the door shut, but not before raking his own tree bark brown eyes *all* over us in our precarious position.

"Uh guys?" I prompted, once the door was closed once more but no one moved. "You can let me down now."

"Yes, I suppose we can," Reg murmured, then stole one more kiss from my swollen lips before sliding free of my body and easing my shaking legs to the floor when Shane also withdrew his industrial sized wrench from my S-bend.

For lack of anything intelligent to say, I cleared my throat awkwardly—because what the fuck did one say to the two supernatural plumbers who had pounded both my drains less than twenty four hours after we met?

"Well, good thing the shower's working ..." I nervously backed toward the bathtub while Shane and Reg watched me like predators, their eyes hot and their dicks hardening once more.

Nope. *Definitely* not human. Where the fuck were their refractory periods?!

"No!" I scolded, suddenly finding the mental fortitude that I must have dropped here earlier when my inner sex fiend had taken over. "I am going to wash up—*alone*—and then we're going to discuss how to get me out of this mess that you all caused."

Stepping into the tub, I quickly whipped the curtain closed before I could be tempted *again* by those otherworldly bodies and ended up dragging them both in here for round two under my newly restored water pressure.

"Alright, sweet thing, we'll just meet you in the kitchen then?" Shane very wisely responded. "How do you like your coffee?"

Good old Southern manners.

"Britt knows," I responded, stepping under the hot water and lathering up some soap between my hands. There was a whole lot of bodily fluid slicking down my thighs that needed cleaning up.

"Give us a yell if you need help scrubbing your back, ST," Reg snickered, "or just if you want to play hide the plunger again." Then the fucking asshole snaked a hand through the shower curtain and slapped me on the ass before following his buddy out of the room and leaving me in peace.

What the ever loving fuck had I just done? I mean, aside from the incredible double-teaming threesome that'd left me totally and utterly *ruined* for any human man, ever again.

Thank Christ neither of them had started chanting anything or drawing runes on me while we fucked, because I would not have been in any position to stop them.

Unless Reg was making that shit up. Fuck, what if Reg was making that shit up? Had I just been played?

Nah. Nah. There was no way.

Right? Right?!

5

CHAPTER FIVE

I decided it would just bother me if I found out I'd been 'marked' and besides—it was too goddamn early in the morning to ask. I would worry about that bit later. Avoiding legit problems was kind of my thing. Plus, you know, orgasmic afterglow and all that.

"Thank you, hun," I said to Britt as I accepted a mug with a picture of a fox that said *For Fox Sake,* only you know, with the picture of the animal instead of the word. It was a euphemism for *fuck,* in case you'd missed that.

I took a sip, assuming Britt's sniggering a-hole face was just about the whole 'caught you getting double-teamed in your Gram's bathroom' thing.

But nope.

"*Gawd,*" I gagged as I practically choked on a mouthful of whiskey. "You spiked my coffee?!"

"Hair of the dog," Britt said and then her eyes lit up. "Get it?! Because I'm a werewolf it's *extra* funny."

"Is it even funnier if I call you a *bitch*?" I said, but she just glared at me.

"No, actually, that makes you sexist."

I rolled my eyes and ignored her, padding into the main living room area where all four men were sitting. I tried to pretend like two of them hadn't just snaked my pipes, but that was damn near impossible. Just *looking* at them got my water flowing all over again, if you catch my drift.

"Alright, rent is due … today," I said, glancing up at the crumbling ceiling and admiring the old, rusted tin tiles. If these dickwads *actually* paid up, maybe I'd have enough money to fix up the old place? "And every thirty days after that—plus a security deposit."

I dropped my chin to look at the guys.

"You're not serious, are you?" Reg asked, lounging on my couch like he owned the place. Apparently that's what he did best—*lounge*. He just draped himself over everything like it belonged to him—including me.

"*Non-refundable* security deposit is what I meant to say," I continued, taking in a deep breath. "Considering you all can turn into, like, elemental *things,* I need to have a nest egg in case you set something on fire or cause water damage or … whatever air and earth elementals do."

"I could regrow all the tree roots in your pipes again?" George said, slicking a hand back through his woody brown hair. He was the only one of the four that wasn't covered in tattoos—just a single tree of life in black on his right bicep. I couldn't stop staring at it.

"Money," I said, taking another large gulp of my more-whiskey-than-coffee coffee. "Five hundred each—"

"That's in *Australian pesos*," Britt said, and I felt my lips purse. I didn't bother to correct her—some things just weren't worth arguing about. "Or whatever it is they use down there."

"And ... a thousand each for security deposits."

"Sugar," Shane said, eyeing me up and down in a way that would've been criminal if he didn't look all Southern and cute and whatnot. The fact that he'd just unclogged the wad of celibacy I'd been harboring for months didn't hurt much either. "Honestly, that plumbing job we just did was worth about seventeen grand ..."

"That's right," Reg continued, snapping his fingers while Billy smirked quietly in the corner. I tried not to look at the bite mark etched into the perfect curve of his shoulder, right above a stylized anchor tattoo. For some reason, I felt much less amicable toward him than I did Shane—more than likely that's because he was a prick. "In fact, you owe *us* money."

"I never signed anything," I said indignantly and Reg grinned.

"Neither did we," he replied, just as smoothly. See, prick.

"The fact is," Shane continued, and I got the sense that he was sort of the 'leader' of the group, "we're not exactly wealthy, you understand."

"Oh, you didn't just get one scrub, but four of them," Britt inserted, not at all helpfully.

"You're poor?" I asked, and I felt this sinking feeling inside my stomach. If I was going to have to entertain four elemental men in my life, I just sort of assumed they'd be wealthy, like vampires or something, stashing money away centuries ago and living off the interest.

"We just started this business," George said carefully, glancing at the others. "And frankly, with Charlie in town, it's hard to get a lot of work."

"Charlie, the plumber?" I asked, remembering the man I'd spoken to and his reluctant suggestion that I hire these four assholes. "And why's that? You're supernatural beings for Christ's sake, shouldn't you be blowing him out of the water?"

"Charlie's Reg's father," Shane explained as Reg scowled and crossed his arms over his chest. The motion was somehow sexy as fuck, seeing as how he was tattooed and wearing a tight navy blue wifebeater that clung to his copious muscles. "And his quad is head of the *elemental storm* in this area."

"What the fuck is an elemental storm?" I asked, sucking down the rest of my coffee. It gave me a nice, lightheaded feeling that seemed to distract from the distinct soreness between my thighs. And let's just say—one pipe was a little bit sorer than the other.

"A storm of elementals is like ..." Britt started and then snapped her fingers. "A chaos of succubi."

I just stared at her.

"Not helping," I whispered, finally relenting and taking a seat on the arm of the couch next to Reg. Even from here, I could smell him. Truthfully? He smelled fucking *good,* like a rainstorm after a long, hot summer.

"A pack of wolves," Reg said, giving Britt a look I'd seen a million times. He thought she was stupid. In reality, she was willfully ignorant. Big difference there. "A murder of crows. A herd of cattle. A flock of birds. A lead of foxes. A kindle of kittens."

"A kindle of kittens," I said with a chuckle, but then I waved the laughter away. Nope. The ovs were still pumping estrogen into me at astronomical levels, and it was making me go a little loopy. "Right, so a storm is just ... your word for a group of elementals?"

"More like a city or a state," George explained, ever the helpful one. "It's elemental law that we obey Charlie."

"So you went into business as his direct competitor?" I asked, trying not to be a snarky bitch but failing miserably. "That makes perfect sense."

"Charlie won't *let* us do anything else," Reg responded, and I could see that this was a sore spot with him. "This is the only storm-sanctioned way for us to make money, and to be honest, you were our first real client and we turned you into a shimmer. Things aren't exactly looking up for me and my boys."

"I … am now jobless," I began, trying not to get hysterical. "Penniless." I flung my hand out to indicate Britt. "My best friend is a sequined cocktail dress wearing werewolf and now I have four moneyless bums squatting inside my Gram's crumbling old house?"

"The toilets work," Billy supplied, head parked on his fist as he spoke up for the first time. His eyes burned like embers, this orange-brown color that bore right into my soul. Made me want to punch him a little. The leather jacket made me want to punch him a little less.

"This is what you're telling me?" I asked with a hysterical little laugh.

"Oh, and also," Reg continued, nodding his head like he'd just simply forgotten this little detail. "You're now an elemental, too. Spirit, to be exact."

"You …" I dropped the mug, but it didn't shatter all dramatically. Actually, it just sort of hit me in the big toe and hurt like a bitch. "You're telling me … that this is basically *Captain* fucking *Planet*?"

"No, that was earth, air, water, fire, and *heart,* silly," Britt said, and then her brows went up. "Um, sweetheart …"

I glanced down at my hands and noticed that they'd turned ... a very odd purple-black color that was quickly becoming see-through.

I did not stay conscious long enough to figure out what *that* meant.

"So ... fucking Elementals is like asking for an STD?"

That was the very first thing I said when I awoke.

Reg and Shane may not have *marked* me per se, but they did a whole lot of other things that I wanted *un*done. Now.

"Not quite how I'd put it, Blossom, but yeah similar ..." George's gentle voice accompanied the sudden arrival of his unnaturally bronze face an inch in front of mine. "How are you feeling? You might be a bit light-headed for a while."

"Blossom?" I scowled at him, not liking all these new nicknames I seemed to be earning from the asshole elementals.

"Yeah," he grinned, "because you're so pretty, like a freshly opened cherry blossom in spring ..." His hand smoothed over my wild blonde hair, which probably looked like I had just been fucked sideways. Which, I guessed, was appropriate.

Pushing George gently aside, I sat up from the floor where I had obviously landed when I fainted ... or dematerialized ... or whatever the fuck had just happened.

"Okay, so point me in the direction of some magical penicillin because I am *not* on board with being the pink power ranger here." Narrowing my eyes at the four broke-ass plumbers staring down at me, I tried really hard to ignore the nagging suspicion that whatever they'd done to me, it was totally irreversible.

"Ohhhh, if Ari doesn't want to be the pink power ranger, could I?" Britt asked, practically bouncing on her toes with excitement as Shane, ever the gentleman, helped me up off the floor. "I look soooo good in pink PVC!"

Billy and Reg both gave my bestie a look that spoke volumes to what they thought of her and I stifled an eye roll at her expense. It wasn't her fault: she genuinely did look great in PVC.

"Here." Shane passed me my mug of spiked coffee that someone had refilled after my, um ...

"Guys, what the shit just happened? I could have *sworn* my hands disappeared ..." I wasn't even sure if I really wanted to hear the answer to this but Britt, the helpful puppy that she was, piped up excitedly.

"OMG girl, it was *mental*. Your whole body turned this like, really pretty eggplant color and then you just disappeared. One minute you're standing there in all your just-fucked glory, and the next you were gone!" She nodded at me like I had just pulled a rabbit from my ass ... which I suppose I sort of had, in a magic show kind of way.

Sitting my ass back down on Gram's sagging sofa, I took a gulp of my fresh coffee then coughed as the whiskey burned my throat.

Jesus, is there even any coffee in here?

"Boys," I prompted, giving them all a serious death glare, "please tell me where to get the cure for this Elemental STD so that I can go back to being a normal human?"

"A normal human with a giant target painted on her forehead for being an unmarked shimmer, you mean?" Reg smirked, drawing my attention to his lush lips and mesmerizing me for a moment while my brain skipped off to replay him going down on me in the bathroom.

The asshole knew it too, as he dragged his tongue across his lower lip, then winked one clear blue eye at me.

"There is no cure," Billy responded in a dickish tone of voice, making me want to punch him in the beautiful face. "I can't believe you didn't stop to ask questions before letting two unknown supernatural plumbers pound your drains unprotected."

"What?" I shrieked. "You told me we didn't need condoms!" Shane and Reg were so lucky they were out of reach or I really would have started throwing punches.

"Oh, sweetie," Britt sighed, "how often have you heard *that* line before?"

Billy rolled his burning coal colored eyes and rubbed a hand over his stubbled chin.

"Fuck me, for a chick who's best friends with a slutty rogue werewolf, you're seriously clueless, Arizona Smoke."

"Do. Not. Slut. Shame," I snarled the words at the sultry fire elemental, but couldn't really disagree with his assessment. My actions had been firmly motivated by my hungry cunt rather than my common sense.

"Tell her the rest of it, Skeeter." Billy met my angry gaze with a mocking eyebrow raised, and I got a sinking feeling in my stomach for what 'the rest of it' was going to be.

Shane cleared his throat uncomfortably and Reg leered at me with a look that was *pure sex*, making my cheeks flush with heat and my o-ring clench at the memory of being double-teamed by their dip tubes.

"Sugar, it's sort of one of those things, where the water only runs one way …" He was clearly trying to be tactful and it was making me even more nervous. "It's like, when a pipe gets clogged and the only way to clear it is to force the obstruction through …"

"What Skeeter is trying to say, Blossom," George interrupted, taking a seat next to me on the couch and casually taking my hand in his, "is that you broke the tap off after turning on the water."

There was a long pause where no one spoke, but I was officially confused as fuck. These plumbing metaphors were starting to get obscure and this was just *not* the time for obscurity.

"You're going to have to fuck me and George, too," Billy clarified with a wicked look in his eye. "Until you do, you're going to have no control over your elemental powers and you'll keep spontaneously turning into your spirit form."

"Yes, queen! Gang bang for Ari!" Britt screamed. "I'll get you more whiskey girl, you're gonna need it!" She took off back into my kitchen and started clattering around.

Turning to George for confirmation that this was true, my gaze snagged back on his tree of life tattoo. Damn, that was some beautiful ink. I was so glad George seemed to be allergic to wearing shirts while he was in my house.

Snap out of it, Ari, you horny bitch. You have some major leaks to plug right now!

"So, Reg lied then." I glared at Reg, extracting my hand from George's hold and folding my arms across my chest, pretending to be angry but really just covering up the evidence of my *own* taps being turned on. *Mental note: buy padded bras.*

"Lied about what, ST?" he asked, aiming for the picture of innocence and failing miserably. The way he tousled his short blonde hair with his fingers and flashed white teeth in a handsome face, he looked anything *but* innocent.

"I told you not to *mark* me. You said we could '*just fuck*'. Those were your words, Reg—*just fuck*." My body was practically shaking I was so mad, and I wasn't positive half of my ire wasn't directed at myself for being such a gullible twit. "And now here I am, turning fucking *invisible* ..."

I held up a shaking hand and sure enough, it was darkening to purple-black again.

A small, scared whimper slipped from my throat.

"Ari," Shane started, but I was already backing up and turning away, heading for my purse and the front door like ... well, what the hell kind of metaphor is there for a half-invisible woman that's slowly changing color?

Not a whole lot, that's for fucking sure.

"Arizona!" Britt called out, but I was outside and down the steps before she could catch up to me. I flung open the door to my hearse (I know, I'm clichéd as fuck, typical tortured soul driving a death cab) and noticed my neighbor, a woman named Alberta O'Sullivan (also clichéd) going through the massive blue bin that held my glass recyclables.

"Sure are a lot of booze bottles in here," she said when she caught me staring at her. I knew Alberta because even Gram had had problems with her and she'd been nowhere *near* as screwed up as I was. She had her shit together. Mine ... well, it wasn't overflowing from the toilet onto the floor but it was getting pretty damn close.

I glanced down at my hands and realized that I was still half-purple and almost completely see-through from the neck down.

Alberta didn't seem to notice.

She was more concerned with digging through my glass recyclables than actually looking me in the face.

"Can you please get the hell off my property and go *home*? Believe it or not, I've got more important shit to worry about today than whether or not you approve of my drinking habits."

"Rubbish is public property once it's been set at the curb," she said, and then she mumbled, "*Fumblin' Dublin,*" in her thick Irish accent, just quiet enough so that she could at least *pretend* to be whispering.

I narrowed my eyes.

"I know what a fumblin' Dublin is," I said, crossing my (very see-through) arms over my chest. "I'm not a drunk."

The lady doth protest too much, methinks, a voice whispered in the back of my mind. Now, if my subconscious was quoting Shakespeare, I knew I was in serious trouble.

"Ari!" Billy called out, clomping down the steps in black work boots and a frown. His gray hair was artfully mussed and a small flame tattoo peeked up just over the edge of his jacket collar. "You can't just run away from this." He grabbed the driver's side door when I tried to close it and held it with preternatural strength.

The old Irish lady from next door was now fully gaping without any sense of shame.

Fan-fucking-tastic.

"Please remove your"—*ridiculously long and sexy*—"fingers from my car door," I said with a slight growl. But damn it. Billy had this musky, charcoal scent to him, like a campfire on a cold night. I just wanted to lean into him and ...

No.

No, no, no,

Bad ovaries! Bad uterus! DOWN GIRLS!

"I just need to get some space. This whole thing is making me feel like there are kangaroos loose in the top paddock," I said and Billy cocked an eyebrow.

"I have no idea what that means," he told me, his voice this lazy West Coast purr that made me think of my time at Uni in Santa Cruz. Go Banana Slugs! Seriously, though. He sounded like the boys I went to college with. And I liked that. *A lot.* It made me feel young and carefree … and like my body wasn't fading and morphing and twisting without giving two fucks how I felt about it.

Oh, and also, there was *still* an old Irish lady staring at me and Billy. Fortunately for me, she was looking mostly at Billy.

"But you can't run, Arizona," he finished finally, sighing and raking his fingers through his charcoal gray hair. For a second there—just a split second—he looked like he might actually say something genuine, something serious that I could hold onto, cling to in all of this chaos.

But like Leonardo DiCaprio's character, Jack, in *Titanic* … I guess that floating door was just not big enough for the both of us.

"Besides, you don't *want* to run from this, do you?"

"You don't know what the fuck I want, dickweed." I slammed the door shut on his fingers, hit the locks, and peeled out of the driveway whilst flipping off a ninety-five year old woman.

Yep.

Today was already lookin' to be a fun one.

6

---◆---❖---◆---

CHAPTER SIX

I made it about … two blocks before I reversed, called Britt from my cell, and had her tag along for protection purposes. After all, I was a lot less keen about getting ripped apart by a succubus than I was having Britt along to nag and make fun of me all day.

"So, when are you leaving?" I asked casually, even though in my heart of hearts, I didn't really want her to go. Britt lived in Montana and worked—get ready for it—as an environmental scientist who helped balance the ecology of Yellowstone National Park with the massive influx of tourists.

Yeah, I didn't get it either.

Or wait … werewolf … environmental scientist. Okay, wow, my best friend was starting to make a whole lot more sense now. I always wondered how she survived in Middle of Butt-fuck Nowhere, USA.

Wolf stuff …

"Are you part of a pack?" I asked, and then wondered if that was rude. Eh. Britt didn't much care if she was rude to me ten, twenty, or two hundred times in a single day. Might as well just go all-out and ask.

But all of a sudden, my best friend, the most confident woman in the entire world, clammed up like a deep-sea crustacean and glanced sharply away from me.

"I was," she said, and the gentle melancholy of her voice gave me the chills. In a distant sort of way, it reminded me of a wolf's howl, that soft, sad sound that echoes through the forest at night, a desperate whimper for company, contact, for *family*. "But now," she said, sucking in a sudden, sharp breath, "I'm moving in with you!"

I almost crashed the car.

And not just because of Britt's statement (although that was part of the problem), but because a man with *wings* had just stepped into the middle of the road.

"Oh, shit," I said, but when I tried to put the pedal to the metal, the engine in the old hearse coughed and sputtered like the bodies it had used to transport (I'm morbid as fuck, I get it). "Britt," I said softly, but she was already growling low and deep in her throat.

But I'd already sort of figured it out.

I was an idiot.

Clearly, succubi (aren't the dude ones incubi?) didn't like me.

I should've just stayed home and let Billy light me up.

"Stay here, Ari," Britt snarled, her teeth already elongating and her cheeks sprouting fur, "I've got this."

She threw open the passenger side door and shifted into her wolf form while in midair—the pink heels fell off, but the crop top and booty shorts stayed. It should've been funny, watching my best friend leap toward a stark naked man with enormous bat wings, furry wolf butt cheeks hanging out of her shorts, but in my current state, all it did was make me anxious.

Maybe because I knew I'd fucked up? Yeah, that was probably it. *I should've stayed at home with the crazy supernatural plumbers.*

Wide-eyed, I watched from behind my steering wheel as Britt sunk her gleaming fangs into the naked man's arm. With a violent snarl, he turned his death glare to the rabid wolf hanging from his limb, shaking her loose with a spatter of blood across the pavement. Fortunately, we were still in suburbia so there weren't a *ton* of people around, but I could only wonder what the hell would happen if one of the neighbors called the police.

Britt stood up, shaking her charcoal and ash gray coat out before circling the naked weirdo in a low crouch, looking for an opening. Seeing as she'd taken out the woman in the alleyway without much pomp and circumstance, I just sort of figured she had this in the bag, too.

The naked incubi simply stood and watched, blood dripping from the wound in his arm, as he waited for Britt to make her next move. When she did, launching herself at him and going for the throat, he turned at the last minute and swatted her with one of the large, leathery bat wings decorating his back.

Breath catching in my throat, my heart froze as I watched Britt's wolf form slam into a power pole then crumple to the ground in a lifeless pile of fur. Terror pushed me forward and I tore out of my seat, stumbling towards her deathly still form.

I was so focused on my bestie that I didn't even notice the incubus stepping directly into my path. My momentum was enough that I just plowed straight into his rock-hard chest, sending us both tumbling in a rolling ball of arms and legs and wings and penis (just one—his) until we came to a grunting halt against a parked car.

Sadly, a ninja I was not, so when we eventually stopped, it was with his hand wrapped around my throat and his weight firmly centered on my chest, his knees pinning my arms.

"Any last words, *shimmer*?" he spat (also clichéd) as he tightened his hold on my neck and I knew my eyes were bugging out with lack of air. I couldn't have spoken even if I did have something amazing and memorable to say.

His hand tightened around my throat, and I knew he was getting perverse pleasure out of killing me slowly. How did I know? He was stark bloody naked and straddling my chest. His boner was practically whacking me in the chin with every gasping breath I struggled to take.

As my airway constricted, my lungs started screaming for oxygen and my vision clouded over. Hot tears began streaming from my eyes, which only seemed to make him more excited. Eyes gleaming, a twisted smile curved across his lips.

"Fucking human trash. That's it—show me how *scared* you are." A little drool dripped from his lips and landed on my cheek as he spoke. His words were panted with excitement and I seriously hoped he would succeed in killing me before I ended up wearing his excitement on my face.

"Nigel!" A sharp voice snapped, jerking the jerk-off's attention away from me. "We want her alive, remember?"

"What?" he protested, his sick smile sliding from his face as he frowned up at my possible savior. "No! Standing orders are to kill any unmarked shimmer. This is an unmarked shimmer, and I am killing it."

"Not this time. Release her neck or I'll tear your bloody cock off." Whoever this newcomer was, he was seriously saving my bacon. Surely being taken alive had to have more opportunities for escape than the situation I was currently in?

The perverted incubus straddling me reluctantly eased his grip on my throat and I dragged in several panicked, gasping breaths then started coughing violently. My almost-killer gave me a disgusted look and backed away, looking considerably less excited now that I wouldn't be dying in his hands immediately.

"Seriously?" I squeaked out between coughs. "Nigel the incubus? I would've thought demons who fed on sex or whatever would have sexy names, like Antonio or Damien or something."

"Don't be ridiculous," my savior scoffed stepping into my line of sight and holding out a hand to help me to my feet. A wicked smile curved across his lips, dripping sex. If I hadn't almost just died or been contaminated by elemental cum, I might've thought he was hot. "Damien is such a clichéd name— I'm Adonis, by the way."

I cocked a brow.

"Adonis ... as in the word for *very handsome young man*? No, you're right, that's way less clichéd than Damien." Warily, I eyed him up. He was clearly also an incubus, with the same huge leathery wings, godlike good looks, allergy to clothing, and cold, cruel looking eyes.

"Uh, thanks," I muttered, brushing aside his hand as I hauled myself back to my feet and looked over to where I had last seen Britt. She was still lying comatose on the pavement, sending a thrill of fear down my spine.

"What the fuck did you do to my friend?" I demanded, noticing the smear of blood on the sidewalk next to her crumpled lifeless body. Panic rushed through me once more as I started toward her, only to be stopped by tight fingers curling painfully around my wrist.

"A rogue werewolf isn't exactly of much concern to me," the new incubus drawled in a bored tone of voice that said, *quite frankly, my dear, I don't give a damn about your missing werewolf friend.* "Shimmer, we don't have time for your delusional ranting. You've been summoned by the COCS, and no one keeps the COCS waiting."

Stunned, I blinked at him a couple of times before replying. "Sorry ... did you just say I've been summoned by *cocks*?" Maybe the oxygen deprivation was messing with my hearing ...

"COCS. C.O.C.S. Committee of Combined Supernaturals." He rolled his eyes like I was some sort of flaming idiot for not knowing what the fuck he was on about.

"This is bullshit, and you know it," Nigel the Pervert muttered, scuffing the pavement with his toe. "I earned this kill; you should've let me have it."

"Shut up, Nigel," the clearly more superior incubus snapped, then turned his cruel eyes on me. "Now then, shimmer, we can do this the easy way, or the hard way—"

He had barely even finished that word before I began hollering at the top of my voice, hoping that someone in this godforsaken area of town might come to my aid.

"Hard way it is," the incubus muttered, then punched me hard in the face.

When I woke, my face was pounding like I had just been punched. *Oh, wait ...*

My cheek was pressed against a hard concrete surface and when I tried to move, I found that my arms and legs were bound tight, so the best I could manage was a wiggling shuffle to roll over.

Given a bit more visibility, it became clear I was in an underground cell of some sort, complete with iron bars and dripping tap somewhere.

Pity they couldn't call a plumber to come and fix it, then maybe I'd get rescued by accident ...

Total life events worth mentioning before meeting those assholes: zero.

Total life events worth mentioning now: a succubus with a gun, a werewolf as a bestie, men who can turn into elemental dragons (and seem to have, like, zero refractory period when it comes to getting hard again), and a kidnapping.

I'd never really been the sort of person who craved a normal, boring existence, but now ... I was sort of craving a boring, normal existence.

Being a minimum wage earning barista in a crappy apartment had never really been glamorous, but it was certainly better than lying on a cement floor in the middle of some secretive incubus hideout waiting for *cocks*. Er, COCS. Sorry.

The more I thought about cocks—the other kind this time— the more pissed off I became. It was like, who the *hell* did those assholes think they were? Clearly, leaving the bathroom door open whilst performing supernatural acts was going to cause problems. I mean, if *I'd* grown up as a supernatural fully aware of all the rules, I sure as hell would've kept my elemental ass a bit of a secret.

I smelled a rat.

Not, like, literally (although I *did* smell evidence of rats from my current position of nose-to-floor). But ... there was something else, a revelation that was starting to sink in at the absolute *worst* possible time.

I felt like I'd been set up.

73

With that new surge of righteous indignation, my hands came completely free of the ropes and within thirty seconds, I was standing in the middle of the small, damp room.

"Now *that* was easy," Reg's voice said from somewhere near the ceiling. "Do you need a Staples' Easy Button?"

"Please, no office supply store jokes right now," I said, glancing up and trying not to gag at the strange blue water dragon clinging to the wall. Evidently he'd come in through the pipes running across the ceiling. Guess plumbing was a pretty useful skill after all.

I glanced down and happened to notice that not only had I managed to shed the ropes, but my clothes as well.

I was, however, still primarily human in appearance.

Reg hopped down from the ceiling and shifted back into the fine, masculine specimen I'd taken advantage of that morning. He, too, was naked but I was pretty sure that was by *choice.*

"Where's Britt?" was the first question that popped out of my mouth. There wasn't really a second question because my brain was actually more concerned with how good it might feel to get picked up by Reg, slammed into a wall, and fucked until I was as liquid as his elemental form.

"Dealing with the local alpha male," he said, and there was something in the way he said it that sounded like he was pissed off. Him. The guy whose fault it was that I was even standing here wondering about Britt in the first place. "Because *he* detected an unmarked shimmer, went to check it out, and found a visiting werewolf tagging along with her."

"So this is my fault?!" I asked, crossing my arms over my chest and trying not to marvel that I even had a chest at all. I mean, I could *feel* it, but I could also see the floor through the perfect, round shape of my tits (they were pretty awesome, I must say). "It's *my* fault that you guys don't know how to close and lock the door to the bloody water closet?!"

"Bloody water … closet? Whoa, you really *are* British, huh?"

I shoved him in the chest with both palms.

"*Australian,*" I growled out.

"Australians don't say water closet. I lived there for like five years once and I never heard that."

"FINE! My dad was British; mum was a kiwi transplant that lived in Australia, and I'm a fucking American. Have a problem with that?"

I shoved him again and he captured my wrists in his hands, tugging me close. I was still see-through, that same odd shade of glimmering aubergine, but Reg had no problem wrapping his long, warm fingers around me.

"You just have a, uh, *unique* vocabulary is all," he whispered, and then his lips were crushing mine. Reg was hard and hot, and all of a sudden, I was just *aching* for him. I wanted him even though I knew I also kind of hated him.

"How are you touching me right now?" I asked him, our lips so close that each word I spoke brushed the full, swollen curve of his mouth. "The ropes … and my clothes …"

"Do you really give a shit?" he asked, but the answer was no: I distinctly did *not*.

Reg released my wrists and angled us so that my back was to the wall.

I made a mental note to rethink the first day that we'd met … something was afoot here, and I needed to get to the bottom of it. But for now … I was just going to let Reg get to the bottom of *me*.

He picked me up with his hands under my ass, and lifted me against the wall, slamming my bare back against the rough concrete. Surprisingly though, in whatever strange spirit form I was currently inhabiting, it didn't hurt.

"We don't have a lot of time," he warned me, but I didn't care. Honestly, the fact that I'd been kidnapped by angry winged men didn't seem to matter so much anymore. In this form, my face didn't hurt at all.

"Then hurry up," I growled, and Reg grinned. With a single powerful thrust, he filled me with every inch of his cock, taking me as hard and fast as he had that morning—only this time, he didn't have to share.

My mouth slanted against his, our tongues tangling as we engaged in an animalistic frenzy that I just *knew* my psychologist would want to hear all about. Clearly, I had issues. Screwing a penniless elemental bum one time could be counted as a mistake, but twice?

Nope.

I felt a conspiracy lurking.

Unrestrained sounds escaped my lips, moans that echoed off the walls and mingled with the sound of dripping water and the fierce, wet joining of our bodies. Reg's groans were deep, male, and tainted with this utterly frustrating sense of satisfaction.

God, I hate him.

He moved inside of me like he had a mission, slamming our pelvises together and working my body up into a frenzy of pleasure that almost *hurt.*

When he came with a loud grunt, and a tight squeeze of his hands on my ass, I almost killed him.

"You can't be done," I said as he pulled away and set my feet back on the floor. "You are not fucking done."

He just smirked at me.

"Let's go. The sooner we get home, the sooner George or Billy would be *more* than happy to give you that orgasm."

I squeezed my hands into fists and gritted my teeth.

"I'm going to fucking *kill* you."

Reg gave me a long look, one eyebrow raised, his tongue running across his lower lip. "As hot as that sounds, ST, if it's rough sex you're looking for then Billy will sort you *right out*."

My lips pursed in frustration as I desperately tried not to feel unbelievably turned on at the suggestion that Billy was into a bit of the *Fifty Shades* sort of stuff. Despite Reg's insinuation that I was not as innocent as I made out to be (he was right, I wasn't), I had yet to hook up with any guy who really took it past the light spanking and handcuffs stage.

"Reg," I coaxed, "come on ... you're a water elemental. Surely you can appreciate how cruel it is to leave me so *wet* right now?"

"Au contraire, Sugar Tits," he smirked wickedly, tugging me by the hand over to the dripping pipe in the corner of the room, "it makes me all the more turned on, being able to sense all that moisture ..."

Dropping my wrist he ran his fingers several times up and down my swollen lower lips, making me moan, before stopping. *The absolute bloody fucking bastard.*

"Come on, sweetheart. Sooner we get home, the sooner the boys can unplug that drain of yours!"

Huffing an angry sigh, I clenched my thighs together in an effort to tell my pussy to *calm the fuck down, girl!*

"Fine," I muttered from behind clenched teeth, "point the way out of here and I can finish myself off when we get home. God made vibrators for a reason, after all."

Reg's ice-blue eyes flashed dangerously for a second, then he nodded thoughtfully and pointed to the tiny crack from which the water was dripping.

"There's the way out," he informed me, and I stared with narrowed eyes.

"Reg … swear to god, if you're fucking around right now and those incubus dicks find us escaping, I am going to be madder than a cut snake." My lip was curling a bit in frustrated anger and I was already borderline 'cut snake' mad anyway. How dare this asshole elemental doom me to a five-way forced marriage, then get me almost killed *twice* and then have the utter gall to leave me without my orgasm?

Despite my momentary lapse in judgement, letting him snake my drain against the wall just moments ago, I couldn't shake the suspicion that this whole thing, this whole damn fuckup, was not an accident.

"Sugar Tits, don't be so suspicious all the time," Reg sighed, almost as if he could hear my thoughts, "that's our way out. You've just gotta turn elemental again and then I can take you with me."

Apparently sometime during or right after our quickie … I'd solidified.

Oh. Okay, turn elemental again? Well, that sounded reasonable. Except …

"How the fuck do I do that?" I hissed, bordering on panicked. What would happen when the incubi found us here, trying to escape? Being sentenced to death had *seemed* like the worst that could have happened but finding myself tied up in a dungeon—awaiting judgement by COCS—led me to thinking there was something worse than death.

Like not getting an orgasm for example.

Reg gave me a calculating look.

"What have you been thinking about the last couple of times you turned elemental? Maybe it'll work again?"

What had I been thinking about? Just then when I'd been lying on the floor, my hands and feet bound, and the smell of rat shit … rats … I'd been thinking about smelling a rat. Because this whole unwilling elemental bullshit seemed like a set up! Indignation flared through me, heating my belly and whipping my furious glare at Reg, who was … clapping?

"Perfect, Sugar Tits! Now let's make like George and *leaf.*"

Without waiting for my response, he snatched my translucent, sparkling, aubergine wrist in his hand then shifted into his water dragon form with a shimmering of light. Dragging me with him, he *dove* toward the tiny dripping crack.

Being forcefully dragged through a water pipe barely thicker than … er … Shane's *pipe*, was an experience I hoped to never repeat again, as long as I lived. It felt like I was being both compressed and torn apart all at the same time, while also flying through space at a zillion miles an hour.

Needless to say, when we finally made it free of the COCS building and into the trees behind it, I promptly vomited all over the ground. My regurgitated breakfast narrowly missed Reg's feet by inches and I kind of wish it had hit him. *Bastard.*

"Fucking hell, Sugar Tits, what is that just coffee and whiskey? We need to get some real food into you if you're going to keep drinking this hard …" Reg's voice and hand ran over me in a surprisingly soothing way, sending tingles down my spine and exploding near my frustrated and aching pussy.

God-fucking-damn him for leaving me unfinished.

"Come on," the infuriating water elemental chuckled, "let's get home before I change my mind and pound your pool like a waterfall after a monsoon."

The trip back home was a relatively easy one—I just rode Reg again.

But like, on his back instead of his cock this time.

Still, my cunt was pressed into the strong muscles of his body, muscles that were made of *water* and yet still felt warm and firm between my thighs. I didn't pretend to understand—I was a barista, not a chemist—but let's just say that snaking through the ice-cold drafts above the city completely *starkers* on the back of a sinuous water dragon with horns and a long whiplike tail was a little, how should I put it, *weird*? Fucked? Let's go with fucked.

In an odd way, it sort of reminded me of how the Care Bears used a rainbow bridge to travel between ... fuck, I 'm showing my age now, aren't I?

Reg carried us all the way back, through the front door, and into the living room at Gram's mansion where he dropped us both on top of the coffee table—completely and totally on display for the other three elementals who sat around eating pizza and drinking beer.

"Are you all bloody bonkers?!" I screamed, seeing them all just *chillin'* while I'd been nearly killed and then kidnapped by naked winged men. "Thanks sooooo much for coming to look for me, you useless sacks of shit! Jesus fucking Christ on a cracker, I didn't think *Reg* would be the only one worried enough to come and save me."

"Calm down, Blossom." George smiled, and I wanted to punch his fucking lights out. "We knew you were safe; Reg wasn't going to let anything happen to you. Although we sort of expected you back sooner than this. What held you up?"

"We were fucking against the wall of ST's cell," Reg smirked and I reflexively smacked him in the stomach with the back of my hand. It undoubtedly hurt me more than it did him though, because his abs were tensed and rock-hard.

"Reg …" George narrowed his eyes at the naked blonde standing next to me on the coffee table and I suddenly remembered I was *also* naked—and horny *as fuck.*

"What?" Reg shrugged one ripped shoulder and stepped down off the table, gallantly holding out an inked hand to help me down also. "I didn't let her finish if that's what you're worried about. You were *particularly* interested in hearing about Billy's tendency toward rough sex, weren't you, Sugar Tits?"

The fucking bastard winked at me while I stood there speechless, my jaw flapping like a naked grandma on a bike.

"I'll get you some wine," he stage-whispered to me, then sauntered his naked butt into my kitchen, whistling.

"Is Britt here?" I asked, and George immediately pursed his lips. "I'm taking it that's a no …"

"She was caught wanderin' around with an unmarked, shimmer, sugar," Shane said grimly, like I was supposed to understand the implications behind his words.

News flash: I didn't.

"And that means what?" I asked, planting a hand on my hip and not giving two fucks that my nipples were hard as rocks and I had elemental cum on my thighs… Note: it was just as gross as the regular stuff. "I don't speak supernatural, remember? So, she was hanging out with me? What does that mean?"

"Depends on the local pack's alpha," Billy supplied, standing up in rugged, faded jeans and a white wifebeater that showed off his own headlights, so to speak. *Jesus Christ.* I snatched one of my Gram's knitted blankets off a faded green chair and threw it around my shoulders.

God, if she could see me now ... she would be pissed.

Gram was this uptight English lady that'd hopped the pond and left her son (my dad) and husband behind; Dad was only ten at the time. He'd eventually forgiven her, forcing a relationship with my grandma on me that I never really wanted. But at least I'd gotten the house, right?

One of the tin ceiling tiles disconnected from the roof and promptly smacked me right in the face.

"*Fuck,*" I cursed as Billy grabbed my shoulders in his tattooed hands and didn't even bother to hold back a wild grin. "What the hell ..." I looked up, but I couldn't for the life of me figure out how the tile had come loose from the ceiling. Simple coincidence? Hmm.

"You okay?" Billy asked, sliding a pack of smokes from his back pocket. He withdrew a cigarette and in the span of a blink, it was lit. No lighter, no match, nothing. I raised an eyebrow.

"Yeah, fine," I said as I kicked the tile away and tried to keep my right breast from popping out of the blanket. "Now, details please. What do you mean 'depends on the alpha'?"

I got another noncommittal shrug in response.

"I'm really not in the mood for games ..." I began through gritted teeth, but just then, the front door swung open and Britt came walking in like nothing at all had happened.

"Where the hell is my car?" I asked her, because even though I drove a death cab, I wanted it back.

"Parked outside," she said with a slight shrug, her dark hair in perfect glossy waves, her four inch pink stilettos free of dirt and scuffs. Here I was worrying my fucking arse off, and she was completely fine. More than just fine, really. She looked like she was about to hit the red carpet for a smutty reality TV show premiere, and I'd just lost my best *7 For All Mankind* jeans that

I'd been wearing. Those things cost like two hundred bucks. They were my *only* nice pair of pants. "Why?"

"Why?!" I asked and I realized I was starting to get hysterical. When Reg came back with a wine glass in one hand a bottle in the other, I snatched the bottle and stormed up the stairs before anyone could follow me.

I'd sort of learned my lesson about leaving the house without the guys, but I sure as fuck didn't have to sit there and feel like I was so far out of the loop I was about to hang myself with it.

7

CHAPTER SEVEN

Safely tucked away in my bedroom, I slipped into a pair of pajama pants and a white tank top and settled on my bed with my computer in my lap. I strongly considered grabbing my Hitachi Magic Wand from under the bed and, uh, taking care of things down under, but I just … needed a moment to myself.

I swept my hair back from my face and tried to decide what to start Googling first.

Werewolves? Elementals? Succubi? Did it matter?

Would there even *be* any actual information available on the internet?

Probably not.

Wikipedia couldn't even get the story of George Washington right. No chance I was getting dirt on the elementals.

Instead, I Skype-called my mom. She was currently living on the Gold Coast in Australia with some hot young boy toy she'd picked up on her travels. The last time I'd visited her, she'd been living in a pink house on Tamborine Mountain with way too many wind chimes.

At that moment in time, I missed her fucking terribly. After a nice, long Skype call though, that feeling usually went away. I didn't like using anti-woman insults like *bitch,* but let's be honest—Mom was a bitch. Britt was a floozy. And I was ... totally out of my *element.*

But even puns couldn't help my mood in that moment (although the wine sure helped!).

"Oh, you're drinking again?" was how my mom—Katelyn Fischer—answered my call. Fortunately by that point, I was half-cut and didn't give a shit.

"I love you, too, Mum," I said, not even bothering to hide the bottle tucked in my lap. Why should I? I was approaching thirty; I could make my own damn decisions. "What are you up to?"

"Well you're the one that called," she said with a slight scoff. I recognized the hideous orange paint of her living room wall behind her head. "You look *awful,*" she continued in that special way of hers. "You've got a black eye, you know."

I pursed my lips.

I'd almost forgotten about being punched in the face by *Nigel,* too wrapped up was I in Reg's big, sturdy pipe. He really knew how to get a girl's faucet running ...

"Yeah, thanks, I'm fine. I appreciate the concern." I swigged another drink of adult grape juice. "I'm finally moved into Gram's by the way, in case you actually cared what your only child was up to."

"That old shack?" she asked with a raised brow and a shiver, like being forced to live here was akin to being cast into the furthest depths of hell. "Why not just sell it and move in with me?"

Speaking of the depths of hell ...

"Because, *mother*, you live in a one bedroom house which permanently reeks of weed." I rolled my eyes at my computer screen and took a healthy swig of my wine while my mum spluttered her denial at me.

"It wasn't a judgement, Mum, you know I'm not against the stuff; your house just smells *really* strong." Also, wasn't about to say this out loud, but uh, hearing your mom's sex noises echo down the hallway really traumatized a person—even at age thirty.

She huffed at me but then proceeded to blather on some inane story about her neighbor which I didn't hear a single word of while I steadily sipped my way through a good two thirds of the bottle Reg had given me. One thing Gram's had going for her: she had great taste in wine, and her cellar was *stocked*.

"Are you listening to me, Arizona Morgan Smoke?" My mother's sharp tone snapped me out of my slightly buzzed musings about Gram's wine cellar and dragged me back to the Skype screen in front of me.

"No ..." I admitted, squinting at her grainy image, "but I have no doubt you'll repeat yourself ..."

"I asked," she snapped, "if you've found yourself a boyfriend yet? You're not exactly in your prime anymore, darling, so maybe it's time to be a bit less choosey? Next thing you know you'll be shopping for adult diapers all alone."

"Nope," I flat-out lied to the woman who raised me. "No boyfriend here." Punctuating this with another swig of wine seemed to be appropriate.

"Well, I can't say I'm surprised," my darling mother continued in a patronizing tone, "you drink far too much for a girl your age. I hope you've been exercising. The *last* thing you need is to be a drunk and have a fat ass, dear."

Resisting the urge to slap my laptop closed on her condescending ass, I forced a pained smile onto my face. *Why the fuck did I call my mum again?*

"Arizona!" Billy shouted, bursting through my bedroom door and standing at the foot of my bed wearing a seriously sexy scowl on his face. "You need to come back downstairs and talk about this shit. Dealing with COCS is no laughing matter, and you sulking up here like a kid with a drinking problem isn't fucking helping."

My eyes bugged out and I tried to slam my hand over the little microphone on my computer, but let's be honest, does anyone *actually* know where that fucking thing is? It was too late anyway as my mother's voice cracked out of the tinny speakers.

"Arizona? Who was that? It sounded like a man talking about his cock ..."

Growling under my breath, I gave Billy a rude hand gesture that said both *get the fuck out* and *fuck you* all at the same time.

"It was no one, Mum. Just the TV." Stupidly, I took my eyes off the sneaky fire elemental for a second and the next thing I knew he'd landed beside me in my bed, leaning against the headboard with his shoulder pressed to mine.

"Hi, Mrs. Smoke?" Billy smiled at my Skype screen and I paused for a moment, trying to think if I had actually seen him smile yet. On that stubbled bad boy face of his, it was *electric.* "I'm one of Ari's new boyfriends, William."

"It's Ms. Fischer, dear, and oh really? How very lovely to meet you ..." Her silver eyebrows were raised so high they practically disappeared into her hairline. "*One of* her boyfriends, you say? Just how many does she have?"

"Mum, the line is breaking up. I can't quite hear you … hello?" I waved my hand back and forth in front of my screen, pretending like the picture had frozen.

"Yes, Arizona, I can still see you. Can you not see me?" My mum frowned at her computer and I saw her stabbing at some buttons so I took the opportunity while she was distracted to end the call. She'd more than likely think it was just her internet connection, seeing as I do things like that all the time to her. Cruel, perhaps, but necessary.

"Well that was awfully frigging rude," Billy drawled, scooting down to get comfortable against my pillows and tucking another magically lit cigarette between his lush lips. "I was only being polite, introducing myself to my new *mum-in-law*," he said with what was probably intended to be an Australian accent but came out more … British … sort of. Either way it was kinda hot on him.

"Do you mind not smoking in my bedroom?" I growled, snatching the cig from his mouth and leaning over him to stab it out in my potted plant beside the bed. Okay fine, it was a cactus. But he had a happy face drawn on his yellow pot and I called him Mr. Plant.

"Arizona *Smoke*," Billy purred my name, running his inked hands up my sides as I leaned across his torso to reach Mr. Plant, "even your name is begging for some fire elemental action … it's a shame you decided to put clothes on. You looked so good in your outfit earlier."

"What?" I snorted, in such a ladylike way. "You mean bloody starkers?" Having disposed of his cigarette amongst Mr. Plant's hair, I moved to sit back on my side of the bed but his hands held me firm.

"Exactly." My face was scarce inches from his smoldering stare, and I could feel my frustrated and frayed nerve endings igniting.

Shit! I should have taken care of business before calling Mum.

"You know, you and I haven't really gotten to know each other yet, Firebug," he murmured, one of his hands slipping beneath the soft cotton of my tank and trailing across the bare skin of my lower back. Where his fingers touched, little bursts of sparks seemed to crackle across my body while I tried and failed to stifle a groan.

"Firebug?" I questioned, trying to deflect attention away from the over-sexualized noise that had just slipped out of me. "What's with you dragons and these nicknames?"

"Just shut up so I can kiss you, infuriating woman." Billy's hand snaked up to the back of my head and used a firm grip on my hair to drag my face closer to his.

I started to lean in, my body reacting to him the way it had to Reg and Shane that morning, and then again in the little concrete room. Sure, I was a healthy red-blooded young woman (guess that young part was debatable if you were to ask Kate), and I had a damn strong sex drive, but the way I was reacting to these men … it was weird.

Putting a hand on Billy's *incredibly* firm chest, I pushed him away a few inches.

"Am I going to be attacked every goddamn time I walk out the front door?" I asked and his mouth twisted into a small frown.

"Pretty much," he said, his face crinkled with some sort of emotion I was having trouble deciphering. I'd sort of pegged both Reg and Billy as the sluts in the group, but it was starting to look like Billy might be more 'tortured bad boy'.

Uh-oh.

I'd had more than my fair share of those in the past and while the sex was fucking out of this world, the relationship bits were substantially more tricky. Plus, guys like this ... they always had a lot of trouble learning to 'adult'. And since I, too, sucked at that, the last thing I needed was to get involved with a man who had the emotional maturity of a sixteen year old.

And yet ... he was so damn fine.

"Then just do it," I said, because yeah, I'd finished my wine, but also because I just didn't want to deal with winged people trying to kill me again. "Mark me."

"Are you fucking serious?" he asked, raising a charcoal brow. His eyes, those orange-brown embers in his face, looked me up and down, like he couldn't quite believe what he was hearing. "I thought you were throwing a shit fit about this?"

I clenched my teeth and tried to breathe through my nose.

"A shit fit? That's what you call it when your friends *accidentally* show their supernatural forms to me and then try to force me into some kind of weird ... magical marriage *thing*?"

I rolled off the opposite side of the bed and nearly knocked Mr. Plant onto the floor. Catching him at the last second, I whirled around and lifted my chin defiantly.

"Look, just mark me—fuck me and chant and cast spells or whatever it is you need to do. But don't you *dare* pretend like this isn't a big deal. It's huge, okay? Fucking huge. Bigger than Shane's cock."

"If you want to see bigger than Shane's cock ..." That was Reg, standing in my now open bedroom door. *Hadn't I locked that goddamn thing? How did these two assholes get in in the first place?* Probably some more weird elemental magic, like the kind that lets grown ass men travel through leaky pipes.

"It's not like you were doing anything with your life anyway," Billy said, and I swear to fuck, that was the last straw.

"Screw you!" I shouted, and then the next thing I knew, I was standing in broken glass, Mr. Plant's pot scattered to pieces at my feet. The shutters on my windows blew open and the panes exploded *inward* with a violent, swirling gale. In the ceiling, a pipe burst and showered my entire bedroom—computer, TV, and phone included—while I stood completely dry in the center of the chaos.

The next thing to go was the candle beside my bed, the one I'd lit for ambiance in case I wanted to, you know, *rub one out.*

Instead of extinguishing in the wild winds and the deluge of water, it grew bigger, climbing up the wall and melting a few old pictures inside their frames. I was so busy gaping at it that I didn't notice Mr. Plant growing until his needles stabbed me in the armpit.

With a yelp, I dropped the cactus—which was now roughly the length of my entire arm—and stepped back, bare heels crunching across broken glass as I stared at the tangled roots, reaching their gnarled fingers across my bedroom floor, curling themselves around the wrought iron posts of my bed.

For about thirty seconds, nobody moved; we all just stood there and took in the chaos around us with gaping mouths and wide eyes. It was Billy who got his shit together first, and with a quick wave of his tattooed hand, the flames sputtered and died, and the smoke drifted out the window as if he'd commanded it.

"The water, Reg," I heard him say a moment later, and then that, too, stopped. By that point, Mr. Plant had reached the ceiling and was on his way to becoming the world's largest fucking cactus. I had to back up against the far wall of the room to avoid getting stabbed by his needles (almost made a sex joke there, but then … I was about to die via cactus impale).

"Christ on a cracker," I heard Shane breathe in that sultry Southern drawl of his. The winds died down immediately and Mr. Plant stopped growing, but he did *not* shrink. I carefully put a hand between his spines and pushed him out of the way.

"What the shit was that?" I asked, my voice high and breathy, my feet dripping blood across the floor from all the broken glass.

"You're a spirit elemental, Arizona," George said, calm as a cucumber like fucking always. Well, if he was so damn good with plants, I wanted the giant spiny cucumber behind me back in his pot and back to normal.

"Great, fantastic," I said, sitting down on the edge of my bed as my hands began to shake. Surprisingly, my blankets were already dry. "But I don't know *what* that means if you won't tell me."

A few of the guys exchanged glances, but it was George who stepped forward, his shirtless, bronzed godlike body kneeling before me. He put a single hand on my knee and I suddenly wished with violent fervency that I wasn't wearing fuzzy pj's with cartoon foxes all over them.

"A spirit elemental has the ability to access the powers of an entire quad," he said, looking me straight in the face with eyes the color of wet earth. "Arizona, you can do everything we can do—and more."

"Because I had unprotected sex?" I asked, just staring at him like I was waiting for Ashton Kutcher to pop out and yell *punk'd!* "Why not just offer up elemental powers to anyone that'll pay?" I snapped, raking my fingers through my long, blonde hair.

"That's not how it works," George continued with a small sigh. He glanced over at Mr. Plant and then refocused his attention back on me. I could hardly look away from his face, that same sense of needy attraction rolling over me like a wave. Even with the acrid scent of char filling my nostrils, I wanted him. Them. I wanted *all* of them. "We can only make a spirit elemental *once.*"

"You used your one trump card on me?!" I asked, still not fully grasping what he was saying. "You were virgins?!"

"*Unprotected* sex, ST," Reg added, sauntering into the room and standing next to me with his arms crossed over his blue tank. "You're not the first woman we've ever slept with—you don't get this good without a little practice, obviously. But yeah, first one to have us nice and bare and—"

"Reg, shut your damn piehole," Shane said, giving him a look that'd freeze hell over.

"Shut up, shut up, shut up," I chanted under my breath, squeezing my eyes shut tight and rubbing at my temples. Fuck, my head felt like I had been caught in a storm drain during a cyclone.

"Where's Britt? I want her in here *now.*" My voice came out in a low whisper and I could sense the panic rising up in me again. Why was the room spinning so badly, and why was I *so bloody horny*?

"Blossom," George said in a gentle sort of way, like he was a yoga teacher or some shit, "it's going to be okay, I promise. Let's just talk this out, shall we? We'll get through this together."

George sat down on the edge of the bed beside me, wrapping his arm around me, enclosing me in his warm bronze embrace; I just glared at him.

Good god, he smells incredible, like wildflowers and sunshine.

The thought froze me in his tempting arms. Of *course* he smelled like wildflowers and sunshine—he was a *fucking elemental!* And now, so was I apparently.

A sudden gust of wind whipped through the room, ruffling my hair and picking up random bits of debris off my floor.

"Honey doll, you're going to need to get a grip there," Shane muttered from behind clenched teeth as he countered the wind and all the bits dropped back to the floor. It was the wrong thing to say to me though, and my temper flared hot, causing sheets of rain to fall from my already sad looking ceiling and drenching the guys.

On the upside though, it also caused their t-shirts to cling to their insanely chiseled bodies in a way that should've been illegal. All except George, that is, who seemed to never be wearing a shirt.

"Do *not* tell me to get a grip, *Skeeter*," I hissed at Shane, rising to my feet and letting my anger drive my actions as I advanced on him, poking an accusing finger into his chest. "This is *all* your fault. If you hadn't just casually left the door open while you did magic, *and then* decided to fuck me six ways to next Sunday without protection, then *we wouldn't be in this mess right now!*" Little fires burst out all around my room again and Mr. Plant continued his growth spurt while the elementals scrambled to counteract my out of control new powers.

"Well, be that as it may, darlin'," Shane gave me a stubborn look, his eyebrow raised, "if you *don't* firstly get a grip so you don't tear down your Gram's house, then secondly complete the *marking*, you will die."

"And so will we," Billy added, leaning against the headboard and playing with a little ball of flame in his palm. He looked like a douche in his leather jacket, tattoos playing across his hand like an oil painting. But, like, a really sexy douche.

A long, tense silence filled the room after he said this, and I stared wide-eyed at the devilishly handsome fire elemental. It felt like the plug had just been ripped out of the bathtub that was my life, and I was powerless to stop the flow of water leaking out.

"So you're telling me," I spoke quietly and calmly, which was at total odds with the raging storm happening inside my head, "that if I don't go ahead and let you all *mark* me, that not only will I die, but you all will too? Is that ... the gist of it? Am I understanding you correctly?"

Billy shifted uncomfortably under my unblinking stare and I saw from the corner of my eye, the others were all watching me like some sort of wild animal as well. Like I was just going to snap at any second.

"Yep. True story." Billy had balls, I'd give him that. He met my gaze dead-on with a stubborn tilt to his chin.

Well, fuck

It was one thing to chance my own life with murderous succubi and incubi and fuck knew what else hunting me, but even as furious as I was, I couldn't willfully let these four die. Could I?

My head was pounding again and my eye twitched in anger. How dare they put me in this position?

Outside my shattered bedroom window, there was a huge storm blowing, which the elementals seemed to be keeping from entering the room as not a single breeze touched us until a booming *crack* echoed and a jagged bolt of lightning slammed into the tree directly outside. It must've shocked the guys just as much as it did me, because their hold on the elements dropped momentarily, allowing the storm to drench us all again before they got it under control.

"Sooner rather than later, would be good, Sugar Tits," Reg drawled, seemingly relaxed but I could clearly see the muscles in his neck and shoulders bunching as he held the torrential rain outside.

"He's right," Shane agreed, chewing on the full curve of his lower lip. Mixed in with some of that worry was a little … anger? Was I reading him right? And what the *hell* did he have a right to be angry about anyway? "A power surge like this … well, it's liable to attract the wrong kind of attention. We best get this shit under control—and *fast.*"

"What does that mean? I don't understand what the fuck is going on?" I turned my attention back to Shane, the leader in his merry band of plumbing misfits.

Jesus, he's hot.

My whole body flushed with heat and my stomach started flipping around like butterflies on a trampoline. Was it a crime to have a chest that wide, that flat, with pecs that sculpted and delicious? Because it damn well should be.

"It means that you just painted an even bigger target on your back, Blossom." George slid his hand into mine and tugged me gently toward the door. "Come on, your bedroom is a disaster. Let's head through to one of the guest rooms and finish this marking."

"Before we, you know, get fucking murdered," Billy grunted, extinguishing the little fire fox in his hand. I wondered if he realized that Chrome was a much more reliable internet browser these days. "Or worse."

"What could possibly be worse than death?" I hated to ask, but got my answer anyway, sort of.

"COCS," Reg spat, then led the way to one of Gram's many guest rooms.

How very ... true.

Cocks *were* deadly, this irresistible addiction that was ten times more dangerous than meth and heroin combined. As far as *C.O.C.S.* were concerned, I highly doubted they were more trouble than the four penis-wielding magicians standing around my house.

So fine. Fine. I'd let them mark me and then maybe I could get some peace. I had a friend with an apartment in New York City. Maybe I'd head over there for a weekend of peace and quiet? Hopefully Siobhan wasn't a werewolf, elemental, succubus, or any other assorted supernatural creature. It'd be nice to have a friend who was, you know, *human.*

"We need a few things for the marking, don't we?" Reg was saying, putting his hands on his hips and looking up at the ceiling. Hopefully he was contemplating the best way to fix the new leak in my bedroom. "We better hit up the Wicca shop on Washington. Shane, you want to come with? Billy and George can, uh, get started without us."

With a smirk, he waved a hand dismissively and dried all of our clothes ... except for *my* white tank.

"You pig," I growled, but he was already on his way out, leaving George, Billy, and me in one of Gram's creepy guest bedrooms.

"This is your grandma?" George asked, lifting up a picture of Gram. I took the gaudy gold frame from his bronzed fingers and stared at the woman contained within. Considering I was about to have some kind of weird, ritualistic fivesome with a bunch of strange dudes, it was an odd moment.

Her severe face glared out of the picture and sent an icy little chill down my spine.

"That's her," I said, remembering hard swats, boring afternoon tea times, and summers without TV, music, or reading material that wasn't historical romance or non-fiction. Honestly, I didn't much miss my grandmother. She'd been a harsh, judgmental woman with a quick temper and little patience for the antics of children.

I moved over to the dresser, pulled open the top drawer, and shoved the picture inside.

Sorry, but this girl was not about to get busy with her Gram's cruel, green eyes glaring out at her.

"So," I said, turning around and giving the two remaining boys my best bitch face. "How do we do this?"

"Well," Billy began, playing with some old perfume bottles on my Gram's nightstand. "Sometimes, when two consenting adults feel things for each other, they take off their clothes …"

I picked up a small statuette of a naked cherub and chucked it at him.

The bastard caught it in midair.

"Cheeky bastard. Now, how does this ritual go and why is it necessary? Telling me you're going to die if I don't do it sort of reminds me of that one time my ex-stepfather said he had cancer so my mum would take him back after he cheated."

I cocked my head to one side and quirked a brow.

"Listen, doll face," Billy said as he sat down on the edge of my bed and kicked off his boots. "Elementals aren't like humans—we can't exist in our own little world. We're all connected. And now that you're one of us …" He paused and the corner of his lip quirked up in a dirty smile. "It's like how the toilet and sink meet the soil stack. There are different ways for the water to flow, but it all ends up in the same place. Energy, Arizona, that's what this is about. You're like a leaky pipe, draining all of us. And if you die, you take the rest of us down with you."

"If I'm such a liability, why'd you bring me into this shit at all?" I snapped, crossing my arms under my breasts and noticing that both Billy and George followed the motion with smoldering gazes.

"Because you're the only—" he started, and then paused when he noticed George giving him a *look*.

"The only what?" I ground out through clenched teeth. After all this shit was over, I was going to have to pay the dentist a serious visit. Hopefully I wouldn't grind off all my fillings. "This whole thing, you showing yourselves to me ... that wasn't an accident, was it?"

"Blossom," George began, but the look I gave him stopped him dead in his tracks.

"Only. What," I repeated, but it was not a question this time —it was a *threat*.

"You're the only woman we've ever run into with elemental blood," Billy said, raking his fingers through his hair. "Mostly human, sure, but all we need is that one percent." He glanced over at me, but not at all like he was sorry for what'd happened. "We're a dying race, Arizona."

"One percent?" I asked, trying to make sense of what he was saying. So ... back in the day, some ancestor of mine had played hanky-panky with an elemental?! "You ... did this on purpose?"

The idea that this whole mess was intentional made a fuck of a lot more sense than some stupid accident.

But it was also *fucked* six ways to Sunday.

"You did this to ... what, make babies with me?" I asked, putting together *dying race* and *only female* into one logical conclusion.

Billy frowned, his brows pinched as he stood back up and turned to look at me. George, meanwhile, stayed just out of punching range. Good for him because the first guy whose nuts I came in contact with, was getting kneed right in the junk.

"There are maybe a million of our people left worldwide, and most of those are *male* and in quads. You're literally almost one in a million, Arizona."

"And I'm supposed to care?" I asked, noticing that my hands were once again see-through. A bolt of lightning crashed into the bricks of the back patio. Huh. What the fuck must the neighbors be thinking? Lightning in early winter in New York? That was kind of ... not normal.

Eh, maybe they'd just blame global warming and be done with it?

"I'm not a savior for your dying race, and I'm not a baby making machine, so eat shit." I closed my eyes and sucked in a deep breath. Despite my rage, I knew I was still going to go through with the marking. Fool me once, shame on me. Fool me twice, fuck me running. Not getting fooled a third time. I wasn't going outside again without completing this stupid ritual. "Let's just get this over with."

"Over with?" Billy asked, and it looked like that brooding bad boy side of him was starting to take over. "This is a sacred ritual, Ari. It's not something you just slog your way through."

"Oh? A fivesome is now a sacred ritual? Puh-lease. Then I guess I had plenty of sacred rituals in college then." *Total lie.* Closest I ever came was that one time Britt and I made out with the same guy and then took turns with him. Alcohol was involved. "Just do what you need to do so I can head into the city and have some time to myself. COCS will leave me alone if we do this, right?"

"It's more complicated than that," George began, but I was already shaking my head.

"Don't care. I am seriously fucking done with you guys right now. Fucking *done.*"

I dragged my sopping wet pajama top off and threw it against the wall with a wet *slap*, then faced the two dangerously handsome men with my hands on my hips. Tits standing out proudly, I glared at the two of them.

Billy smothered a grin by rubbing a hand over his stubbled chin. He made no attempt to cover the fact that he was taking a good long look at my hardware before meeting my defiant stare. His inked fingers split open over his grinning lips.

"We can't complete the *marking* until the boys get back, which could be a while yet … but if you're that eager to practice in the meantime …?" His hands went to the heavy leather belt slung around his hips, that sly grin darkening seductively.

My hands flew up instinctively to cover my breasts and I whirled around to face the dresser, my face flaming. In line with my current run of luck, the dresser had a mirror so I could clearly see Billy smirking at me while I dug around for a clean shirt and threw it over my head.

"I'm not," I lied, "I just didn't want to wear a wet shirt while we waited." *Lie, lie, lie.* "I'm only going to go through with this whole *marking* bullshit to save my own ass." If I were Pinocchio, my nose would be giving hardcore sex toys a run for their money right now.

"Sweetie, I feel like you haven't fully understood—" George tried again but I cut him off with a wave of my hand.

"Will I die if we don't finish this? Yes or no answers here, Woody." I was referring to the little wooden cowboy from *Toy Story*. Honestly, my mind wasn't *always* in the gutter.

"Yes," he nodded, then tried to say something else.

I cut him off.

"If I let you *mark* me, then will COCS stop trying to have me killed? Yes or no?"

"Well, yes …" a frown creased his bronze face and he ran a hand through his hair, like he was annoyed at me. For what, I had no idea.

"George, why don't you go and get Arizona some more wine?" Billy smoothly interrupted, jerking his head toward the kitchen. "She looks far too sober for what's about to go down."

Oh fuck, what the hell did that *mean?*

"Don't look at me like that, Firebug," the smoldering hot handyman chuckled, stepping in closer and boxing me against the dresser with arms on either side of me. "We never did get to finish our chat upstairs before we were so rudely interrupted by your powers. Are you sure you didn't want a bit of a *warm-up* before the boys get back?"

His scalding breath feathered across the skin of my neck, sending shivers curling through me and I forced myself to shove him away. I was still madder than a cut snake, and this *asshole* was one quarter to blame for this shit flood I was currently wading through.

"Not on your life, *William*," I sneered. "I will go through with this marking, this … group sex thing … but as soon as it's done, I am out of here. You all can stay and fix up all the damage you've caused to my beautiful house, but I'm getting some space from all of this crazy."

"We'll see," he answered cryptically, flopping onto the bed and folding his arms under his head. Refusing to take the bait, I just shook my head and stared out the window. The storm outside was still raging hard, and the poor old oak that had been hit by my lightning was steaming and smoldering under the deluge.

A soft hand caressed my arm, sliding down to my hand and placing a glass within it. George had arrived so silently I hadn't even noticed he was back.

"Here." He smiled, his bark brown eyes sympathetic. I noticed he'd filled my glass way over the socially acceptable point. "Don't worry, I brought backup." He gave me a sexy wink and nodded to the bedside table where three more ancient looking bottles of red wine sat.

Taking a long sip of my wine, and moaning a little as it warmed my belly, I gave George a bit more of a genuine smile.

"I think you might be my favorite," I murmured, running my tongue over my teeth and savoring the fruity, acidic aftertaste that this wine had. Tasted like a Chianti or one of those old-world styles, but what would I know? I was a barista, not a sommelier.

"Why, because he brings you alcohol?" Billy snickered from his position on the queen-size spare bed.

"Exactly," I replied, not bothering to look over at him. My gaze was firmly held by the earthy depths of George's eyes.

"You're welcome, Blossom," he whispered back with a heated look in his gaze, like he was already thinking about where he wanted to plow his wood. He tucked a stray piece of my wild blonde hair behind my ear, then smoothly leaned in and kissed me.

Totally contradictory to the hot and demanding way Reg and Shane had kissed me, George's kiss was sweet and unhurried. He took his time, massaging his lips against mine and letting me set the pace while all my pent-up anger and frustration seemed to slip off me like dirt in the rain.

Probably sensing the shift in my mood, George slid his hands underneath my fresh shirt and slowly started tugging it up my skin, not once losing contact with my lips. The sheer patience he showed in removing my shirt so damn slowly was almost painful, but it did allow me a minute to second-guess things.

"Wait," I gasped, breaking away from his kiss and flicking my wild eyes between the two elementals, "aren't we waiting for Shane and Reg? I'm serious about only doing this once. Just to complete the marking and then we're *done*."

"I just thought maybe this would be a bit less intimidating if we started before they got here? You weren't fooling anyone that you've participated in group sex before, Blossom."

He was right, of course he was right, but this seemed all really daunting. Nervously, I chewed my lower lip and stood mesmerized as Billy deliberately unbuckled his belt, then slid it from his pants and set it on the bedside table.

"Well, Firebug?" he challenged. "What's it going to be?"

Complete the ritual by getting laid by four hot but admittedly annoying liars? Or get killed by naked, winged incubi and succubi bitches with guns?

It was kind of an easy choice.

What the hell.

"Fuck," I cursed under my breath, trying not to love the feel of George's fingers on my bare skin. His fingertips were soft, but firm, like he knew his own strength and was being careful to regulate it. "Whatever. Let's just get this over with as soon as possible."

"Why don't we focus on making it enjoyable instead?" George asked, lifting a hand up to put a finger against the side of my face. Without using any pressure whatsoever, just the gentle burden of his touch, he turned me back to look at him.

"No matter what you do, I won't enjoy it," I said, but I was already getting off on the hard press of his body against my own. My last boyfriend hadn't exactly been ... how should I put it … *in shape.* Now, I wasn't trying to be judge-y or anything, but having a guy with a rippling eight pack and arms strong enough to pick me up and fuck me against the wall—priceless.

"That's an awful way to go into it," he said, giving me a look and a quick flash of smile, teeth white in his bronze face. "Humans just fuck with their bodies; elementals bring a little magic into the mix."

I pursed my lips, but I didn't say anything. Sure, the sex I'd had thus far had been … fine. Okay, it was fucking awesome. But it wasn't any *different* (except for maybe the whole DP situation, but that was just my lack of experience talking). If there was magic in all of that, I hadn't felt it.

"You have to be marked first," George told me, like he could read the thoughts straight from my brain.

Wait …

"You don't happen to have mind-reading powers do you?" I asked and he just laughed, pulling me in close for another kiss. His mouth was so gentle when it slanted over mine, it was like my lips opened on reflex. *Nice guy,* they said as I kissed a man that smelled like flowers but was far from feminine (not that there's anything wrong with that since, you know, feminine and masculine are largely societal constructs). *Nice guy,* they repeated after I was done with my inner socio-political rant, *very rare.*

Lifting my hands up, I curled my fingers around George's broad shoulders and wondered what'd be like to see him *in his element,* so to speak, on his knees in the dirt, his skin shimmering with sweat under the hot, hot sun. I could just imagine his hands cloaked in thick gloves, his arm swiping across his forehead as he plowed my flower bed.

Whoa.

Okay, this was happening.

George's tongue expertly teased against mine, neither subjugating nor acquiescing, but simply *tasting* me. A groan escaped unbidden, but I was so into the kiss that I forgot to be embarrassed. Half of my brain screamed that I met these guys, like, yesterday, but the rest of me (mainly the throbbing warmth between my thighs) did not care one bit.

As we kissed, George eased my shirt up until it was breaking the vibrant heat between our mouths, chucking it aside and then pulling me close, the taut points of my nipples scraping against his chest.

"This can be weird," he began, which was not a good way to start a sexual romp with four random supernatural dudes, "or it can be sensual."

"George," I began, but he was already backing me up so that my thighs touched the edge of the bed, pushing me down gently with a single palm between my breasts. I sat down on the end of the guest bed, a puff of dust rising off the rose pink comforter. Damn. It'd been a long time since Gram had had any company.

I tossed a quick glance over my shoulder and found Billy sliding his hand down the firm expanse of his tummy, right underneath those faded jeans … Shit. Okay, I held up the white flag to my ovaries and decided that, hey, even if these elemental weirdos wanted to make babies with me to save their dying species, that I was pretty a-okay with that.

Just *look* at them.

"Take your pants off for me, Ari," George said, the intensity of his gaze making me squirm. Knowing Billy was polishing his wrench behind me did not make this any easier.

"All the way off?" I asked, and he quirked a brow.

"Normally, I'd say no, let's do it with them half-on, half-off, but …" George's soft smile turned wicked at the edges. "But for the marking, we need you completely nude. Want some help?"

I just sat there and gaped at him like a goldfish, watching as he knelt down between my thighs, curling his fingers around the waistband of my fox covered pj pants. Slowly, like he *wanted* to torture me, he dragged the fabric down my thighs, taking my rainbow panties along for the ride. Tossing them aside, George glanced up at me.

"Ready?"

"If you have to ask that, then probably *not,*" I said, sucking in a sharp breath.

George held out his hands and as I watched in awe, they went completely see-through, just like I did when I was elementing all the way out. He didn't go full dragon like I'd seen in the bathroom, just see-through, *ethereal.*

The dual scents of wet earth and growing things filled the room, like a flower garden after a spring rain.

"Sit still," George commanded, and even though I wasn't much for taking commands, he was so damn nice about it, I decided to listen and see what was going to happen.

His hands found my upper arms, his effervescent palms pressing against my flesh. As he dragged them down and over my wrists, along my thighs, I felt this … breathtaking sensation pass over me. It was something I'd never experienced before, like pure energy made flesh, traveling through his palms and into me, lighting me up like the night sky in a summer thunderstorm.

And in his wake, a small dark line of earth was left, clinging to my skin like I'd just applied a mud mask to my arms. Even as I watched, tiny little green things rose from the dirt, grew buds, blossomed into beautiful flowers.

"That feels … really weird," I whispered, my voice coming out in a gasping breath. I tried to liken the feeling to something I'd experienced before, but my mind came up completely blank.

The closest sensation I could relate to it was that one time Britt and I went to Vail, Colorado for a skiing trip and got *really* high on pot chocolates.

I felt like I was floating, but grounded, too. Like I could soar if I wanted and yet come straight back home with a single thought. Yeah, like *that* doesn't sound like a high person's thoughts.

Maybe someone had spiked my wine?

"George," I managed to gasp out as he stood up and pushed me forward with a hand on the chest again, straight into Billy's arms. His hands, when they came around to cup my breasts, were also see-through, completely covered in flames. It didn't hurt when he touched me though. No, quite the opposite—scalding warmth washed over me, like I was slipping into a hot tub.

"Got started without us, I see," Reg said, his voice just barely registering in my brain. I was too far-gone at that point to think clearly.

"Hurry," Billy said, his breath warm against my ear. As he held me in his arms, I saw flames transfer from his skin onto mine, dancing along my breasts and down, down, *down.* There were flames *everywhere*—if you know what I mean.

Reg and Shane appeared in my field of vision, taking their clothes off like they had *business* to attend to—i.e. me. *I* was their business.

"You found what we needed?" George asked as Shane produced a fucking *knife* from the bag.

"What the hell is that for?!" I asked, trying to move away and finding myself wrapped in Billy's arms.

"It's an athame, sugar, relax," Shane drawled, freeing his half-erect cock from his jeans and kicking them aside. "It's a ritualistic representation of the *phallus.*"

Holy fuck.

I'd never heard someone say *phallus* and sound sexy before.

"And this," Reg said, withdrawing a metal goblet. "What do you think this is?"

"It's a goddamn cup," I said, gasping as Billy ran his thumbs over my nipples. At this point, they were hard as fucking diamonds. Add a little water and I could cut granite.

"This is a ritualistic representation of the feminine aspect in nature."

Reg handed the cup to George

"And you're gonna fill it," Reg said with an evil smirk.

"Fill it? With what?!" I asked, but then Shane was taking up a position on my left, Reg on my right.

I was surrounded by four hot naked men.

Correction—four hot naked *plumbers.*

Shane reached out and dragged a single fingertip across my lips, causing the air in the room to shift, teasing my hair around my face. As he moved his finger, little swirls of white clouds clung to my skin like snow. He traced a long, tingling line all the way down the side of my jaw, along my throat, straight to my belly button.

At the same time, Reg was taking a much dirtier route, reaching out and pulling my right knee wide. He teased his fingers along my inner thigh and straight toward the promise land.

I didn't do a thing to stop him.

Meanwhile, George was setting up some sort of … altar with the athame and the goblet near my feet.

I guess Reg had warned me—chanting and runes and shit. Well, that's exactly what I was getting. As soon as George was done with his setup, he rejoined the others, taking up his place between my thighs and tracing several runes on my stomach with his finger.

He spoke a single word and then the others repeated it. I couldn't quite understand what they were saying, but I guess I didn't need to—George took that moment to find my opening with the thick, hard length of his cock, thrusting into me and grabbing hold of my hips with his gentle but firm grip.

I arched my back and lifted my pelvis into him, my head laying back onto Billy's shoulder.

The chanting around me could've come across as one of two ways—creepy or hilarious.

I mean, really? A bunch of elemental plumbers chanting in a foreign language while they gangbanged me? Stupid, right?

But no.

Whatever was happening right now felt *right.* It had this primal, earthy quality to it that made my blood sing and my heart pound. Outside the windows, the storm raged, thrashing the sides of the house with sheets of water. Lightning crashed into the tree outside my grandmother's window *repeatedly,* and yet … it never burned.

The mens' voices rose in a wild, primal chant, mixing with the howl of the wind and the cracking of the wooden shutters against the windows.

As he fucked me, nice and slow and deep, I could feel the others tracing more runes onto my body, their fingers leaving glowing marks on my skin that shimmered like sunshine on water, brilliant and liquid and organic.

George moved inside of me to the sound of the storm and the breathless chanting, hitting me so deep, I swear I could *feel* him in my womb.

Guess that's what it felt like to fuck an earth spirit.

As he pleasured me between my thighs, Billy took over my breasts, massaging them with his hands, teasing the nipples with his thumbs. His lips eased down the sides my throat, burning a hot trail of pleasure with his mouth.

Shane took it upon himself to kiss me, putting one of his big hands on my belly as he leaned over and slipped his tongue into my mouth. He tasted like honey and whiskey, and his kiss was as thick and drawling as his accent. I wanted more of it. More of him, George, Billy …

And Reg.

On my left, the water elemental took up kissing the side of my neck that *wasn't* being scorched by Billy's hot mouth. He traced the pulsing throb of my pulse, running the tip of his tongue along the veins and arteries that gave me life.

His right hand snuck down between my thighs and even though it should've been weird, having him touch my clit while George fucked me, it wasn't. It just felt … right. Like the rest of this strange, ferine ritual we were involved in.

Those tattooed fingers of his were putting just the right amount of pressure on me, enhancing the slick slide of George's cock. All I had to do was relax into it, arch my breasts into Billy's touch, tangle my tongue with Shane's.

It was the most exquisite form of pampering I'd ever endured.

George was right. I didn't have to suffer through it; I just had to let myself fall.

The boys continued drawing on my skin, bringing the strange runes to life on every inch of my body except for my feet, face, and hands. I was glimmering like the ocean on a warm day, gold-yellow symbols flickering like fireflies.

A sharp, low sound slipped from George's lips as he came, spilling himself inside of me and filling the air with the sweet scent of pine. Dripping sweat, he immediately moved to the side and traded places with Shane.

"What are …" I whispered, but I felt like I might burn up from the inside out if I didn't get any release. Besides, it wasn't exactly like I *hated* what was happening to me at the moment. Fuck, I could do this all day everyday and never get bored.

In fact, getting marked by elementals may very well have been my newest pastime.

Shane slid his warm hands up the inside of my thighs, chanting the same strange words as George. My hair swirled around my face in a warm breeze, a gentle gust sliding off the surface of the Caribbean. I could smell that fresh, electric scent of a storm brewing, like the very molecules in the air were charged and ready to *strike.*

Shane's blue eyes met mine with an almost physical sense of force, like he was touching me through that sharp gaze of his. The edge of his mouth quirked up briefly in a smile, but then he was grabbing my hips and there was nothing *cute* or *kind* about his facial expression. No, the Southern manners were wiped aside for that universally annoying male smugness.

Unlike George, he took his time sliding into me, just like he had in the bathroom, slipping his inked cock in inch by careful inch until he was fully sheathed inside the hot slickness of my pussy.

"Fucking shit," was all I managed to get out. I wasn't about being coy or flirty at that point. No, I was acting on pure instinct. Thoughts and logicality just didn't seem to be present here. Hell, I didn't *need* them.

Wrapping my legs around Shane's hard, hot body, I drew him closer, the colorful wash of tattoos on his chest blurred in the semi-darkness of the room. With only candles and lightning to illuminate us, the stormy evening was quickly bathing the house in blackness.

Reg maintained a slow, even pace on my clit, increasing the pressure of his lips on my neck to the point where I *knew* I was going to be left with hickeys galore. On the other side, Billy did the same, like he was trying to match Reg's intensity.

All of that sensation—Shane's thick, hard shaft and the slow, easy kisses George was laying across my sweaty stomach—brought me to climax with a sudden burst of pleasure, filling my body from head to toe and dragging a scream from my throat.

For a few seconds there, it was almost painful, almost felt *too* good. But I couldn't stop it. Whatever this was that was happening—this weird, supernatural plumber *thing*—I had to see it to the end.

Based on the event thus far, I had a pretty good idea of what that might entail.

Two guys down ... two to go.

The chanting continued around me, a slow sensual song adding a soundtrack to our lovemaking. And I swear to god, even though he was chanting in a foreign language, I could still hear Shane's Southern drawl.

He drove into me with purpose, hard and fast, fucking me with a fury that matched the storm outside the walls of Gram's house.

Heh.

Bet she'd never banked on something like *this* happening in the dusty rose and cream guest bedroom?

Probably not or else she would've invested in a better bed ... With each thrust of Shane's powerful hips, I could hear the springs inside the mattress creaking with that primal rhythm. It could've been funny in a different situation, but honestly, it was just sexy as fuck.

Shane's orgasm took me by surprise, bursting from him with a gust of wind that knocked my grandmother's perfume bottles to the floor. The sharp, frosty scent that filled the air—just like a good, crisp Northeastern autumn—mixed all of those floral scents and made me feel like I was in the middle of a rose garden.

"Stay strong," Billy whispered in my ear, and then he moved over for George to take his place, rotating the circle of men around me like they were simply planets and I, I was the fucking *sun.*

Sliding off the bed and taking his place in front of me, I saw that Billy ... Billy, shit. What was his last name? I was having an orgy with four dudes whose last names I didn't know?! Christ on a cracker...

Anyhow, Billy What's-His-Name, had pierced junk.

Like, all over pierced junk.

Oh, and the man was *hung* like a goddamn horse.

"Fuck me," I whispered as the lushness of his mouth twisted into the signature smirk of a bad boy who knows he's got the goods women want. Screw him for that.

"Planned on it," he said, stepping between my thighs. By this point, I was drenched in sweat and saliva and ... other things. I could feel that liquid heat between my legs, but I didn't care. My body knew that we weren't finished here.

I caught a brief glimpse of silver in the firelight, Billy's piercings winking back at me from the long, curved length of his shaft. He was as big as Shane, thick and hard and ready for me.

I was going to be seriously fucking sore come morning.

"Ready, Firebug?" he asked, but I was pretty sure he didn't give a shit if I was or not.

He slipped inside the warm, aching tenderness of my body, raking a fervor with the tip of his shaft. I could *feel* all those bits of metal, warm from his skin, arousing me in places I hadn't known were cold and wanting until now.

The way *he* chanted sounded possessive, and the grip of his hands on my hips was firm, unyielding. He didn't look at me like a stranger that was interested in a quick fuck, but like a man who'd spotted something that was supposed to be *his.*

That is not at all sexy, I tried to tell myself, but hey, even feminists can have kinky fantasies, right?

And this whole thing?

It was so a fantasy come true.

George threaded his fingers into my hair and drew my head back, breaking Billy's gaze as he kissed all the sore places the fire and water elementals had left. For a few moments there, I breathed in through both my nose and mouth, absorbing the vast array of scents in the air—some of them pleasant and sweet, others base and animal.

But then George was turning my face to the side and kissing my mouth with that firm but insistent press of lips that had started all of this shit in the first place.

In the back of my mind, I was still aware of the knife— sorry, *athame*—and chalice that were sitting on the floor, but it was hard to care *what* the back of my mind wanted when my body had everything she desired.

Billy rocked the bed with his frantic, angry thrusts, coming hard and fast inside of me and pulling away with something that sounded suspiciously like a growl. With that sound, that campfire scent of his perfumed the air, mixing with the tang of spent fireworks, like it was the Fourth of July or some shit.

"Hurry Reg, I'm freaking out," I heard him say, but I didn't watch as the men switched. My eyes were drifting closed as a strange sort of heat fell over me, mixing with that odd, detached feeling I'd gotten earlier when the men had first started to touch me.

I knew then that I was being kissed by magic.

As soon as Reg entered me, I could *feel* it.

The marking was coming full circle.

Two mouths pressed hot, wet heat to my nipples, sucking and biting and drawing pleasure up through my spine like... well, okay, like water through pipes.

These plumbers really knew how to keep the flow going.

My eyes opened wide and when I glanced to my right, I could see the five of us reflected in the mirror, this primal mix of bodies, our limbs tangled, flesh wet with sweat. The runes glimmered on the surface of my skin like tattoos, and my heart beat so frantically at the sight of Reg fucking me that I almost passed out.

"I'm going to whisper some words in your ear," George told me as I watched my eyes go from green to *purple,* a faint glow emanating from them and tinting my cheeks with color. "Repeat after me." In a language as fluid as the stars, he told me beautiful, beautiful things I could not understand.

My lips ... they seemed to move of their own accord.

I spoke the words, Reg came inside of me, and my orgasm hit at the same moment the runes began to glow, casting away all the shadows and filling the room with light.

Above our heads, another fucking pipe burst.

116

8

CHAPTER EIGHT

A cool breeze across my naked back woke me and I opened my eyes, frowning. How could there be a breeze when the window wasn't open?

The room was dead still, the only sound coming from the deep breathing of the four naked elementals scattered around the room. No one had really wanted to return to their own rooms after the, ah … magic happened, so here we all were. My body was aching in the most delicious way, one that reminded me how damn clean my pipes must be, after all the plunging they'd just taken.

Head on my arms, I'd been sleeping flat on my belly, which was not the easiest task when one was as busty as I was. Exhaustion had taken over quickly though so I must have crashed before noticing how uncomfortable my position was.

I lifted my head, looking around for where the breeze had come from. The lacy curtains fluttered with the same breeze, yet the window was still closed tight.

What the shit ... is my power still going rogue?

The guys had said once we finished the ritual that I would have them under control though, so it shouldn't be causing wind without my conscious decision.

Rolling over carefully so as not to wake the two burning hot bodies either side of me, I sat up to get a better look.

"You ought to be ashamed of yourself, my girl!" Grams scolded me, suddenly appearing beside the bed and making me scream with fright.

All four elementals woke at the sound of my girly shriek, bursting into action and scanning the room for what had just caused my alarm.

"What's going on, darlin'?" Shane asked, his voice thick with sleep as he stood in the middle of my Gram's guest room, stark naked and ready to attack any intruders.

At a loss for words, I simply squeaked and pointed a shaking finger at my recently deceased grandmother, who stood beside the bed dressed to the nines in the skirt suit she'd been buried in and wearing a *very* pissed off expression on her face.

"What are you pointing at, ST?" Reg coaxed with a yawn. "There's nothing in here." He had just been efficiently checking all the dark corners of the room, anywhere someone might hide, and clearly came up empty-handed.

Of course, he came up empty-handed. Grams is standing right there, *only a foot or so in front of him!*

"H-her!" I stuttered, my shaking finger still pointing at my dead grandmother, but all I got from the elementals were varying looks of confusion ... like I had just finally lost my last marble.

"You don't see her?" I shrieked, now second-guessing whether I *had* in fact, let kangaroos loose in the top paddock. Or found myself a few sandwiches short of a picnic.

"See ... who, Blossom?" George asked gently, running a soothing hand down my back. "There's no one in this room except us."

"They can't see me, stupid girl," my Grams snapped with a roll of her eyes. Now that I was a bit more awake, it was becoming clear that she was somewhat see-through. "Although *you* might show the common decency of covering up your lady bits while speaking to your grandmother."

Arching a vaguely translucent eyebrow at me, she waved her spectral hand towards my nakedness and I scrambled to yank a sheet over myself. *No one* needed their grandmother to see them stark naked, covered in glittering runes and elemental semen.

"You all don't see my dead grandmother standing beside the bed?" I hissed, blushing furiously. Obviously, I knew she was dead and possibly a figment of my wine addled brain, but some things are just ingrained in your DNA. Being embarrassed when your Grams caught you in post gangbang afterglow was one of those things.

"There's no one there, babe," Billy drawled, yawning heavily and stealing Shane's recently vacated spot in the bed. "Just go back to sleep or I'll start thinking we need to wear you out again ..."

His hand snaked up and grasped my breast under the sheet I'd been clutching to my chest, deftly locating my nipple and tweaking it teasingly. A yelp of surprise squawked out of me at the same time as Gram hissed in anger.

"Seriously! She's right fucking there!" I smacked Billy's hand off my breast and tucked the sheet tighter to my body. "Grams, what the hell?"

"I beg your pardon, Arizona Morgan Smoke?" The old woman's eyes almost bugged out of her ghostly head. "I will thank you not to use such foul language when speaking to me."

"Grams, *seriously*?" I muttered. "I'm nearly thirty, and you're dead. You'd think I would be allowed to say *fuck*."

"Goodness knows you clearly know the meaning of the word." She gave a pointed look at all the naked men occupying the room with me. "I would have expected better from you than *this*, Arizona."

"What? Group sex?" I blurted, the shock and exhaustion weakening my filter. Gram narrowed her eyes at me in disapproval.

"Elementals," she snapped, giving the guys a dirty look. They, meanwhile, were all staring at me like I'd just transformed into a seven-boobed cyclops.

"You guys really can't see her? She's standing right there being all judgmental and condescending." I waved my hand at where my Gram's ghost—because that's what I assumed she was—stood.

"Where?" Reg asked, taking a step closer to the bed and coincidentally ending up with his dick touching Gram's butt.

"Ah yep, right there." I cringed. "Your wrench is right on top of her sewage."

"Oh for the love of Christ." Grams rolled her eyes again. "These plumbing jokes are out of control, Arizona. They need to stop. All I've heard in this house for the last two days has been *snake my drain* and *hide the plunger* and frankly, my dear, it's severely lacking in class. As if you shacking up with an elemental quad wasn't bad enough, surely my afterlife doesn't need to be haunted by your appalling puns too?"

My jaw dropped open, at a loss for what to say—my puns were *excellent*.

"Wait, Grams, you knew about the elementals? Why the hell didn't you ever tell me?" I screamed, anger flaring hot in me as I frowned at the elegant old woman.

"Would it *really* have made a difference?" she sniffed, giving Reg's dick a curious look as he moved to where he probably thought was a safe spot but actually ended up halfway inside my ghostly grandmother. I made a *scoot over* gesture to him, because the sight of his naked body practically wearing my Gram's ghost was beyond disturbing.

"Yes, it really would have." I ground my teeth together hard. "Maybe if I *had* known to watch out for the sexy plumbers, I wouldn't have ended up in this mess!"

"Now wait one hot second here," Shane demanded, glancing at the other men, "is it possible Ari's exhibiting some of her spirit powers? Talking to ghosts isn't exactly much of a stretch —I've heard of weirder manifestations."

The ghost in question gave Shane a withering look which probably matched the one I was giving him. Surely it was painfully obvious that was what was happening—either I was crazy or you know, ghosts.

"Stupid *air* elemental," Grams muttered. "Oh don't give me that look, Arizona. I did my best to keep you out of this mess and look at you. The second I'm gone, you're in my guest bedroom letting an *entire quad* have their wicked way with you. My body is barely cold in the ground for goodness sake!"

"What do you *mean*?" I growled, growing increasingly frustrated with the cryptic ghost in a twin set and pearls.

"Sugar Tits, do you mind filling us in on what's going on?" Reg frowned. "We're only hearing one side of this conversation and it's a bit hard to follow."

"What do you mean, that you did your best to keep me out of this mess, Grams? You never mentioned anything about elementals or magic or any of this crazy bullshit. Yes, I said bullshit. Get over it woman, you're dead already." I narrowed my eyes at her, trying to convey my best death threats through my gaze but this old bird was a pro at that game and just gave me a bored look back.

"I mean that I had you spelled to cover your elemental blood. No supernatural creatures should have sensed anything more than human on you … but I guess that started to wear off when I died." She pursed her lips and frowned. "These boys weren't wrong that you carry elemental blood, but it's a whole heck of a lot more than the one percent they're talking about."

"What? Grams, I'm ..." I rubbed my hand across my eyes, careful not to drop the sheet in the process. "Sorry, but a little elaboration might me nice. Color me confused here."

"I can imagine, dear. Excessive drinking does tend to kill off brain cells." The smug old bitch smirked at me, but she *had* reminded me that there was still wine on the bedside table.

Reaching over to grab a bottle, I yanked out the cork that George had helpfully removed earlier, and took a long swig from the bottle.

"Oh lord," my Gram's ghost groaned, "tell me you're not drinking a three thousand dollar bottle of wine like some sort of homeless lush?"

Shrugging, I turned the label to show her, then took another healthy gulp. The guys were all watching me, waiting patiently for me to fill them in.

"Ok, Gram, explain. What percentage of elemental blood *do* I have, and more to the point, why is this house practically falling down when you can afford to have wine this expensive sitting in the cellar?" It really was good wine too. Nice and smooth.

"Because the only handymen in this entire bloody state are elementals, aren't they?" she muttered, sulking a little. Guess she didn't discover this until *after* she bought the house.

She cocked her head to the side, her pearls sliding across her wrinkled neck as she seemed to be listening to something we couldn't hear.

"Sorry, Duck, I have to go. I'll be back though, so try not to destroy anymore of my house in the meantime. And for goodness sake, tell these boys to start wearing pants!"

And with that, she was gone.

Shocked, I blinked a couple of times at the space she'd just disappeared from, then took another long gulp from the wine bottle.

"So ...?" Shane prompted, folding his massive arms over his chest and frowning down at me. Damn, he was a sight to behold, standing there all stern and in charge. Tattooed waves crawled across his chest, bordered by some elaborately detailed scroll with words in a language I didn't recognize—probably the same way they'd been chanting in last night while they fucked me.

"In a nutshell: my Gram is haunting us, I have *considerably more than one percent* elemental blood in me, and this wine costs more than my car." I paused. Did I miss anything? "Oh and she says you all need to start wearing pants, but ... that's optional I would say."

Yeah, yeah, I know I said we would have this one orgy and then I'd be done with them. But a girl can look, right? There was no harm in looking ... Right?

"That's it?" Billy grunted, still laying back with his head on my pillow and an arm thrown over his head.

"Pretty much, then she said she 'had to go' and disappeared." I chewed my lip. "Is this really a spirit elemental power? Like how I can make lightning and shit?"

There was a pregnant pause, a moment while no one responded, then Reg ran his hand over his short hair, sighing heavily.

"Short answer, Sugar Tits ..." Reg frowned at me, then hunted around the floor for his clothes. "Yes and no."

"Yes *and* no?" I repeated. "Where are you going?" He was pulling on his jeans, and buckling his belt up while looking exceptionally concerned.

"Reg is going to go speak with Charlie, hon," Shane answered for him while Reg located his phone and started tapping out a text. "If anyone knows more about this, it's Charlie."

"I don't understand, is this a bad thing?" I wasn't sure if they were talking about the ghost thing, the lightning, or the elemental blood. Maybe all three?

Their worried expressions were freaking me out. George also pulled on his pants, then left to find a shirt I presume, seeing as he hadn't been wearing one earlier, and I turned to Billy who was still lying in the bed beside me.

"Billy, what's the drama? Do you know more than you're letting on?" I felt stupid still sitting there stark naked while everyone else was getting dressed, so awkwardly scooted off the bed with the sheet still wrapped around me.

Uh, before I seriously considered heading downstairs, a shower was in order. Because, you know, juices from the ritual and all—theirs *and* mine.

"Firebug, I think the time for modesty has long since passed, don't you?" Billy grinned, ignoring my question completely and raking his burning coal colored eyes all over me as I shuffled around hunting down my clothes.

Somehow, my fox printed pajama pants had made it on top of a lamp and my top was halfway under the bed. I bunched them up in my arms while still struggling to hold the sheet in place. Bare tits plus bare Billy ... that would only get me into trouble again.

"Yes, well, that was *before* I knew my Grams was watching me," I muttered, then cringed when I remembered everything that had just gone down in this room earlier in the night. Fuck I hope she didn't see *everything*.

"What are George and Shane doing?" I asked, noticing they had both now left the room leaving Billy gloriously naked and sprawled across the bed by himself.

"George will be going with Reg," he told me, yawning, "otherwise Reg and Charlie will end up in a fistfight. Water might seem like a gentle element, but it's not. Those bastards give fire a run for our money in the aggressive stakes. Actually so does air, come to think of it. Earth are the only ones who are even remotely *grounded* ... so to speak ..."

"Oh Billy ..." I whispered, "that was awful. Maybe leave the puns to the professionals, yeah?"

He scowled and threw a pillow at my head, which I just managed to catch while laughing at his hurt expression.

"Alright, so Reg and George have gone to see Charlie. What are the three of us doing in the meantime?" I considered his relaxed pose, and he raised his eyebrows at me suggestively.

"I can suggest a thing or two ..." His hand dropped south to his hardening dip tube and I threw the pillow back at him, leaving the room to go find Shane.

I had to step over the fucking *pentagram* drawn on the floor, the one with the athame and chalice inside of it, but I decided that was a mystery best left for another day.

Regardless of what we'd all just gone through, magical gangbang and all, I still wanted nothing to do with these assholes and the drama they were raining down on my life. Never thought I would see the day that I missed being *just a barista.*

"Shane!" I yelled out once I reached the corridor. Even though they'd said I should be safe now that the ritual was over, I didn't trust another freak storm not to rip the roof off, or another winged executioner to come knocking at my door. Padding cautiously down the hall and dragging the sheet behind me like a ghost (pun intended), I followed the sound of Shane's voice when he yelled back.

"What are you doing?" I asked, finding him standing in the middle of my destroyed bedroom with bits of debris floating around him.

"Just cleaning up a bit," he murmured, giving me a small smile. "It's sort of the least we can do, right?"

"Oh." I was stunned. It was actually a really thoughtful thing for him to do. Didn't come anywhere close to making up for everything that his dodgy plumbing team had caused, but it was a start.

"I can only really clean up a bit, but when the others get back we can fix most of the damage together." Shane shrugged, like it was no big thing, but my resolve to ditch their fine asses ASAP was weakening a little.

"You can do that?" I was suitably impressed and Shane just nodded, his attention on the flying bits of shit as he directed them back where they belonged or into small piles to be dealt with later. "So … could you fix up the rest of my house? Seeing as you're not paying any rent ..." Maybe these handymen would turn out to be handy after all?

"Yes ... but it couldn't be in place of rent. We're not *allowed* to work in any trade other than plumbing, so it'd have to be simply improving our own home—which *is* allowed." He turned his curious, denim blue eyes my way. "So, Arizona Smoke ... are you asking us to officially move in with you?"

Oh flaming dingo shit, I'm going to live to regret this.

"Yes ...?" It came out as a question, because I couldn't believe what I was actually saying. Just minutes ago I was thinking about the quickest way to get the fuck out of dodge, and now I was asking the source of all my troubles to freaking move in with me ... permanently... I must be going barmy.

"Well, we accept." He grinned, then grabbed my face in one huge palm and sealed the deal with a hot, wet kiss. His mouth slanted across mine as his tongue slipped in, tasting like Johnnie Walker Double Black and sweet tea. No wonder my resolve was crumbling so hard, with kisses like that.

"Shouldn't you discuss this with your ahh crew?" I asked, pulling away from his kiss in an effort to regain a bit of mental fortitude.

"My crew?" he snickered, rubbing a tattooed hand over the lower half of his face. "You mean my quad? Well, technically *quint* now that you're a part of it."

I decided to ignore the last part of that statement, clutching the sheet and my crumpled clothes against my chest.

"No, I mean your plumbing crew. But same same, whatever." I certainly wasn't admitting I'd just forgotten the word for their collective.

"Silly sugar plum," he chuckled, planting another kiss on my lips. This time it was just a sweet, gentle meeting of mouths before he pulled back and met my gaze. "I know you're new to all of this, but as far as my quad is concerned, we're married now."

"All of us?" I squeaked, my chest tight. Why this sent me into a panic worse than the prospect of a gangbang had, I do not know.

"You know it, wifey," Billy answered from where he stood propped against the door frame, "and as my first husbandly duty, I have ordered us pizzas. Figured you might be … *famished* … after last night's activities." His smoldering stare said everything I needed to know about where he thought the rest of the day might be heading. And damn if my greedy cunt didn't want to agree with him.

Down girl, I scolded myself and calmly made my way to the newly repaired bathroom across the hall. I was, however, careful to make sure I locked the door behind me. The runes the boys had drawn all over my skin were still glittering faintly, and I worried they were having some influence over my actions.

Had I known then, what was to come, I would have made the most of the little magical buzz we were riding. More fool me.

9

CHAPTER NINE

Reg and George arrived home with a bang. Literally. I thought Reg was about to take my entire damn door off he kicked it that hard.

"Chat went well with Charlie then?" Shane asked in a dry tone, while Billy smothered a smile behind a slice of cold pizza. He'd ordered enough for everyone, but when the other two hadn't returned home after a couple of hours we'd decided to eat it ourselves.

As far as Britt was concerned, she was still fast asleep upstairs, drooling all over one of the shiny pink pillows she'd brought with her—I'd checked. When I'd tried to wake her earlier, she'd slapped me away and mentioned something about needing the extra z's to heal from her fight with the incubus. Whatever.

Surprisingly, I'd managed to keep my hands off both sinfully sexy plumbers while they combined their air and fire talents to do a bit of repairing around my beautiful old home. Mainly just in securing the tin ceiling tiles that had so nearly decapitated me just the day before. Now that I thought about the moment objectively, I blamed Gram's ghost.

"As well as can be expected," George answered for Reg, who looked like he was having a hard time controlling his rage. He stalked back and forth across the floral print carpet of my living room, his fists clenching and unclenching in time with his jaw.

"So ... what does that mean?" I asked. Clearly I was the only one here that couldn't read minds, because I had no idea how well Reg and his father got along.

"He wants us to formally present you to the COCS head." Reg spat the words with disgust, stopping his pacing and staring hard at me.

"Umm ..." *Come on, was I seriously the only one that just heard Reg say I needed presenting to the* cock's head*?*

"Committee of Combined Supernaturals," Shane reminded me, rolling his beautiful blue eyes. "Honestly, honey doll, it seems like we're becoming a bad influence on you."

"Bad influence? Have you *met* Britt yet?" I asked, popping out my hip and planting a fist on it. Speak of the devil ...

"Jesus Christ," she said, in that usual proprietorial way of hers, "how long did you guys fuck for? I mean, the noise of those *springs*. Next time you plan on doing it all night, can you get a hotel room or something?"

She waltzed past us and into the kitchen wearing nothing but a pink thong and see-through babydoll nightie. Fortunately for all four guys, they didn't so much as glance at her. Lucky them. I was feeling as possessive as Billy had looked last night.

Even though I hated these guys and was totally going to try to eradicate them completely from my life, I felt ... slightly jealous at the thought of Britt getting any action with them. I mean, that's just simple girlfriend etiquette, right? Never scoop up your sister's sloppy seconds.

"Congratulations on being marked!" she shouted out just seconds before I heard the distinct sound of a wine bottle being corked.

If I'd been a werewolf, my ears would've pricked up. I could recognize that sound *anywhere.*

Note to self: maybe look into attending some sort of *meeting* after all this supernatural business is done and over with.

"Why would I need to see a COCS head?" I asked and then sniggered, taking a bite of the cheese pizza in my hand.

"Besides the obvious reasons?" Billy asked, lifting his brows and giving me another of those stupid *you are mine* asshole looks. "Just to keep the peace, prove that you're now marked and one of us so they can get off our dicks—and so you can climb right back on."

"Wow," I said, lifting my brows and giving him a *look.* "I thought you were better than Reg, but really, you're just as big of a slut as he is."

Reg didn't take the bait, heading up the stairs and slamming one of the doors loud enough that it echoed around the entire house.

"He okay?" I asked, but George just shrugged.

"Give him twenty and he'll forget what it was he was even angry about in the first place."

Sitting down on the edge of the couch, I watched Britt flounce into the room with her nipples showing through her nightie. She deserved a purple nurple for that …

"Isn't COCS the same group of people that tried to kidnap me and kill Britt yesterday?" I asked, pausing to chew my food and take another bite.

"Yup," Billy said, rubbing at the flames tattooed onto the right side of his neck with an inked hand. He didn't have nearly as much ink as either Shane or Reg, just a few well-placed designs, but add in the stubbled masculine jaw, the charcoal hair, and those abs ... he had the bad boy look down pat. "Same, same. But you're marked now, so you know, they won't try to kill you this time."

I narrowed my eyes and continued scarfing down my food, but I didn't correct Billy in that technically, the one pervy incubi *stopped* the other pervy incubi from killing me yesterday—they *hadn't* exactly wanted me dead.

I smelled another rat.

"You seem to know each other pretty well," I said instead, telling myself that I'd pack up and head into the city to see Siobhan *after* I asked a couple of questions, for informational purposes only of course. It's not like I was developing *crushes* on these assholes. No way, not even if they claimed we were 'married' now.

Lifting up a hand, I glanced at the runes on my arms and wondered when they were going to fade.

"Well, we've known each other our whole lives," George said, giving the pizza a careful look and then almost reluctantly extracting a slice from the box. "As soon as four compatible elements in an area are born, they're put together into a quad. Reg is the youngest, so the rest of us were sent to live with Charlie and his family. They basically raised us."

"So ... you're like brothers then?" I asked, wondering if it was creepy that they were all, you know, *inside* of me last night. Speaking of, showering this morning was a *bitch*. There was an awful lot of cleanup.

"Brothers?" George asked, giving me a weird look. "No. More like lovers."

"Lovers?" I asked, the word coming out in a squeak. I mean, not that I cared, but …really? "You four?" I glanced between George, Shane … and Billy. "You suck dicks, Billy?" I said, just trying to clarify. He didn't really seem like the dick sucking type to me.

"No," he said, glaring at me. For what reason, I wasn't sure. But whatever. Screw him. "But I sure as hell hope that you do."

I threw my pizza crust at him and turned to Shane.

"Lovers? Like … you're polyamorous or something?"

"More like …" Shane started, glancing up at the ceiling. "We're together for life, and on the sliding scale o' sexuality, we're all at least ten percent bi." He shrugged his broad shoulders, dropping his azure gaze to mine. "Trust me, sug, we've been looking for the right woman for a *long, long* fuckin' time. We'd much rather please a woman."

"Oh, no," I said, shaking my head and wondering if I was simply fighting the inevitable. I'd known these guys for all of two days and they felt like old friends. I should probably just listen to my ovaries and start dating them, just to see what might happen. But no. Nope. Stubborn is as stubborn does, okay? I had to at least make a show of it. "I am not that right woman, no way. I said you could *move in,* not have my hand in marriage. We are clearing up all of this, you know, *this.*" I gestured at the glimmering runes on my body, the streaks of blue and green, white and red, trails of elemental magic left by the guys. I looked like I'd been tattooed like my favorite rockstar, Paxton Blackwell—color from head to fucking toe.

"Clearing up?" George asked, and he raked his fingers through his brown hair before chucking a worried gaze in Shane's direction. "She thinks it's coming off, Skeeter."

"Think … what's … coming off," I whispered, my mouth and throat already dry. "I'm not really liking that statement, George."

"Arizona," he said, and I tried not to like the way my full name rolled off his sexy lips. "The runes are permanent."

"Oh, *snap,*" Britt said, making me jump. For the first time in what was probably her entire life, she'd been quiet for more than two seconds and I'd forgotten she was there. "You really *are* screwed"—she paused to give me a lascivious leer—"blued, and tattooed, Ari."

"How the *fuck* am I supposed to get a *job* when my entire body is covered in glimmering runes?!" I shouted, standing up and ignoring that sweet carnal soreness between my thighs.

"A job?" George asked, still sounding confused. "Arizona, you're our mate. We're supposed to take care of you; you don't have to work."

I couldn't decide if that was … old-fashioned and sexist, adorable as all fucking hell, or stupid because not a one of these four bums had money and they were all living in *my* crumbling old house.

"Except you're forgetting just one goddamn thing here," I growled, my anger spiking again and setting the runes—or *fuck,* tattoos—sparkling and shimmering.

"What's that, honey doll?" Shane drawled. The stubborn set to his gaze told me he was supremely confident in this idea of them 'looking after me' like I was some thirties housewife. Fuck them, if they thought they'd be coming home to a hand cooked meal and sparkling house every night. I couldn't cook for *shit.*

"You're all broke ass motherfuckers! You can't even support *yourselves*!" I snapped the words at them and had the satisfaction of seeing Shane's cocky expression slip a tiny bit.

"That's irrelevant now," George helpfully responded. "Now that we've completed our quint, we're entitled to a certain cut of the plumbing contracts."

"Why?" Britt asked, cocking her head to the side like a slutty spaniel.

"Why?" George repeated, looking a bit confused. "Because we have a wife to care for now. Charlie can't edge us out of the market now because our women are so priceless. We're honor bound to do *everything* in our power to give them a comfortable life."

"Cool." Britt nodded. "Don't suppose you have any other woman-less friends that like it doggy-style?" She threw George a saucy wink, but I knew my bestie, and she wasn't kidding.

There was a brief pause where no one quite knew what to say back to her and then Shane turned to George, changing the subject.

"So when are we due at this meeting with the Head?" he asked, his confident drawl back in place. Casually, he trailed a finger down my arm, tracing over the air runes and making my whole body break out in gooseflesh.

"Tonight," George said, checking his wooden Fossil watch. "Seeing as it's now almost mid-morning, Arizona will need to get a dress. You know how formal these things are ..."

Shane grunted, clearly not a fan of formal events.

"I'll take her shopping," Billy volunteered, making everyone stare at him in surprise.

"Ah no," Britt snapped, "if anyone is taking little miss jeans over here shopping for a dress, it would be *moi*."

"You can come along, if you want, but it needs to be a very specific sort of dress. So you'll need one of us to make sure it's ... *appropriate*," Billy informed my indignant bestie while simultaneously casting me a *come-hither* look.

"Oh, well. Fine. But I'm coming," she sniffed. "Not like I'm getting to *come* any other way. Girl, are you sure you need all four of these hunky meat sticks?"

Possessiveness flooded me like someone had just run over a fire hydrant and I had to clench my teeth to keep from snapping at my bestie. Clearly, my ride or die bitch was just joking— she'd never take a man that I was even remotely interested in, not even if he *begged.*

"Whoa, girl," Britt whispered, her eyes wide as she noticed the tightness of my jaw and the fact that my fingers were curled into fists. Guess magic really *was* involved in that ritual last night because I was acting like a serious crazy person. "Your stance is like, way aggressive—and trust me, I know body language. Part wolf, remember? Anyway, I thought you were dumping their asses as soon as you were safe from the executioners?"

"Firebug can't help it," Billy said with a smug look on his devilishly handsome face. "She's had a taste of the quad and now she's addicted."

"Ugh, whatever. Let's go get this fucking dress." I threw my hands up and headed into the kitchen to find wherever Britt had left my keys. Billy had said it needed to be a specific sort of dress, and I had the sinking feeling that *specific* meant *slutty.*

Whatever it took to get this magic mess sorted, so be it. Surely whatever Billy selected wouldn't be *that* bad ... right?

George ended up tagging along on our shopping trip, so it was a good thing we took my hearse. Years ago when I first bought the morbid vehicle, I had added some extra seats into the ah, coffin area, so there was plenty of space for all four of us.

Billy directed us to a fancy looking boutique on the main street of town, which I hadn't been into yet. Since moving here, I'd spent most of my time taking care of Gram, then planning her funeral after she was gone, and then trying to recover from the stress of it all. Just as I was starting to feel like myself again, the plumbing packed its shit in so I really hadn't checked out the shops at all.

"Well this doesn't look so bad," Britt murmured, echoing my thoughts as we entered the shop. "The way he said *specific* I was imagining some sort of like ... leather bondage type getup. Which like, don't get me wrong, you'd still look *smoking* in." She gave me a long look, and I just knew she was picturing me dressed like that. Dirty bitch.

She was right though—the store seemed like a totally normal, upscale fashion boutique. Billy was at the counter, speaking with the shop assistant who was giggling like a hyena and twirling her greasy hair around her finger.

That same flare of possessive anger swept through me as I watched Billy lean on the counter, giving her sexy bedroom eyes. Those were *my* sexy bedroom eyes, god-fucking-damn it!

"Relax," George murmured, placing a calming hand on my arm before I could leap at the ratty looking slut and tear her fucking eyes out, "she's a sewer troll. He would *never* go there. He's just getting any new supernatural news. Everyone knows sewer trolls have all the best gossip."

"What the fuck is a sewer troll?!" I whisper-snarled back, but George just smiled like he thought I was playing around. These boys had a tendency to forget that before all this shit, I'd been a normal human. And like, sewer trolls weren't exactly part of the cast in *The Lord of the Rings* so I didn't have much reference material to go off.

Britt, the bitch, snickered at my scowling face and flipped her hair before wandering off to look at clothes. My feet stayed glued to the spot though, watching Billy flirt, until he finally turned back to us and nodded his head to the heavy velvet curtain behind the cashier's desk.

"Come on, Firebug," he said, "let's find you a ... ah ... dress."

The way he just said 'dress' was not inspiring much confidence in me *at all*, but I followed him through the curtain all the same. On the other side, I pulled up short.

"Oh *hell no!*" I yelled, while Britt burst out in peals of laughter from behind me.

"Girl, oh my god," she howled, "I was just joking about the bondage outfits!"

Sure enough, the room beyond the curtain was filled with racks of leather, chains, PVC, and fuck only knew what else, as well as a serious assortment of toys in the display cases and cabinets.

"Told you it needed to be specific," Billy grinned, "and it needs to show off as many runes as possible. It's the best way to keep you safe, if everyone can see we've marked you."

"If it helps," George added, "we have to wear this shit too ..."

"Have I mentioned lately how *stupid* I think supernatural rules are? First, forced marriage. Next, a mandatory orgy. And *then* ..." I took a few steps forward and fingered some hideous hot pink latex suit. "Bondage wear for uniforms?"

"I happen to look really goddamn good in bondage wear," Billy said, sauntering through the little den of iniquities like he'd grown up there. Hell, for all I knew about the boys, it was possible that he *had.*

138

"Don't do that," Britt whispered in my ear, pausing to heft a large, chocolate colored dildo in her hand. The way she stroked it was a little disturbing, like maybe I should look away and give her some privacy.

"Do what?" I hissed as George and Billy disappeared into the sea of handcuffs and *Fifty Shades of Grey* themed sex toys.

"That *thing* that you do, like when you ran out on—"

"Don't say his name," I whispered under my breath, smoothing my hands down the front of my wrinkled long sleeve top with the fox on it. It was part of that pj set I'd been wearing the other night, definitely not meant for public consumption.

Maybe getting dressed up in bondage wasn't such a bad thing? Clearly I didn't have a lot of room in my fashion repertoire to argue.

Then again, my body *was* covered in magical runes so you know, fashion choices were limited.

"I'm just *saying* that after you and … you-know-who fucked for the first time, you had this same face on. I call it your 'I'm-really-happy-but-I-refuse-to-accept-my-own-happiness face."

"Please don't call him you-know-who," I whispered as I stared at a display of condoms. Jesus. How many different ways could you really wrap a cock? I picked up a glow in the dark rainbow one and squinted at it. "Makes him sound like Voldemort or something."

I chucked the condom back onto the display and grabbed another. *This* one had weird purple spikes along it. Huh. Didn't … exactly look like it would, you know, *fit*.

"So what the hell am I supposed to call him then?" Britt said, *way* too loudly for my own comfort. I tried to shush her, but the woman at the counter was staring right at us, at *me* specifically. At least I knew she had no context in which to judge me. I glared right back at her until she glanced away.

"Don't call him anything," I said, trading out the spiked condom for one that said *Grab a Sock for your Rock!* on it. "Don't mention him, don't bring up my college days, just don't talk at all."

"Oh, you kidder," she snorted, slapping me so hard on the back that I fell boob first into the condom display.

"You won't be needing any of those," Billy said, reappearing by my side and sliding the square package from my fingers. He tossed it aside with a stupid smoldering half-smile.

"Why not? I'm marked now. You said I could pregnant if I were marked." I picked up a handful of square packages and dropped them into one of the paper bags next to the display, a little condom goodie bag.

"We'd have to actually *try,*" he repeated, taking the bag from my hand and dumping it out. The rainbow condoms got mixed up with the spiked ones and now I could *really* feel the saleslady glaring at us. "For you to get pregnant, we'd need to do a spell, *and* make sure all four of us were coordinated."

"Wow, where did you grow up? Texas? Didn't anyone tell you how the birds and the bees work? It only takes *one* guy, Billy."

"Not for elementals," he said, grabbing my wrist and pulling me away from the condoms.

"Then *good,*" I said as he dragged me into the back of the store, toward a row of curtained changing rooms. "Because I don't want kids. You hear me? I don't care if your species *is* dying out. Consider it a socio-political statement on the environment."

"Jesus, shut up," Billy said with a bemused half-smile. He dropped my wrist and turned to me, putting his warm hands on either side of my face. It was too familiar of a gesture for someone I'd just met … but maybe an okay gesture for someone I'd had an orgy with? I wasn't sure. "Do you ever stop talking?"

"No, I don't," I said, trying to slap his hands away. It was futile, like batting at a steel beam. "Besides, the world *is* overpopulated—"

"With humans," Billy corrected with a sharp grin. "It's overpopulated with *humans.*"

"If you think I'm going to be some little elemental breeding —" He smothered my mouth with his own, slipping his tongue between my lips and making me completely and utterly forget what the hell it was that I was saying in the first place.

Heat licked up my spine, but I couldn't tell if that was plain and simple lust or his fire magic or what the hell ever.

When he pulled back slightly and cocked a brow, I glanced down and saw that I was *glowing* through my wrinkled pj shirt. The runes were bright enough to attract the attention of the sales clerk and that guy in the trench coat lurking near the porn section.

"We'll have to teach you how to control that …" he started, pushing me into the changing room and dragging the curtain closed between us. "Now try on some of that shit and tell me what you think."

Licking my lips, I lifted a hand to my face and tried to ignore the tingling feeling on my mouth, one that I hadn't felt since … you-know-who. You know what I'm talking about, that special college guy that rocks your fucking world and then your fucking bed and then you just…run away and never speak to him because you're afraid of intimacy? That guy.

I groaned and put my forehead against the shiny vinyl of a miniskirt and tried to suck in deep, soothing breaths. I'd always been sort of a mess and a fuck-up, so now that I was like, some kind of 'chosen one', I was having trouble dealing. I couldn't be the one and only female elemental, savior of a dying race—especially not when the idea of birthing *anything* made me want to puke: elemental *or* mini human.

And then all this business with COCS and plumbers and …

"Fuck a nun's dry cunt," I growled out, standing up and tearing the skirt off the hook it was hanging from. "Billy, this won't even cover *one* of my ass cheeks, let alone two."

"That's sort of the point, Firebug," he called joyfully, clearly having the time of his damn life. I stared at the contraption in my hands, a skirt of lace and vinyl and straps. I had no idea how to even put the damn thing on. I was a barista, damn it, not a dominatrix.

"Do I need to give you a hand?" Billy teased, slipping inside the curtain and sliding his hands under my fox printed pajama top, making as though he was going to pull it off until I slapped his wrist away.

"Thank you, no. I have this." I glared hard and opened the change room curtain for him. "If you don't mind?"

"Yell if you need me," he offered, then retreated with a heated look and yanked the curtain shut behind him.

Taking a deep breath, I turned back to the clothes that had been set out for me to try on. If they could really be called that. Clothes. There were so many damn buckles and laces I feared for my own safety just trying them on.

"Here goes nothing," I muttered, stripping down and struggling into the skirt. It took a whole lot of wriggling, and failed lacing but eventually I was in. And kinda liked it. The little scraps of lace and chain made it into a sort of steampunk meets bondage style which was actually really sexy, and it made my ass look spectacular. Different underwear were a must though, as my *I HEART Paxton Blackwell* printed panties were way too obvious in the mirror when I bent to pick up the top that had fallen from its hanger.

The top half was surprisingly easier to get into, thanks to the almost non-existent back of it. All that held the leather contraption together was a tiny clasp at the back of the neck, and a pathetic *why bother* sort of zipper above my lower back. One thing was for sure, my *marks* definitely would not be missed. Neither would my tits because holy fucking cleavage Batman!

The 'top' had them boosted so high I could practically rest my chin on them if I felt so inclined, but *damn* I looked hot.

"How we going in there, Firebug?" Billy called through the curtain, startling me out of my thoughts and making me yelp.

"Um, good?" I replied, not altogether sure of what an appropriate response should be here. God knows I didn't want them to realize I was okay with this outfit. I looked like a whore. And not a figurative one, a literal I-get-paid-for-sex whore. My inner feminist was bashing her head against a wall.

Without further warning, the curtain whipped aside and Billy stepped back into the small cubicle holding a pair of deadly looking stiletto boots.

He took a long moment, running his burning gaze all over me and sending the sparkling runes off in a frenzy before he knelt in front of me.

"To complete the look," he informed me, helping me put one foot into a calf-high black leather boot and lacing it up professionally. Without a word, he did the same for the other foot and I was forced to use his broad shoulder for balance so I wouldn't fall flat on my ass.

Once finished, he sat back on his feet and gave me another shrewd, considering look.

"These won't do at all," he scolded playfully, sliding his hands under my barely-there skirt and gripping the edges of my cotton panties.

"What's wrong with *Beauty in Lies* underwear?" I asked, a little breathlessly but determined to defend my choice of undergarments, even if I did already know they looked silly. They were fan panties, which I had bought at the merchandise store during a concert I'd been to last year, and I kinda fucking loved them—also, they were *signed.*

Billy clicked his tongue, not answering but at the same time dragging the panties in question down my thighs, *slowly*, then moving my boots one at a time until they were completely off and leaving me bare.

"Much better," he murmured, trailing his fingers back up my leg until he reached my already throbbing pussy and slipped inside.

"Billy," I hissed, "someone will catch us. We're in a store for fox sake!"

"Yeah, doll face … a sex store. Now shut up for a sec …" He spoke quietly but with an edge of authority in his voice that told me he demanded obedience. Every part of me wanted to slap him and tell him where to shove his domineering attitude, but instead all that came out was a girly moan when he sat forward on his knees and pressed his lips to my aching cunt.

"Shit, Billy …" I don't know what I was about to say, because his tongue had just located my clit piercing and was playing me like a goddamn fucking violin. One hand gripped my ass, underneath the pathetic excuse for a skirt, while the other pumped two fingers inside of me, perfectly in sync with the motions of his lips. My orgasm was building fast and the runes on my skin were glowing to an intensity that could light up a dark room.

ELEMENTS OF MISCHIEF

I leaned my back up against the mirrored wall behind me and hooked a leg over one of Billy's thick, muscular shoulders. Briefly, I wondered if all that muscle was from plumbing jobs or if he just spent, like, six days a week working out.

Somehow though, that question didn't seem all that important with his hand shoved up under my skirt, his teeth tugging my clit piercing in a way that was criminal.

"Excuse me," the bitchy saleslady said from outside the curtain. "But we have a very strict rule—one person per dressing room. I'm going to have to ask one of you to come out of there."

"Billy," I tried to say, but he ignored me, lifting up his one free hand and cupping my ass in an iron grip, locking me in place as he teased an orgasm loose, pulling all of that coiled energy from the base of my spine, unleashing it in hot waves across my skin.

"Excuse me," the woman repeated. Clearly she needed to get a life; she took her job way too damn seriously. I mean, she worked in a sex shop for fuck's sake. "If one of you doesn't come out of there right now, I'm coming in."

My fingers dug into Billy's charcoal colored hair, nails scraping his scalp. I *should've* been using my hands to punch him straight in the face, but damn I was going to wait for this orgasm first. If he tried to screw me over like Reg though …

"That's it," the woman said, jerking the curtain back at the same moment I felt all of that pleasure and feeling inside of me break to pieces, my climax coming over me like a roar. Tears prickled at the edges of my eyes as I sagged against the wall and Billy caught me around the waist, lowering me to the floor.

Unfortunately, there was no one to lower the saleslady slowly down to the black carpet. She just … collapsed right there in the doorway to the dressing room.

"Billy," I breathed at the same moment George appeared in a … a black collar and leather pants.

"William," he snapped, angry for the first time since I'd met him. "What the *hell* are you doing?" He knelt down next to the sex store employee and lifted her into his arms. I tried not be jealous at the way her head lolled onto his shoulder. She did look a little pale though. *My orgasm face isn't* that *scary is it?* I wondered as I pushed the asshole fire elemental aside and put my granny panties back on.

"Sorry if I'm excited about actually finding our fucking wife," Billy said defensively, getting out a cigarette and lighting up. I was pretty sure he wasn't allowed to smoke in here, but what the hell? As long as he put it out before this bitch woke up… "You know how many quads *ever* get that sort of privilege?"

"Ari," George said, the alarm in his voice making *my* alarm bells go nuts. "You need to give her spirit back," he said carefully, lifting up his face and locking those earth brown eyes of his on mine.

"Her spirit?" I asked, feeling the color drain from my own face. I crawled over next to the woman and realized that not only was her skin sallow and ashen, but her eyes were open and blank, empty. Like she was … "Is she fucking dead?" I asked, feeling my heart thunder away inside my chest. "Please tell me she's not dead, George."

"She's not dead," Billy said, frowning, his cigarette hanging limply from his lips as he talked around it. "You must've accidentally used your magic when you came …" His mouth twitched a little. "Musta been a good one."

"Eat shit," I said as I smoothed the girl's hair back from her face.

"What's going on back here?" the other employee asked, the one from the front of the store. As soon as she saw us kneeling on the ground around her coworker, her face blanched.

"Okay, sweet cheeks," Britt said, stepping out of a different dressing room. As promised, she looked *really* good in pink vinyl. "Back your troll ass up and forget what you've seen here."

"Like I'm going to listen to some rogue ass werewolf," the woman said, going into full-on bitch mode. "I'm calling Charlie."

"Like hell you are," Britt said, storming across the room in four inch heels. She snatched the troll chick by the arm and dragged her back through the curtain and into the front of the store. I didn't pay them a whole lot of attention—I was far too concerned with the fact that a woman was literally laying here dying in front of me.

"What do I?!" I asked, looking imploringly at George. "How the fuck did I take her spirit in the first place? Oh God, is her soul trapped somewhere?"

"Not her spirit, like her incorporeal self, Blossom, but her spirit energy."

"Her magic, basically," Billy said, waving a hand at the woman's comatose form. "And since this chick is a human, she doesn't have a whole lot of it. Whatever you took, just give it back."

"How am I supposed to give it back when I don't know how I took it in the first place?!" I snarled at him, hating him at the same moment I was lusting after him. Bastard. Wonder how he'd cleaned up his hands? Probably wiped 'em right off on his jeans. Fucking men. So gross. Why couldn't I have been born gay?

"Hey, Blossom!" George snapped his fingers in front of my face. "A little bit of focus here. This chick has maybe a minute left before this becomes a permanent thing."

"Well, okay but fucking *how*?" The guys both gave me blank looks and I had to resist the urge to scream.

"We haven't got a clue, babe," Billy offered up, oh-so-helpfully, "you're the spirit elemental here, in case you forgot? We only know what you've done because we've heard about it from Reg's mom. But just hearing stories doesn't exactly give a play-by-play of how your powers work, you know?" He paused and glanced at George. "Should I try to call Joan?"

"No time. Arizona, just … take a deep breath and try to let your instincts take over," George urged, his fingers pressed to the lifeless girl's throat. "She's almost gone."

Clenching my teeth against a smart-ass retort, because time really didn't allow for it, I screwed my eyes shut, clenched my teeth, and … tried.

"What are you doing?" Billy asked impatiently, breaking my … er … concentration.

"I'm trying," I muttered back, not opening my eyes.

"Looks like you're trying to take a really hard shit," he muttered and I cracked my eyes to glare his way.

"Quit it, you two," George snapped. "Now or never, Blossom. Maybe try and look inside yourself? When I'm doing earth magic I find like a metaphorical seed, then coax it forth. Try that."

It sounded like a crock of hippy shit, but I had no better ideas so I shut my eyes again and tried to 'look inside'. However the fuck one did that. What I found wasn't a little seed waiting to be *coaxed forth*, but instead a blinding ball of light just bobbling around inside my consciousness.

Almost as soon as I acknowledged it, the ball started bouncing around like a happy fucking puppy so for lack of anymore *spiritual* ideas, I just sort of mentally pointed at the shop assistant's body. Thankfully, that seemed to be all the encouragement the glowing ball needed and it happily *whooshed* back into the girl, leaving me with the overwhelming feeling someone had just ripped a giant Band-Aid off my soul.

"Did it work?" I asked, cracking one eye open cautiously.

"I think so …" George still had his fingers pressed to the girl's throat, so when she sat up abruptly with a dramatic gasp, she nailed him right in the nose with her forehead.

"Take that as a yes," I muttered. "That was surprisingly easy, too."

"Good. Now you'll know what to do next time you steal someone's spirit when you come," Billy snickered, helping the shop assistant back to her feet while George clutched at his bleeding nose in pain.

"You okay?" I asked tentatively, trying not to laugh as he pinched the bridge of his nose to try and stem the bleeding. It *had* been pretty funny, seeing a girl come back from almost dead only to deliver a Glasgow Kiss to George's face when all he'd been doing was trying to help.

"Fine," he grumbled, looking anything but. "Let's just get these clothes and get the hell out of here before Billy tries to suggest a three-way at the coffee shop down the road."

Ugh, I couldn't believe my tap actually turned on a little at that suggestion. Swear to fuck, my lady bits had developed a mind of their own since meeting these godforsaken dragons. Sorry, sorry, *not* dragons. *Elementals*.

"Sure thing," I agreed, struggling to my feet and giving George a solid eyeful of my swollen lips—not the ones on my face either. "You look seriously sexy in bondage wear, by the way."

"I might say the same to you, Blossom," he said, wiping his nose on a piece of fabric that was on the floor. The bleeding seemed to have stopped now, but his nose was purple and swollen, so probably hurt like a motherfucker.

Billy, meanwhile, had sat the confused salesgirl down on what looked like some sort of saddle and was speaking to her in a low voice, too quiet for me to hear. Whatever he was saying, she seemed to be okay with, because she was nodding up at him with a dazed look on her face.

"Alright, get changed and I'll pay for these. You don't need to try on the other outfits, Firebug. That one is perfect." Billy's eyes smoldered into me as he returned from the spaced-out sales chick.

"Just maybe with different panties?" I joked, but neither Billy nor George were laughing.

"As much as I'd love to say wear none at all, I don't really want Charlie and the rest of COCS catching a glimpse of what's *ours*." *Yep, there he is.* Billy the domineering asshole was back. I wanted to say it wasn't sexy in the least but once again, I'd be a big fat liar.

Rolling my eyes, I decided against taking the bait this time, because I was suddenly overwhelmingly exhausted. Yawning heavily, I retreated to the changing room and looked around for my clothes.

"Hey, have you guys seen my shirt?" I asked, popping my head back out of the curtain, "the one with um … with the fox on it?" *Fuck that was really embarrassing to say out loud. Maybe I really did need a new wardrobe?*

"Oh …" George looked awkward, holding up the fabric he'd just cleaned up his bloody nose with. "It wasn't this was it?"

The wad of fabric he held was covered in splotches of blood and yup, definitely had a cartoon fox on it, too. Great.

"Here, take mine," he offered, holding out his own shirt for me. "I hardly ever wear one anyway."

Huh, he had a point. I accepted it gratefully and struggled my way out of the ridiculously whorish outfit.

Back out in the less *adult* section of the shop, Britt had somehow found the time to change and now had the troll bitch giggling and flirting way harder than she had been with Billy; when she rejoined us my bestie had a *very* smug look on her face.

"Why the grin, Fluffy?" Billy asked as we all climbed back into my hearse.

"Well, *William*," she teased, "I am *so* glad you asked, seeing as I know you came up empty-handed from the troll gossip channel ..." Clearly she'd won the troll over far more than Billy had, because his eyes narrowed at her.

"If you're such a fucking lady-killer, then tell me, what the hell was she so freaked out over?" Billy lit a cigarette, and I promptly rolled down the window, stole it from his fingers, and chucked it outside. He glared daggers at me.

"My car, my rules, you useless bum," I told him, realizing that the boys had rolled into my life with a fucking van with toilets emblazoned on the sides and nothing else. Okay, well, there were a few other things the guys were packing that were worth something, but that was another subject altogether.

I still planned on leaving them. Er, if it was even possible to leave someone that you weren't really with in the first place.

"There's something happening in the underground," Britt said, digging through the large shopping bag she'd carried out of the store. I had literally no desire to know what was in it ... and every confidence that I'd find out anyway. "Like, literally as well as figuratively." Britt paused and leaned up between the front seats. "Hey, can we stop at a Starbucks or something? I'm jonesing for a chai tea latte."

"Britt, focus, please," I said, driving back towards Gram's place and wondering when she was planning on making her next appearance. Why not when I was on the toilet? That would be just my luck. Or rubbing one out in my ... er, her old bedroom.

Eww.

Okay, I was so changing rooms.

"Mmm, sorry, right," she said, flopping back into her seat. I still had yet to hear what'd happened with Britt and the local ... alpha, was it? How medieval ... Anyway, it wasn't like her to withhold information from me. Usually it was the other way around—me, trying to escape while she laid it all out, completely unrestrained. "The Hudson Valley pack mentioned something similar ..."

"Mentioned *what*?" Billy asked, lighting up another cigarette. When I reached out to take that one next, he stuck his hand out the window to keep it from me.

"Relax, William," George said from the backseat. "I'm sure Brittany's working her way up to it."

"Jesus Christ," Billy growled, leaning against the door so he could smoke his cigarette in peace.

"There's been some weird shit happening in the supernatural community." Britt paused, reconsidered her words, grinned big at me in the rearview mirror. "Supernatural—your people's word for non-humans, not ours."

"Not her people," Billy said, flicking his cigarette out the window. I cringed. God, he might be calling me *Firebug,* but I was going to start calling *him* litterbug. "She's one of us, remember? According to dear old Gram ..."

"Does anyone else feel like we're in an episode of *Charmed*?" I asked and Billy snorted.

"What do you mean by 'weird shit'?" he asked as we pulled into the line for Starbucks. Somehow, even at three in the afternoon, the fucking place was packed.

"Disappearances, fluctuations on the power grid, unexplained *deaths.*" Since the windows in the backseat didn't roll down (the hearse was made for dead people, remember?), Britt leaned back into the front and practically fell into my lap trying to check out the specials. "Is it pumpkin spice latte time?"

"Wow, you really are a walking cliché, aren't you?" Billy asked with a smirk. "A promiscuous pink vinyl wearing gossip with a penchant for oversharing and coffee drinks with more water and sugar than actual caffeine."

"And you," Britt said, putting on her best California girl bitch accent, "are the typical bad boy—angry, brooding, tattooed, and so insecure with himself that he insults others to bolster confidence in his four inch dick."

"Hey, Ari," Billy said conversationally, "you tell me—is four inches an accurate estimate?"

I rolled my eyes to the car's gray felt ceiling and tried not to make a plumbing joke, something like *four inches? sorry, but Billy was packing one hell of a pipe.*

I swatted Britt in the backseat again and eased up on the brake as the cars in front of me scooted forward.

"What's a power grid?" I asked, praying that it was George who answered this time. He seemed like the only adult human in the entire group, someone capable of answering questions with more than sarcasm, snark, or inappropriate wordplay.

"That's not an official term," he said, and I had to wonder if maybe some god—gods?—were listening in and decided to answer my prayers. "Not all non-human species get along; we all have our own culture, rules, ways of explaining things …"

I pulled up to the window.

"Pumpkin spice," Britt repeated.

"Coffee, black," from Billy.

"Can I get an unsweetened iced tea?" And George.

"You don't happen to have some whiskey to spike the coffee with?" I asked into the speaker, and there was a long, strange pause with some unintelligible mumbling from the barista. "Just me give me an iced mocha," I said with a tired sigh, and then repeated the orders for the others.

The total was … fucking expensive. Screw you, Starbucks.

We pulled forward again.

"So power grid …" I started and George continued his explanation.

"Generally, there's a certain amount of power, raw energy, *magic* in an area. Any major addition or subtraction to that is going to draw attention."

"What would that mean anyway?" I asked as we *finally* hit the fucking window and got our drinks. I passed them around and then pulled back onto the street, sipping my mocha and wondering if this is what heaven tasted like.

No, heaven probably tastes more like elemental c—

I stopped that thought in its tracks. Fill that word in however you choose.

Home, packing, driving to city to see Siobhan.

Those were my orders.

As soon as I saw the COCS head, that is.

"I don't know," George said, and there was a weird tone in his voice, "but bringing out your powers, that's a fluctuation that a *lot* of people are going to take notice of."

We drove the rest of the way back to the house in silence.

10

CHAPTER TEN

"Should I be scared of COCS?" I asked as Britt attacked my face with gobs of makeup, doing her best to cover up the black eye I'd gotten from the incubus. She was obsessed with those makeup subscription boxes, the ones that send surprise cosmetics in the mail every month. She was a member of like four different clubs and had brought a literal duffel bag to my house filled with makeup.

"I don't know? Think you're maybe a little closer to gay on the Kinsey scale than you first thought?"

"COCS, Britt. C.O.C.S.," I said, knowing she was just being a cheeky bitch. I adjusted myself on the chair and heard my outfit *squeak*. Outfits should not squeak. I wanted my cotton pj pants back.

"Right," she said with a stupid grin, "you're *clearly* not afraid of cocks, considering you had four of them in your—"

"Finish that sentence and I will punch you right in the tit," I growled out, slapping her hands away. I was having a hard enough time being in this house with all the guys, my body covered in runes, and constantly fucking *aching* for them. One afternoon. One. That's how long I'd been stuck in a house with them after the marking and it was *torturous.*

Alright, Ari girl. One step at a time. Get through this meeting with COCS, then get changed and drive to the city to stay with Siobhan. Surely a bit of distance would help ease the addictive pull of these otherworldly handymen?

"Girl, I gotta tell you," Britt said, stepping back and narrowing her eyes at my face, "you look ridiculously bangin' right now. Like, you've always been a pretty hot piece of ass, but since your screaming orgy last night your shit is just seriously on point."

"Uh thanks," I muttered, "but can we not call it a *screaming orgy* please? It was a sacred ritual to complete our magical bonding." Jesus I sounded like I'd been drinking the magical Kool-Aid.

"Pah!" Britt coughed. "If that's the case, then I must have participated in a *sacred ritual* or two myself!"

Um, pretty sure that was the line I used last night. Had she actually heard us that well? Ewww ... she'd heard my sex noises?

"Anyway," I hedged, frantically changing the subject, "are we done? I want to get this meeting with the cock head over with so I can get the hell outta dodge."

"They're called COCS, Ari," Britt said, correcting *me* this time. I just shrugged; I meant what I said. "Sure, whatever. You're done, you beautiful bitch." She gave me another considering look, her lips pursed. "You sure there's no room in your little reverse harem for another girl? The rumors about dogs and cats not getting along are all false, you know. I lick pussy like a champ."

Fuck me, I'm too sober for this shit already, although that was kinda funny.

"No, Britt. I like my drains pounded by real plungers thank you." I rolled my eyes at my own plumbing joke. It was like I couldn't help myself anymore!

"Suit yourself, girl." Britt tossed her long dark hair over her shoulder and led the way downstairs with a sexy sway to her walk. She had decided to tag along on our introduction to the COCS Head, and seeing as she was already a card-carrying member of the supernatural community, no one could stop her.

She'd bought her outfit from the sex shop earlier and was now decked out in neck to ankle hot pink PVC.

"Hooooooooly shit," Britt exclaimed as she entered my living room where, presumably, the guys were waiting. "Damn, someone better call a plumber because I think I just sprang a leak!"

My eye twitched a little with that possessive jealousy and I pushed past her into the room myself.

The guys were all decked out in their own versions of my slutty bondage wear and looked like a smorgasbord of pure sex just draped all over my living room.

Must. Not. Maim. Best friend.

She better stop looking soon though, or shit was going down.

"Brittany, maybe you want to wait for us in the car? We just need a moment with Arizona." Shane phrased it as a question but it was clearly an order. "Alone."

My bestie gave me a knowing look and a wolfish grin before flouncing out of the door. She clearly thought I was in for some sort of group quickie before we headed out, which was *so* not happening. I meant what I said. It was a one time thing. Absolutely never again. Not even if the fate of the world depended on it.

The little changing room incident didn't count, obviously. That was just lingering madness from all the um ... all the drain snaking ... but I was better now. All out of my system. Nope, no lingering horniness here. I was done. D.O.N.E. Done.

Dear lord, is Reg in hot pants right now?

Moisture flooded my new panties and made a big fat stinking liar out of my own brain.

Fuck. I truly was screwed, blued, and tattooed.

"So ah, what did you want to tell me?" I found a particularly interesting pattern on the rug and inspected it thoroughly in an attempt to avoid looking at any of my new husbands in their fetish wear. Oh geez. I just called them my *new husbands* in my own inner monologue. This was bad. Bad, bad, bad. The sooner I got some distance from them, the better.

"George and Billy passed on the information that Britt gathered," Shane started, moving to stand closer to me. There was something odd about his pants, but I stubbornly refused to take a better look, for fear of trying to rip them off him with my teeth.

"Uh-huh." I nodded. "And?"

"And we made some calls. It seems similar disturbances— disappearances and unexplained deaths in the supernatural community—have centered around other quints completing their groups in the past." He paused and my gaze swung back to him involuntarily. He looked worried; Shane *never* looked worried.

"Okay, that's good in a way, isn't it?" I frowned. "Then someone knows what's causing it?"

"Not ... exactly. It appears that in several quints, sexts, or septs"—the hell if I knew what he meant by all that (we were considered a quint, right, because there were five of us?)—"the disturbances start slightly before and continue long after the spirit elemental comes into her powers ..." Shane paused, his deep blue eyes locked on my face.

"... and stop right after the same spirit elemental turns up brutally murdered and drained of her magic," Reg finished for him, a bitter twist to his words.

"Ahhhhh ..." What the actual dingo-loving fuck did one say to that?

"We wanted to tell you now, because we aren't sure the COCS Head will be honest with you, and we need you to be alert." Shane's mouth tightened and his jaw clenched. "We just found you, sugar plum, we can't lose you now."

"Can you elaborate please?" My tongue darted out to lick my suddenly paper dry lips. "When you say 'brutally murdered' ..."

"We mean, torn to tiny pieces and stuffed down a storm drain," Reg replied, his face dead serious.

A sharp spike of panic rippled through me and my runes sparkled. Outside the living room, a single lightning bolt slammed into the grass.

"That's ... odd," George murmured, frowning at the spot through the window where my bolt had left a sizzling scorch mark. I noticed that he, too, had covered up his facial injury with a bit of makeup—I could hardly tell he'd been head butted by a sex shop employee. "Did you mean to do that, Blossom?"

I had no words; they just told me I might be ripped into little pieces and stuffed down a storm drain. Were they fucking serious?

My head shook frantically. No, fuck no, I hadn't *intended* to let my lightning loose. What if it had hit Britt?

"You shouldn't be having any power spikes like that now that the *marking* has been completed ..." George mumbled to himself, frowning thoughtfully. "I need to look into this more."

Shane turned toward the window, to get a better look and I almost choked on my own tongue. He wasn't wearing *pants* at all. He was in ass-less chaps with a matching man-thong. He looked a little like he was about to attend a gay pride parade in San Francisco, but like, in a good way.

"Lightning's pretty standard for a spirit elemental, right?" I asked, but nobody looked convinced and I was already flummoxed enough as it was. Best to just let sleeping dogs lie ... "Can we go now?" I asked, glancing over at George in his leather pants and collar. Now if there was only ... oh my god, there was! There was a *leash.*

I wondered if I got to hold it ...

My eyes wandered over and found Reg in an unzipped leather jacket, a set of black straps in an X over his muscular chest and some ... like, leather dude panty *things.* Sorry, but I was a barista, not Anastasia Steele. I didn't know what all this shit was called.

"We better get out of here," I said, swallowing back my hormones and sneaking out the front door. Of course, I *thought* the cool crisp air outside would calm the aching heat I felt creeping over my skin. But then I saw Alberta O'Sullivan, my bitchy Irish neighbor, and the heat in my skin just turned to anger instead.

"I dinna think I would ever say this to a complete stranger," she began, but I was already about two hundred percent sure that however she was about to insult me, she'd said it many, many times in her long, long, long, long, *long* life. Bitch was ancient. "But you look like a common floozy."

I paused there on the steps in a miniskirt and vinyl top, my skin painted in runes, and thought up some quick lie about body paint or …

"Elemental slut," she continued, digging through my garbage.

Wait. What?

"Brownie," Reg whispered, licking the curve of my ear as he passed by.

"Brownie?" I asked stupidly, still staring down at Mrs. O'Sullivan in surprise. "You just ate."

"Brownies are a type of fae, sug," Shane said, pausing next to me in all his ass-less glory. I was just glad Mrs. O'Sullivan was the only neighbor on the block. We were at the end of a cul-de-sac in an underdeveloped area, the old houses still clinging to part of the vast estates that had once been theirs.

"You better not be thinking of selling this house," Grams whispered from behind me, sending a bright shiver of ice down my spine. I glanced over my shoulder and found her standing there with a cup of tea in one hand. I'd almost forgotten about her in all the, uh, excitement. George and Billy waltzed right through her, making Gram frown. "Arizona Smoke," she started, but I just reached out and pulled the door shut behind me.

One thing at a time.

One bloody cocksucking thing.

"Mrs. O'Sullivan … is a faerie?" I asked, heading down the steps with George and wondering if Grams was going to make me pay for my rudeness later. "Why is everyone in my life suddenly an obscure supernatural being I've never heard of before? I thought you said you people were rare—where are all the humans?"

"Like to like," Shane said, opening the sliding door of his plumbing van for me. It would've been, like, chivalrous or something if it didn't have a toilet emblazoned on the side. "Those of us in the know tend to stick together. Now hop in."

"I canna even imagine what yer poor dead grandmother would say if she saw ya now," Alberta continued, clucking her tongue at me. *I can,* I thought, glancing over my shoulder and watching as the woman, er, *brownie,* extracted several pieces of broken pipe from the trash can.

"You're judging me?" I asked, crooking a brow. "While you dig through the rubbish bin?"

"Rubbish bin," Britt giggled as she leaned against the side of the van and fucked around with her phone. "You're so cute and British."

I gritted my teeth and climbed inside the car, noticing as I did that there was absolutely zero equipment in here, just a bunch of seats. Actually, it was a lot nicer than I'd expected.

"You guys don't have any equipment?" I asked as Reg climbed in the front seat and flashed a grin over his shoulder.

"Oh, I wouldn't say *that,*" he purred, cupping his junk and winking at me.

I frowned and then did a double take as I looked and saw *wings* protruding from the back of Mrs. O'Sullivan's baggy shawl. They looked like they were made of bark.

"What ... the ... are you taking the piss with me?!"

"British," Britt chuckled again as she climbed in next to me and took a glance out the window. "Oh, that? Those have always been there. She's just glamoured against humans. Now that you're an English elemental instead of a human—"

"I'm still human," I inserted, but it sounded like a feeble attempt at self-denial, even to me.

"Now that you're an English elemental," Britt repeated, just to piss me off, "you can see what's really there. Brownies are house spirits."

"That's ... nice," I said as I put two fingers up to my temple and rubbed therapeutically. "No, really. More supernatural stuff. I love it. Keep it comin'."

"Mmm," Britt murmured as she reapplied her glossy pink lipstick. "Did I mention I have a date with the local alpha male?"

"You ... what?!" I asked, giving her a look. "Can't you read sarcasm? I was being *sarcastic*. Don't tell me anything else. I feel like my head's about to explode."

"I'd sure like *my* head to explode," Reg murmured from up front as Shane took the driver's seat. Behind me, Billy lounged like he was on his way to the club, and George studied Alberta with a curious expression.

"Come on, girl. You're all worldly and shit, right? You've seen exotic places I've never even dreamed of visiting," Britt continued, doing nothing to ease the headache building between my eyes.

"We've been over this before—Sydney does not count as an exotic locale."

"No, but Cleveland does," Britt said, flashing me a grin and then laughing when I raised a skeptical brow. "Come on, cheer up! Your world's just tripled in size, sweetie."

"Quadrupled, actually," Billy corrected from behind me.

I ignored him.

"Right," I said, leaning back in my seat and trying not to notice the smells in the van. Like, I was seriously in heat or something because I swear, I could taste each one of the guys' scents on the back of my tongue, this heady, masculine display that had me dripping ... sweat. Okay, and other things. "First, I fucked you guys because you said I'd die. And now that I've fucked you guys, you think I might die. Do you see where maybe I'm having just the teensiest little issue here?"

"Maybe you should fuck us again and see if things balance out?" Billy suggested, dragging his tongue across his lower lip suggestively.

Fuck. Me.

I wanted so badly to be furious, but my thighs were clenching with a life of their own and my nipples were so hard they actually hurt in this death trap of a 'top'.

"What Billy means, honey doll, is that we'll get some answers from the COCS Head when we get there. Until then, you have the four of us"—Britt's fake cough interrupted Shane —"*five* of us, to keep you safe."

"You're in good hands, Blossom," George assured me with a gentle smile.

"And if you really need reassurance, I am more than happy to show you just how *good* these hands can be," Reg suggested and I rolled my eyes. How the hell did I get into this mess? Oh yeah, that's right. Fucking dragons in my drains.

"Hey, you guys don't think that there was a *supernatural* influence over those tree roots that ruined my plumbing, do you? It kind of seems coincidental …" It was another idea that had been gnawing at me since discovering their exposure was less accidental than they made it out to be. The awkward silence in the car told me everything I needed to know.

Mother. Fuckers.

"Seriously?" I hissed, anger flaring hot once more, "You fucked up my pipes, causing *thousands* of dollars of damage, for *what*?! A supernatural fuck-fest?"

"It wasn't us, sug," Shane drawled, sighing heavily, "but we suspect Charlie's sext had a hand in it."

"That particular species of tree doesn't have mischievous roots like that," George explained. "I knew there had to have been elemental involvement the second we saw them."

"Well then Charlie can fucking well reimburse me the seventeen thousand he quoted me to fix them!" I was a raging inferno of anger now, which was thankfully putting my lust on hold for a few seconds. Probably a good thing—I was halfway ready to rip off my panties and let Billy and Reg fuck me fast and dirty right there in the van while we drove.

"Uh, I don't think that's quite how it works, Sugar Tits," Reg told me with a small, amused smile. "But I would fucking love to see you tell him that."

"Good," I muttered, "I fucking will."

"And make him pay you in *Australian pounds*," Britt piped up from beside me, "'cause, ya know, the exchange rate means you get more money that way."

"Jesus, wolf-girl. Other way around," Billy snickered from behind us, reaching out and tugging on Britt's hair playfully, "she'd get *less* money if he paid in Australian *dollars*."

"Is that right, babe?" she asked me, blinking her big doe eyes at me and cocking her head like a confused puppy.

"I don't know," I said tiredly back, "I'm a barista, not a fucking accountant."

"Not anymore, you're not," Shane said firmly, his eyes on the road as he drove, but his knuckles white on the steering wheel.

"Oh, yeah I know right?" Britt agreed. "Sucks about you getting the sack. People are fucking assholes. That's why I prefer animals."

Shane's knuckles eased up in his death grip and I knew he thought he'd won this round.

Asshole.

"Let's just get to COCS without anymore arguments, okay?" George suggested, running a finger underneath his collar uncomfortably. "The sooner we can get changed, the better. I still don't understand why I always have to wear the collar and leash."

"Because you also don't mind sucking a bit of dick, hon," Shane drawled and met my eyes in the rearview mirror. Damn if I wasn't suddenly turned on again. How did they fucking *do* that?

Britt made an over-sexualized groan from beside me, so she clearly seconded that opinion. Apparently the idea of my husband sucking my other husband's dick really did it for her. I gave her a look and she shrugged innocently back at me.

"Yours are so hot, I might have to get four of my own," she whispered as I rolled my eyes and crossed my arms underneath my breasts.

"Hey, Firebug," Billy's smoky voice whispered in my ear as his hand slid over the back of my neck, "no need to feel jealous. Our plumbing tools are reserved for one job only, now."

"Lucky you've got more than one pipe to work on, though," Reg added, turning in his seat to wink at me.

"Alright. No one speak for the rest of the drive." It was the only way we were all going to make it there in one piece.

No one spoke again until we pulled up at the literal sprawling mansion that must be Charlie's house, but Billy kept his hand on my throat, gently stroking the skin every now and then.

166

One thing was for fucking sure—plumbing must pay *well*. An actual, honest to god butler answered the door. A butler. Silly penguin suit, British accent, and all.

"Seriously?" I muttered under my breath to Reg as I sashayed into the marble floored foyer of his father's house. In six inch stiletto lace-up boots, there was only one way to walk —*sashay*.

"The master is waiting for you in the great room," the butler told us with his nose upturned, "can I take your coats?"

Sort of a stupid question, given we were barely in clothing, let alone coats. Reg just flipped a hand at the elderly man dismissively and led us deeper into the house.

"There was really no need to be rude," I whispered, scolding the water elemental's appalling manners, but he just gave me a crooked grin and a quick ass grab.

"He's not a person, Sugar Tits, he's a golem." He managed to retract his hand just before I smacked it. Bad enough knowing Grams witnessed my group, ah, plunging, without Reg's parents catching us playing grab ass in the hallway.

"Sorry," I told him, giving Reg a lippy little smile, "but I'm not taking the bait. I don't know what a golem is and I don't care."

"Sure you don't," Reg said, folding his hands together behind his head, "and *I'm* not interested in fucking you in my childhood bedroom. We all tell lies every now and again."

I bumped him with my shoulder, knocking him off course a little. It was a familiar sort of move, like we'd known each other forever. I didn't like that; it scared the shit out of me. I mean, I was all for insta-lust, but insta-love or even insta-friendship? Gross.

"So, do you like, have a mom or something?" I asked, and Reg laughed. "Billy already tried to explain your totally fucked-up birds and the bees …" I paused, reconsidered. "And the bees and the bees and the *bees* situation, so … do you really have four dads and a mom?"

"No," Reg said, and I felt a slight rush of relief. Maybe Reg'd been dicking around with me … "I have five dads and a mom."

"You have *five* fucking dads?" I asked as he flashed me a sharp grin and pushed open a pair of doors into a room that looked like it was sucked right out of the he-man lodge on *The Stepford Wives.* Yep. Yep. Looking at all this, uh, masculine décor (and I say that ironically since, you know, gender is a social construct and all that), it was pretty obvious there was only one woman in this house. "Where did the fifth come from?"

"This is my mom's hunting lodge," Reg said, ignoring my question with a loose shrug of his left shoulder. "She programmed the butler to call it the 'great room'," he made little quotes with his fingers, "because she thinks it sounds all formal and shit."

Well.

His mom's hunting lodge.

That would teach me to make gender-based assumptions.

I only had a few seconds to think on that because as soon as I stepped over the threshold and into the room proper, I felt it. Power. Magic.

My lips went dry and my throat constricted with nerves.

As *soon* as I saw her, I knew that this mother-in-law would be a real *son of a bitch.*

"Oh god." I almost turned around and started running. Would have, too, if I hadn't taken a few steps backward and slammed into Shane's sweet, soapy smelling man chest. Grr. "Please tell me I don't have to meet three more women like this," I whispered as Shane put his big hands on my shoulders and kept me facing forward.

"No, sweet pea. Reg's family raised us all; remember?"

That was comforting…ish. But then, the fact that my very first time seeing Reg's mom's face was when she turned around and cocked a shotgun in my direction did not bode well for future engagements.

"Reginald," she said with a tight smile, her face as youthful as, well, mine.

Like, basically we looked like we were exactly the same age.

"Do elementals not … get old and kick the bucket?" I whispered to Shane.

"Later, baby cakes," he drawled in my ear, making me nice and hot and bothered … in front of a woman who looked like she wanted to blow my head off.

"Mom," he said and then hooked an evil sideways grin, "or *Mum* as the new Mrs. Copthorne might say."

I whipped my head over to gape at Reg, unsure as to whether I was more concerned by the fact that I'd *just* now learned his last name—or because he called me Mrs.

Gross.

"This is her then," Reg's mom said, and I noticed that *she* was wearing khaki pants and a white button-up. Here I was, basically naked in bondage wear and wet panties. Fan-frigging-tastic.

The woman—Mother Reginald let's call her—flipped some long blonde hair over one shoulder and moved across the massive room toward me, her brown leather boots slapping a stern rhythm across the marble floors. She was smiling, but I noticed she didn't put the shotgun down.

"You are so fucked," Britt said from behind me, doing little to boost my confidence.

"She's so …" Reg's mom looked up and down and gestured randomly. "She's a spirit elemental, that's for sure."

Hmm. That didn't exactly sound like a compliment, now did it?

"Boys." Mother Reginald kissed Reg on the cheek, then Billy, George, carefully craned around me for Shane. "I'm so proud of you."

My new mother-in-law beamed at the guys … and then just sort of dropped a soggy gaze onto my face.

I guess you'll have to do, that's what that face said.

"You really are … one in a million," she told me, looking me up and down again. Her blue gaze traced the runes on my skin carefully. "I'm Joan, by the way," she continued, holding out a hand for me to shake. "I wish we were meeting on better terms, but honestly, this issue with C.O.C.S.," she said, saying each letter in the acronym individually. Hmm. Yet another issue where I had to wonder if I were being duped … "Is something we need to take seriously."

Joan stepped back, still resting the barrel of the shotgun on her shoulder.

"Really, though, waiting so long to mark a shimmer? That was asking for trouble." Joan turned around and moved over to a rack on the wall, resting the shotgun against the green velvet backdrop. There was nothing unusual about displaying guns, but fully loaded ones? Hmm. This was a woman I was going to have to watch out for. "Now get upstairs and make nice. We have more important things to worry about."

"That's it?" Reg asked, stepping into the room in his … leather banana hammock, boots, and jacket. "That's all you have to say? We found our soul mate, Mom, for fuck's sake. Show a little good cheer."

My cheeks flamed all the way out at the words *soul mate.*

"Wow, you really move fast. One day, they're plumbers. The next, soul mates," Britt whispered in my left ear.

"We are not soul mates," I hissed out, but Joan was already talking again

"Soul mates?" she said, one blonde brow quirked in mock surprise. "Well, I don't know about that."

I gritted my teeth. Hey, it was totally cool for *me* to be doubtful about a bunch of strange plumber dragon weirdos, but for her to question it? Now that just pissed me off.

Lucky for *her,* Reg grabbed me by the hand and stormed out of the intimidating room before I could snap back at my new mum-in-law.

Fuck, I still couldn't believe Reg had just called me his missus. My stomach felt a bit off, like I'd been riding a roller coaster after eating half my bodyweight in cotton candy.

"Reg, I think I just ..." Tugging my hand out of his, I backed away from him a couple of steps. "I think I just ... um ..."

"What's wrong, ST? Was it my Mom? You can't take that shit personally. She's a raging bitch to everyone except us boys." He reached out to take my hand again, but I pulled it out of reach.

"No, no I just need a minute. I think. To get ... um ... fresh air ..." I was backing away from him again and had almost made it past the other three confused as fuck looking elementals before Britt grabbed a handful of my messy blonde hair and yanked me face to face with her.

"Don't even think about it, *chica*," she growled. Like … literally growled it like some sort of talking dog. Which, I suppose she was.

"What's going on, honey doll?" Shane asked suspiciously. "What does Britt think you're about to do?"

Britt glared at me with a *don't fuck with me, girl* look on her face but I stubbornly tightened my lips and glared back at her.

"She's about to run," Britt, the *fucking traitor*, snapped. "I've seen her do this once before, and I guarantee the fact that Reginald over there just called her *Mrs. Copthorne* has her tying her mental jogging shoes as we speak."

The weight of four sets of eyes settled on me, and I could feel the radiating disappointment from all of them. I refused to look at them though. Refused to feel bad for wanting to get the fuck off this crazy train. These plumbers were *hot*, don't get me wrong. They were possibly the hottest things I had ever seen in my life, except maybe that one guy.

"She did this once before. In college. She slept with our best friend and then bolted when he said he loved her." My former best friend was just spilling secrets all over the place tonight, and I was fucking livid.

"Do. Not. Speak. Of. Him." I snarled back at her and she at least had the grace to look a little apologetic. Not nearly enough though.

"Are you going to quit trying to run?" she challenged back, and the pressure of the guys stares held me glued to the spot. Not that I could have moved anyway, with Britt's death grip on my hair.

"Yes …" I ground out from behind tightly clenched teeth.

"And are you going to stop freaking the fuck out over Reg calling you their soul mate?" she continued, clearly not drunk enough yet or she'd have let this go already. "Because news flash, Arizona, you *are* their soul mate. Just like they're yours. Fuck, even a blind ass human could see the five of you are made for each other."

Our gazes remained locked for a long, tense moment where no one uttered a sound. We were all just ... frozen in the middle of this crazy expensive looking hallway with an honest to god suit of armor standing behind Billy.

"Fine ..." I finally muttered and Britt released my hair.

"Excellent! Now lets get this party started! Mama needs to get some dick in her tonight or she's going to lose her howling mind." Britt flicked her hair over her shoulder and proceeded down the long hallway without checking that anyone was following her. The exaggerated sway to her hips said she expected we were though.

Shane clamped a huge hand over my wrist, like a socket wrench over a bolt.

"Just in case," he told me, giving me a look that I couldn't quite decipher. It was pointless arguing now though. The second his skin touched mine, I could barely remember why I was so freaked out to begin with.

11

CHAPTER ELEVEN

Upstairs was actually the roof. Reg led us up there and we found Charlie, along with four others, waiting on a wide platform framed with a low wrought iron fence which wouldn't save a chihuahua from falling, let alone a person.

"Well isn't this dramatic," I groused, still feeling furious at Britt, despite no longer wanting to flee.

"Supernaturals tend to be a bit … eccentric," Shane explained, still maintaining his tight hold on my wrist as we approached the waiting group.

"No shit," I replied, eyeing up some of the absurd outfits being worn by the people who comprised the COCS Head. Clearly, everyone was assigned a theme. Ours happened to be bondage, but I didn't envy the waiflike girl on the far left who was dressed as a clown.

Shane just flashed a grin at me and lifted his chin in the direction of a slightly overweight plumber that I recognized right away—you don't forget a man who hands you a quote for seventeen grand that easily, especially not when it pertains to flushing toilets and walking through ice-cold weather to antique stores just to piss.

"That's Charlie, and the other four assholes next to him make up the rest of Joan's sext," he told me, gesturing with a tattooed hand in the direction of Reginald's ... many dads.

"Reg, boys!" Charlie boomed, holding out his arms as if he was air hugging them, seeing as none of the 'boys' moved any closer than we were already standing.

"Charlie." Reg's tone conveyed just how much he thought of his father—or rather, *one* of his fathers? "We're here to formally declare our mate, our spirit, and our wife, Arizona Morgan Smoke."

"Oh, hah, right to the formalities hey, Reginald?" Charlie coughed out a fake sounding laugh and darted his eyes nervously at the people standing with him. "Arizona, nice to see you again." Charlie smiled at me and I bared my teeth in more of a snarl than a smile. "This group here," he gestured at Reg's other dads as well as a small cluster of people standing behind him, "is comprised of the Heads of the Committee of Combined Supernaturals."

"You owe me seventeen thousand dollars you manipulative fuck," I replied, without really stopping to think through what I was saying. Hey, what can I say? I was a barista, not a diplomat, damn it!

"And spousal support," Britt added, and my anger toward her softened just a fraction. The girl did always have my back ... I *guess*.

Charlie spluttered a little, then with a slightly embarrassed flush to his cheeks, regained composure.

"Very well, Arizona," he said, with a shrewd look about him that I just knew wasn't going to be good for me. "You want money; I want something in return."

"Huh?" I asked, completely and utterly unsure as to where this was going.

"A grandchild!" he said, and then he guffawed like that was the funniest damn shit he'd ever heard in his life. I just stared at him. The urge to run was … overwhelming. Charlie came forward and put his arms around me, a totally awkward moment since, you know, I wasn't wearing a whole lot of clothing. "Welcome to the family," he said, patting me on the back with a meaty hand.

It was a little weird, snuggling up to the plumber who'd literally tricked me into marrying his sons. Dickhead.

"Let me introduce you to my sext," he said, and I cocked a brow. Hmm. Okay, unfortunate name … but six elementals a sext makes, I supposed. Frankly, I was glad I only had to deal with a quint. The slightly overweight man (who, now that I looked at him, also appeared way too young to be Reg's dad), turned to the others standing next to him and started to introduce them one by one.

"I feel like there's an extra element here," I whispered, but Shane acted like he didn't hear me. Fucker. I distinctly saw his lips twitch. Yet again, I had the sense that I was being tricked. And I didn't like it. Not one fucking bit. "Skeeter …"

Before he could answer though, a waiter whisked by with a platter of champagne glasses. Hah. You know what happens next, don't you? I snagged three in one go, drained the first in a single drink, and then made Shane hold the empty glass. Why not? He wanted to act like some machismo fuck, then he could hold my used glassware.

"So, Reg is like … part each one of these guys' sperm?" I whispered, and this time, Shane actually grinned at me, running his fingers through the darkness of his hair.

"Yep."

"Huh." I glanced down the row of dudes, all fairly average and—thankfully—not wearing quite as revealing of outfits as we were. Did not want to see my new father-in-laws decked out in leather and collars and ass-less chaps.

"Let me get Adonis and Rachel over here and we can get past this unpleasantness," Charlie continued, waving us forward. Britt had already disappeared into the crowd, but that was to be expected. She was a wolf on the prowl … quite literally, actually.

"Who the fuck is Rachel?" I asked as the five of us trailed along behind Charlie and over to a cluster of—you got it— naked winged people. Okay, so maybe they weren't *naked* per se, but they were wearing less than we were, and that was quite the feat.

"Rachel is the Chaos Queen," George said from behind me, sliding a hand over one of my bare shoulders and making me shiver. It was like these boys couldn't keep their hands off of me. "The queen of the succubi."

"Ah," I said, but I still didn't really get it. So, what? Each supernatural species had its own club with rules and a leader and shit? Like the Boy Scouts or something?

"Excuse me, Rachel?" Charlie said, clearly annoyed at having deal with the issue of my unmarked shimmer ass. Although I suppose I technically *wasn't* a shimmer anymore. Nope. Now the deal was sealed with magical tattooed runes, and I was up shit creek without a fucking paddle.

Sealed to the supernatural.

The thought made me shiver.

At least in that moment, I felt like I was coasting, like this whole thing was just the result of a weekend spent partying too hard, like maybe the boys and the magic, the werewolves and the sewer troll ... like it was all just a bad LSD trip.

I still didn't quite believe it was real.

"Rachel, this is Arizona," Charlie said proudly, putting a hand on my shoulder. He was beaming at me like I was his own daughter. Cute, I guess. But maybe a little soon?

Rachel turned slowly to look at me, her hair as red as rubies, collected on the top of her head in an artful chignon. The once-over she gave me was ... lascivious?

Uh-oh.

I think I'm being checked out.

"*Guten tag?*" I said, but I couldn't exactly remember what that meant; it'd been years since I'd taken German.

"*Guten abend, Arizona Smoke. Ich bin Rachel,*" she said with a shark's grin, her purple painted lips pulling back from white-white teeth. She was pretty. No, no, she was *devastatingly gorgeous.* Even though I was pretty sure I was like a ninety-five percent on the Kinsey scale, Rachel the Chaos Queen was kind of hot.

"I don't actually speak German ..." I said slowly and she threw her head back with peals of laughter. Even that was pretty, her guffawing. When she dropped her chin to look at me, I realized Adonis was staring as well, his gaze sweeping me with appreciation. Either I cut a pretty figure with the stretch marks on my thighs and the birthmark on the back of my right calf, or incubi and succubi were just kind of ... slutty.

I was betting on the latter.

Reaching up to rub at my still slightly sore nose, I glared at Adonis. I had not forgotten about that son of a bitch punching me in the face (I still had the black eye to prove it). And this guy was their king? That did not bode well for my future relationship with his people.

"As you can see," Charlie said, seeming like the derpy but friendly type, "she's finally been marked."

"Of course she has," Rachel said, giving Reg's dad a poisonous look. "Anyone with an ounce of talent could tell the moment that connection was made." The way she was looking at me, with eyes too purple to be human, I knew I needed another drink or ten. I chugged the two glasses of champagne in quick succession and traded them out for fresh ones off the next passing tray.

"I just wanted to see this for myself, another completed ... *sext*." Rachel paused for a moment and then frowned at the same moment I did. Sext? Wait, I thought we were a quint? Fuck my life—I couldn't keep up with all these damn terms.

The exaggerated expression on Rachel's painted lips had bits of glitter sparkling inside the purple like diamonds. Hell, I wouldn't be surprised if they *were* diamonds. The bit of nothingness draped over her curvy form was covered in sparkly bits too fine to be Swarovski. "Where's the other one?" she asked, and I noticed Reg choking on his champagne. He started coughing as Billy pounded his back with what sort of looked like a fairly unsympathetic fist.

"What other one?" I asked, and my skin broke out in goose bumps.

There was another one?!

My heart started to race and sweat dripped down between my breasts.

"What other one?!" I asked again, and Rachel smiled.

"The energy elemental," she said, and I swear, if the look on Billy's face could kill ...

"Rachel," Billy purred, pouring a healthy dose of sex into his voice as he took the succubi (succubus? *fucking terms*) queen by her arm and tugged her away from me while murmuring something in her ear that I didn't pick up. Reg followed them close behind and George looked undecided in what to do with himself, like a spare nut when the bathroom was completed.

"Go with them," Shane said quietly, "and I'll take Ari on a tour of the house."

Charlie looked like he was about to say something, but George cut him off as Shane tugged me away from the little rooftop party and back inside.

"Shane, you'd better tell me what the fuck is going on right this second or—" My threat was cut short by Shane jerking to a halt and whipping around to face me.

"Or you'll *what*, Ari?" he challenged, his jaw set and his shoulders tensed and rippling. "If I don't tell you what's goin' on, what are you possibly gonna do that's worse than what you *just* tried to pull downstairs?"

"Downstairs?" I was a bit gobsmacked … Uh, change of subject much?

"Yes. Downstairs," he repeated, and I saw clearly just how pissed off he was with me. "You tried to leave us. You're *it* for us, Arizona. You're our soul mate. We will *never* get another opportunity to love and you're just ready to throw that all away because you panicked when Reg called you Mrs. Copthorne? So whatever this new threat is for not spilling our secrets, it can't be anything on your attempt to leave."

"Ah hah! So you admit there *is* a secret!" My attempt to lighten the mood went down like a lead balloon. Shane leveled his hurt glare at me, then dropped my wrist and stalked off down the corridor.

"Shane! Wait! Come on, I was just kidding …" Okay, I wasn't, but clearly now wasn't the time to push his buttons. He ignored me though, and kept stalking. "Shane, where are you going?"

How dare he walk away like that? I had questions—lots of them. About this … energy elemental, about Reg's parents, about why COCS was such a danger then they were part of the fucking shiny pink head of it.

"To my room," he snapped back. "I need a minute to clear my head before we go back and deal with all of that crap up there." He waved an angry hand in the direction of the roof, then continued striding away from me until he reached a door near the end of the hall.

Without pausing to invite me in, he opened the door, entered, and slammed it shut on my face.

What. The actual fuck had just happened?

I was supposed to be the one mad at them, not the other way around! But Shane'd looked really hurt by my little moment of cold feet downstairs … I guess I hadn't really considered how they might be feeling towards me?

Fuck it.

Not bothering to knock, I twisted the handle and let myself into Shane's childhood bedroom, slamming the door behind me. The tattooed air elemental stood in the center of his room, still fucking fuming, and shooting me crazy death glares.

"Oh, fucking stop already *Skeeter*," I snapped. "I think we're about even, considering the manipulation you went to in order to mark me as your mate, don't you?"

"Ari …" Shane growled. "Just give me a minute to calm down, okay? I have the temper of a bull in heat sometimes."

"No, Shane. Not okay. I'm falling to pieces bit by bit here. I didn't realize I was hurting any of you with my actions and now

I feel really fucking awful about it. At the same time, can you *please* stop with the 'soulmate' talk? It feels like it's bordering really fucking close to 'love' and we are sooo not there yet."

"Yet?" he repeated, and I froze. Had I said yet? I meant full stop. Ugh, fucking Freudian slip!

Shane prowled closer to me and I instinctively backed up. My back hit his bedroom door and suddenly I had nowhere left to run as he slid right up against me, his hard hot body crowding mine in a way that wasn't entirely unpleasant.

"You said *yet*," he murmured into my ear, his hands braced on either side of my head and his warm breath fanning across my skin. My heart seemed to stutter and skip for a second as all the tiny fine hair on my neck stood on end.

"It's just a word, Shane. Doesn't mean anything." *Yeah, that sounded* really *fucking convincing, Ari. Bravo. You're selling this well.*

Clearly Shane agreed—with my brain, not my words. His lips descended onto my neck, pressing a hot kiss over my pulse point before grabbing a small bit of my flesh and sucking lightly.

"Shane," I breathed in what I think was meant to be a protest? I don't know. It came out sounding sexy as fuck, which I doubt was what I'd meant to happen.

"Yes, sugar?" he drawled, really playing up that damn accent of his and making me whimper low in my throat. How the hell was I supposed to say no to this? Especially when the runes on my skin were sparkling like I was a vampire in the fucking sun.

"We're in your childhood bedroom … with a party waiting for us …" My reasons really didn't sound all that important when said out loud. "With a COCS Head waiting for us."

"They won't notice us skipping out for a long, hot moment …" Shane chuckled, sliding his hands underneath my pathetic excuse for a skirt and hooking his thumbs through the sides of my panties. "And you were right about one thing, sugar plum— there *is* a cock head waiting for you."

"Few minutes?" I arched an eyebrow at him. "Cock head?" He grinned back before claiming my lips in a scorching kiss.

"Few minutes, half an hour … trust me, sweetness, they won't mind." Well … when he put it like that …

Fuck it. This was happening. Again.

"So, sugar? What's it going to be?" He ran his thumbs along the top of my panties, just inside the waistband but not pulling them down … yet. "Are we going back to this stupid party frustrated and worked up, or are you gonna let me fuck you fast and dirty on my race car bedspread?"

A low groan slipped from my throat as my hand, with a life of its own, found the heavy-duty pipe wrench that Shane was smuggling in his man-thong.

A sound outside the door made me pause, and the door cracked open a smidge to reveal Reg with a small unbent paper clip in his hand.

"I used to pick this lock all the time when we were in high school, found Shane in here jerking off …"

"I ain't knee-high to a grasshopper anymore, shithead," Shane told his … boyfriend? Shit, I had no idea what to call the relationship these four guys had with each other. "I can still kick your ass."

Reg let himself into the room and closed the door with that fine ass of his.

"Question," I said, trying to pretend like I wasn't all hot and bothered by having two fine men in leather standing next to me.

"How does Shane have a Southern accent if he grew up here with the rest of you?"

"Is that a diversionary tactic, sug? Because it's not gonna work." Shane grabbed my wrist and put it right back on his wrench.

"He lived in *Texas* for a few years before his family moved here and joined the storm. Guess the unfortunate country bumpkin thing just sort of stuck."

"I'll whoop the pretty right off your ass, Reginald," Shane said with a sharp grin, encouraging me to, um, twist his wrench.

"Why? Am I interrupting something? You spirited our new wife away to your old bedroom for what purpose? To show off your childhood collection of NASCAR memorabilia?"

Reg sat on the edge of the massive California king bed and folded his arms behind his head, ever the consummate slut. The grin he flashed me was nothing short of lascivious. I should've found it annoying, but I had my hands full, so to speak.

"I haven't seen all of the COCS Heads," I reiterated, realizing full well how dirty that sounded. "Shouldn't we, you know, make our rounds? I thought you said they could be dangerous ..."

"We'll get to it," Shane said, sliding his hand down the bare skin of his belly and under the leather of his thong. "But maybe we should share an orgasm or two first?"

"Oh, really?" I asked, but he was already freeing his shaft from the leather and giving me this sultry, Southern grin.

"We skipped right to the final act with the marking. I thought maybe we could backtrack a bit?"

"Right?" I said, cocking a brow and taking a small step back, folding my arms over my chest. "You want, what, to be sucked off?"

"Not saying I'd be disappointed at that," he purred, as my own mouth twitched up at the edges.

"Good," I said, nodding my chin sharply, "then Reg," I continued, gesturing over at the water elemental, "will take care of that for you."

"Aw, man," Reg groaned, sliding his hands down his face. "We just got a *wife* and now you want me to blow this guy? Please."

"Then I guess I'll just be heading back to the party ..." I started, reaching for the door and pausing when Reg rose to his feet, tossing a cocky smirk my way.

"You think I won't rise to the occasion?" he asked, crossing his arms over his chest in challenge, the leather of his jacket creaking with the movement.

"Shane certainly did," I said suggestively, leaning my back against the wall and watching the two men as they glanced at each other. Shane raised a brow and Reg just shrugged.

"Fine. Watch a pro and see how it's done," he said with so much asshole swagger that I almost forgot he was about to suck another dude's dick.

Reg swept a tattooed hand through his short, blonde hair and knelt down, leaving his jacket on and turning my entire body into a vessel for hormones. I was just one walking, talking horn-ball. Fantastic. As if being unemployed, broke, and covered in magic runes wasn't enough.

Sucking in a deep breath, I stared completely enraptured as Reg curled his inked fingers around the base of Shane's long, thick pipe. Even though I could tell he was trying to hold back a little, a small moan escaped Shane's throat as he glanced over and made eye contact with me.

"Watch and learn, Sugar Tits," Reg said, sliding his tongue in a circle around the head of Shane's cock, paying special attention to the underside. Not only was it hot as hell to see the two men together like that, but Shane's dick was a work of art, a swirling storm of tattoos that disappeared into Reg's smirking mouth inch by careful inch.

Oh, God. I could say goodbye to these panties now; they were soaked. *He's fucking deep throating?! Fucker.* Now I knew Shane was going to be disappointed—that particular move was a little outside of my repertoire. Gag reflex and all that.

"Fuck," Shane cursed, letting his head fall back. His hands found the side of Reg's head, like he just couldn't help himself. "Sugar, take over," he begged, but I was just fine standing there and watching.

My hand slipped up and under my skirt, pushing my panties down my hips and letting them fall to my ankles. I kicked them aside before seeking out the warm heat between my thighs. I'd watched guy-on-guy porn before, but this was the first time I'd ever seen it in person and it was *hot.*

Reg slid back, a small strand of saliva connecting the full curve of his lips to Shane's cock. He slicked his hand up and down the long length of my new … um, husband? … lubing him up and then twisting his hand in a corkscrew motion.

Inked fingers against an inked cock …

As soon as my fingers found my clit, I was fucking *lit.*

"Holy crap," I whispered, noticing the corner of Reg's mouth twitching into a grin. He knew *exactly* what he was doing to me. I teased my hardened nub in circles, using my own lube to work myself up into an aching frenzy. My skin had that hot, achy tight feeling again and my runes … they glittered like stars. Wow. *This* was going to be an awkward adaptation, lighting up like a fucking Christmas tree every time I saw something sexy.

I was never going to be able to see a Ryan Reynolds movie in theaters again.

Reg continued to turn his hand in a clockwise motion, drawing these deep, sultry sounds from Shane's throat. His head dipped low again, taking the air elemental into his mouth again —but just the tip. I'd never seen that joke look so sexy on anyone.

Meanwhile, my fingers found the molten heat of my core and dove inside.

I bit my lower lip to try and stifle a groan, but it came out anyway, echoing around what was actually a cavernous fucking room—especially for a kid. If Shane and the guys had really grown up in the lap of luxury like this, why were they poor as fuck now when I coulda used a sugar daddy or two or four …

"Come here, ST," Reg murmured, his lips against Shane's dick. Somehow though, even on his knees with his hand on another man's cock, it was clear that he was in charge. I moved forward a few steps, curious to see what he was planning … and yelped when he grabbed me by the waistband of my skirt and dragged me a few steps closer.

Reg's hand slid up my thigh and then took over for me, sliding inside my pussy with two tattooed fingers. For a moment, we were in there together, but then I decided I needed to put my hands on Shane's shoulder to stay standing upright.

"Arizona Smoke!"

I heard the voice before I saw it. Gram. Standing next to Shane's bed and glaring at me through round, silver spectacles.

"I've caught you bang to rights, my girl," she said in that upper-crust British accent of hers, throwing a bucket of cold water right over me.

With a scream, I stumbled back, tripped, and fell ass first into a metal basket filled with firewood. Great. I was going to get splinters right in the coochie.

"What in the name o' Christ is going on?" Shane asked, tucking his cock back into the leather chaps. Good instincts. Wasn't really comfortable with Gram seeing my new husband's junk. Or me with my other husband's hand up my skirt. *WHY THE FUCK AM I MENTALLY CALLING THEM MY HUSBANDS?!*

Reg, apparently, didn't do well with surprise ... or maybe really well with it? ... because he'd turned into his water dragon form. Just wasn't sure if it was the shock of my sudden scream or a defense mechanism.

This time, though, he was kind of ... sexy? A sleek, watery beast growling and flashing a mouthful of teeth ... in the complete wrong direction of Gram's ghost.

"Reg," I muttered, my eyes glued on my scowling grandmother. His scales shifted and glittered in the light, making it look like his whole form was comprised of crystal clear water. "Over there." I nodded towards my Gram's ghost and Reg did an awkward sort of shuffling to turn around, then bared his teeth at the potted plant in the corner of the room, some three feet to the side of our unwelcome visitor.

"Grams, what the hell are you doing, popping in here unannounced like this?" I yelled, recovering a bit from my fright and trying to pull myself out of the firewood basket. Unfortunately, my butt had landed low enough that my balance was all wrong, and I found myself kind of flailing.

"Here, sug." Shane gallantly gripped my hand in his and tugged me up and out of the damn basket.

"Girl, don't pretend I didn't just catch you getting finger blasted by this one," Grams waved a hand at Reg's dragon form while he still snarled at the potted plant, "while *that* one had his knob gobbled by another man!"

The look on her face made me pause a second. Was she … disgusted or amused? Crazy old bitch.

"Grams, do you mind telling me what the fuck you're doing here?" I tried again, deliberately calmer this time as my thundering heart rate slowed a fraction thanks to Shane's warm hands on my skin.

After he had liberated my ass from the firewood, he'd placed one massive palm on my lower back and it seemed to be doing wonders for my temper—even if it did still set my runes glittering faintly.

"Arizona, what did I tell you about using that sort of language?" my dead ancestor snapped prudishly, and I rolled my eyes.

"Grams, I'm not going to stop saying *fuck* after you just saw my husband's cock halfway down my other husband's throat." I raised my eyebrow at her in challenge and she pursed her lips in anger. The old bat might be a stubborn bitch, but it was hereditary.

Oh, and I was saying husbands *aloud* now, too. Yep. That was it—I was seriously fucked.

"Fine, then perhaps I'll just make myself comfortable, shall I? I bet you're all kinds of worked up right now, getting interrupted like that. You must just be dying for me to disappear so you can finish getting your rocks off with these two studs …" *Ugh, she wasn't seriously threatening what I thought she was threatening … was she?*

"Maybe I'll just sit right here"—she sat her ghostly butt on the end of the bed and folded her ankles like she was at tea with the queen—"and talk about the weather."

"Suit yourself," I bluffed. "There are plenty of other places in this house we could fuck. Fuck, fuck, *fuck*."

The mean old hag smirked at me.

"I'm your guardian ghost, my girl. There's nowhere you can go that I can't follow."

Sighing, I rubbed at the bridge of my nose. Why did the talking ghost of my grandmother always seem to give me a splitting headache. Fucking shit, I was going to *need* that orgasm when this was over.

"Fine, Grams," I ground out, "I will stop swearing if you just tell me what the … penguin … you're doing here?"

"What the *penguin*?" the old bat snorted, and even Shane gave me a look that said he thought I'd lost my mind. "Very well, Arizona. Seeing as you seem so *desperate* to finish your sordid little tryst, I'll cut to the point."

"Thank you," I sighed, then realized Reg was still focused on the potted plant. His long antennae-like whiskers quivering and drool dripping off his razor-sharp fangs. His tail flicked back and forth like an angry cat's. That's kind of what he looked like, too … a cat-lizard-dog combo. No wings, just clawed feet, a long muzzle, and a mohawk of ice down his long, curved spine.

"Reg, hon," Shane said, noticing where my attention was focused and calling out to his friend, "it's just Ari's grandmother. You can change back now."

Reg's beautiful blue head whipped back to look at us, then in a shimmering of light he was back in his human form, leather hot pants and jacket perfectly in place.

"I knew that." He shrugged, leaning against the dresser like he hadn't just been so shocked he'd changed forms.

"Grams, you were saying?" I prompted, leaning a little into Shane's touch as his hand slid up to the back of my neck and rubbed little circles in my tense muscles.

"I came to warn you that you're in grave danger," she announced, then didn't elaborate.

Obviously. Because, you know, why not just warn someone and then *not* explain a lick about *why.*

"Let me guess, something is going to try and chop me up into little pieces and stuff me down a storm drain?" I was halfway joking, but the dead serious set to Gram's mouth made me double take.

"Not something. Someone. *Kuntemopharn*, to be precise." She scowled, and spat the foreign word like it left a bad taste in her mouth.

"Sorry." I squinted at her. "Did you just say ... *cuntmuffin?*"

"Arizona!" she barked. "Now is *not* the time for your foul language. I just told you your life is in danger; can you never take anything seriously?"

"I am taking this seriously!" I yelled back. "But you just told me off for swearing then you said a *cuntmuffin* is coming to murder me and I don't really know what to do with that information!" I was getting a bit hysterical maybe, but I blamed it on the blue ovaries (that's the lady version of blue balls in case you were curious).

"Arizona ..." Shane started and I shushed him. I know it probably sounded all a bit odd to them, but I couldn't be assed relaying everything Grams was rambling.

"I did not say a *cuntmuffin* was coming for you." Gram rolled her eyes. Guess that's where I learned it from. "I said, *Kuntemopharn* is coming for you. I would spell it but frankly, my dear, I don't have the time. And neither do you. He's already caught your scent and is on the hunt. You need to kill him before he kills you, or the fate of the elemental race is doomed."

There was a long pause, in which I just squinted at the ghost sitting on Shane's NASCAR bedspread in her twinset and pearls.

Uh-huh.

Mm-kay. So ... this really was an acid trip then? Because the things people were starting to tell me bordered on lunacy. Either they were all crazy or I was. And frankly, I was betting on the latter.

"Sugar Tits ..." Reg started and I shushed him as well with a flap of my hand.

"Right. And ... do you have anything more to tell me?" I asked the old bat. Of course she did—she just loved dragging it out for dramatic effect.

"Yes. You're the last living pure-blood elemental female, and if *Kuntemopharn* consumes your magic he'll gain your sext's magic—all of it. You'll be little more than pawns in the scope of the game he's playing, and I can assure you, no one wants that." Her wrinkled lips pursed together in what looked eerily like a cat's bum, while she scowled at me from behind her spectacles.

Wait ... did she say pure-blood?

Now I was really confused.

"Your little ceremony last night gave the last spark needed to awaken him; he's been sleeping for centuries." Gram sighed and looked at me like this was entirely my fault. But if you made the assumption that if she'd told me a lick about any of this *before* she died that the whole of the situation might've been avoided. Nope. I was so not taking the blame for this one. "You'll want to find him while he's still weak, or you won't stand a chance."

"So, basically a *Dungeon & Dragons* campaign then?" I asked, but either Gram didn't find me funny or she didn't get the joke. "Ooookay, fine. Be that way. And um, how exactly is he building his strength?"

"He's slaughtering weaker supernaturals, draining them of their power then tearing their corpses to pieces and shoving them into storm drains," she told me, looking a little green around the gills. "Just, stop him, Arizona. You're the last bloody hope for this world." Gram stared at me for a long moment and then muttered something under her breath that sounded suspiciously like, "God help us all."

"No pressure though, right?" I joked, and she frowned.

"All of the pressure, my girl. If you fail ... well. Let's not let it get to that, hmm, Duckie?" She patted at her perfectly curled hair nervously. "Oh and you've probably guessed by now that you're adopted, so your mother doesn't know anything about this world. Let's keep it that way, shall we?"

And with that little grenade, she was gone again.

I stood there a moment after she *poofed* out, waiting to see if she was just messing with me and about to rematerialize and give me a bit more information, but she didn't. Bitch.

Adopted. Adopted? *Adopted?!* The thought didn't bother me so much in that I was opposed to the idea just ... pure-blood elemental? *I* was a pure-blood elemental? Then who the penguin were my bio parents?!

I had a serious headache on the way—like FedEx overnight delivery fast.

Groaning, I rubbed at my face to try and ease the hectic migraine that had been building ever since the old prude had startled Reg's tattooed fingers right out of me.

"Ari, can you tell us what's going on now?" Shane prompted, clearly frustrated at only hearing half the conversation. I didn't even know where the fuck to begin.

"Uh, have you guys ever heard of *Kuntemopharn*?" I asked, sounding out the word the way I had heard my Grams say it.

"*Cuntm*—" Reg started and Shane glared at him to shut up.

"*Kuntemopharn*?" he repeated, and I nodded. "No, never. But Charlie has all of the storm's historical tomes in his library here. Surely if the COCS Head hasn't heard of it, then there'll be information in there?"

It was actually a good suggestion. Of *course* an entire species that I never knew existed would have archives. But hey, what could I say, I was a barista, not a historian!

"Alright, good plan." I nodded, then eyed up my two new husbands in their ridiculous bondage outfits—ridiculously sexy that is. Oh, and *husbands* ... That word again. "Now, which one of you two is going to clean out my pipes? I get the feeling we may not get another opportunity for a while, and dear lord, save you if I am stuck feeling this unsatisfied for much longer ..."

"You still want to screw after seeing your dead grandmother's ghost as she warned you about cuntmuffins? Holy crap, Sugar Tits, you're hardcore." Reg slicked his hand over his hair and grinned at me. "Fuck, you're as bad as I am."

"I'm sort of ... operating under the notion that this is all a drug induced dream." I flashed Reg my best *take-no-shit* smile. "Might as well get some D while I've got the chance. Lord knows my pipes had basically zero running water before meeting you guys."

Reg laughed and slung an arm around my neck, running his tongue up along my jawbone. It should've been gross, but ... it was actually pretty flipping hot.

"Threesome?" Reg said with a quirk of brows. "Like in the bathroom the day after we met?"

"Do you *want* me to kick your ass?" I asked him with a sassy bump of my hip. I wasn't kidding—I really did believe that at some point, my ass would wake up on Gram's couch, my mouth tasting of last night's wine, my head spinning like crazy. Because that was my life—normal, average ... well, maybe even a little below average? I'd never been special or good at anything in my life. I was about as run-of-the-mill as they came.

Adopted.

I was so not going to delve into that shit.

Nope.

How the hell am I adopted?! Why would my parents not tell me that? Where the bleeping fudge did I come from?

If I were to stand there and psychoanalyze, I'd probably realize that I was trying to screw these guys to get my mind off my grandmother's words. I wasn't necessarily *hurt* by them; being adopted didn't bother me. But ... I also didn't like being lied to—especially not about a subject as sensitive as, say, *not being fucking human.*

"I think you promised me a blow job?" Shane asked, climbing onto the bed and sitting up on his knees, freeing his cock from his pants again. It was a shock every time, seeing his junk all tattooed and shit.

"Bleeding hell," I whispered under my breath, and I swear, I heard Britt say *British* somewhere in the mansion. Maybe being a spirit elemental meant I was psychic or telepathic or some shit? I hadn't exactly asked many questions about my own power.

Reg swatted my ass as I crawled up onto the bed. I didn't know a lot about threesomes—that was more Britt's thing—but

I had *some* idea of a position we could try. I was hoping the guys would just *get it* so I didn't have to explain.

"I just want to warn you that I'm not as, er, talented as Reg …" I started, but Shane was gently fisting his fingers in my hair, making my scalp tingle. He was being firm, but not domineering. And I *liked* it.

Shane put the warm head of his cock against my face, traced my mouth with the tip, sliding pre-cum across my lips. I could taste the salty sweetness of him, and it turned me on like fucking crazy—especially when I felt the mattress shift with Reg's weight.

My black vinyl skirt was pushed up with a crinkling of cheap fabric and I wondered for a second why the hell the boys all got real leather and I got this shit … bastards … *oh*. But then I felt a warm hand cupping my cunt, squeezing tight.

"You are *soaked,* Sugar Tits," he said, and I could just imagine him grinning dickishly at me. "As a water elemental, I must say, that's fucking *hot.*"

I couldn't exactly drum up a response because Shane was sliding into me, the thick length of his shaft heavy against my tongue. With my hands on the bed, I was balancing on all fours. It was kind of awesome, knowing I didn't have to do any of the work. Good. At least then Shane wouldn't see that a dude was better at BJs than I was.

"Relax, honey doll," he said, his voice soothing along my skin like a balm. "You're so tense."

"No, stay tense," Reg said, as I felt him sliding his cock between my folds, wetting his shaft with the molten desire from my body. "Stay *real* fucking tense."

Caught between a rock and a hard place.

Heh.

Well, it was funny to me.

My breath hissed out in a strangled moan as Reg slid his cock into me, the exhale making Shane growl like a ... well, a *dragon.* There was something about the fact that these guys could turn into beasts that was sexy as all get-out, like they were monsters on the cusp of breaking loose, using what little willpower they had to hold back.

That was about the last sentient thought I had as Shane and Reg began to thrust, their bodies moving in and out of me, making me wonder why the *hell* I'd never tried this before. It was a lesson in exquisite torture, a taboo sampling that had my brain shutting down and my body taking over.

My runes flared, bright enough to cast shadows in the room, and I could only fucking pray to whatever god the elementals worshipped that Gram would stay the *fuck* out of here.

"Oh yeah," Reg moaned, grabbing my hips in *just* the right spot, just over the bone. The feel of his fingertips pressing into my skin made my back arch, my ass pressing into the hard, hot heat of his body.

The position I was in could've be construed as ... vulnerable? I felt anything but, like *I* was the one being serviced. Yes, Shane's hands were in my hair, Reg's holding my hips in place, but I still felt like *they* were mine.

Uh-oh.

Fucking shitballs.

There I went again, getting all possessive over dudes I didn't even *want* to be mine.

Shane was the first to come, and the hot saltiness of him coming in my throat made me forget to question what was happening. I swallowed and as he pulled away, I reached a hand out and dragged him down to me, using the straps on his chest to bring his face to mine.

Shane leaned down and let me kiss his mouth, the taste of his body still clinging to my lips. His tongue took over the interaction, bringing soft moans from my throat, drawing them straight into his.

Fortunately for him, Reg didn't finish quite as quick, working my body with a quick, but steady rhythm, bringing forth that orgasm I was so desperate to get. After all, maybe when this was over I'd wake up and find out that I was alone again. No Britt, no boyfriend, no money, no job, just … me.

Maybe I'd rather deal with cuntmuffins and plumbers than go back to that shit …

"You ready, ST? Because I'm like, thirty seconds from blowing my load."

I pulled back from Shane's lips and saw him flash a grin.

"Ain't he a dumb shit?" he asked, pulling away and tucking his cock *slowly* back into his leather thong—right at eye level. I think that's what did it, the accent and the view—well and the fact that I was getting my ass pounded *hard.*

My fingers curled in the NASCAR bedspread and my back arched, drawing a sharp groan from Reg. I think we came at right about the same time, but it was hard to be sure because as soon as I felt that release, that uncoiling of energy from the base of my spine, my runes flared and literally blinded me.

Lightning crashed *inside* the bedroom and *another* fucking pipe burst in the ceiling.

"Fucking hell, ST!" I heard Reg shout, stopping the rainstorm of water before it hit either of us. I collapsed forward and rolled onto my back, turning over and looking up at a sheet of water, frozen in midair. As I stared, it retreated right back into the hole in the ceiling.

The lightning had set a small fire, but I supposed it wasn't *that* big of a deal considering I was dating a fire elemental.

"Christ on a cracker ..." Shane murmured, hoisting me up into a sitting position and nodding with his head in the direction of the flames. "Can you put that out, doll?"

"Me?" I asked and Shane raised both dark brows at me. I was still lying there, panting, trying to put myself together and he wanted me to do *magic*. "I don't fucking know how!"

"I heard about what happened at the sex shop," Reg told me, looking for the briefest of moments like he might *actually* be serious about something. But then he just grinned like an asshole. "Stealing that woman's energy and putting it back. Come on, this is *easy* shit. Just dig deep, ST."

I sat up, all sex muddled and hazy in the brain, and I stared at the small fire on the rug, the runes patterned across my skin glimmering metallic.

Dig deep, my ass, I thought as I looked inside, searching for that bit of *something* I'd found when I was at the clothing store. Instead, all I got was this violent rush that swept over me and made me gasp.

"Shit," Reg said, and I noticed the color draining from his face. When I opened my eyes back up, I saw several more lightning bolts slam into the *carpet* inside the room. Inside. Lightning. Shit and fuck. "We need Warden," he told Shane, and I managed to glance back just in time to see his face twist with frustration.

"Fuck Warden," he said as I stared between the two men and tried to figure out what was going on.

"Who the hell is Warden and why are we fucking him?" I demanded, my breath coming in short, sharp gasps as prickles of pain coursed all over me. "What's happening?" My skin was lit up like a bloody Christmas tree, with little tiny spider legs of electricity pulsing and dancing in the gaps between the runes, almost as though the gaps were left specifically for this electricity to fill.

"Honey Doll, you just need to calm down. It'll be alright." Shane's syrupy voice dripped over me, soothing a little of my panic and making me take more notice of the scowl on Reg's face as he stomped out the little fires caused by the lightning.

"Maybe I did it wrong?" I murmured. It had seemed *so* easy at the sex shop. Just … look inside, find the glowing ball thing and *voila*. "I'll try again …"

"No!" Shane and Reg both screamed at the same time as a dozen more bolts of lightning hit the carpet all around the bed and my body convulsed. It felt like I was being hit by a Taser. Or … I imagine that's what it would feel like. As I said, my life was below average, and I really hadn't been hit by any Tasers before to compare against.

My muscles all seized up and my skin felt like it was burning. Like I had just been shoved into a rotisserie oven which was a little ironic, given I'd just been spit roasted and enjoyed it a whole hell of a lot more than whatever was currently happening to me.

"Shane, we *need* Warden," I dimly heard Reg repeat to Shane. The pleading edge to his voice was not something I'd heard from the water elemental before, and it spiked my panic higher. My jaw was locked up hard and I couldn't speak to ask *what the fuck* was happening, so could only lay there on Shane's NASCAR bedspread while the electricity on my skin wrecked fuck knows what sort of havoc to my insides.

"We *don't* need him," Shane snapped back. "Just go get Billy and George. Between the four of us we can ground her."

"Shane—" Reg started again.

"Go! Now!" Shane boomed the command at his ... partner? lover? ... I really needed to work out what they called each other.

"Don't worry, sugar," he murmured to me when Reg slammed the door behind him, "we just need all the elements here to balance you out and then you'll be right as wind." He lay on the bed in front of me, our faces just inches apart, but I noticed he didn't make any attempt to touch me. Smart move. This shit hurt like a raging bitch.

It could only have been a matter of seconds and the door burst open once more, with my three remaining husbands all piling into the room.

"Shit," Billy swore, throwing an angry look at the back of Shane's head. "Shane—"

"No!" Shane snapped, sitting up and whirling to face the fire elemental. Whoever thought air would be a weak element had *clearly* never met Shane ... fuck, *seriously*? I didn't even know Shane's surname! "Everyone just help ground her; it shouldn't be that hard with all of us here."

I couldn't see what their responses were, but the four of them fanned out around me in a sort of sex fetish group hug or something. From my awkward position it looked like they were joining hands as they started to chant in their magical language.

Oh fuck, this is totally a dream... right? BDSM dressed sexy hunks of men who fix toilets and chant *in magical languages?*

Either it was one hell of a drug induced dream, or I had gone certifiably crazy and was currently running down Main Street with my knickers on my head.

As they chanted, the little swirls and loops of electricity dancing over my skin seemed to lift off a little bit and hover over the surface. My four husbands increased the speed of their lilting words, and I could *feel* the magic being poured into me, pulling the shattered pieces of my soul back together and easing the pain.

My jaw freed up just a fraction and I sucked in a gasping breath, my eyes pleading with George to keep going. He was the one located in front of me and his gaze stayed locked on mine as they chanted their magic words, his warm wood colored eyes reassuring me that I would be okay. George would never let anything bad happen to me.

After what felt like half a year, the lacework of glowing electricity hovering above my skin sort of intensified then, in a sharp stab of pain, sucked back inside and left me panting as the pain dissipated completely.

"Blossom?" George asked gently, brushing a soft hand through my hair. "Are you okay?"

"I think so," I whispered, facedown on Shane's bed. "What the fuck was that?"

When no one answered me, I pushed myself up to sit, so I could give them all the stink eye.

"Someone start talking now, or else …" I growled the threat, not really knowing what I would do to follow through on it, so *of course* Billy called me on it.

"Or else what, Firebug?" he smirked. "What *will* you do if we don't start talking?"

"Or else …" I racked my brain. I'd already promised not to run again, and honestly I couldn't even if I tried—not in my current state. "Or else all of this," I indicated my still soaking crotch, "is closed for business."

Billy's gaze darkened in challenge and Reg snorted a laugh.

"Let's not go making threats we have no intention of keeping, Sugar Tits," Reg snickered and I turned my death glare on him.

"Oh, I am *dead* serious, Reginald Copthorne," I assured him. "I let it slide on the roof when that slutty chick mentioned 'the other one' but shit just got real. I felt like I was about to fucking die and y'all are keeping secrets from me." Pausing, I sucked in a deep breath, mentally preparing myself for the trump card I was about to play. "I thought we were supposed to be married now? Married people don't keep secrets. Not big ones that impact their *wife*."

Fucking. A. I almost choked on that word, but it hit home. Even Billy looked sufficiently chastised.

True to my run of luck though, just as I thought I was getting through to them, the door to the bedroom flew open, almost knocking over the little display of race cars on the shelves near the door.

"*There* you all are!" Reg's mother exclaimed, sweeping into the room in her stylish hunting outfit. Bitch. "I've been looking for you *everywhere;* do you have any idea how rude this is?"

The scathing look she gave me said just who she considered to be the rude one here. My eye twitched a little with the desire to slap this bitch and tell her where to shove her judgements but a small part of my brain recognized that this woman was, in fact, my new ... mother-in-law. *Gag me with a fucking spoon— am I really buying into this crap?!*

"Boys, why don't you head back up to the roof so your ... *spirit* and I can get to know each other?" The sharklike smile curving across her face said she would rather tear my eyeballs out with her perfectly manicured nails, but none of my husbands seemed to pick up on that.

"Sorry, Ma." Reg shrugged, the movement nice and fluid and easy. *Gah, those muscles, those beautiful, beautiful muscles.* "Ari actually needs to speak with the Head. We just found out about some cocksucker—er, sorry, cuntmuffin—that wants to try and kill her; we wanted to ask if you or Charlie or any of the others knows anything about it."

The irony of Reg calling anyone else a cocksucker was not lost on me, and despite my resolution to stay mad at them, I couldn't help the small smile pulling at my lips. Or the pooling heat between my legs as my mind replayed the image of Shane's inked up dick between Reg's lush lips.

Reg's mother snorted a rather unladylike noise and curled her lip in disbelief.

"Oh really? And who would want to kill this girl already? She's not even complete."

What the hell did *that* mean?

"Someone literally called *cuntmuffin.*" Reg shrugged and Shane whacked him in the shoulder.

"He means *Kuntemopharn.* Have you ever heard that name before?" Shane asked, and the Copthorne matriarch's face seemed to drain of color.

"You know something," I observed, narrowing my eyes at her. "What do you know?"

"Where did you hear that name?" she whispered, her eyes huge in her perfectly made-up face as her hand fluttered near her neck. "Because whoever told you he was a danger, they were lying—he's dead. Has been for a long time."

"I'm inclined to trust my source," I snapped, feeling a bit defensive of my dead grandmother. How dare this bitch tell me Grams was lying. Could ghosts lie? Or was that faeries? I didn't know—I was just a barista, not a folklorist.

"I think you've been misinformed, but if you don't believe me, you can see for yourself." She pursed her lips and gave a decisive nod. "Come on then."

Joan Copthorne spun on her riding boot heel and stalked out of Shane's bedroom, clearly just assuming we would all follow her like puppies. Which we did, but that wasn't the point. This wasn't about her; I just really wanted to know what the fuck kind of creature was out there calling itself cuntmuffin—dead or alive.

12

CHAPTER TWELVE

The library was exactly what I would have expected, given the ostentatious décor of the rest of the house. It was a near perfect replica of the library in *Beauty and the Beast*—or at least it was in my head. The shelves of books were stacked from the floor to the soaring, vaulted depths of the ceiling, with long ladders on sliding rails dotted around the room.

Reg's mother was even more annoyed at me, if that was even possible, after I made them wait outside the guest bathroom so I could er ... mop up a little. What? Girl's gotta do what a girl's gotta do!

"Master, how can I be of assistance?" the butler asked, popping out from behind a desk and giving us all a blank, glassed over look.

"Golem," Reg whispered in my ear. "Still don't care what it is?"

Ugh. Curiosity was biting at me, but I couldn't give him the satisfaction.

"Nope," I lied, "do not care." But I watched with fascination as Reg's mum rattled off a list of books, then the smartly dressed man sketched a little bow and went to gather them all.

"You're trying to work it out, aren't you?" George grinned. "What it is about him that makes him not human?"

I glanced at the golem's retreating back, quirked a brow and tried not to be bothered about the fact that I couldn't find my panties before we came down here ... Honestly, I'm pretty sure they were incinerated by a lightning bolt. *Fuck, those were expensive Victoria's Secret ones, too.*

"Um, he's too polite to be human?" I asked and heard Billy chuckling behind me, his laughter the sound of leather and chrome, the voice of a motorcycle growling to life. Speaking of ... I'd only seen the boys' hideous plumbing van. But four grown ass dudes? They had to have their own rides *somewhere* right? Like, uh, maybe in the garage of this gigantic mansion?

"He's made out of clay, Ari," George said, reaching out and putting the end of his leash in my hand. I seriously appreciated the gesture. "Animated with magic; he has no soul."

"Sort of like Reg's mother," Billy whispered, and I heard the water elemental growl at his friend ... boyfriend ... Jesus, whatever. Billy sauntered past us, pausing to glance down at my bare cheeks hanging out of the skirt. Not that it mattered—even *with* the skimpy panties I'd been wearing, there were cheeks. "By the way," he continued, lifting the burning color of his eyes to mine. Even though I'd *literally* just been, um, plowed, I felt a stirring of heat in my belly and my runes shimmered stupidly. Can something even do that? Shimmer stupidly? "Your friend left with the alpha male of the Hudson Valley Pack."

He shrugged one of his deliciously broad shoulders, like that statement told me anything at all. I knew ... zero about packs

… zero about alpha males … Well, okay, I knew *something* about them—they were dicks. And usually had big dicks. Fuck.

"Well," Reg's mom said from a table near the fireplace, "are you just going to *stand* there or are you going to come over and take a seat?"

"She'll grow on you," George promised, letting me lead him by the leash over to the table. That improved my mood substantially. The thing that *didn't* improve was the look on Joan Copthorne's face.

"I'm sure she will," I said, and then under my breath, "like a fungus."

I pasted on a smile and sat prettily in a velvet chair, careful not to flash Reg's mum all my good parts. The boys took seats along the right side, leaving me at the head of the table with Joan on my left. The fact that she was wearing a long-sleeved shirt, scarf, khaki vest, and matching pants … that scared me. I couldn't see any part of her body that would have runes on it, so I had no idea if this was like permanent, permanent.

"*Kuntemopharn* means storm dweller in *our* language," Joan said, emphasizing the word *our* like I was some kind of alien creature invading her planet. "The storm dweller," she continued, taking a book from the returning golem's arms and dropping it on the table, "was an elemental who absorbed the energy of his sext."

I bit my lower lip for a second … and then it all started to sink in.

Sext.

We didn't have a sext (hah, sext…), but a quint. Where the fuck was our sixth person?

Warden.

Oh shit.

There really *was* another one.

My skin prickled with goose bumps and my throat went dry.

I curled my fingers around the edge of the table, but decided not to say anything in front of Reg's mom—she'd enjoy my shock and dismay too much.

The pages of the book swirled in an otherworldly wind as Joan smirked at me. Like, *see I can control* my *powers.*

I glared at her.

"Mom, just cut to it, please," Reg groaned, looking like he wanted to puke. Something about the scene in Shane's bedroom had really upset him. "Storm dweller. Cuntmuffin. Who cares? What's this book gonna tell us about all that?"

Reginald's mom opened to a page with a really creepy *Alice's Adventures in Wonderland* type ink drawing of a large dragon-esque creature. It vaguely resembled the boys in their dragon forms, but there was just something *off* about it. It smiled with a gaping maw, teeth sharp and tongue lolling. Honestly, it looked like some sort of creature from one of Britt's hentais (you know, the pervy Japanese cartoon porn).

"The storm dweller," Joan said again, like she simply enjoyed having information that I didn't, "is an anomaly, a mutation. It's what happens when a single elemental uses their connection with their unit to absorb every ounce of magic."

"Yeah, duh," Reg said, pulling a Billy-esque hissy fit. "So what?"

"So for there to even *be* a storm dweller alive today, the last one would've had to have been resurrected from the dead." Joan paused to give a genteel laugh, like this was the most ridiculous thing she'd ever heard in her life. "Or a new one would've had to have been made."

Her eyes snapped up to Reg as he stood up and knocked his chair over.

"We know where you're going with this," he snarled as his mother took the rest of the books from the golem and placed them in a stack in front of me. "So let's just go down there so we can go home."

Home, he said. Hmm. I wasn't sure how to feel about that.

"Down … where?" I asked, getting a little tickle at the base of my spine. I didn't like this. I didn't like it at all.

"There's an entrance to an underground tunnel on the back of the property," Reg said carefully, tapping his fingers on the glossy wood surface of the tabletop. "It used to be part of the city's sewer system, but when they upgraded in the sixties, it was closed off and left to rot." His mouth twitched and he sucked in a deep breath through his nose. "Along with the last storm dweller's skeleton. I used to play in there as a kid."

"In the sewer?" I asked, but Reg just shrugged, his mouth twitching, like he was recovering some of his usual cocky attitude. "You played with a skeleton in the sewer?"

"He evaded the nannies and snuck down there," Joan said with a sniff, standing up from the table and pointing at the stack of books. "I'll take you to see the corpse so you can be sure that you're *wrong*," she emphasized, "but I want you to read these. If you don't learn more about who you really are, you're not going to last long."

Speaking of … I wondered vaguely if this was the right time to bring up the whole *adopted pure-blood* argument. The boys had thought I was a mere one percent? Huh. Guess even in death, Gram's spell was slow to fade. Wonder if knowing I was an elemental through and through would wipe the twisted scowl off Joan's face?

"Mom," Reg warned, but she wasn't done.

"You'll end up another storm dweller that we'll have to—"

ELEMENTS OF MISCHIEF

"*Mom!*" Reg shouted, slamming his hand on the table. "Stop it," he snarled, giving her a look that was almost scary.

"Without Warden ..." she continued, flicking a glance my direction. Clearly, she didn't intend to finish that thought because she turned on her heel and headed for the back doors of the library.

"Let's get this fucking over with," Reg growled, stalking off after her as Billy shook his head and lit up a cigarette with magic.

"Warden is our sixth," I said carefully, looking George straight in the face. Of all the guys, he seemed the most likely to tell me the truth. His brown eyes met mine and held steady. "Warden's another elemental," I confirmed and George smiled softly.

"Yes, Warden is an energy elemental," he said slowly, keeping his attention on my face. "But he left about ten years ago and we haven't heard from him since."

"What happened to make him leave?" It had to have been something big. From the little I had seen so far of this ... community? Species? ... they tended to stick together like glue. Their bond was something I was borderline envious of—or would be, rather, if I didn't already have a foot in the door myself.

"He used to be the leader of our quint," George started and I frowned.

"But, I thought Shane ...?"

"Now, yes. But back then it was Warden. He was the strongest of us, and our leader is always the strongest, not the oldest." George shrugged and then smiled softly. "Like you are now."

I quirked a brow, but I didn't know how I felt about being *anyone's* leader—I could barely manage to keep my dresser stocked with clean socks. But I decided to keep my mouth shut and let George continue.

"None of us know exactly what happened, but the two of them got into it about something or other and the next thing we knew, Warden had packed his shit and taken off. We just sort of left him for a while, thinking he would come back eventually but then months turned into years and … here we are."

"And Shane never told you what it was about?" I prompted as we fell into step together, following behind the others as they led us out of the warm library and into a cold New York night. George and I kept our voices low as we walked across the wet lawn, supposedly heading toward some ancient fucking dragon skeleton. Insert eye roll here if you will.

"He won't speak about it, barely even tolerates us saying Warden's name." George's mouth pulled down at the corners in a mournful expression. "We all miss him though. Bad."

"That doesn't make sense, George," I muttered, narrowing my eyes. "You must have *some* idea what caused their fight?"

"Of course." He smiled with those full lips of his, their lushness the only thing keeping my eyes away from the rounded curves of his biceps and that beautiful tree of life tattoo. If I was going to get anything done around this man, he was going to have to start wearing a shirt. "We're plumbers, not stupid." He winked at me, but it was a playful one, not a pervy lascivious slut shutter like when Billy or Reg did it.

"Well?" I prompted, seeing as we were almost at the edge of the property already and I was pretty desperate to hear the rest of this story. If there was a fifth dude out there that I was *fated*, or whatever, to be with … well, I kinda wanted to know what the deal was!

"We always suspected it had something to do with … a girl." George paused and ran his fingers through the nut-brown color of his hair, the starlight above highlighting natural streaks of chestnut and darker strains of mahogany. He was limned in the light coming from the house, emphasizing the near perfect shape of his body, trimmed and toned, muscles in places I didn't even know muscles could grow.

"Warden met her in school," he continued when I stayed silent, stirring up memories of my own ill-fated college romance. "He came back for summer break totally different, and then a week later he was gone." George gave me a sympathetic look. "I know it wasn't right of us to keep this from you, but … it's sort of a nonissue now. None of us would even know where to begin looking for him—even if we wanted to."

"And you don't?" I challenged, holding his gaze. "None of you have any interest in tracking him down now?"

"He's made it pretty clear he doesn't want us to find him." George's brow dropped in a frown and he broke eye contact with me. "Come on, let's go look at skeletons in sewers."

"Is that a euphemism for something?" I waggled my eyebrows at him suggestively, trying to lighten the mood as I grabbed his leash and continued across the garden to where the others were already waiting.

"If it is, Blossom, it's a bad one." George chuckled and I saw a bit of the tension drop out of his shoulders. This Warden had really done a number on my new husbands … er, boyfriends. Or whatever.

Mental note: *grill Shane further when he's feeling vulnerable.*

Maybe another blow job from Reg was in order …

"Here we are," Joan said as we caught up, giving George a warm smile that most definitely was *not* extended to me. She waved her elegant hand at the vegetation growing halfway over a metal grate lodged into the side of a small, grassy mound. If I hadn't known to look for it, I'd have probably missed it completely. Even now, the only reason I could see the slight shine of metal through all that green was because Billy had a dancing bundle of flame in one hand, casting brilliant orange and yellow light across the darkness of the yard.

That must be the poop shoot—er, sewer entrance—we're looking for, I thought as George shifted into his dragon form and carefully coaxed the vines and weeds covering the gate out of the way with a single breath. He simply leaned forward, exhaled, and swished the tree bark brown length of his tail and it all just ... gently peeled away.

George took a step back and shifted into human form with a sigh, casting a glance my way, like his being human was more for my benefit than his own.

"Why did he need to dragon-out?" I asked Billy, who stood closest to me. "Seems like a sort of easy task?"

"It is," he nodded, "but we used an absolute shit ton of magic grounding you earlier and he's probably exhausted. Using our dragon or elemental forms gives us an extra boost of magic. I'm barely keeping it together as it is." He twirled the flame around and had it alight on the tip of one finger.

"Oh." Well shit, now I felt bad. I hadn't even considered what toll that ritual in Shane's bedroom might have had on the guys, but now that Billy mentioned it, they were all looking a bit rough.

"Don't sweat it, doll face." Billy smirked. "It's our job to keep you alive now."

Shane hauled the metal grate open, his thick pipes bulging as he pulled at it, and we all paused for a moment, no one really offering to go first.

Hey, don't blame me! There was a skeleton in there for fuck's sake!

"Come on then," Reg growled. "Billy, the light?"

Billy's eyes tightened a little but he stayed in his sexy leather clad human form as several little balls of fire ignited from nothing and bounced through the air to line the tunnel, lighting our way as we followed Reg through the foul smelling slosh.

At least it smelled more *earthy* than *old shit* to me. That, and Reg went see-through on us, using his elemental magic to push the water away from my six inch stilettos. Didn't do a lot to remove the slippery sludge though. Let's just say—if the cuntmuffin guy wasn't out to kill me, the shoes probably would.

"Are you okay?" I whispered to Billy, noticing the slight sheen of sweat on his forehead.

He nodded tightly, but took my hand in one of his.

"Fine. Just ... let's be quick."

"Ah hah!" Joan yelled, her voice echoing sharply down the sewer tunnel. "See! What did I tell you? Exactly where it's supposed to be."

The 'where' she was talking about was a wide opening in the middle of the tunnel, a circular room with a stone slab raised in the center like an altar. On top of the slab was, as promised, a skeleton. The bones of the skeleton were shackled to the stone with several rusty looking chains and even had metal spikes hammered between the wrist and ankle bones. However this *Kuntemopharn* had died, it hadn't been pleasant.

"Huh," Reg muttered, clearly not expecting to have found the skeleton where it was supposed to be.

"I don't get it." I frowned. "Why would Gram say this dude was trouble if he's, you know, *not*. I mean, the mighty cuntmuffin's just a pile of old bones for fuck's sake."

"Maybe she *lied*?" Joan rolled her eyes dramatically. "Ghosts have been prone to mischief before, you know?"

"Something … doesn't feel right about this …" I was murmuring mostly to myself as I took a couple of steps closer to the skeleton. There was a heaviness to the air that smacked of magic, but maybe that was whatever had protected this … ah … grave … for so long? My hand was still held firm in Billy's grip, so I tugged him along with me as I got closer to the altar.

One foot, in deadly stiletto boots, slipped on fuck knows what and I almost ended up with my bare coochie in a pile of old shit.

"Careful," Billy hissed, catching me just in time and placing me back on my feet. "It's bad enough our shoes are getting destroyed; you do *not* want that fine ass in this crap."

"Thanks." I smiled wryly, then continued forward to the altar, stopping just a foot from the remains.

"Does anyone else *feel* that?" I asked, looking around at my four new husbands … and shiny new mother-in-law. Of all of them, she seemed to be the only one who knew what I was talking about. Her brow was drawn low and her lips were tight as she looked around the room, almost as if she suspected someone else were here with us.

Not knowing why, I reached out my free hand to touch the skeleton. Right as my finger *should* have met bone, the whole thing just flat-out disappeared. The chains dropped to the stone with a clang, and the sound of Joan's bloodcurdling scream bounced through the room.

"It's just a fucking glamour!" Billy said, right before his foxfire went out, and in an instant, I felt *something* sweep through the tunnel at me, a force of energy, like a warm gust of wind. It knocked me flat on my ass, my head cracking against the wet cement floor.

"*Mom!*" I heard Reg shout as I struggled to stand up, long fingers curling around my wrist and yanking me to my feet.

Based on smell alone, I knew it was George—that night-blooming jasmine and musky wet earth scent of his was unmistakeable. Even in the middle of a reeking sewer, I was sure of it.

"Stay close," he warned me, putting one of my hands flat on his shoulder. Beneath my fingertips, I felt him shift, his smooth skin roughening, limbs elongating. Considering the fact that I hadn't known shifters even *existed* a few days ago, the whole thing should've freaked me the fuck out.

Instead, I found it *comforting.*

"Climb up," George said, but he didn't wait for me to try. Instead, I felt the rough, muscular length of his tail curl around my waist, hoisting me up and onto his back. I mean, I'd ridden dudes before, but I was so not used to this.

My fingers curled around the rough horns protruding from George's head as he snaked forward, muscles bunching beneath my thighs, sending us flying toward the entrance to the sewer at a speed I could hardly even comprehend in the dark.

We burst out of the half-open grate, back into the yard, and then up, up, *up.* I screamed because well, shit, I was afraid of fucking heights. George took us up in the air and swirled, the long sinuous length of his body curling around itself as he spun to face whatever the hell was going on back at ground-level.

"Stay sharp." Gram's voice said near my right ear, her clipped British accent snapping me out of my brief moment of shock.

Water cascaded out of the large pipe, carrying with it at least two bodies that I could see—Joan and Reg. They landed in a heap on the grass, but neither was moving. And even from here, it was easy to see that the water was tinged with red.

"Somebody's bleeding," I heard myself choke out, glancing over at the semi-translucent expression on my grandmother's face. The stern Englishwoman I'd known my whole life, this stoic being made of stone and Earl Grey tea, she looked fucking *terrified.*

"Joan," George said as I glanced over my shoulder and saw the entire wall of glass windows in the library explode outward in a sea of glass. Two different dragons, ones I didn't recognize, came flying out, one of them sparkling with white-hot flickers of electricity and the other, a shimmery emerald green with leaves for scales.

Since I knew they weren't *my* boys, I just assumed they were Joan's.

George dropped us down so fast my stomach bottomed out, my thighs clenching tight to keep from falling off. His large, clawed feet gripped the grass as we landed, tail lashing out and cutting a bush right in half. I couldn't see what the hell it was he was aiming at, but in the next moment, I heard a sound, a crackling rush that preceded a massive wave of orange-red flames.

For a second there, I was completely stunned. I just sat on George's back like a useless lump—hey, I was a barista not a ninja.

Fortunately, Billy was there in a split second, the sinuous flaming whip of his body sliding into place in front of us, cutting the wall of fire off in its track. It shot skyward, like a fireworks display, the ground beneath it steaming, a few nearby bushes crackling with flames.

"Arizona, wake up!" Gram snapped as I blinked a few times and came to, sliding off of George's back and landing in the mud. No sooner had I done that then he was being rolled over by *another* dragon, this one a shimmery pink, blossoms sprouting from its scaled hide.

218

As pretty as it was, as soon as its body hit George's, I heard the awful crack of bone and a howl escaped his fanged maw, more animal than human. Were we ... losing?

"Who the hell are these people?!" I asked as I whipped my head around and saw several more individual scuffles happening amongst all the madness. It was time for a simple mathematics equation. If I had four dragons, and Joan had five, and I saw *six* more ... then what? Who the hell were they?

"You should shift," Gram told me as I stumbled forward and knelt down next to Reg and Joan. Neither of them were moving and that scared the shit out of me. I didn't exactly *know* Reg, and I was definitely not onboard for the whole 'arranged supernatural marriage' thing, but I didn't want him dead.

I really, *really* didn't want him dead.

"Reg," I said, turning him over and checking his pulse with shaking fingers. He was alive, just unconscious. *Thank fuck,* I thought as I breathed a sigh of relief and tried to do the same for Joan. She was ... oh god. As soon as I turned her over and saw that one side of her face was mutilated, I felt myself getting dizzy, my stomach twisting itself into knots. I was definitely *not* cut out for this shit.

"Shift, Arizona," Gram snapped at me again, reaching out and grabbing onto my arm with a ghostly hand. I could actually *feel* her fingers wrapping around my arm, shards of ice cutting into me and jump-starting my heart.

"I don't know how to fucking shift!" I screamed back, because Jesus H., *shifting* into a dragon wasn't exactly a trick they taught you working the counter at Starbucks. I crawled closer to Joan, ignoring the raw meat that was the left side of her face, and I untied the scarf around her neck, using it to staunch some of the bleeding. The woman was a bitch, for sure, but that didn't mean she deserved to die.

Gram reached out and took me by the chin, her ghostly nails digging into me like they used to do when I was a child and being punished for something.

"Keep calm and carry on," she said, and I almost laughed. That was a joke, right? An ill-timed one maybe, but still … "Arizona, if you don't get up and fight now, at least three people are going to die here tonight—possibly more."

"How could you know that?" I shouted back, trying to make sense of all the commotion happening in the yard—and believe me, there was a *lot* of it. "You can't possibly know that," I whispered as Reg groaned and rolled onto his side, coughing up a healthy amount of blood.

"Arizona, I'm a witch," Gram said, kneeling next to me in her houndstooth patterned skirt and jacket. "I get premonitions; I always have. Now, you can bloody listen to me or you can sit here and watch several people die—your choice."

With a sigh and a tight smile that stretched the wrinkles on either side of her mouth, she disappeared.

"Reg," I said, after I'd tied Joan's scarf around her head, stopping up at least *some* of the bleeding. "Are you okay?" Stupid question maybe to ask someone who'd just coughed up blood, but I wasn't exactly feeling *rational* in that moment.

Reg didn't even get a chance to answer me because suddenly, there was this strong pressure around my waist, like I'd been grabbed by a fucking anaconda. Up and off the ground I went, whisked away like a doll.

When I came face-to-face with the thing that was holding me, I just about lost it completely.

It was yet *another* dragon, but not one of the ones I'd seen before—a new one.

Its face was split in half like fucking Pac-Man or some shit, and its teeth were black, rotted and oozing pus from its gums.

When it hissed at me, the stench was almost unbearable. Bones protruded from the thinly stretched skin across its body, and its eyes ... they were just sockets of darkness, like pockets of shadow.

I knew right away that I was looking at the ... cuntmuffin? Shit if I could remember its proper name.

From behind the creature, a beautiful woman appeared, her hair the color of sunshine, her lips a crooked red smile that I was pretty sure was *not* lipstick but *blood.*

She paused next to the monster holding me and laid a hand on its side, leaning in close and whispering something in that mystical language the boys had used on me during the, uh, marking.

Slithering up next to her was a dragon that looked like it was made of fucking *metal,* its skin a shiny silver that was as unnatural as it was beautiful. It hissed at me when it caught me staring and I froze up completely.

"Whoa!" I yelled, holding my hands up defensively. "I really feel like there's been some sort of misunderstanding here? Maybe we all need to sit down and discuss it over whiskey?"

The woman with the bloodied lips, and the metal dragon both bared their teeth at me in a snarl, and the *thing* holding me tightened its grip. Sharp spikes of pain shot through me as its claws penetrated my flesh and I let out a yelping scream.

"Arizona, you shift your lazy ass into dragon form and teach this festering heap of shit who's boss around here!" Gram's ghost was hovering near my head and as she spoke, the grotesque creature turned his attention past me like he could see her.

For some reason though, the sound of my straitlaced grandmother swearing gave me the push I needed, where the threat of certain death had failed.

Screwing my eyes shut, to try and block out the distraction that was *kuntemopharn*, I searched frantically for the *seed of magic* that George had described to me in the sex shop and thankfully found it, sitting there in the dark of my mind, waiting for me. It wasn't as big or as bright as the ball I had returned to the shop assistant, but I instinctively knew it was *mine*.

With a quick mental high five for finally remembering this wanker's name, I stretched out my intentions toward the glowing blob and *willed* it to understand what I needed.

A warm shudder radiated through me starting from deep within my chest and flowing to my extremities, and I knew I must have succeeded when Grams whooped near my ear.

"Yes!" she yelled. "You did it, Duckie! Now kick his ugly ass!"

Oh yeah, just like that, huh Grams? Just ... kick his ugly ass. Yeah sure, no worries. I'll just ... ugh.

When my form had shifted, I'd slipped through the tight grasp Kuntemopharn had on me, my whole being turning to a sparkling aubergine colored mist before reforming me into my newly acquired dragon form on the grass some several yards away from the bad guys.

The woman with the bloody lips snarled something in that language I like, super needed to take Rosetta Stone classes on, her voice sounding like barbed wire scraping down a blackboard.

"Daniel," she said, and although I had no idea who she was talking to (maybe cuntmuffin had upgraded to a less humiliating sort of name), I could tell she was pissed. "Let's get the little bitch and drag her fat ass out of here."

Well shit. If that wasn't a bit brutal, then I was a purple dragon. Oh wait ...

My brain was teeming with new information, new skills that I could now use, and I realized quickly that this form had the collective knowledge of the men I was now connected to. It was a little unnerving but useful as fuck, as it taught me how to tap into my elemental powers without the trial and error of getting ripped into tiny pieces and then shoved down a storm drain.

Around me, the good guys were losing. Reg was out cold again, with a worrying pool of blood spreading beneath him while George and Shane took on another strangely elegant looking dragon, one that was simply a dance of smoke and shadows in the moonlight. Billy, ever the badass, had just stopped another one of the fuckers from biting Joan's head clean off her corpse ... er, body? I had no idea if she was alive or not by that point.

It was do or die. Literally. If I didn't do *something*, then we could all very well die here on this lawn.

Following my instincts, I drew up water from the ground, forming it into a hardened spear of ice and hurling it at the deformed and decaying dragon. The spear flew faster than any human could have thrown it, but at the last second the metal plated dragon threw a wing in its path, shattering it, the tiny pieces sprinkling all over the grass.

"Really? You're going to make this difficult, you little cunt?" the woman with the bloodied mouth snarled at me. I guessed she must not only be a misogynistic slut-shamer, but also their designated voice box.

Her powers must really suck if that was all she was good for.

Hell, maybe the only skills she had had to do with her mouth?

Rising to the challenge though, I pulled sparks from the fire Billy was wielding and fed it with wind to ignite the blazing ball before sending it hurtling toward cuntmuffin and his bitches. This time I followed the ball of fire with a hard gust of wind, forcing the blaze hotter so that when it hit the metallic lizard it melted a satisfying hole straight through her wing and splattering across Kuntemopharn's rotting face.

I was permitted a short moment of glee, watching the big bad guy collapse and struggle in the grass before he was back on his feet and flying at me. In his face, I saw my death, and it wasn't pretty.

Right as his full, rotten weight should have connected with me, a snarling mass of fur and teeth knocked him clean off course and tumbled with his momentum across the grass a small distance. Another blur of fur leapt over me to join in the fight and quickly I noticed we had gained some more allies. Suddenly, we were back on the winning team, and this wanker *knew* it.

His backup dragons retreated from their individual battles, attacking the wolves instead, who were ripping chunks of decaying flesh from Kuntemopharn's hide with their razor-sharp fangs. There were certainly some interesting outfits draped over those lupines, but I could tell right away that none of them were Britt—from the lack of pink vinyl, obviously.

The pony-sized wolves tore into the battle like they had a personal vendetta to take care of and hell, for all I knew, they really did. Glancing over my shoulder—it was a big, scaly, purple, muscly shoulder but a shoulder nonetheless—I noticed that more people from the party were coming our way.

A shout sounded in that ethereal elemental tongue, and I noticed right away that several of the dragons were pulling back and heading for the sewer grate—Kuntemopharn's rotting corpse among them. Eight separate forms slid into the shadows and disappeared into the sewage—a few dark shapes taking off after them.

Shifting back into my human form with the practiced ease of a dopey, gangly teenager with knobby knees, I scrambled to my feet and half-stumbled, half-sprinted across the grass to Reg's lifeless body. He was facedown in the sopping wet grass, his mother's mutilated body only feet away from him.

"Reg," I gasped, gently turning his face to the side, for fear of him drowning in the inch or so of water surrounding him. Okay, wait, maybe that was dumb. He *was* a water elemental after all.

As I brushed some of his blonde hair off his forehead, Charlie and several of Joan's other husbands came over and knelt beside us. I heard what sounded suspiciously like supernatural cursing in that strange, eerie elemental language (there it is again!), and then they were lifting her up like she was made of glass, carrying her in the direction of the house.

Either Reg was totally okay or else his dads cared more about his mum than him because they left him right there on the muddy ground in front of me.

"Where's Shane?" I asked when George appeared on Reg's other side, also in human form. He was missing a *substantial* chunk from his left arm. Like, *meat* was showing. I felt my stomach turn over and dropped my eyes back to the comatose elemental in front of me.

"I don't know," George said, and it sounded like he was panting pretty heavily. "We need a healer though," he continued through gritted teeth, flicking his brown eyes up to mine. "Let's get Reg inside."

"I've got him," Billy said, appearing from the bushes and bending down to grab his friend. He tossed Reg over one shoulder and stood back up, muscles ripping. It would've been, like, seriously fucking sexy in a different context. "You guys look for Shane; I don't feel him nearby though." Billy started walking and then paused when he noticed the wound in George's arm; one charcoal brow cocked up. "But don't take too long—you need a fucking healer like *now.*"

"I'll be fine," George said, and there was something about his face that was almost scary, a quiet simmering anger underneath that made me wonder what would happen if he was pushed to the edge. "Arizona, you're the spirit elemental here," he continued, lifting up his right hand and touching the bleeding wound with tentative fingers. At least it was on the side *without* the tree tattoo, right? Small miracles and all that. "Search for Shane's essence."

"His essence?" I asked, realizing then that I was breathing just as hard as he was. Glancing over my shoulder, I saw several werewolves sniffing around the grounds. Still no Britt— no way I'd miss that hot pink miniskirt. Guess she really was off doing the *Dances with Wolves* thing with the alpha male. I could only hope the sex was good and that he didn't have an ugly penis because I was going to have to hear *all* about it.

"How do I do that?" I asked, knowing there wasn't going to be an easy answer. A lot of this magic shit was sort of … intuitive. I slicked some wavy blonde hair behind my shoulders and tried to breathe. "Look deep inside yourself, you must," I whispered and George raised his eyebrows.

"Are you … making Yoda jokes right now?" he asked, but at least he almost smiled. That was something. "Yes, look inside and find the connection you have to each one of us. Try to follow that to its source. It should be easy to designate which belongs to Shane."

"I'll do my best!" I said, realizing that my hands were starting to shake. I think spare adrenaline was still coursing through me, making me feel like I'd downed ten large cups of coffee. I was hyper-fucking-active. Closing my eyes—because it just seemed right to do magical things with one's eyes closed —I searched for that glowing ball inside of me. I realized it was probably just my mind's way of rationalizing an impulse that felt natural but yet was impossible to understand. There was no *actual* glowing light ball inside of me, but that was the easiest way to perceive it.

I felt around for some sort of *connection* to the guys, not really expecting to find much. I mean, I'd known them a handful of days. That wasn't long to feel anything for anybody, was it?

But I guess when George said *connection,* he meant *magical connection.* Our little orgy had opened up all sorts of magical pathways inside of me.

Searching around, I felt the slightest tug in George's direction. When I probed at it with my mind, I could feel the cool, easy earthiness of his magic. Touching on that, I could almost feel my mind blooming with growing things, wet earth, the sweet heady scent of floral blossoms.

"I think I've got it," I said. Either that or this was just another part of my hallucinatory dream sequence and I'd soon wake up ... I opened my eyes, but the sight of the bloody water near my feet, the broken metal grate from the sewers, George's arm ... it was all too distracting. I snapped them closed again, took a deep breath, and felt for that wild twist of tornado that was Shane. If someone were to ask me to picture an air elemental in my head, I would've thought soft, wishy-washy, weak. But that wasn't Shane at all.

I kept searching, touching on the hot flaming brand that was Billy, the ... sultry ... fluidity that was Reg (of course that asshole would find a way to make water sexy), and something else … There was an electric tingle that traced right up my spine and into my skull, making me feel on edge, my teeth gritting against the buzz of energy coursing through my body.

Lightning struck several places around the yard; I couldn't *see* it with my eyes closed, but I could feel it.

"Fuck," George whispered. "Ari, are you alright?"

I was fine. But I really fucking wanted to know who this Warden guy was and why I was connected to him even though I hadn't met the fucking asshole. Guess our orgy was powerful enough that I vicariously had had sex with him, too. Figures.

"Fine," I breathed, moving on with my search until I found Shane.

As soon as I ran into the essence that was his, I could feel a slight breeze picking up stray bits of my hair. I wasn't sure if it was real or not, but it was comforting in a way. Shane was okay; he was alive.

And he definitely wasn't anywhere near here.

"He's not here," I said, opening my eyes again. This time, I didn't get distracted; I had a good lead on Shane's magic. It felt … like it was underneath us. "He's in the sewers," I said, paused, wetted my lips. "I think."

"The sewers," George said, and although there were a lot of plumbing and pipe jokes I could've made with that, I said nothing. You know, plumber lost in the sewers is funny and all that … "Okay," George said, and then he shifted back into his dragon form. "I'm going to look for him," he told me, flicking the long, curved length of his tail. Tiny leaves sprouted from it here and there. "Tell the others."

Before I could respond, he whipped forward and disappeared into the tunnel.

Fuck me running.

I was going to have to go after him, wasn't I?

I jogged back to the house, through the herd of werewolves, and inside.

"Billy," I snapped, relieved to see that Reg was actually sitting up, blood trailing down one side of his face. His mother ... I didn't see her anywhere. "Shane's in the sewers," I said, stomping one heeled foot for emphasis. "Like, way, way down in the sewers. George went after him, and so am I."

I turned before the boys could stop me and got about fifteen feet before there was one asshole on either side of me.

"Slow your roll, ST," Reg said, and I had a hard time explaining to myself why I was so fucking glad to hear him speak, see him standing up next to me, even if he *was* covered in blood. "You're not going anywhere without us."

"You're injured," I told him, trying to pull my arm from his grip. He was strong *as fuck,* Reg was.

"I'm fine," he said, but he didn't look it. I wasn't exactly sure how healers worked, but he didn't seem like he was ready to take on cuntmuffin again. "Once I shift, I'll be fine ..."

"Until you shift back," Billy said, sounding pissed off. He gave me a look and I swear, there was more than just metaphorical fire burning in those eyes of his. He was fucking madder than a wet hen, as Shane might say. "Our dragon forms are fluid, *elemental,*" he stressed, dragging me across the wet grass toward the sewer entrance. "But our human forms ... they're fucking meat sacks."

"Wow, Billy, really, your talents as a poet are simply *wasted,*" Reg said, scowling at him. "I know my own limits, okay?"

"Yeah? Well I know *your* limits better than you do. Sit your ass back and wait for us. Go round us up some backup." Billy pulled me from Reg's grip and toward the sewer entrance. I had no idea what we were going to find down there, but I could *feel*

Shane slipping further away from us, George chasing after him. "Stay close," Billy warned, crossing his arms over his chest. "And *stay* in dragon form."

He cocked a brow, like he was waiting for me to shift. Again.

"*Well,* I don't fucking know *how* I did it the first time, do I?" I half-shouted and Billy's eyes tightened, like he was really trying not to shake the shit out of me.

"Doll face, now really isn't the time for your self-doubting shit. Just give into it and it'll happen naturally. It's a part of who you are now …" He nodded encouragingly to soften the hard words. He was right though: Shane was lost somewhere deep in the sewer and an injured George was chasing after him. I needed to pull my shit together *fast* and go save them.

Taking a deep breath, I squeezed my eyes shut tight, as it was how I seemed to be getting all my 'magic' done these days. I let the tension and worry drain out of my body and instantly felt the *shift* washing over me like one of those fancy rainfall showers. Mental note: make my new husbands upgrade the bathroom when this was all over.

"'atta girl," Billy murmured, shifting into his own dragon form and nodding his huge scaled head at me, flames dancing down the back of his neck and spine like a mohawk. He tapped shiny black claws against the ground and ran his long tongue over white-white teeth. It shouldn't have been sexy, but … it kind of was anyway. "Come on then, Firebug. Stick close and point the way."

"Yes sir, my dear dragon captain," I said, slopping on a heavy dose of sarcasm—just to maintain my usual norm. Couldn't let a crisis derail me from snark and sarcasm, now could I?

230

"We're not fucking dragons." Billy's indignant voice echoed around the walled confines of the sewer as he took off with me tight behind him. Mm. After this was all over, I think maybe I *would* like to be tight behind him. Or rather, maybe I'd like him tight behind *me*?

Whoops, might take a bit of getting used to not to let my hormones derail *every* thought I was having down the road of sex, sex, sec. Fuck knows I didn't need to be thinking about Reg deep throating Shane earlier ...

"Never thought I'd find two men going at it as fucking hot as if they were doing me," I mumbled, like way louder than I intended. Shit echoed down here—it wasn't my fault!

"Seriously? Just ... focus on finding Skeeter, would you, doll?" Billy said, the flaming orange and red shape of his body twisting around corners and lighting up the darkness ahead.

It was a good thing my dragon form couldn't blush, or I'd be the color of a slapped ass right now. At least I assumed we couldn't. Shaking my head to clear it, I focused again on finding my connection to the air elemental.

He was even further away this time, and I had to carefully dodge the live wire that was my connection to the mysterious Warden.

"Got him!" I called to Billy and saw him cringe, as much as a dragon can cringe. Sorry, echoes again. Having sex down here would definitely suck; I was already loud enough as it was. And then there was that ball slapping thing ... in echo? No thank you.

"Lead the way, Ari—it'll be quicker than you trying to direct me."

Together, we flew through that sewer pipe at what felt like the speed of light, taking each turn and intersection with unwavering confidence that we were heading in the right direction. It was as easy as holding that thread that connected me to Shane and just … *pulling*. All of a sudden we were almost on top of them, both Shane and George.

At some stage, we'd crossed from the sewer into the storm water system and had just almost landed right on top of our missing lovers. The shock of it sent me straight back into my human form, and given my human form couldn't *travel the elements* like my dragon form could, I ended up plunged into a deep pool of ice-cold water.

For a moment, I flailed wildly under the water, freaking the fuck out that I was going to drown, but then remembered I could now control the elements—water being one of them. Trying to be delicate about it, I politely coaxed the water to bring me back to the surface, but must have thrown a little much *oomph* behind it because my body shot out like someone had just detonated a stick of dynamite.

"You okay, sugar?" Shane coughed as I landed *hard* on the concrete ledge both he and George were resting on. "Looks like you're getting a handle on those powers pretty quick?"

An incoherent groan bubbled out of me as I pushed myself up to sitting. I was still in my ridiculous bondage outfit and somehow even the stiletto boots had survived all the fighting and shape-changing, but I was soaked. My hair hung in front of my face in wet noodles and I had no doubt all of Britt's carefully applied makeup was halfway down my face. I bet my black eye looked particularly awful right about now.

"That bad, huh?" I muttered, noticing the looks on both Shane's and George's faces and interpreting it as *holy fuck, Ari, you look like death warmed up.*

"Don't be ridiculous, Arizona," Shane scolded with a gruff voice. "You're as pretty as a peach—always are. We're just starin' because your, ah ..." He waved his hand toward my chest and smirked.

"Oh for the love of fucking Vegemite," I growled, tucking my boob back into the stupid pleather top where it belonged. I guess it took just a smidgen more practice to get *all* my clothes back in the right place after shifting.

"Need me to check everything's in place at the other end, sug?" Shane winked at me and I fought back the urge to take him up on the offer. Damn sexy air elemental.

"Thanks, but I never did find my panties earlier." I meant it as a shutdown but there was a long pause while both George and Shane stared at me with heated gazes.

"I see that," Billy chuckled from behind me, where he must have just shifted back into human form. Of course after my abrupt exit from the water I had ended up on all fours with my ass in the air.

"Ahem," I fake coughed, sitting back on my ankles to hide at least a *little* bit of my dignity, "so what the hell, Shane? What are you doing down here? You had us all really fucking worried and George needs to see a fucking healer!" George was holding his arm awkwardly, but it didn't seem to be bleeding out which was odd, given the severity of the wound.

"I know," Shane grunted. "I'm holding an air bandage on it for him. We just couldn't quite work out how to get back to Charlie's house from here. These tunnels and pipes really all look the same ..."

"So what you're telling me"—I held back a smile—"is that you were up shit creek in a barbed wire canoe with a rusty teaspoon for a paddle until Billy and I found you?"

"I actually understood that one," George said, lighting up a bit. "She means we were fucked."

"Exactly!" I winked at him; George got me. "What were you doing all the way down here anyway?"

"Ah, when Kuntemopharn did his little disappearing act, I caught the tail end of him disappearing down the sewer, so I decided to follow and see if I could find out where the fuckers were camped out or some shit." Shane shrugged. I couldn't argue; it was sound reasoning.

"So did you?" I hated when people dragged out the suspense in their stories. Drove me nuts.

"No, but I did get some pretty useful information. Can we go back to the house though? I'm worried George and I won't make it back if we use much more energy down here." Shane really did look beat. His dark blue eyes were packing so many bags it was like he was going on holiday, and his broad shoulders were slumped with exhaustion.

"I guess so …" I grimaced. "Back into dragon form then?"

"Correct—although we're *not* dragons," George said playfully and I just rolled my eyes, sliding into my dragon form with considerably more ease than the last few times. Although, you know, still like a stumbling newborn calf.

"If it walks like a dragon, and talks like a dragon," I muttered under my breath.

"Still not a dragon, sugar." Shane's voice slid into my head like honey over a biscuit. "Let's go on and get back before we get caught in a turd-floater."

13

CHAPTER THIRTEEN

The four of us made quick work of getting back to the house as all I needed to do was follow the thread connecting me to Reg and we were back inside the library in no time. It was a pretty nifty trick, come to think of it.

"George you should get that arm seen to." I frowned as we all rematerialized into our human forms and he clutched at it, groaning.

"I'll take him to the healer and then we can reconvene in Reg's room. Sound okay, sugar plum?" Shane asked, raising an eyebrow at me. Thing was, last time one of us had used the word *reconvene,* we'd ended up in an orgy.

Not sure if that bothered ... or excited me.

Like I was going to argue the point now, while George was bleeding out.

"Of course," I said smoothly, my unconscious mind repeating *orgy, orgy, orgy* over and over again. "Go. We need to make sure Reg is okay anyway ..." I trailed off and gave Billy a look. Did we know if Joan was alive or not? Billy gave me a small head shake so I kept my mouth shut, waiting until the other two men left the room.

It wasn't my place to tell Shane and George that their foster mother might be dead.

"Do you think Joan ..." I began hesitantly, surprised that I even cared if the bitch was dead. Thing was, if she went now I wouldn't get the chance to prove her wrong about me.

"There you are," Charlie interrupted, coming into the library and pausing for a moment, staring down at the glass beneath his feet like he'd just realized this room was a bloody mess. When he lifted his face back up to stare at us, there were lines there I hadn't noticed before, like he'd aged a decade in the short time since I'd met him upstairs.

"Is Joan ..." Billy started, breathing in sharply, like he was preparing himself for the news.

"She's alive," Charlie said softly, rubbing both hands down his face, "but in bad shape." He paused for a moment and gave his pseudo-son a long look. "We have a couple of big jobs next week—including all those new bathroom installs down at the rec center. Do you think you and the boys can handle it?"

"As soon as I see what condition Reg and George are in," Billy told him, his boots crunching across the shards of glass as he walked over and gave the older man a one-armed hug, patting him roughly on the back in typical dude fashion. "Where's Reggie right now?"

"Upstairs with Joan," Charlie said, expression tight. "I think he had a concussion, a few broken ribs, a punctured lung. He's fine now, but he needs to sleep. And please, for the love of god, we owe that poor man a bathroom remodel—pro bono obviously."

"Healers have a *take no payment, creed,* Charlie," Billy said, lighting up a cigarette and nodding with his chin for me to follow. "You know that."

"Just install his new shower for me, William," Charlie said, grabbing a glass decanter from a cabinet against the far wall. "And stay the night, would you—just in case."

Billy stiffened, but I wasn't sure what that *just in case* was for—in case Joan died? In case Kuntemopharn and his allies came back? I had no idea.

I followed Billy out of the library and up the curved staircase, past the entrance to the veranda where we'd had our drinks, and then down the hall and up *another* set of stairs. He knocked lightly outside a pair of double doors that'd been left partially open, and then slipped inside.

Me, I just stood in the hallway feeling nervous and out of place. Felt a little weird to go into the boys' mother's bedroom and just, you know, *stand there.*

"You did well tonight," Gram told me, materializing next to me in her spectacles and houndstooth suit.

"Did I?" I asked, moving over to the banister and leaning my butt against it. All along the wall, various oil paintings were lined up, hanging from a picture rail. They were all predictably themed but also sort of ... *weird*—a fireplace with little fire lizards (salamanders, right?) crawling out of it, an ocean with mermaid tails protruding from the water, a tornado with a *face,* a tree crawling with small doll-like creatures hanging from its branches. The last one featured an electrical storm with purple, blue, and pink strikes dropping from thick, gray clouds.

Electricity.

I had another ... elemental, uh, boyfriend out there somewhere ....

"Are you even listening to me?" Gram asked, drawing my attention back to her. I kind of wasn't, but I nodded anyway. "There's not a lot I can do for you in my current state, but I will tell you this—for once in your life, please take this seriously."

"I take things seriously," I said, still unsure as to how I felt about Gram's ghost following me around. I mean, I was sorry she'd died but we were never really *close*. Having her around now ... I doubted much would change. "Are you going to tell me who my biological parents are?" I asked, but when I glanced over at her face, her expression was dire. "That bad, huh?"

"Arizona, your parents ... you just met them."

"I ... wait, *what*?!"

I felt my stomach drop and suddenly, my heart was racing like crazy again.

"That ... rotting thing was my parent?!"

"Not the *kuntemopharn*," she said, using the word easily, as if she was fluent in the elemental language, too. "But Daniel, and his wives."

"His *wives?!*" I asked, feeling a whole bunch of emotions rush over me at once. I was simultaneously disgusted *and* fascinated at the same time. But then something occurred to me ... "Wait, which one is my mother?" I asked, remembering Billy's wild story about *all* the elementals needing to, uh, come inside of me to get me pregnant.

"All of them, Duckie," she said, raising her eyebrows. "But I'm not going to explain how six women and one man collect their fluids in a single place. You can figure that one out on your own."

I just stared at her.

"My dad's a sexist polygamist prick with six wives?" I asked, and then realized that the cherry on top of my shit sundae was this—who the fuck was that metallic dragon?! I'd sort of been laboring under the impression that there were *four* elements, then I was told about a fifth and then a sixth ... and now a *seventh?!* Did I have *two* fucking elemental a-holes out there connected to me?

"Pot calling the kettle black," Gram warned, and then paused when Billy and Reg exited the room. Reg was clean, and wearing a fucking Pokemon shirt that was probably left over from his childhood. He smirked at me as soon as he saw me, so I figured everything was okay.

"Are you talking to yourself, ST?" he asked, glancing roughly in Gram's direction.

"How you're allowing that man to disrespect you like that ..." she began with a tired sigh. Gram pushed her silver spectacles up on her face.

"Gram was just explaining how I had *six mothers* and one father," I said, feeling the right side of my face twitch. "Weren't you, Gram?"

"Your father and your mothers were here tonight, yes. They're the ones that raised the *kuntemopharn* from the dead," she added, tucking that little nugget of shit into her explanation like it wasn't particularly important.

For me, you know, finding out that things could be raised from the dead at all came as a pretty huge shock.

"Necromancers?" I asked with a slightly dry, skeptical sort of laugh. "You're telling me that my parents are *necromancers?*"

"Your father is," Gram said grimly, "he's the spirit elemental."

"If women are so rare in this world," I scoffed, crossing my arms over my chest, "then how the *fuck* does that asshole have six wives?"

239

"Male spirit elementals are like male calico cats," Billy said which was sort of unhelpful since I didn't know shit about pussy. Heh. That was more Britt's thing than mine. Although there was that one time my senior year of high school … "Male calico cats are a one in three thousand phenomenon. Because being a spirit elemental is tied to the sex chromosomes, only women can technically fill that niche. That means your dad has an XXY chromosomal disorder called Klinefelter syndrome; only one in *ten thousand* male spirit elementals is fertile."

"Dude, you just lost me there," I said as Gram harrumphed next to me.

"If you'd paid more attention in school," she began, but I was already blocking her out—just like I'd done when she was alive.

"Does it matter?" Billy asked, lighting up yet another cigarette. "Who cares about that fucker anyway? As soon as the COCS Heads get ahold of him, he's fucking done for."

"He's my biological dad," I said, and felt satisfied when Billy actually choked on his next inhale. "And those crazy women—like the metal dragon—are my bio moms."

I crossed my arms over my chest, effectively propping up my tits and drawing Reg's eyes to the creamy mounds (I had to admit—I did have pretty sweet boobs).

"So, you plan on telling me why there's a metal elemental? Do we have one of those, too?"

"We don't know," Reg said, crossing his hands together behind his head. "And if we did, you've never fucked him so we have no way of tracking him down."

"The hell is that supposed to mean?" I asked, not caring that Gram was still standing there listening to the conversation.

"Well, clearly you've nailed Warden in the past," Reg continued even though Billy was giving him a *shut the fuck up right now* look. "Talk about a fucking coincidence …"

"*What*?!" My shriek bounced down the corridor and both men shushed me, glancing over their shoulders at the bedroom where Joan was recovering.

"Ari, just …" Reg took me by the elbow and quickly steered me down the hall to what must have been his bedroom. Inside, I found an adult's room, not a child's leftovers like with Shane. Hmm. And in here, it was just as grand, just as opulent as the rest of the house—four-poster bed, velvet curtains, heavy rugs, a fireplace as tall as I was.

"No, I will not *just* anything, Reginald!" I was yell-shouting, causing the words to lose a little of their impact, but my point must have gotten across because Reg sighed dramatically while Billy groaned and flopped himself down in an expensive looking leather armchair. The entire fucking house was *minted* and these four were trying to tell me they had to move into Gram's mansion because they didn't have a pot to piss in? Yeah right.

"Look, Sugar Tits," Reg started again, holding his hands up defensively, "I don't know why you're acting so surprised here. You're a smart girl—surely you've noticed you have a connection with energy? Otherwise, where the fuck all the lightning coming from?"

"I thought that when we all … *you know*"—this was my not so subtle euphemism for *screwed five ways to Sunday*—"with the runes and the magic orgasms …" Okay, it sounded a bit silly out loud, now that I thought about it.

"You thought what, Firebug? That you'd somehow magically fucked Warden through the cosmos?" Billy snorted at

241

his own joke, but that was exactly what I *had* thought happened.

"But ... I've never fucked a Warden before ..." I flailed and then petered off. How could I have slept with another elemental and not even known? I mean, surely the *magic* would've been a dead giveaway?

Gram's spell, maybe? It made sense, didn't it? If she'd cloaked my true identity from the world ...

"Are you sure?" Billy asked with a brow cocked, his smirk as sharp as sin. "Because I'm pretty sure half the girls I've fucked in the past gave me fake names."

"Yes," I growled, "I *am* sure—I'm not nearly as big a slut as you. And honestly? That doesn't come as much of a surprise, *William*—if we'd ended up in a one-night stand, without all this magic shit tying us together, I'd have given you a pseudonym and then cut and run, too."

"Wow. Defensive much? Not what I meant, Ari." He flicked his cigarette butt into the air and snapped his fingers, incinerating it completely. "I just meant, it's unlikely Warden's using his real name, you know? If he hadn't wanted us to track him down, then it stands to reason he was operating under a fake name."

My knees suddenly seemed incapable of holding my weight any longer and I sat heavily on the edge of Reg's king-size bed. If this really *was* his childhood bedroom repurposed then *damn.* What *kid* needed a king-size bed, I had no idea.

"Ok, let's ... let's look into that later." Digging up skeletons from my shitty dating past didn't exactly seem like the most relaxing way to end a stressful day. For now, what are we going to do about Kuntemopharn?" See, I could be serious when I needed to be. Grams didn't know what the hell she was talking about.

"Well, we need to kill him. Isn't that what your dead grandma told you?" Reg asked, stretching out on the bed beside me. His Pokemon shirt lifted to show his smooth expanse of abs, highlighted with swirling ink.

I lost my focus momentarily.

"Well that's an awfully rude way to refer to your guardian ghost." Grams sniffed, touching her pearls like she was terribly offended, then disappeared again. Old bitch knew how to act, I'd give her that.

"Ya'll need to hear what we just found out from the COCS Heads," Shane said, letting himself into the room without knocking. George followed close behind him and gave me a small smile.

My heart flip-flopped, but I just tossed a bundle of dirty blonde curls over my shoulder and pretended I was too cool to care.

"George, is your arm okay?" I asked, running my gaze over him for any lingering signs of injury. He seemed totally fine though.

"Good as new, Blossom," he said, and took a seat next to me on the bed. His freshly healed arm brushed against mine and the addictive scent of wildflowers and moss reached my nose.

"What did you learn, Skeeter?" Billy asked, and I cringed at Shane's nickname. It was so hard to picture myself ever falling in love with a man named *Skeeter*.

Whoa. Where the *fuck* had that thought just popped out of? *Ugh, focus, you lust-blinded fool!*

"Turns out the elementals helping Kuntemopharn are the same ones that went rogue from the California storm back around thirty years ago. They've raised him using their male spirit's necromancy power," Shane informed us, not having heard the information Grams had just dropped on me, about them being my bio parents. "They know about Ari somehow, know that she's the strongest damn spirit we've seen in a while; they'll be coming back for her. No doubt about it."

"Yeah, they know about her because she's their kid," Billy informed Shane and George, flicking out another cigarette. He must be really stressed, I hadn't seen him smoke quite so many in quick succession before.

"What?" George asked, shocked, and I just shrugged.

"Oh, and Reg spilled the beans that I've probably fucked Warden before and not even known who he was." I was pissed. This whole thing was bullshit. I wished Grams would reappear so I could wring her scrawny neck. Obviously I knew that wouldn't solve my problems,but it'd damn sure make me feel better. Besides, she was dead anyway, so no harm done, right?

"I see …" Shane drawled, watching me with curious blue eyes, "but you don't know who and when, huh?"

"Jesus fucking Christ, you make me out to sound like Britt." I wasn't dissing my girl—she just really loved the dick. "I wasn't exactly a virgin when I met you guys, so stop acting shocked that I could've slept with your buddy somewhere down the line."

"That's for sure," Reg snorted, probably thinking of our very first time together. You know … when I let him and Shane double plunge my drains in Gram's bathroom? Yeah. That time.

"There's no 'could have' here, sug." Shane's honey-like voice softened the words. "You *have* fucked Warden somewhere along the line or we couldn't have completed the *marking* ceremony when we did."

I racked my brain. There was that one guy at the rock concert, when we fucked in the bathroom. Or the dude I went on all of three failed dates with from my yoga class? A handful of others, too, but all of them, *all of them*, I had used protection with. In this day and age, you couldn't be too careful so I had never gone without … except once.

Groaning, I dropped my head into my hands. Surely not. What were the odds? Fuck a hairy dingo.

"You thought of someone?" George prompted, sliding his warm hand onto my knee in what was probably meant as a comforting gesture, but my over-sexed body took as a come-on.

"Yes, no, I don't know. I need to talk to Britt. In the meantime, what are we doing about cuntmuffin?"

"Kuntemopharn," Shane corrected, "is hiding out in an abandoned pipe system on the far side of town. I suggest we take the fight to him before he has a chance to strike at us unawares again."

"I agree." Billy nodded, giving me a long, lingering look and then lighting up yet another smoke. "Reg, let's go and see what sort of backup COCS is willing to provide. They're the Committee of Combined Supernaturals, after all. Maybe the wolves or vamps want to pitch in and help?"

"I *guess,*" Reg agreed reluctantly, rising to his feet and tossing a sexy look my way before following the surly fire elemental from the room. I sort of felt like I was being set up— left with Shane, the original instigator of the supposed fight with Warden, and George, the mediator.

Fucking Billy.

Dickhead.

Or rather, *pierced* dickhead to be more accurate.

"So do you want to talk about who this guy is?" George prompted, his thumb drawing small circles on the inside of my knee, making me groan. I *still* wasn't wearing any fucking panties.

"Not particularly," I said, trying not have a full-blown meltdown. I mean seriously? Of all the men in this world, the one guy that I'd actually totally fallen for … was an elemental? And not just any elemental, but one of *my* like, destined chosen or whatever?

Warden, huh? I mean, there had to be a time or two that I wasn't thinking of that I didn't use protection, like a drunken one-night stand or something … There was just no friggin way that Max Cornwall was Warden. Just no. Nuh-uh.

"You know," George said, leaning back on the bed and looking for all the world like a fucking god. I mean, who has abs like that? And body fat? Psh. Not on this guy. No human being looked this good (except for Channing Tatum, of course). His skin was that shimmery bronze that all pathetically pale people (myself included) go for at the tanning bed but can never quite achieve. "You can talk to us about anything; we're in for the long-haul, Arizona."

"So you *say*," I told him skeptically, even though in reality all I wanted to do right then was put my head on his chest and go to sleep with the sound of his heart beating against my ear (totally corny and lame, I know). "But I don't know you guys from Adam. Theoretically, I get that we're supposed to function as a unit or some shit, but …"

"Then get to know us," George said, lifting his brown eyes up to stare at Reginald's ceiling. He frowned and I was prompted to follow his gaze. Then I saw what he was looking at, and I frowned, too.

"It's a mirror," I said, feeling my right eye twitching.

"It's a mirror," George confirmed as Shane kicked off his boots, pants … okay, wow. Shane was taking off *everything*. Once he was fully stripped down, he just climbed up Reginald's king-size bed like we owned the place, tucking all eight inches of … I mean all six foot whatever of himself beneath the covers.

"What would he need a mirror for?" I asked as George dropped the burnt umber color of his eyes back down to me and lifted the corner of his mouth in a slight smile. It was almost enough to make me forget about Warden-who-couldn't-possibly-be-Max-Cornwall.

"I thought you said you were experienced?" George joked as Shane chuckled from beneath the covers, propping his face on one sculpted, beautifully masculine arm.

"I mean, I get that a mirror on the ceiling is like, the typical sleazy dude fuck fetish, but you're telling me he used it as a teenager? Teenagers don't need fetishes—they're all just massive bundles of hormones. When did you guys move out? After college?"

"Well," George started, dragging the word out long enough to make me suspicious. "We've been looking for our spirit elemental for so long that we haven't had much of a chance to set up a permanent place of residence."

He smiled at me, like *that* would make things better.

My eye was twitching again.

"So … when did you move out? Twenty-five? Twenty-six …?"

George paused and ran his fingers through his hair, gently tousling the brunette strands before he stood up and started stripping. As I looked around, I realized that not only was this room bigger than Shane's childhood bedroom, but also … it didn't have any race cars. Or like … like any childhood things *at all*. Plus, the mirror …

"Oh my god, you guys live with your parents still," I said, feeling a wave of disgust roll over me.

"Not anymore, sugar," Shane drawled from under the covers, rolling onto his back and putting his hands behind his head. "Now we live with *you*."

"But … you had cars in your room …" I said and the corner of Shane's lip quirked up on one edge.

"That was *our* childhood room," he explained and then gestured up at the ceiling. "Would you mind getting the lights, sweet thing? I'm worn slap-out."

I stood up, but George put a hand on my arm and stopped me from heading for the switch.

"Practice makes perfect," he said, and I realized then that he wanted me to *magic* the lights off. I just stared at him.

"So you guys just all live in the same room?" I asked, wondering if their jokes about being ten percent bisexual were maybe a little off the mark. If they slept in the same bed together every night, didn't that make them at least twenty or thirty percent? Thank you Kinsey sliding scale of sexuality …

"We did as children," George said and when he realized I was definitely *not* going to be using my Warden-please-don't-be-Max-Cornwall powers, he moved over and turned off the lights himself. But not before, you know, slipping his pants off and exposing his, um, tree branch and berries to me. "We even cuddled up in that giant bed together. But when we got a little older, we started moving into our own rooms."

"And Warden?" I asked as George sighed and cast a glance over at Shane. It was dark, but silver beams of moonlight were slanting into the room and illuminating the two mens' faces enough that I could see their expressions. Shane … was really not fucking happy.

"And Warden," George confirmed, and before he could stop me, I was heading out and into the hall where I bumped into Billy and Reg having a private conversation. Fuckers. Off to check out backup, my ass.

"Where's Warden's room?" I asked and they both paused to stare at me like I'd sprouted antlers. Not that that would be too crazy weird or anything, considering all the shit I'd been through lately. I mean, shapeshifting into an elemental dragon was totally cool, so why not a big velvety rack o' moose horns?

"Why the fuck do you need to see his room?" Billy asked as I crossed my arms over my vinyl barely-there top and stared him down. "What does it matter? It's not like he's planning on coming back anytime soon."

"Tell me or I'll just start opening random doors and looking."

Billy sighed and shoved his hand through his charcoal hair like I was the most annoying creature to ever walk the planet. Reg just stood there and looked at me like he felt sorry for me which was pathetic—*he* was the one with a mirror on his ceiling.

"Third door on the left," Billy said, and I was gone, heading for that room like it would hold all the answers. Without hesitation, I opened the door and stepped inside, shutting it behind me and then flicking on the lights.

As soon as electricity bathed the room ... I knew.

I fucking *knew.*

"Jesus H. Christ," I whispered as I moved into the room and paused at the edge of a black bedspread, neatly made and dust free, as if Max ... *Warden* had been here just hours before. On the nightstand, there was a picture of all five boys, four of those faces newly familiar to me ... and one of them dear. "You motherfucker," I said, gritting my teeth. Even though I knew that *I* had been the one to run away, somehow that didn't make Warden's absence in my life hurt any less. I wanted to maybe castrate him and shove his balls down a storm drain ... That is, if I ever saw him again.

He had no social media presence, no online presence at *all* really, and if he didn't even bother to contact his mother … How was I ever supposed to find him?

Not that I wanted to, you know, because I so didn't.

I studied the picture, Warden's hair black with a red streak down the front, haphazardly spiked into some sort of stupid mohawk or faux hawk or whatever the fuck. But it was his eyes, those two sharp pools of liquid jade that had my heart pounding.

"Max …" I whispered to the picture, feeling like he was right there staring back at me. "You fucking asshole."

"Sweetheart?" George's soft voice called through the door. "Do you mind if I come in?"

Did I mind? I didn't even know … My brain felt like it was exploding.

"Sure," I replied hesitantly and he slipped through the door, closing it behind him. He'd thrown on a pair of loose boxer shorts with *My Pipe Can Make You Gush* printed across the butt. They hung low on his hips, drawing my attention to his drool worthy V that pointed down at the good bits …

"Ari, are you thinking dirty thoughts right now?" George grinned, snapping my attention back to his face. My own heated a little at getting caught out like that, but I just shrugged and held up the picture.

"Warden, huh?" *Yes, good work, Arizona—change the subject.*

"Yup." George sat on the edge of the bed beside me and took the picture from my hands. "I take it you recognize him then?"

"*Max Cornwall* is what he said his name was. We were best friends in college. Max, Britt, and I were practically joined at the hip. We did *everything* together until we all got really damn hammered one night." I could hear the bitterness in my voice as I said it. It wasn't Max that I was mad at after all these years—it was myself.

"And what happened?" George prompted, not pushing me for answers but just … softly suggesting that it was okay to confide in him. And I wanted to. George got me. Or at least he got *this* part of me. The messed up, closet-introvert, commitment-phobe that ran from her first love.

"After Britt passed out in the bathroom—probably the *only* time she's ever passed out—Max and I kept drinking and one thing led to another … He told me he loved me and I just *panicked*. The second he fell asleep I grabbed my shit and ran." Rubbing my eyes, I groaned and lay back on Max's bed. Warden's, I mean. *Warden's* bed. "I took a semester off school and went to stay with my mum in Australia. When I came back, he was gone."

"So I take it you must have …" George paused, raising his eyebrows suggestively and I grinned.

"Fucked bareback? Yeah, Woody, we did. I guess that's how I got these powers, huh?" George was still sitting on the end of the bed, looking down at me where I was lying on my back, and for a moment I got a bit distracted in the calm of his tree bark eyes.

"I imagine so …" he murmured, shifting to straddle my legs. He leaned his weight on palms planted on either side of me, so his face was directly above mine. "So what now, Arizona Smoke? Are you going to run from us, too? When we tell you that we love you, will we find your shit gone in the morning?"

"When?" I squeaked, a little breathlessly. This wasn't fair, asking me questions like this when I was already in shock with the whole bio parents news and then the Max-is-Warden dumped on top of that! Not to mention with George's delicious body so close to mine I could practically feel his body heat warming me from the inside out. My skimpy pleather outfit was still soggy, and an involuntary shiver raced through me.

"Yes, Blossom. *When*. What do we have to do before then, to convince you to stay?" George moved his weight onto one elbow, picking up the other hand and trailing it ever so gently down my bare arm.

"Aren't we getting a little ahead of ourselves here?" I laughed nervously, my skin pebbling under his fingers and sending flutters to my belly.

"Are we?" He raised an eyebrow over one rich oak eye. "Sorry, Blossom, I didn't mean to come on too strong ..." Abruptly he pushed up off the bed and stepped away from me. His sudden absence was filled with a rush of cool air and I mentally kicked myself for being such a fucking scaredy cat. What the hell was so wrong with me that even the *idea* of love from these guys sent me into a tailspin?

"I didn't mean ..." I trailed off in a huff of frustration, because that's exactly what I *did* mean. Ugh, why couldn't I get my shit together? These four incredible, gods of men wanted to be with me. Britt would have been out ring shopping to seal the deal already, but here I was agonizing over the *prospect* of them using the L word.

"Don't worry about it, sweetheart." George smiled and the expression lit up his face, like sunshine on flower petals or some shit. "We aren't going anywhere; we'll wear you down sooner or later."

"I shouldn't *need* wearing down," I muttered, mostly to myself, but sat up and grabbed his hand to tug him back to me. George was like valium to my anxiety. Something about touching his skin just calmed me like nothing I'd ever experienced before.

"Come on back to Reg's room, Blossom. You're exhausted and probably dying to get out of that outfit ..." He raised an eyebrow at me in a teasing way, running a single palm down the smooth, bronze perfection of his belly. Basically, it was impossible to look away. "Which I have no issues assisting you in, but I'll understand if you need some space." George paused with his fingers teasing the waistband on his borrowed shorts before slipping them inside and running his tongue over his lower lip in pleasure. "I wouldn't ever want to pressure you."

"Fucking Christ, I can't decide if you're a nice guy or a perv ..." I grinned, letting George pull me to my feet with the hand he removed from his shorts. As I regained my balance in the stupid boots that I couldn't wait to take off, I braced my other hand against the smooth expanse of his chest.

"Maybe a little bit of both?" He smirked, dipping his head just the fraction of space between us and pressing his lips to mine. It wasn't a demanding kiss, or even a particularly passionate kiss. It was more of an invitation kiss ... and it was an invitation I *badly* wanted to accept.

Sliding my hand up from his chest, I gripped the back of his neck, pulling him closer and answering his unspoken question with a parting of my lips. A small, surprised noise slipped from him as he clearly hadn't expected me to reciprocate, but as his mouth slanted over mine and his tongue slipped inside, I felt a tingling rush all over and knew my runes had just lit up.

"Damn, Blossom," George chuckled, pulling away after a moment, "we're going to need sunglasses if this keeps happening."

I snorted a laugh. Fuck, he was right. My skin was all kinds of lit up like a goddamn Christmas tree, but now that I knew about Max—*Warden*—I could see the now obvious gaps in between the other four swirling patterns. Bloody hell. Max really *was* an elemental, wasn't he?

Guess I had a type and it wasn't as simple as dark or light hair—it was a species thing.

"Come on, let's get out of this room. It feels like Warden's watching us in here …" George murmured, taking my hand and leading me out of my former best friend's, first love's, and missing husband's bedroom.

Back in Reg's room, stretched out underneath the pornographic ceiling mirror, Shane was waiting for us. His tattoos danced in a wicked splash down both arms, across his hands, his chest … his junk.

"Where are the others?" I asked, looking around for Reg and Billy, and seeing no one else in there. Shane was still gloriously naked, his ink demanding attention; it would have been rude of me *not* to look… right?

"They're speaking with COCS, Honey Doll," Shane drawled, raking his eyes all over me where I stood at the foot of the bed in all my drowned rat glory. Maybe they were into this look? They were plumbers, after all. Drowned rat might be right up their pipe?

"Hmm, well maybe the two of you might help me out of this wet outfit?" I suggested. Fuck it. Maybe all I needed to break through my emotional hang-ups was some seriously good pipe cleaning.

"Well, shoot," Shane said, letting his mouth turn up at the edges in a good ol' boy grin. "That just dills my pickle, seein' you all excited like that."

"Don't let your pickle get … too dilled," I said, even though I had no fucking clue what that expression meant. It sounded dirty though, right? Like way dirty. "Because this doesn't *mean* anything—it's just sex."

I turned around and scooped some soggy, muddy blonde hair over one shoulder.

Heh.

Glancing down I could see some dried blood and bits of leaves between my tits. Not the most attractive look in the world ... As George's fingers found my zipper, I let out a deep, long exhale that sounded a little desperate—even to me.

Damn. Guess almost getting murdered sort of ... wet my plumbing, so to speak.

"Any chance I, uh, might be able to take a shower first?" I asked as George took all of, you know, two seconds to pull my zipper down. I was basically wearing a top made for a fucking doll; there wasn't exactly a lot of fabric involved.

"Shower?" Shane said with a small sigh. I didn't say anything, but you know, he *had* sort of climbed into bed right after being down in the sewers ... At least he was naked, so hopefully he hadn't tracked shit in there. "Sounds like a plum fine idea."

Swinging out of bed, I could very clearly see the full, er, erect length of his wrench, covered from base to head in ink. Musta hurt like a bitch, getting his Johnson tatted and all that.

Before I could even muster up a single logical thing to say, George's hands were on my skirt, pulling the zipper down ... pushing the fabric over my hips. And since I was no longer wearing underwear, that basically left me ... nude and in stiletto boots.

I spun around quickly enough that I smacked George in the face with my hair. Didn't look like he cared though. In fact, he didn't quite look like *such* a nice guy anymore either. There was this primal male energy about him, this desire that was palpable. I could taste it on the back of my tongue.

George wanted to fuck me.

Like, *now.*

"Shower?" I said, raising a brow and moving around him, circling the foot of the bed and pausing on the other side to take off my boots. I wasn't sure if it was an earth magic thing or what, but something about George made *me* feel primal too (me? primal? I was a barista not a wildcat). But still … There was this answering feminine heat inside of me that wanted George to take me, claim me … and that wanted to take him and claim him, too. Eww. "My women's studies professor would so kick my ass right now …" I murmured as I chucked the boots and watched George push his boxers—they *had* to be borrowed from Reg, they were just too stupid—down his muscular hips.

My breath caught, and I turned away, feeling the already semi-soreness between my legs throb with more want, need, desire. *Greedy bitch.*

Moving over to the half-open door where Shane had disappeared, I pushed aside the elaborately carved wood and just … sort of stood there gaping.

"There are *some* perks to living in a family of professional plumbers," George whispered from behind me, coming up close and putting his hands on my shoulders. He kneaded my sore flesh with firm fingers, untangling about a million knots that I didn't even know I had.

"This isn't a … bathroom," I whispered, licking my lips and feeling steam from the running water kiss across my face. Wait … hadn't I done something pretty similar to this with Reg the other day? Shane in the shower … another man standing beside me …

Uh-oh.

"This is a palace," I finally finished, groaning as George crowded in even closer, teasing my lower back and ass with the hardened length of his shaft. If he were to push me over and just get to it, well, I wouldn't exactly complain.

"Shall we get in?" George whispered, replacing his cock with his hand and putting just enough pressure on my lower back to guide me across the seamless marble floor beneath my bare feet. It was *heated.* That was sort of a thing for me, heated floors. I'd once read an article that my favorite rock band of all time—Beauty in Lies—had heated floors in their tour bus. I'd become obsessed.

One entire wall of the massive bathroom (it was larger than Gram's living room, kitchen, and dining room combined) was a gorgeous polished soapstone counter, the jade color reminding me disturbingly of Max's ... *Warden's* ... eyes. There were *six* fucking sinks there, too. Six. Six sinks.

"Talk about prepared," I whispered, but it was sort of hard to care about the twenty foot ceilings, stained glass windows, massive soaker tub and ... never mind. I no longer blamed the boys for refusing to move out of their parents' house. Shit, I was selling Gram's place and moving *in.* "You knew I was coming, huh?"

I gestured lamely at the row of sinks.

"We hoped for it," George whispered, voice low and sultry, almost a *growl.* A growl. But not like a bad boy Billy asshole growl, but ... something bestial, animal. It called to every instinct I had inside of me and my runes flashed bright, reflecting off the wall of mirrors, the shiny floors, the huge glass doors that showed me every inch of Shane's naked form wrapped in steam.

"Hop on in and don't be shy," Shane said, lathering a loofah with *lots* of soap. I wondered what he was planning on doing with that ... As long as he didn't try to stick it up my cooch like

Christian Grey did to Ana Steele in *Fifty Shades*, then I was good with it.

He held out a warm, soapy hand and I took it, stepping into the marble expanse of the shower and letting him pull me into the hot stream of water.

There were fucking jets *everywhere*—including the ceiling and three of the four walls.

Really though, who could blame me for wanting to get in? It was a shower to die for and I was a *very* dirty girl.

The hot water pounded down on my aching muscles with a pressure that could only be described as supernatural while George stepped in behind me, his hands on my waist.

"Here, let me help you clean up a little, Sugar," Shane purred, letting a little dragon bleed through into his voice so it came out rough and wild. Using his soaped up loofah, he began scrubbing gentle circles on my skin.

He started innocently enough at my shoulder, then quickly descended his soapy sponge to circle lower, dragging its rough surface across the skin of my chest and then lower, dipping between my breasts and then skirting beneath one of them. My breath caught in anticipation as his knuckles brushed lightly across the underside on my left boob, but that's all he did before switching hands and soaping the other side.

The look in his eyes told me everything I needed to know about how much he was enjoying torturing me, even if his rock-hard wrench hadn't already given it away.

"Shane …" I hissed, as his loofah circled closer to my nipple but dodged it right at the last minute.

"Yes, Arizona?" He smirked, using his empty hand to cup my other breast but still avoiding my granite nipples which were practically begging for attention.

"Shane, don't be mean; Ari's had a hard day," George murmured from behind me, his own *hard day* pressing against my lower back and making me lean into him instinctively.

"Ah, of course, where are my Southern manners?" Shane drawled, turning up the charming gentleman routine which was so deliciously at odds with his tattooed pipe tapping me on the stomach. Although it was very gentlemanly of him to *finally* quit fucking around and pay a little closer attention to my good bits.

Squeezing out a bit more soap onto my chest, he then tossed the loofah aside and cupped both breasts in his huge, calloused hands, this time grasping my aching nipples within his thumb and forefinger of each hand and rolling them gently. Sharp waves of pleasure radiated from each peak, rolling through me and soaking my sinkhole way more than the shower had already done.

George tilted my face back towards him and claimed my lips in a kiss which was totally at odds with the gentle one he'd given me in Max's room. Maybe not such a nice guy after all?

"Fucking Christ," I muttered, when he paused for a breath and Shane leaned in to take his place, grabbing my lips in his with more fever, more domination; it only intensified my need for them both.

Shane's fingers still held my rigid nipples and as he kissed me, he tightened his grip ever so slightly, causing my back to arch and push forward in his hands.

George snagged a loofah of his own off the rack under the main showerhead and began trailing it down my spine, scrubbing in gentle circles, then sliding around my waist to my stomach.

"So, is this how you guys shower normally, soaping each other up and all that?"

Shane chuckled and dropped his soapy hand to his cock, curling his fingers around the inked length of his shaft, sliding his fist up and down *niiiice* and slow.

"Not exactly, sweetheart," he said with a slight smirk, "this is just for you."

I swallowed hard, feeling my lids flutter closed as George dropped his hand lower ... lower ... slicking the soapy loofah across my landing strip—I know, tacky, but Britt convinced me over the phone to get it waxed like that. Pretty sure she still had that lightning bolt down there—unfortunately she'd sent me a picture and I'd had to actually see it.

"Your mind's wandering," George said dropping just a *little* lower and teasing my clit with the tips of two fingers. "I think we need to teach you to focus," he whispered, sliding his tongue along the shell of my ear, sucking my lobe between his teeth.

The whole bathroom smelled good—like jasmine rustling in a night breeze—but I couldn't decide if it was the men or the soap ...

"My mind always wanders," I whispered, voice barely audible above the sound of the running water. "I guess I'm just complicated like that."

"Maybe you've never had the right sort of attention?" George said, dropping his loofah and sliding his fingers down and between my thighs, parting my folds and pushing into that desperate ache between my legs.

"Maybe not ..." I breathed as George pushed in all the way to the knuckles, and I leaned back into the warm, wet planes of his body. If these guys wanted to try to top the best sex I'd ever had then go for it—whether they did or not, this was sort of a win-win situation for me. Unfortunately, when I thought really hard about my favorite sexual experiences, I kept landing on two: the magic orgy (I know, I know, but it *was* good) and that night with … Well, *you know.*

George kissed along the side of my neck, water running down my throat and across my bare body, droplets teasing my nipples, slicking all the soap down the drain. I watched as Shane worked himself up with his hand, fingers sliding along the inked length of his shaft.

He did it with this *look* on his face, like he knew how fucking hot he was.

Asshole.

George added a third finger, and this little gasp burst from my throat, making Shane chuckle.

"I think you found the right spot," he said, leaning his back against the wall and putting on a show for me. I didn't want it to work, but it did. As George worked my body with his hand, I watched Shane do the same to himself. Even though we weren't touching, it was like we were in sync. As his orgasm approached, I felt mine sneaking up right along with it.

And then George *stopped,* pulling his hand away. I was instantly reminded of Reg leaving me high and dry inside the incubi/succubi hideout.

"You're not leaving me like this," I said, panting heavily. But George was already capturing my face in his hands, turning me to face him, and kissing me, his tongue teasing along the bottom curve of my lip before slipping into my mouth. The way he kissed me … I knew he wasn't done yet.

Behind me, Shane stepped close, wrapping his hands in my hair. At first, I was just surprised he'd managed to pry them away from his cock, but then I realized what he was doing.

He was *washing* my hair for me, firm fingertips digging into my scalp and massaging in slow, easy circles.

Screw hand jobs, oral, double penetration … now *this* was the shit.

"Nobody's leaving you all hot and bothered, sugar," Shane whispered in my ear, making me shiver. It wasn't enough that I had hot naked men on either side of me, but one was holding my face and kissing me with this easy possessiveness that I should've hated, but actually sort of liked and the other was washing my fucking hair.

I almost came right there, orgasmed in their arms without a single person touching me anywhere below the belt.

George continued to kiss me as Shane washed the soap from my hair, conditioned it, and then rinsed it again, teasing the back of my scalp with his fingers, trailing them down my neck … poking me in the back with his massive pipe.

"There," he said as George finally released my lips and drew an aching groan from my throat. I wasn't *done* kissing him. I felt like a teenager when he was around, like I could lay there for hours and just kiss. I hadn't done that since I was seventeen years old. "All clean. Now, sugar, you ready for this?"

He hit a button on the wall and all the jets stopped, just like that, leaving the three of us in a sudden quiet with nothing but heartbeats and steam to distract from the nakedness of our bodies.

"Yeah," I managed to say, "bed."

Before I could even think to take a step out of the shower, George was scooping me up and *carrying* me against the bronzed perfection of his chest, laying me out flat on the bed beneath the horrible mirror. Looking up, I could see that every inch of my skin was covered in runes, the shapes glimmering gently, like gold leaf in a beam of afternoon sunshine.

"These are never going away, are they?" I asked as George crawled over and took up my left side while Shane knelt on the edge of the bed. They both followed my gaze upward and stared at my naked body, reflected back at me with wet blonde hair curled around my face, my nipples pebbled and hard, my skin pale against the dark bedspread.

"We'll make you a glamour," George said, laying his body out alongside mine.

"Like the old Irish bitch from next door was using?" I asked, feeling my heartbeat pick up speed as his dark eyes met mine.

"Exactly. It's a form of magic that cloaks a person's true form from the outside world." George ran a single finger down the length of my body, over my rib cage, the curve of my hip … The pleasure was exquisite. "We can get one that lasts months for relatively cheap …"

He smiled at me, this sweet slow smile that promised dirty things would happen in the dark.

"Lights?" I asked and George raised his brows like he was waiting for me to do it, goddamn it. I could've sworn I'd turned those off … but some asshole had turned them back *on* again after we'd headed off to shower. I felt like it was on purpose.

"Or you can leave them on," Shane drawled, leaning forward and raising a dark brow at me. "I don't mind havin' a clear view where the sun don't usually shine."

The lights snapped off with a little spark, and I had a feeling they might not turn on again without some intervention in the, uh, electrical panel. I think I'd blown a few spark plugs.

Shane chuckled.

"Looks like all we gotta do to get you to use your magic is piss you off. Seems easy enough." Shane paused and even though I couldn't *see* him smiling, I could feel it. He was smirking at me. "Now, about that blow job you promised …"

I sat up and pretended to glare—hoping he could see at least *some* of my pissed off facial expression in the few stray shafts of moonlight. I didn't want him to know exactly *how* tempting that offer really was …

"Straddle me, Arizona," George said, drawing my attention back to him. He laid back into the pillows and gestured at his chest. "I want to taste you."

Oh. Shit.

I bit my lower lip and felt my entire body flush hot.

And I was bitching about having four hot husbands … why? With all the D in the room with me, I was struggling to remember my hangups. Forced marriage? Eh. I just I could live with that …

So I did what George asked. I mean, if he wanted to go down on me, who was I to complain? I slid one leg over his chest and gasped when he grabbed onto my hips and pulled me toward his face, his hot breath feathering against the swollen wet heat of my pussy. He hadn't even *touched* it yet and I was shivering with the anticipation.

"Well, look at that," Shane said, straddling George's legs like he didn't give a shit that there was another man between us. I mean, I guess he *did* let Reg suck him off earlier … Shane leaned forward until his lips and mine were almost touching … "You're in just the right spot to suck me off, sweet thing."

He captured my mouth at the same moment George's tongue flicked out along the length of my cunt. The gasp of sheer ecstasy that escaped my lips disappeared into Shane's mouth as he kissed me hard and fast, reaching down and taking my hand in his before positioning it around the base of George's cock.

"Think you can handle us both, little spirit?" he asked as he moved back and sat up on his knees, putting the thick, tattooed length of his shaft within range of my wet, swollen lips—the ones on my face this time.

My right hand slowly slicked along the length of George's dick, using his pre-cum for lube, pumping him as I leaned forward and oh so carefully took the head of Shane's cock into my mouth.

"Fuck me runnin', Sugar," Shane groaned as I swirled my tongue around his tip, paying extra attention to the underside and then dipping lower. Slowly, I stroked George a couple of times, letting my jaw adjust to Shane's girth, before finding my rhythm.

In near perfect synchronization, I pumped my hand up and down George's cock while sliding Shane in and out of my mouth until George's lips latched onto my swollen clit, sucking and flicking at it with his tongue. A whimpering groan eased out of my throat around Shane's inked up dick and he gripped his hands into my hair, helping me keep my balance and encouraging a faster rhythm.

Following his lead, I increased my pace on both him and George, relaxing as he used his hold on my wet hair to push deeper in my mouth, almost triggering that pesky gag reflex of mine.

"Jesus H. Christ, Honey Doll," he panted, his lower abdominal muscles in front of my face tensing and flexing, "I reckon with a little practice you could go deeper."

As if to prove his point, he pushed his hips forward just a fraction more, seriously threatening my sensitive throat before pulling back to his original depth. I made a growl of annoyance at him, but secretly the idea of this *practice* was making me hotter—if that was even possible.

George was licking at my *lower* lips with a confidence that definitely didn't seem like the *nice guy* I'd pegged him as, and while Shane tested my limits, George slid his hand up my inner thigh, pushing two thick fingers deep inside me while his tongue played my clit like a violin.

Fucking hell, these elementals were going to be the death of me; I could already feel another mind-blowing orgasm building, but was determined to make them come first. Call it a power play, or feminism, or whatever, but I liked knowing I could drive a man to the edge and push him right on over—especially someone like Shane.

Oh god, I'd better be quick about it though because George had some *serious* oral skills going on.

This time when Shane thrust forward into my mouth, I took him a little deeper than I had dared to yet and when I heard a satisfying hiss from his mouth, withdrew by scraping my teeth lightly down his length. Pulling him all the way out of my mouth, I very deliberately met his hooded gaze as I bent and licked the length of George.

Having seen the way he'd *risen* to the occasion earlier when Reg sucked him off, it wasn't hard to imagine that watching me lick George's dick would turn him on even more.

And I was right, too.

"Sugar, you're killin' me here," Shane groaned as my hand wrapped around his throbbing length and stroked him in time with my mouth sliding up and down George. I only managed a couple of quick pumps before Shane muttered something under his breath and pulled me away from George's dick, replacing it with his own between my lips and thrusting urgently.

I tightened my mouth around him, and let him go for it, and within moments he was coming. The salty sweet tang of his cum hit the back of my throat as he thrust deep. At the same time, George slipped a third finger into my throbbing cunt, stroking me into a frenzy with his tongue on my clit and sending me crashing over my own cliff into a mind-shattering orgasm.

God only knew how much time passed while Shane and I came, but when we eventually returned to the real world, both panting and gasping, he met my gaze with a wicked wink.

"George, George, George," he tsked, sliding back down the bed a little and bending until his head was level with mine. "Nice guys always finish last, hey Sug?"

"So they say," George murmured, still teasing my aching cunt with his tongue and sending aftershocks zinging through me.

"Maybe I should lend you a hand, Honey Doll," Shane suggested to me, running a finger down George's rigid length and stopping when he reached my hand at the base. Jesus, it was even turning *me* on again, so I nodded encouragement at him before taking George in my mouth, the same way I'd done for Shane moments earlier.

While I worked him over with my mouth, I watched transfixed as Shane propped himself up on one elbow between George's legs, then proceeded to fondle the other man's balls. From the corner of my eye, I saw Shane lick his lips and it dragged my gaze back to his face. He locked eyes with me and winked again.

I wasn't entirely sure what he had planned, but when George groaned and his balls tightened ready for release, Shane ducked forward and sucked the younger man's nuts into his mouth like a pro.

Holy. Shit.

"Fuck!" George yelled, bucking his hips up and coming hard while the air elemental sucked on his balls. Just watching them sent me into yet another mini-orgasm and the three of us wound up in a sweaty tangle of limbs and saliva, staring up at Reg's porno mirror on the roof.

Seeing it in the afterglow as we were, I kinda understood the appeal. The runes glittering all over my body cast enough light for us to see by and the contours of my husbands' bodies were like a work of art.

"Shit, Billy, looks like we just missed the fun." Reg's voice came from somewhere in the direction of the door. I was too exhausted to look though so I just snuggled my face into George's thigh and yawned.

"There's always more fun to be had," Shane drawled in that goddamn sexy southern accent of his and fuck if my pussy didn't clench at the suggestion.

"Don't tempt us," Billy muttered and I felt his blazing hot fingertip drag a slow line up the back of my thigh and over the curve of my ass. "We probably don't have the time at the moment though. Not until you hear what we have to say."

"Ugh, as much as it pains me to admit it, he's right," Reg agreed, coming around the bed to lay beside us. The fact the Reg and Billy, two of the biggest sluts I'd ever met—Britt included—weren't jumping at the chance to get their ends wet, meant something serious.

"What happened?" I asked, pushing myself up off my two spent husbands and sitting in the center of the huge bed facing Reg. "Is it Joan? Is she okay?"

"Huh?" He frowned at me in confusion then flapped his hand dismissively as his expression changed to a smirk. "Yeah, of course. Our healer is like, literally magic. No, something more serious unfortunately."

I waited for him to continue but his focus had shifted down to my naked breasts and I saw his tongue dart out to wet his lips as he stared.

"Billy?" I asked, exasperated. Maybe I needed to put some clothes on …?

"What Reg was about to say, before becoming hypnotized by your awesome rack, was that Kuntemopharn's killed three more witches. He's on his way to getting a whole hell of a lot stronger. If we stand any chance of taking him down, we need to act quick. But, uh, hate to say it—it gets worse." Billy grimaced and ran a hand through his ashy gray hair before sitting on Reg's other side and leaning on the headboard.

"What could possibly be worse than that, sug?" Shane drawled, shifting to prop himself up on one elbow, totally unconcerned with his nudity in a bed full of other men.

"Warden called," Reg replied, and the smile slipped from Shane's slightly swollen lips. "It seems he felt someone tug on their life bond and he called to ask how the hell that was possible when he didn't *have* a life mate."

Reg turned his attention back to me, focusing on my face this time. "I don't suppose when you were searching for Shane in the sewer you might've accidentally tugged on Warden's thread?"

Ah shit.

"How the hell was I supposed to know he could feel that? I was just trying to work out who was who!" I threw my hands up in frustration. No one told me to watch out for Warden's bond. Maybe if they'd been a little more forthcoming in the first place …

"How is this even a bad thing?" I asked, frowning, "Like yes, it's shit for me because I'm going to see Max again for the first time since college, but how is this necessarily worse than Kuntemopharn killing witches and draining their power?"

"It's not … really …" Reg cocked his head and eyed me up, this time taking in the position that George and Shane were still in, their naked legs still somewhat tangled together. "It'll just be a bit of added drama, but it was bound to happen sooner or later."

"Maybe he can help us sort out this festering sore of a storm dweller," George muttered, rolling on his side and getting comfortable.

"Doubtful," Billy responded, with an edge of bitterness to his tone, "he didn't seem particularly concerned for our wellbeing. Said he had some things to tie up in Manhattan and would be back when he was good and ready."

Judging by the pissed off set to his jaw, I guessed it must've been Billy that took the call.

"Did you tell him who I was?" I asked cautiously, not really wanting to hear the answer. "Did you tell him *who* your life mate is? And that he already fucked her, like, a decade ago?"

"Yeah, Firebug," Billy's voice softened and his eyes gave me a sympathetic look, "that was when he clammed up and told me not to hold my breath waiting for him."

"Oh." My heart sank almost to my knees and my gaze dropped to the comforter in front of me. What the hell had I really expected? That he would be ecstatic to learn the girl he'd loved in college was now fucking his four best friends? Of course he didn't want to see me; I'd pulled a seriously dick move taking off the way I had.

"Hey, chick," Reg said, tapping me on the chin to raise my focus off the bedspread, "none of that. You didn't know what he was, anymore than he knew what you were. He'll get over it … eventually."

"And if he doesn't?" I asked in a small voice as Reg picked me up by the waist, hauling me over to straddle his lap where he leaned on the headboard.

"Well if he doesn't, then it just means we won't have to share you with anyone else." He gave me a cheeky smirk, but the kiss he pulled me into was surprisingly tender and gentle.

"Okay, so Warden is a problem for a whole other day. What are we doin' about Kuntemopharn then? Also let's not forget that Ari's bio parents are the necromancers that raised him in the first place, so they'll also need dealing with." Shane yawned heavily as he finished this sentence, rubbing his eyes.

"I think the best thing any of us can do right now is get some sleep," George suggested, and I swear I wanted to suck him off right then and there for saying it. My eyelids were so damn heavy it felt like I was wearing lead mascara, and I'd ventured into that slightly dizzy stage of exhaustion, where it feels like you've just had one too many glasses of wine.

"Probably a smart idea," Billy said, sliding to the edge of the bed and bending over to pull off his heavy motorcycle boots. As he leaned forward, I was treated to a good three inches of his ass crack, and I felt my hungry cunt tighten.

It was a secret I'd held close, never even told Britt before. But I was totally, one hundred and ten percent, a crack addict. There was something about seeing the top of a sexy man's ass crack hanging out the top of his pants that just *drove me wild*.

Ever since Shane first knocked on my door, I'd been praying the stories of plumbers' cracks would be true, but until now, I'd yet to see it for myself. Admittedly, that was probably because more often than not they wore no pants at all, but *holy fucking damn*, seeing Billy's crack hanging out the top of his leather pants and my pipes ready to *fucking burst*.

"You okay there, Sugar Tits?" Reg asked, his hands sliding up my naked sides to rest on my waist. My breathing had become labored as I'd stared at Billy's ass, and as he

271

straightened, turning to look at me curiously, I had no doubt my cheeks were flushed with heat.

"Just fine," I lied, snuggling into the mess of boys. Wow, boys, plural. That was definitely going to take some getting used to …

It'd been a hell of a long time since I'd snuggled anybody— let alone several somebodies.

"If you want to talk about it …" Billy started, but he didn't sound like he wanted to talk about Max … er Warden, either.

"Nope, all good here." I said, cutting him off. "Goodnight." I flashed a fake smile and laid my head on Reg's chest before things got awkward, all the while realizing that I was going to have a hell of a time falling asleep after his announcement. Knowing that Max was out there, that he knew about me, and that he wasn't coming … Fuck, I had no idea how to process all of that shit.

"Night, Sugar Tits," Reg said, putting his hand on my head. I closed my eyes, expecting to be barraged by awful memories or new fears … but instead, as soon as my lids slid shut, I was fucking *out*.

14

CHAPTER FOURTEEN

I woke up to a hard dick in my face and almost completely lost my shit.

But then I remembered that I was now 'married' to four different dudes. Hell, it was going to be like living on a farm—waking up to a cock each and every sunrise.

I sat up and glanced down to find Reg tangled up in the sheets, completely nude. He was also snoring. Scooting away from him, I swung my feet over the side of the bed and then started digging through dresser drawers, looking for clothes to borrow. I settled on a pair of boxer shorts with frigging Pokemon on them (what was with all the goddamn Pokemon?) and an oversized black t-shirt.

Now … to find my purse.

For the life of me I couldn't remember where I'd left it, but I felt almost desperate to call Britt and update her not only on the supernatural situation, the bio parent thing, and the sex … but also Warden. She was the only one who'd truly understand what I was going through.

"Hey," I said, moving back over to Reg and poking him in the cheek. "Wake up. I need to borrow your phone."

"Nightstand," he grumbled, swatting at me and then turning over, further tangling the sheets around his legs. I grabbed the cell lying there and turned it on, surprised to see that no passcode was required to get in. Huh.

After I called Britt, I was going to have to get nosy and go through all his pictures, just to see what he'd gotten up to before meeting me. I mean, not that I cared. Because I didn't. Seriously.

Dialing Britt's number by heart (it was the only one in the world I had memorized), I waited not-so-patiently for her to answer.

"Girl, you would not *believe* the size of this man's dick," was how my best friend answered the phone.

"Britt," I started, but she wasn't done. I was just going to have to let this nightmare run its course.

"I'd say at least nine inches, and then there's girth. I mean, and he knows how to actually use it. Do you have any idea how rare that is?" That was a rhetorical question that I didn't bother to answer. "Anyway, have you ever met a man who could go, like, ten times in one night? That's the thing about humans—they always finish too quick. That's why I like to stick to my own kind. No other dude has as much stamina as a werewolf —"

"Britt!" I said, when I'd had about enough. "I need to talk to you about something."

"Are you okay?" she asked, snapping into one of her *very* rare bouts of seriousness. That was the thing about Britt—

usually a slutty weirdo, but definitely a ride or die bitch when required. "What's going on?"

I took a deep breath and explained the situation to her, leaving the part about Max/Warden for last.

"Holy mothershitting balls," Britt whispered, exhaling against the phone and giving me goose bumps. The surprise in her voice was just a distant shimmer of the overwhelming shock flowing through mine. Of all the men in this world, Max had to be one of these fuckers, an elemental, some destined, like, soul mate thing of mine.

Figures.

"This is pretty much the greatest love story since ... like *Titanic* or whatever."

"You hated *Titanic*," I told her and her clothes rustled as she shrugged. "This isn't a love story, Britt. It's ..." I glanced over my shoulder at Reg, still fast asleep and snoring. "It's like a Stephen King novel—rotting undead dragons, a polygamist bad guy who also happens to be my biological father, and the only man I've ever loved, a man that *I* abandoned, reentering my life at the craziest possible moment? I really do need to get out of the city for a bit, stay with Siobhan."

"Ugh, I *hate* her though," Britt whined as I pursed my lips. It sucked, but my two besties in the whole wide world couldn't *stand* each other.

"I just need a second to think, Britt. I haven't even gotten a *second.*"

"You'll take those boys with you though?" she asked, sounding unusually concerned. Usually Britt didn't worry over much except broken nails and bad dye jobs.

I sighed and rubbed at my temple with two fingers.

"Yeah, I'll take them with me, I promise," I said, and then wondered if I was going to end up regretting that.

Surprisingly, I thought I was going to have to drag the guys to NYC with me, but instead, they seemed to think it was a good idea to put some space between us and *kuntemopharn* while we tried to figure out a plan.

Before we went anywhere though, I needed this glamour that George had mentioned. The runes looked strange enough on their own, like I'd gone and got a whole body tattoo, but there was just no way to explain them sparkling and glowing every freaking time I got turned on. Which lately, felt like every five minutes.

"This shop is legit?" I muttered quietly to Reg as he held open the door for me to walk through. We'd stopped at the local Wicca store in town—the same one that Reg and Shane had purchased all of the equipment for our bonding ceremony from. I'd been wondering what the hell had happened to that damn cup …

"Don't let the tourist crap fool you, Sugar Tits," Reg chuckled, following me inside with a hand on my lower back. Yep, there went those damn runes again. Fuck me, I looked like one of the vampires out of *Twilight*. This glamour could not come soon enough.

I glanced around the shop, taking in the purple walls and glossy black trim, the tables covered in crystals and the walls of old books. The air was perfumed with a sweet and smoky mix of incense, ancient paper, fresh ink, and herbs, jars of which were lined up on shelves next to the register.

"Ah, I see your bonding ceremony was a success, then?" the middle-aged woman behind the counter nodded as we approached her. She had curly red hair and green eyes that seemed to take in my entire essence with a single once-over. This woman was a witch? Like, a real witch? And Gram was one, too? Fuck me running ... "I guess congratulations are in order? Reginald, your father must so happy for you boys."

"You know how Charlie is, Anita. Never happy with anything these days," Reg said with a smirking half-smile, but one with enough warmth that suggested they were old friends. Maybe she'd needed a bathroom remodel at some point?

If I found out he'd fucked her though ... I might cut a bitch.

"Now, what can I do for you boys today?" She eyed up my husbands with affection and I snorted at her calling them *boys*. The sheer fact that I was wearing their permanent reminders of our orgy proved to me they were *men*.

"We need a glamour for Arizona," Shane responded with a wide smile. "She's having trouble controlling her magic."

The woman, Anita, raised her eyebrows at me then dropped a saucy wink. "I don't blame you, girl," she chuckled, "come on through to the back then. One glamour, coming right up. I trust you brought the chalice and athame back?"

A small cat sneaked out from behind the counter, rubbed itself against a display of tarot cards before it glared up at me with bright yellow eyes. It took me a second to realize it had a headless rat corpse clutched in its jaws.

Heh. How very precious ...

"We did," Billy replied, producing the ornate silver items from the paper bag he carried. I vaguely remembered them bringing both out during our *marking* ceremony, and saying something about me filling it?

Gross.

Musta been a metaphorical fill because all those other, uh, by-products of our orgy had gone either in the toilet or down the shower drain ...

Anita must've caught my confused look because she smiled patiently at me and explained.

"The chalice was used during your marking ceremony as a symbolic capture for all the excess magic in the room. A ritual as powerful as the marking of an elemental leaves a huge excess in the air, which is able to be stored and repurposed in a chalice such as this." She held out her hand and Billy passed her the seemingly empty cup. "As well as in the blade of the athame. They're both symbols for the feminine and masculine aspects in nature."

The woman raised a red eyebrow at me, ignoring the cat as she crouched down and started crunching *bone*.

"Now, I just need a few special ingredients and I can get started ..." Anita trailed off and glanced over at Billy; he nodded, giving me a sympathetic look. Immediately, I felt my guard go up. That feeling was, of course, slightly softened by the fact that the man smelled like a campfire and wore a leather jacket over his broad shoulders.

"Hand, please, Firebug," he told me, lifting up the athame and wiggling it slightly. Light from a few nearby candles reflected off the blade as my runes flickered and then promptly snuffed them all out. Oops. But it was better than indoor lightning strikes, right? "We just need a little bit of blood."

"Uh-huh," I said, holding my hand against my chest and resisting the urge to take a step back. It was either this or miss out on going to see any future *Magic Mike* sequels in theaters with Britt. I looked down at the black cat again and felt my stomach flip-flop at the tiny smatters of blood on the old floor, the rat's tail lying in the center of it all. The rest of its body was now gone.

"You can do this, Arizona," George said softly, coming up behind me as Reg moved his hand away from my back. The earth elemental wrapped his arms around my waist and held me in a jasmine scented hug. Since this particular store was one of a few without a *No Shoes, No Shirt, No Service* sign, he'd taken advantage and gone clothing free up top.

I leaned into his muscular midsection with a small sigh.

"Just do it," I said as my runes went wild and put on a small light show. I noticed Anita discreetly moving over to flick the lock on the front door and flip the sign to *Closed.*

I held my hand out and shivered when Billy's warm fingers brushed against my skin, the few flame tattoos on his skin seeming to dance in the flickering light of my runes. He rubbed a soothing thumb over my palm, pressed a hot kiss against it, and then stabbed me with the fucking knife.

"I've got you," George whispered against my ear, and I swear, I could feel the earth beneath my feet, even through the wooden floor of the shop. It was like I was suddenly surrounded by sweet, natural growing things—such as the hard pipe wrench stabbing me in the back. Guess just like I couldn't help the runes, he couldn't help his equipment, huh?

Billy slid the sharp end of the athame into the tip of my middle finger, drawing crimson beads to the surface of my skin. Normally, I was a fan of getting penetrated, but not so much like this. I scrunched my face up as Anita held the chalice out and Billy massaged several fat drips into it.

It was over in an instant and then the asshole fire elemental was sliding my finger into his mouth and sucking on it.

"Asshole," I said as George pressed a kiss on the side of my neck and released me. I pretended not to like either of those things, but the runes said otherwise. I was *so* ready for this fucking glamour.

The boys each took a turn, letting Billy prick them and add more blood to the chalice. Brave fucker that he was, he did his

279

own hand himself and then wiped the blade off on his jeans before folding it back into the paper bag.

"Thank you, dears," Anita said, bending low, her black dress fluttering as she patted the cat on the head and then … snatched the rat tail from the floor. I watched in horror as she plunked it into the cup and gestured for us to follow her through a beaded curtain behind the register.

Hopefully this glamour wasn't supposed to be taken orally or worse—as a fucking suppository. Like, as much as I didn't want to put rat tail lotion on my skin, that's sort of what I was praying for at this point.

Anita took us into a dimly lit back room as I sucked on my smarting fingertip and wished it was still in Billy's hot mouth. Now *this* is what I had imagined a witch's lair to look like. All manner of things hung from the ceiling, including parts of animals and various plants, and in the little kitchenette there was an honest-to-god cauldron bubbling away on the electric stove top.

Anita hummed to herself as she rifled through cupboards and drawers, grabbing jars of things, and throwing pinches into the cup before picking the boiling cauldron up by the handle and pouring its steaming contents into the chalice.

"What is *that*?" I whispered to the guys, but the witch heard me anyway.

"This, dear?" she clarified, holding up the cauldron, and I nodded. "Hot water."

"Oh."

Well, didn't I feel silly now?

"Here you go!" she announced, holding out the chalice to me. I accepted it warily because, you know, there was a rat tail floating on the surface. That, and the liquid inside was a slimy green sort of color that smelled utterly putrid.

This was so not a fucking lotion.

"You'll need to drink it," Reg smirked, obviously seeing my look of revulsion.

"All of it, sweetie." Anita smiled and nodded encouragingly, her crescent moon earrings dangling with the motion. The cat padded into the room to join us and sat there with a *you can thank me later* look on her snotty face. I had to resist the urge to stick out my tongue. I was, like, totally a grown woman who didn't do that shit anymore.

Well, at least not very often.

Ugh, this was so gross, but surely it had to be better than walking around looking like Edward freaking Cullen? I took a deep breath and brought the cup to my mouth, ready to neck it back like how Britt and I drink *Adios Motherfuckers* at nightclubs.

"Wait!" Anita yelped, snatching the cup back out of my hand. "Sorry, forgot to activate it." She laughed like that was a hilarious little oops on her part. "Wouldn't want you to have to drink it *twice.*"

I glared daggers as Anita waved her hand in an elaborate gesture, muttering something in Latin, or French, or Russian … I don't know. I was a barista, not a linguist.

"You've never fucked her, right?" I asked the boys and got a long moment of silence in response. Turning to glare at them over my shoulders, I saw several looks of revulsion on their faces.

"Dude, she's like *ancient,*" Reg said with a shutter, leaning down to whisper in my ear. "You should see *her* without her glamour on—not pretty. Probably why she forgot to activate the glamour—Anita's gettin' a little senile in her golden years. I think she's like, three hundred and eight or some shit."

My eyebrows went up and I had to wonder, how old exactly *was* Gram when she died then? Clearly she hadn't been using a glamour herself, what with the wrinkles and all.

I glanced back at Anita and found purple flames shooting up from the liquid. It was like bananas foster up in here or something. They flared bright for a moment and then died away before the happy witch passed the chalice back to me with a sigh.

"That was a close one! All done now, though. Bottoms up!"

I put the cup to my lips, closed my eyes so I didn't have to look at its contents, and tossed it back like a badass bitch.

Britt would've been proud.

Well, at least she would have before I dropped the metal cup to the floor and swooned into the arms of the boys, my consciousness flickering for several seconds as a wave of raw energy rolled over me like a storm.

When I came to, the damn cat was in my lap and the boys were fanned out all around. Well, three of them were. I was currently sitting in Shane's lap, his massive dip-tube poking me in the ass. As a wave of hormones hit me like a tsunami, I noticed that my runes were *not* presently flaring to life.

"It worked," I said, sounding surprised.

"Well, of course it did, sweetie," Anita said as she swept the floor with a very witchy looking broom. I ignored her and leaned in to steal a kiss from each boys' lips as a thank you— but not a one of them would kiss me back.

"Rat tail, Sugar Tits," Reg said with a shrug. "Brush your damn teeth first."

I reached out, punched him in the shoulder, and pushed the cat off of me so I could stand up ... just in time to see Anita fish an eyeball from a glass bottle and pop it into her mouth, humming as she shivered with pleasure and then continued sweeping the floor.

Okay, that was it.

Enough supernatural shit.

It was time to head into New York for some girl talk, shopping, and cosmopolitans.

The guys could come, but they better not get in my damn way.

Unfortunately, Gram decided she'd *also* like to tag along for my trip into the city proper.

"This Siobhan character," she said with a scoff, appearing on the sidewalk outside my best friend's apartment building. "I never liked her; she's a terrible influence."

I ignored my dead grandmother and waited for the rest of the boys to pile out of the plumbing van. We were parked in a fifteen minute zone, so somebody was going to have to move the damn thing sooner rather than later, but one of the guys could deal with that. I just wanted to see my girlfriend's face, maybe go out for coffee or something, and have some private chitchat time.

I sooooo wanted to gossip about my new men and their giant dicks. What?! We all do it with our lady friends—you know it's true.

"Oh, also," Gram said smugly as I took my small overnight bag and craned my neck back to stare up at the massive, soaring heights of the building. Standing in the middle of New York City was like … transforming from a human—or elemental—into an ant. You just became so fucking insignificant. I'd always thought of that as a bad thing, but right now, the anonymity felt good. "Your friend is a succubus."

With that bit of shit tossed and splattered on my feet, Gram winked out with a smug smile and left me gaping in the middle of the dirty sidewalk.

"Siobhan ... is a succubus?" I said aloud and Reg cocked a brow.

"You talking to yourself again, ST?" he asked again. "Or just chillin' with ghosts?"

Several people walking by either glanced over to give me a *you fuckin' crazy lady?* looks or *I want to fuck your husbands* looks. Neither of which I much enjoyed.

I glared at Reg and swept my fingers through the blonde waves of my hair.

Succubus, huh? Figured. Really, I wasn't all that surprised.

I decided to ignore that bit of information for the moment, watching as Shane yanked a duffel bag from the back of the van.

"Are you sure *kuntemopharn* isn't going to come for us here?" I asked instead, and it was George who answered.

"In the middle of the city? Probably not—at least not yet. They'll wait for us to come back."

"Clearly your parents in no hurry to do whatever the fuck it is they're planning to do since you're still alive," Billy tossed my way, hauling his own duffel bag over his shoulder and nodding with his chin for me to lead the way. "Show us where to go, Firebug."

I took a deep breath, closed my eyes for a moment, and then opened them back up. Okay, so, Siobhan was a succubus, no big deal. It wasn't like I'd almost been killed by one of her kind just last week or anything ... And surely she wouldn't mind me bringing four random dudes she'd never met in her life to hang in her studio apartment, right?

"Does your friend know we're coming?" George asked skeptically as we took Siobhan's elevator up to the twenty-fourth floor. "I only ask because succubi and incubi often entertain ahh, clients in their homes …"

This made me pull up short.

"Wait, you don't mean … ugh, I always thought she was a bit promiscuous! This makes so much more sense now."

"And coming from someone who's friends with the slutty furball, that's saying a lot," Reg muttered under his breath and I whacked him in the gut.

"Those in glass houses shouldn't throw stones, Reginald," I teased, then turned back to George. "No, I don't know where the hell my phone ended up and don't know her number so …" I shrugged.

We'd just reached her door, so I knocked and waited. Then knocked again. Waited some more. Raised my hand to knock a third time and Shane grabbed my wrist gently.

"I don't think she's home, darlin'," he murmured, stroking the underside of my wrist with his fingers. I shivered with pleasure, but at least my runes didn't go nuts—yay, glamour!

"But … she has to be …" I frowned at him, unprepared for this turn of events. Siobhan worked from home, which I now realized was code for being a supernatural call girl, so where would she be? Maybe just gone out to the shops or something?

"Oh, wait!" I had a spark of memory—I knew where her spare key was. "We can just go in and use her phone to call her," I explained as I fished it out from behind the firehose at the end of the hallway.

HIJINKS HAREM

"Is she not going to mind us just letting ourselves in?" George asked, looking a bit concerned, but I figured, why tell me where the spare key was if I wasn't allowed to use it?

"She'll be fine. Probably gone out to buy more vodka or lube … and suddenly the amount of sex toys she owns makes a whole hell of a lot more sense. Fucking succubus. Why are none of my friends human?" I was mostly muttering this to myself as I unlocked Siobhan's door and let my little harem of men inside.

"Because you're a particularly strong elemental, Sugar Tits," Reg answered anyway, "and like calls to like and power calls to power. I wouldn't be surprised if this succubus is one of the *elites*, and your dress wearing wolf turns out to be the alpha's new mate or some shit."

"Huh." I paused, considering this. "Wouldn't that be fun to see? Britt with a *mate*." Snickering to myself, I headed into Siobhan's little kitchenette and grabbed her phone from the counter.

"Have a seat or whatever," I told the guys. "I'll just see where she's at."

The phone only rang a couple of times before my other bestie's voice answered with an upbeat, "Hello Morgs!"

"How did you know it was me?" I asked, smiling. She always called me Morgs, because of my middle name. Don't know why, she'd just always done it. The two of us had met after college when I'd moved to Oregon and started working at a Dutch Bros.; she'd come in at all hours of the night to get coffee. One of the reasons I'd decided to commit to the New York move—besides Gram, obviously—was because of Siobhan.

286

"Well, it says that my own apartment is calling me and seeing as you're the only one I trust enough to know where my key is ..." she trailed off with a sultry laugh.

"Yeah, fair enough," I replied. "Where are you anyway? I came to er, visit." No point in dumping my whole story about Kuntemopharn at her door just yet. That could wait until after a few vodkas. Or glasses of wine ... Siobhan usually kept some good stuff around her apartment, so I began hunting through cupboards while we talked.

"I'm in Barbados, babe!" She laughed. "I've been seeing this new guy, and he just called up last night and told me we were taking an impromptu holiday, and so, here we are!"

In the background I could hear a man's voice murmuring and Siobhan's throaty sex laugh. It's amazing I hadn't worked out she was a succubus before now.

"Uh-huh," I murmured a bit sarcastically as I fished out a corkscrew to open the bottle of red I had just snaked from her pantry. "New guy? Or new client?"

There was a long pause on the phone.

"Babe, it's not what you think ..." she started, her voice dropping all traces of her laughter, but I just snorted.

"It's not that you're a succubus masquerading as a call girl in order to get easy meals?" I snickered and heard her sigh of relief on the other end.

"Oh thank god, you know about the supernatural thing? That would have been *so* damn awkward to explain otherwise!" Her sex laugh was back and the man with her murmured something else near the receiver, probably kissing up her neck or something. Men couldn't keep their fucking hands off Siobhan. "At your Gram's funeral, I felt that elemental vibe on you, babe. I was wondering how long it'd be before some quad or quint hunted your ass down. I assume that's what happened? Females in your species are rare *as fuck*."

"So I've learned …" I said, trailing off and wondering how much I wanted to get into over the phone. Unfortunately, Siobhan made that choice for me. While Britt was my ride or die bitch, Siobhan was more of a wild card.

"Babe, I've got to go. Stay as long as you want; I don't know when I'll be back! Ciao!"

She disconnected before I had a chance to say anything else, so I put the phone down and took a healthy sip of wine straight from the bottle. Glasses were overrated. Besides, if she wasn't going to give me a little girl time, she owed me booze.

"So when is your friend coming back?" Shane asked. He leaned on the doorframe to the little kitchenette, making the room look tiny in comparison to his massive bulk. When did these guys have the time to work out?

"She doesn't know," I replied, offering him my bottle of wine. "She's in Barbados with a client, but we're welcome to stay here."

"Well then," he said, taking a slow sip from the bottle, then licking his lips like a goddamn porn star, "what are *we* going to get up to here in the Big Apple?"

"I don't really know," I admitted, "I hadn't thought that far ahead. I'd fucking kill for dinner and dancing though …?"

"Seriously?" He coughed, choking a little on some wine and looking at me like I'd just grown a second vagina in the middle of my forehead.

"Uh yeah … why not? We all just nearly died, I don't even know how many times in the last three days. Isn't it about time we cut loose and had some normal human fun?" I propped my hand on my hip, sticking my butt out a little in what I hoped might be a bit of a sexy pose. Probably just looked constipated though, such was the level of my game. How I ended up friends with Britt and Siobhan, I can't even explain. Maybe I made them look good?

"Shane has a *thing* about dancing," Reg snickered, and the Southern sexpot tossed him a dirty look before turning a small smile back my direction. Heck, maybe my hip pop really was working? Shane seemed as if he liked what he saw.

"Aw, hell. You know I can't say no to you, Sugar," Shane groaned, rubbing his hand over his face. "Boys, our new wife wants us to take her to dinner and dancing!"

"Does she now?" Billy grinned, popping out of Siobhan's closet holding a pair of handcuffs and a flogger. "I think we might have more fun staying here."

"Oh, Billy, put down the dirty succubus sex toys, please," George said with a small shudder.

"Lighten up, Georgie Boy," Billy chuckled, whacking him playfully with the flogger. "It's not like I picked up her Ben Wa balls or her butt plugs ... although she does have *plenty* of those back there, too!"

"Quit it you two," Shane said with a small grin. "Billy, stop snooping through Ari's friend's sex toys and George, don't be dramatic. Everyone knows succubi and incubi have natural immunities STDs."

"Dinner and dancing, you say?" Reg nodded thoughtfully, tapping his chin. "Yes, I think that's a pretty damn good idea. I'll call my buddy that runs the Black and White Club down in the Meatpacking District. They've got an incredible restaurant on the ground floor, and a pretty wild nightclub on the basement level."

"Sounds perfect!" I took another swig of wine, then handed the bottle to Billy when he held out his hand for it. What was a little backwash between lovers, right? He gave me a sultry wink and a smile that *almost* made me reconsider our plans.

Almost.

But with Siobhan out of town, there'd be plenty of time for sex later.

Now. What the hell was I wearing to go dancing?

Luckily, Siobhan was almost the same size as me, so I raided her closet (the clothing one) and was feeling pretty damn good about myself as our cab pulled up outside the packed restaurant. Most of Siobhan's outfits had been on the, uh, *less demure* side, but I'd finally settled on a super sexy hot pink minidress that would make Britt swoon with envy. Short enough to barely cover my ass, my long legs were well on display with the matching pink satin peep-toes. I'd taken a shower and used some of Siobhan's fancy hair products, so my blonde hair was shining, with the curls fluffed up in a sexy disheveled sort of way.

Billy had made a *very* tempting offer to make my bedhead more authentic, but I was determined to enjoy a *normal* night out with my four husbands. Well ... as normal as was possible.

"Uh, Reg?" I muttered under my breath as we left our coats with the reception and followed the maître d' to our table. "You didn't tell me there was a dress code here."

Everyone, and I mean *everyone*, staff and patrons alike, was dressed in either black or white, or a combination of the two. Who the hell would have known the name of the club was so damn literal?!

"I know, ST," he chuckled, pulling out my chair for me in a rare display of gentlemanly manners, "but you looked so damn sexy in that dress, I didn't want you to change."

"Everyone's staring." I could feel my face flushing with heat. Being the center of attention was not my thing, at all.

"Everyone is dead jealous, darlin'," Shane said with a wink, then flagged down a waiter so we could start ordering a round of drinks.

"Guys this place is seriously fancy," I said cautiously. "I know *I* can't afford to eat here, and you all don't have a pot to piss in between you, so ..."

"Don't you worry your pretty little head, Sugar," Shane replied, picking up my menu and handing it to me. "Reg is old friends with Hank, the man that owns this joint."

"And Hank is ..." Undoubtedly another supernatural creature the way my life was going these days.

"Incubus," Reg replied, "and a real dirty bastard, too. You'll see when we head down to the club after dinner." He threw me a wink that said all I needed to know. Whatever was downstairs in *the club,* I seriously doubted it'd be a normal night of dancing and margaritas.

Great. I'd tried to run from the supernatural and stumbled right into more of it.

Thus, the new story of my life.

"So, do incubi and succubi have some sort of elemental connection? They seem to be hanging around an awful lot." As the waiter paused next to our table, I ordered some house specialty cocktail called the Bow Tie, because why the hell not? Mama was gettin' drunk tonight.

"Not particularly," Reg said, reclining stupidly back in his seat. Even though he was dressed appropriately for the restaurant, he too stood out with from his sheer lack of propriety. At least there was that. "They just happen to be kind of … you know, populous."

"Meaning there are a fuck of a lot of them around here," Billy added, ordering fireball whiskey, neat, and tossing his menu onto the surface of the table. "Basically if you want to get shit done in the Northeastern United States or eastern Canada, you have to wheel and deal with those assholes."

"Those assholes? Ah, Billy. And you thought I was comping dinner?" I glanced up at the speaking voice, trying not to shiver as a dream of a man paused next to our table in a white suit and black slacks. His smile was liquid sex and as he stretched it across his face, I could tell it was meant to slay. Fortunately, I think elementals were immune to their charms because even though I'd met several, I'd never felt anything for one. And clearly, their powers were sex related since, you know, they had to eat. What exactly it was that they ate was sort of beyond me.

Frankly, I didn't want to know.

Reg stood up to give his friend one of those stupid one-handed man hugs, withdrawing with a small shiver that let me know he, too, could feel his body's resistance to that supernatural pull.

"You didn't tell me you were in town?" Hank said, because this just had to be Hank. "You should come downstairs when you're done eating—Adonis and Rachel will be there somewhere. Nigel, too, if you want to kick his ass for laying hands on your wife."

"Thanks," Reg said, giving his friend a small salute. "Honestly, I feel like he deserves a kick to the balls. Let him know it's coming, would you?"

"You got it," Hank said, lifting a hand up toward the rest of us sitting at the table. "Enjoy your dinner everyone and I'll see you downstairs."

"There's trouble afoot," Gram said, appearing on my right side. I chose to ignore her, accepting my cocktail gratefully from the waiter. "Arizona, it's in your best interests not to ignore me, you know?"

"If there's trouble," I ground out under my breath, realizing that even in a room full of supernaturals, I probably still looked like a weirdo. Fantastic. A freak in both worlds. "Then why don't you ferret it out?"

"I'm bound to you, remember? Duckie, you're a bit of a nitwit, you do realize that, don't you?"

"Are you talkin' to your dead grandmother again, Sug?" Shane asked, looking like some sort of oil tycoon in that suit, dark hair slicked back, accent thick as molasses. The tattoos on his hands were the only giveaway he wasn't quite a Southern plantation prince.

"She says there's trouble afoot," I said, mimicking her upper-crust English accent in my American-Australian-British combo pack voice. I sounded kinda … like I was trying at all times for an accent I never quite reached. Most people thought I had some weird accent from a place they'd never heard of … or else I was mentally challenged. Either way … Kinda lame.

"There *is* trouble, Arizona; I can feel it."

"You can't feel anything, you're dead," I whispered as I opened my menu and tried not to gape at the prices. I mean, if it was comped and all … .I was ordering the most expensive thing on the menu for sure. *Bacon wrapped filet mignon, here I come!* "Did you have some sort of ghostly premonition or some shit?"

"Not yet. But I'm old, Arizona Morgan. I can tell when things just aren't right."

I ignored her and glanced up as I folded my menu closed.

"I'm having steak, how about you boys?"

"I'm a vegetarian," George said with a smile and I raised a brow.

"Of *course* you are," I said as he smiled at me, giving my body this little thrill of memory, of those lips on *my* lips. Oh yes. George might be the nice guy in the group, but I wasn't going to discount his skills in the bedroom …

"Looks like the glamour's holding out," George said, reaching over to take my hand, twisting it over to examine the long, bare lengths of my arm. Not a single rune in sight. I was both relieved and also, sort of, I don't know, *missing* them? I must've been losing my fucking mind.

"It feels a little weird," I said, my heart thundering as George ran his tanned hand up the paleness of my arm. *God that feels good.* "Like I'm covered in foundation or something. Not sure if I'm gonna like wearing this every day, all day."

"We can make anti-glamour in the chalice as well," George said, turning my palm over and running a single finger across the lines in my hand. "You don't have to wear it everyday if you don't want to." He sounded pleased at the idea, like I'd finally said something of intelligence. Maybe he liked me embracing my elemental side or something?

"How many spells can we make before the magic runs out?" I asked as I tried to surreptitiously take in the swanky restaurant digs. I'd never eaten somewhere so nice in my entire life. There were massive chandeliers soaring above our heads, and real wood molding on the walls that probably cost more than Gram's house.

"About a half-dozen small ones like the glamour," Shane answered, drawing my attention back over to him in his sexy suit. "But we can always refill it if need be." His smile was downright fucking wicked. I had to cross and uncross my legs under the table three times to stop the throbbing in my nether regions. And by nether regions, I mean my cunt.

"And to refill it ..."

"Sugar, you just want me to say it—you know how we refill it." Shane flashed me a wide grin and I found myself biting my lip flirtatiously. I think I was actually having *fun* with these assholes. "Group sex, that's how."

"It'd make a hundred spells if fucking Warden were here," Billy said, tapping his fingers on the table. Everyone went silent for a minute and Shane frowned. Great. Warden. Basically the elephant in the room.

Fortunately, the waiter chose that moment to come over and take our food orders.

"Why do you have to bring him up at every god-given moment?" Reg snapped, and I raised an eyebrow. It sort of maybe felt like Reginald and William had a sexual tension thing going on beneath the surface ... Or maybe they were both just dicks?

"Because I fucking hate him," Billy said, and it was pretty clear in his voice that he didn't feel that way at all. "I hope he never shows back up. Good riddance."

George sighed and propped his face in his hand, looking luxe as hell in a white-white suit against his bronzed skin.

"Yeah, you just say that shit because you two got drunk and fucked—"

"You want to keep going?" Billy asked, standing up and looking like he was about to start a fight right there in the middle of the restaurant.

"Just saying, for a guy who says he has zero homosexual tendencies ..." Reg continued, shrugging his shoulders loosely.

"Alright, that's about enough o' that," Shane said, downing his entire tumbler of Johnnie Walker whiskey. "Can we please just get smashed and enjoy the rest of our night? Who the hell knows when we're gonna get another opportunity like this."

"You mean because we might die?" I asked with false cheer, picking up my drink and examining the orange liquid inside. I think the menu said cognac, vermouth, and pineapple juice. I didn't much care so long as it got me drunk.

"We just might be busy is all, honeycomb," Shane said, and I felt the corner of my mouth twitch. I liked that one—honeycomb. Although I'd probably die before admitting it.

"Are we planning on discussing battle strategies or ..."

"Mom said she'd train you," Reg inserted, and I felt all the color drain from my face. "As soon as we get back in town, she'll start working with you five or six times a week."

Chilly spider legs swept over my skin, like icy needles jabbing into my flesh. *That* was how excited I was to be working with Reg's mum.

"Oh ..." I began, trying not to cough on my drink. "That's ... so nice of her."

"I mean, she's a spirit elemental, so ..." Reg just shrugged and picked up his beer—i.e. wheat tea because like, where's all the alcohol?—and continued on like he didn't notice my severe discomfort. "Obviously you guys have different powers. I mean, either that or you're schizophrenic and not *actually* talking to ghosts."

"I'm gonna kick your ass," I told him as I pointed at him with the pineapple leaf from my drink.

"I wish you'd pay more attention to my warnings ..." Gram was saying in my ear, making me feel like I really was going crazy or something. "There's magic here—big magic. I might be dead, but I can feel it."

I continued to ignore her. Frankly, I wasn't sure if I was more concerned with the cuntmuffin guy ... or Reg's bitchy mom training me six days a week.

"Joan is a little rough around the edges," George started, "but you'll get used to her."

I wanted to call his bluff on that one, but then, I didn't want to ruin dinner by telling the boys I hated their mom.

No, I would take care of that part later.

15

CHAPTER FIFTEEN

The stairway that led to the basement level club was this curving majesty of modern architectural design, with glass sides and sleek black steps that seemed to float in the center of a large foyer. Apparently, this club was invitation *only*.

Huge security guards flanked the heavy velvet curtains which must lead into the main club, and a tiny, waiflike girl held a clipboard to check names off. Reg approached her like they were old friends, and judging by the way she blushed, they probably were.

I had to fight the urge to claw her eyes out. This whole jealousy thing was not working for me. Too misogynistic.

She flipped her hair flirtatiously, and dropped the black velvet rope to allow us all past, but the jealous glare I earned from her was enough to strip paint. *Bitch.*

Oh that reminded me ...

"Hey, when this is all over and people aren't trying to kill us, do you guys think you can help do up Gram's house a bit?" I asked Shane, catching up to him and yelling a little to be heard over the booming music.

"Of course, darlin'," he said, taking my hand in his to pull me closer as we wove our way through the crowd, "but I thought you were gonna move in with us?"

Ugh, I had said that in my sex-addled state, hadn't I? I really needed to stop letting my vagina do the talking.

"Yeah, about that ..." How to politely say I'd rather stick rusty spoons in my eyes than live in Joan Copthorne's house ... hmm ... "I think that maybe our own space might be nice for a while? Seeing as we're technically in our honeymoon period and all?"

"And you want to confidently scream at the top of your lungs while we're fucking you, and not have your mother-in-law listening?" Reg popped up on the other side of me, making me jump.

"Um, yeah," I shrugged. "Fairly much. Shots?"

We'd just reached the bar, and I wasn't really ready to have that open conversation about how I was all of a sudden onboard with them moving in, the fact that we were all married, or that I *badly* wanted that screaming orgasm from them all right here in this swanky nightclub. So instead, I hailed down an employee and ordered us a round of tequila.

The smartly dressed bartender lined up five shot glasses and expertly poured out five shots of Don Julio Blanco right before I remembered that I hadn't actually brought my wallet with me, and had no money to pay for them.

"On the house for Reg and company," the bartender said with a wink, somehow reading my mind—or maybe my *I'm poor as fuck* facial expression—before disappearing back down the bar to serve someone else.

Sweet. Who was I to refuse free booze? I handed a shot to each of the guys and we slammed them back, the burning liquid heating a path all the way to my belly and kindling a small fire there.

"We should dance," I suggested, my eyes fixated on the writhing mass of bodies on the heaving dance floor. Every single person in the club was, without a doubt, stunning. Maybe there was an entry requirement that they only allowed beautiful people in?

So, basically, like most ritzy clubs, huh?

"Shane, dance with me?" I grabbed his hand again and tugged him toward the dance floor, only to be met with resistance.

"Good luck, Sugar Tits," Reg chuckled, sipping on a beer that George had just handed him. "Skeeter can't dance to save himself. You'll have to try a whole hell of a lot harder than that to get him out there with you."

That sounded suspiciously like a challenge to me.

I narrow my eyes as George handed a tumbler of scotch to Shane, and another shot glass to both myself and Billy.

"If you're looking for a dance partner," George grinned, "Billy is your man. I figured shots were easier so you weren't spilling a drink all over that lovely dress while you danced."

Billy threw me a wicked look as we slammed our shots back, then took my hand in his and led the way onto the crowded floor. It was set down a few steps from the bar, so when we came to a stop somewhere near the center, I could tell the other guys still had a clear view of us while we danced.

"So you want to get Shane out here, huh Firebug?" Billy yelled to be heard over the music, and his gaze was pure smoldering heat as he grasped my hips and began moving with me. "There's one surefire way to do it."

"And what's that?" I yelled back, letting my body melt into the rhythm of the music and following Billy's lead. All around us, couples and groups were grinding and undulating like they were in some sort of trance, some of them dancing so close they were practically fucking. As I cast my heavy, tequila fuzzed eyes around the room, I thought I saw Rachel and Adonis slipping behind a curtain at the entrance to a VIP lounge. Interesting.

"The *only* way to drag Shane's two left feet anywhere near a dance floor is to get him incredibly, irreversibly, undeniably … turned on." This last part was delivered into my ear with a panty melting growl, and my eyes flicked up to meet Shane's across the dance floor.

He was watching us like a hawk. This could be fun …

Flipping my curls over my shoulder, I stepped in closer to Billy and as my hips rolled and moved with the beat he tightened his grip on my waist.

"Get ready to put on a show, doll face," he snickered, licking a long line up my neck from my shoulder, ending at my ear and sucking the lobe into his mouth. A flutter of excitement flipped in my belly and I shivered.

My arms snaked up around Billy's neck and as he crushed our hips together, I could clearly feel the outline of his stainless steel pipe wrench, straining at his suit pants.

Feeling his hard length pressed between us, I suddenly remembered all of the piercings he had in his junk. Holy fuck, I was dying to get a better look at them all. My clit piercing had hurt like an absolute bitch, but he had *three* different ones!

"Do you think this'll get Shane out on the dance floor?" I whispered against Billy's ear, smearing hot pink lipstick across his skin. My right hand dipped under Billy's shirt, palm sliding against the rock-hard perfection of his abs until my fingers found the waistband of his slacks. And then down I went until I found the pierced perfection of his cock.

The thick hazy warmth of the crowd gave us as much anonymity as a darkened bedroom and as we continued to grind and gyrate to the music, I started to work Billy's shaft with my hand. It was hot enough in here that we were both dripping sweat, the movement of my fingers on the velvety length of his cock nice and slick. Nobody likes a dry hand job, right?

"I think it's working," Billy breathed at about the same moment I felt Shane slide up behind me, taking over Billy's handholds on my hips, grinding the hard bulge inside his slacks against   my   ass.
The music in the club was atrocious, but it'd been so long since I'd partied—and partied in good male company—that I didn't care. I pulled out my inner Britt and jacked Billy off at the same time I got my groove on with Shane.

"If you make me stain these slacks …" Billy started, but it sounded more like a challenge than a threat. I pumped his body hard, teasing the piercing on the underside of his shaft and the one on his balls—I couldn't quite reach the one on his taint. Too bad.

Our mouths clashed in frantic heat, and a sonorous groan slipped from Billy's mouth, adding to the booming bass beat above our heads. When he came, his fingers gripped my hips, hands layered atop Shane's, and he squeezed, causing me to bite his lower lip in response.

I slid my hand from his slacks and wiped it on his white button-up, underneath the black lines of his jacket.

"You sneaky bitch," he whispered as I laughed, smacking him in the face with my hair as I turned to dance with Shane. Two left feet he might've had, but he also had hips like Elvis and a body chiseled from stone. There wasn't a girl in there that would mind the fact that he didn't have the best moves in the room. If it was a choice between a man who could dance ... or one who could fuck, well, it was an easy decision to make.

My arms wrapped around Shane's neck, and I loved that even with heels on, he was like a fucking mountain—tall, strong, sexy. Not too bad for a random plumber turned supernatural soul mate, right?

Billy took a few minutes to recover from his, uh, wrench polishing, but then he was right there at my back, encouraging me with his hips as I ground all over Shane. The feeling in the air was electric.

As I was preparing for another deep-sea diving adventure in Shane's pants, Reg and George reappeared with new shots—slippery nipples this time—and we all took another round. By that point, I was starting to have a really good fucking time.

"Coming to the city was the best idea ever," I drawled, definitely buzzed and edging toward drunk. The room seemed to sway ever so slightly as I hung on Shane, then Reg, George and then Billy. After all, if I was going to be forcibly married to four dudes, why not take advantage of them all?

"Sure seems to have perked you up some," Shane said, and maybe it was my imagination, but he sounded a bit slurred, too, like that honey-molasses Southern accent of his was dripping. It was sexy as hell.

"I'm still planning on, you know, breaking this up," I said as I gestured sloppily at the four men. I don't think a damn one of them took me seriously, but it was in my nature to be stubborn, so ... I was at least going to pretend to still be anti-elemental.

"Whatever you say, ST," Reg slurred, and yeah, he was totally drunk, too.

I just giggled stupidly and kept dancing, the lights flashing around me, sweat slicking down my body. I mean, it wasn't like

I'd never been clubbing before, but this was … wow. Not only was my cunt throbbing like a volcanic explosion of lust was about to hit my panties, but my nipples were hard as rocks, the boys were all aroused, and I felt like I was drowning in heat.

My hands … they just wanted to be all over the guys. And their hands? Well, somebody had their warm fingers climbing up underneath my short skirt.

George ran a single finger across the crotch of my panties, making me shiver and groan, my hands curling around Shane's broad shoulders as I tried to stay standing up. *Maybe I'm a little more intoxicated than I originally thought?*

"You look like a fucking flower," George whispered in my ear, pressing up against my back. Reg and Billy weren't far away, one on either side of me, crushing me together in this protected little circle right there on the dance floor. "Let's part those petals, shall we?"

He licked up the length of my ear, his own voice just as groggy   and   slurred   as   the   others'. But at least he was true to his word.

George slid two fingers under the wet fabric of my panties and straight into the molten heat of my core, teasing my inner walls with these delectable come-hither motions. It vaguely occurred to me in the back of my mind that I was in fucking public, in a club, and that even if everyone here was a supernatural creature—and I didn't know that for sure—I was still getting fingered in public.

"You're so warm and wet, Ari," he groaned, grinding up against me, putting his mouth on my neck, his spare hand on my breasts. I didn't even seem to mind when he pulled my top down and exposed me completely.

That should've been my real warning right there, but … I was too far gone.

So drunk, I thought, my mind a blurry whirlwind of sex and want and need. That's all I cared about in that moment—getting laid. I didn't care who fucking saw me.

"Fuck me with your cock," I begged, still clutching onto Shane, loving the fact that his hand was now sneaking into his slacks, his full mouth parting in a groan as he stroked himself. "Now."

George withdrew his own hand and literally tore my panties off, ripped the fabric to shreds.

So much for being the nice guy.

As I swayed with the music, my breasts hanging fully out of my top, all three of the other men were touching themselves—Reg even had his hard dick out and in his hand. All around us though, everyone else was doing the same.

Clothes were being torn, mouths were clashing, bodies were tangling together.

George shoved my pink skirt up until it was bunched around my hips.

In one smooth motion, he slid inside me all the way to the hilt.

My breath puffed out in a gasp at the sudden feeling of fullness, and I clutched at Shane's shirt for balance when George began to move.

Gone was the nice guy tree-hugging hippy, and in his place was a wild, primal being, pounding into my aching cunt with a force that was almost pushing me off balance in my high heels.

Shane tilted my face up to his and captured my mouth in a searing kiss, dominating me with his demanding lips and tongue.

My head was spinning so hard the room was fuzzing in and out of focus, and I wasn't sure if it was the booze or the sex, or both, but I *never wanted it to end*. Every inch of my body was lit up with arousal and I wanted more. I *needed* more. As I groaned into Shane's mouth, and arched my back to push against George's thrusting hips, Billy must have read my mind, because he stepped in close beside George and grabbed hold of my breast with one hand, while the other rested on the curve of my ass.

While George fucked my pussy, and Shane pillaged my mouth, Billy teased my rock-hard nipples with a roughness that sent sharp spikes of pleasure vibrating through me. Every now and then, perfectly in time with George's motion, Billy's hand came down *hard* on my ass, making my cunt clench and George groan.

"You like that, don't you Sugar Tits," Reg asked, his hooded gaze intense on me. As I broke from Shane's kiss for air, I found him on the opposite side to Billy, cock in hand and stroking it like a horny teenager. "You like Billy's hand on your ass, while another man's dick is inside you …" He trailed off, watching as George readjusted his grip on my hips, allowing Billy access to my other ass cheek.

"Yes," I panted, gripping Shane's shirt tighter in my sweaty grip and crying out in ecstasy as Billy landed another blow, while twisting my captive nipple. "I fucking love it."

Reg's blue eyes flared with excitement. How had I only just *now* worked out that he loved a bit of dirty talk? Although he wasn't likely to get much from me the way I was. My tongue felt heavy in my mouth as I spoke the words, and they came out with a tiny bit of a slur.

"I need more though," I gasped, meeting Reg's heated gaze and begging with my eyes, "Reg, baby, I *need more*."

Somewhere in the back of my mind, that stupid little voice was muttering about this not being right, that this wasn't *normal* behavior. Or at least, as normal as my behavior ever really was.

But surely she was just the frigid, sexually repressed part of me that was the result of single sex schooling through my formative years?

Slamming a door on the whiney bitch in my mind, I turned back to Shane and let him take my mouth once more, in a kiss that could have easily set my panties alight, had I been wearing any.

But who needed panties when you could wear a bronze god's eight inch cock and some seriously warm handprints instead?

I arched my back a little more, shifting my weight in the pink satin peep-toes and allowing George in deeper. He was practically bottoming out, but his dick was stroking my G-spot in just the right way so I pushed back into him, urging him harder, faster, deeper, I don't even know what.

Reg must have taken me at my word, that I needed *more*, and he dropped to his knees between Shane and George. I broke my kiss with Shane once again, curious to see what Reg was up to, and watched as he lifted the front of my tiny dress out of the way. Meeting my eyes, he slowly slid his fingers into his mouth, swirling his tongue over them, then withdrawing them wet and gleaming to rub at my throbbing clit.

The orgasm that he sent me crashing into was so intense it was practically supernatural. As I came, screaming my release, George joined me with several hard thrusts and his fingers gripped my hip bones so hard I knew there'd be bruises tomorrow.

I fucking loved it.

As George slid free of my soaked core, I stumbled a little bit but was caught by eight *very* helpful hands.

"Steady on, darlin'," Shane drawled, his honeyed voice saturating me. "We ain't nearly done with you yet, girl."

A lazy smile crept across my lips and I drunkenly cast my gaze around us. Fuck me, not three feet from us on the dance floor was an all male threesome happening, and not a stitch of clothing was left between them. Where did the industrial-size bottle of lube suddenly come from anyway?

"Good," I replied, turning my attention back to *my* men. All four of them had their dicks out of their pants, and in their hands. Even George. That surely had to be the supernatural in him? No human man could turn it around that damn quick, and there was no mistaking the fact that he'd finished seeing as his cum was sliding down my thigh already.

Somehow, we'd ended up near the side of the dance floor, so when Shane picked me up by the waist it wasn't far to go for him to slam my back up against a wall and sink his massive inked up pipe wrench deep into my drain.

My arms went around his neck, our tongues tangling as he fucked me hard and fast, almost furious. It was like there was this charge in the air and we were powerless to resist it. The more Shane screwed me, the more I wanted. It was like I was insatiable. Even with one orgasm down and another fast approaching, I didn't feel any sense of relief. In fact, each thrust of Shane's cock was making it worse. If the growls slipping from his throat were any indication, he felt the same way.

"Don't stop," I breathed against Shane's lips—although I knew he wasn't going to. No, we would never stop. We'd stay here and we'd fuck until we dropped dead. That much, I knew. That much, I was fucking *sure* of. But in that moment, I wanted it. If I could die wrapped in the arms of these men, my body wracked with pleasure, then surely it was all worth it?

"*Arizona Morgan Smoke!*" Gram shouted from somewhere nearby. I should've been mortified that she was witnessing this and instead, I felt … nothing at all. I didn't care. It didn't mean a damn *thing*. Hell, I just felt sorry for Gram that she wasn't getting any. "Arizona!"

Shane slammed into me with a ferocious grunt, spilling his seed and making me bite my lower lip as I wiggled against him. I was *not* fucking done, damn it.

"Reg," I whispered as soon as my feet hit the ground, grabbing the water elemental by the face and running my tongue along the side of his lightly stubbled jaw up to his ear. "I'm not finished."

He didn't say a damn thing, just spun me around and pushed my face to the wall, sliding his shaft between my folds, teasing me. I wanted to fucking strangle him.

Reg lubed himself up with several thrusts before finding my opening and entering me, taking me just as hard and fierce as Shane, as George. I could barely even breathe, curling my fingers against the wall's smooth surface and pushing my ass as hard into him as I could manage. It wasn't enough. Why wasn't it enough?!

"There's magic here, Duckie—I tried to warn you," Gram was saying and Christ on a cracker, if the nickname *Duckie* didn't snap me out of my sex frenzy, nothing was going to. Instead, I just moaned and sucked on my own lip, enjoyed the sight of Billy doing his bad boy slouch against the wall next to me, stroking his cock with sure, strong fingers.

Reaching out a hand, I curled my fingers around his waistband and drew him just a little closer, so I could take charge. The look on his face was this heavy lidded bloom of sex, like he was about to blow his load and then fall into a never ending sleep. I wanted to join him there, drifting off into oblivion …

"Oh, Duckie …" Gram said, and she sounded almost like she was crying.

Couldn't figure that part out for the life of me because I was having the best fucking day of my entire life. Should've been pretty obvious at that point that magic really was, as Gram put it, *afoot.*

As Reg thrust into me, and I pleasured Billy, George and Shane, well they got a little busy, too, kissing and touching one another. It was quite the sight.

My eyes watered with tears of pleasure as another orgasm crept up on me and broke, like waves against rocks, shattering me to pieces. But, honey, someone must've turned the water on *full blast* because I felt a rush of hormones take over me, twice as powerful as before. I was like a cat in heat.

"More, Reg," I begged, tears streaming down my face. And I *never* cried. It was pretty much the last thing I ever wanted to do. I didn't cry when Gram died, or when I found out I was adopted, or when I was forcibly married to four random men I didn't know, so why now?

Because of the *magic.*

It was turning me into a completely different person, and even with a veil of lusty fog over my gaze, that was a little scary.

"Reg …" I tried to tell him to stop, so we could take a breath and see what the fuck was going on around us … all those people … all those *naked* people … But I couldn't make myself say it. I didn't want to stop. I just wanted fucking more, more, more.

And then, on the verge of another mind-blowing orgasm, it all just … stopped.

The thrumming bass above our heads, the flashing strobes, the colored spotlights dancing over the crowd.

Everything just went still and dark—no lights, no music, just bodies and breathing and cries of confusion.

"What the …" Reg started, and then he was pulling out of me and stumbling away as I scrambled to put my tits back in my top, pull my skirt down, wipe the sweat from my brow with a shaking hand.

Billy created a ball of foxfire in his palm, lighting up the severe line of his frown. I could just barely make out Shane and George to his right.

"What's happening?" I whispered, just before total chaos broke out in the room. People were groaning—not happily anymore—and screaming and shouting and cursing each other out. Personally, I don't know how they had the energy for it. I felt like I'd been hit by a fucking Mack truck. "God, I feel like shit."

"We need to get out of here—now," Shane growled from behind me, curling his fingers around my upper arm and pulling me into the darkness. Billy threw an even bigger ball of fire up, lighting the way through the crowd and all the tangled bodies. Some of them were moving, fighting, putting their clothes back on, but some were also completely passed out on the floor, snoring and moaning in their sleep.

"What the … what the fuck is going on?" I asked as Shane continued to drag me ahead of the others, straight over to an emergency exit whose sign was no longer glowing. He shoved his way through and within a few minutes, we were back out on the cold, wet New York City streets.

"Guys," I said, trying to remain calm as I stumbled down the sidewalk in my heels. "What the motherfucking fuck was that?" I was starting to sound hysterical, but really? Really?! I'd just gotten down and dirty in a room full of people *and* I'd loved every second of it. On top of that, I wasn't the only person doing it! "My head is *killing* me."

"It would," Billy said, vanquishing his foxfire and storming down the sidewalk ahead of us, raking his fingers through his charcoal hair repeatedly, like he was about to freak out or something. Inside, even though I was exhausted and having a hard time putting one foot in front of the other, I could feel this … I don't know, electric tingle, like a sharp kiss from a lightning bolt. It both frightened me and intrigued me at the same time. "Those fucking demons were draining us dry."

He glanced over his shoulder like he thought someone might be following us.

"Those … the incubi?" I asked and got a curt nod in response. "Why would they do that?"

"Who the fuck knows?" Billy responded, walking faster, almost running. I struggled to keep up, leaning against Shane's massive muscular form to keep myself from falling over. He didn't seem in much better spirits really, but at least *he* didn't have high heels on. Apparently the heels I'd borrowed from Siobhan were magically attracted to sewer grates and kept getting stuck in the metal bars.

"This is really bad," George was saying from my right side. As I glanced over at him, it occurred to me that we'd just *rutted* like animals in the middle of a New York City club. Hmm. If I hadn't felt close to collapse, I might've been embarrassed. "On top of the storm dweller, we're going to have to deal with this, too? It doesn't make any sense. They *knew* we were in the club tonight."

"Which means we were targeted," Reg said, picking up his pace so he could walk backward next to Billy and face Shane, George, and me. "They wanted us in there."

"So … the incubi and the succubi … they did that on purpose? Made us … you know …"

"Horny as shit?" Billy asked, lighting up a cigarette and pausing at a curb. "Yep."

"Why?"

"Oh, honey doll," Shane said, sounding like he was about two seconds from falling face first onto the pavement. "They eat that shit; they live off it."

"They drained us and then just … stopped?" I asked, but the weird vibe I was getting off the men didn't seem to be going anywhere.

"They didn't stop, Blossom," George said, his voice filled with this quiet heat that said that even if he *was* a tree hugging hippie, he wanted to kick some ass. "Somebody stopped them."

"How?" I asked, feeling completely left out. It felt like I should *know* these things when in reality, I didn't know shit.

We were in New York, so of course, even at this late hour, it was kind of *loud,* but the silence amongst my new hubbies was deafening. My heart skipped and lurched inside my chest and that's when I realized—that spark beneath my rib cage, that was Max. Warden. Whatever.

"He's here?!" I chirped, and that's when I *really* felt like I was about to lose it. "Where?" I touched that little string of energy inside myself on accident, just sort of flicked it, and felt the answering wave of magic that traced straight to its owner.

Standing on the opposite side of the street.

Right there.

Not fifty feet away … was the first man I'd ever fallen in love with.

16

CHAPTER SIXTEEN

Max Cornwall aka Warden cursed loudly enough that it echoed in the nearly empty streets, and swung his gaze straight over to me. Crouched low in a white hoodie and jeans, he was almost invisible in the grimy New York evening. But those eyes? I'd never forget those fucking eyes.

They were this magnificent mosaic of jade green and gold and gray, the most perfect hazel, like a spring morning when everything's covered in dew … Hey, still a barista, still not a poet.

"Max?!" I squeaked about ten seconds before several sewer manhole covers exploded upward in bursts of water, the sound of the metal plates clashing to the street a deafening boom that made my ears ring. "That's not good, is it?" I asked, feeling my heartbeat start to thunder and my head swim. "That's really fucking bad."

"It's plum awful, Sug," Shane said, jerking me close as several pairs of arms dug out of the various holes in the pavement. And the stench that came with them? It burned the hairs out of my nostrils. It was a sickly, sweet smell like death and disease and shit all mixed together. Like, well, a big city sewer might smell.

"You need to get Arizona out of here," Warden was saying, all of a sudden just *standing* next to me like he'd never left. The sight of him so close, those eyes, the curve of his lips, the spiky tuft of dark hair sticking out from under the white hood of his sweatshirt ... it all took me back to my time at UCSC. That night. Those feelings ...

"Let's take her back to her slutty friend's apartment—there were wards everywhere," Billy said, clearly speaking with clenched teeth as he glared at Max/Warden and *I* tried really hard not to look at the things crawling out of the sewer.

"First off, please don't slut shame ... and wards?" I managed to spit out, still desperately enthralled by Max's presence and the idea of one of my best, good friends casting *spells*. Siobhan had ... wards? My entire world felt like a lie, like I'd been living in one big dream cloud from birth until now, a hazy fog that obscured all the things that really mattered.

"Let's go, sweet stuff," Shane said, pulling me away from Warden as he turned to face the monsters slipping out from underneath New York's city streets, clawing at the cement with slimy fingers and pulling their gaping mouths and rotten faces to the surface.

What the fuck was a human going to think when they saw this?!

I resisted Shane's grip for a minute, reaching out a hand and just barely managing to slide my fingers across the back of Warden's. Our touch ... it was electric in more than just a magical sense. His gaze snapped over to me and I could see so

315

many things taking place in his eyes, so many emotions warring for supremacy.

"Get the flip out of here, Smokey," he growled, looking like he was about to shit his pants. Whether it was me or, you know, the *zombies* I wasn't sure.

"I …" Words failed me as Shane started to pull me away from him, down the sidewalk away from the stinking, rotting, loping things that'd just burst forth from the sewer. It didn't take a genius to put it all together—necromancer spirit elemental, undead things, zombies.

Shane managed to get me to the end of the block, George tagging along with us, as we left Billy, Reg, and Warden behind. After being drained from those fucking winged whores (who must use glamour *a lot* because I like, didn't see any wings in there), I knew they weren't going to have an easy time fighting. I could barely stay awake let alone go full dragon …

"We gotta run, babe," Shane said, sounding like he wanted to shake me.

I looked up and caught faces peering down off balconies, a shout here and there, the honk of a horn down the street. Like I said, it might be nighttime, but it was still New York.

"What's going to happen to all these people?" I asked, and I really didn't enjoy the silence I got from George and Shane.

"Pick her up and carry her," George said after a moment, but I was already wrenching my arm from Shane's grip. There was no way in *hell* I was abandoning these guys to fight and possibly die, to let random completely derpy humans get killed in the crossfire—especially not if this all somehow had to do with … me.

Before Shane or George could grab me, I went spirit elemental on their asses, letting my skin go to that dark purple color that basically turned me into a living ghost.

316

Unfortunately, Gram was nowhere to be seen or else I was sure she'd have been proud.

"Don't do this, honeycomb," Shane warned, but I was already taking off in the direction of the zombie horde. There were dozens and dozens of them, some swarming toward Reg, Billy, and Warden, and the rest wandering off to god only knew where. A substantial portion were coming straight at *me,* but fuck 'em—they could try to eat these invisible brains.

Several zombies went right through me, their clothing rotted and wet and hanging in tatters from their discolored flesh. They were fast, too, clearly powered by magic and not some weird unknown disease. These things were pawns, like a flock of birds with one mind. Sure, there were a few *different* flocks going in opposite directions, but I could see a single hand behind it all.

Had to be my bio dad.

How nice was that?

"Arizona, what in the wicked fuck?" Warden asked as I jogged my way back over to him and the other boys. God, I'd always loved his unusual cursing habits. If I'd been wearing panties, I'd have wet them. Then again, it was already pretty wet down there as it was … Like, sort of gross wet. I needed a shower. "Get the bleeping Christ out of here!"

"Eat a dick, Max," I said, puffing like I'd run a marathon, barely able to tear my eyes off of him … and there were like, zombies. Lots of zombies. The man had a magnetism to him that I couldn't seem to resist.

"Holy bleeding hell hole," he breathed, like I was already draining the life right out of him. "You're going to get yourself killed!"

As soon as those words, left his lips, he swung his arm out and all the lights on the street went out—the apartment buildings, the streetlights, even nearby cars lost their headlights. An arc of energy followed the movement, sweeping out and hitting the wave of undead things like a ton of bricks.

The stench amplified about a hundred times, the sweet scent of decay now gently roasting in an electrical fire. Billy made it worse, taking the flames that'd sprung up from the creatures and sending them roaring into the sky. As soon as he did that though, he collapsed.

"Christ, sugar pea, gettin' you to do somethin' you don't want to do is like herdin' cats."

"I have no idea what that means," I said as Shane scooped Billy up into his arms and I felt the glamour sliding off of me like water off a duck's back. Even though I was in invisible elemental form, the runes popped up across my skin like beacons, shimmering faintly. "But can you just get him the hell out of here?"

"We're not leaving our spirit elemental to fight alone, are you crazy?" Reg asked, panting like he'd already run a triathlon and was now being asked to do an ironman. "You die, we all die. You did understand that part, right?!" He paused and worried at his lower lip for a second. "And besides, I like, sort of like you …"

"This isn't a goddamn Bar Mitzvah!" Warden shouted, sweeping his arm down and sending another wave of energy at the next horde of zombies. I had literally no idea what a Bar Mitzvah had to do with the situation, but that was Warden for ya. His cursing and bitching slang made even less sense than my American-Australian-British combo pack.

"Just tell me what to do," I said, wishing I could just fucking reach out and *touch* him. Being see-through sort of made that part a tad difficult. "As long as it isn't *run* or *hide*, I'll do it."

"For Satan's sake," he said, nibbling at his lower lip and casting me a sharp glance with golden eyes ringed in dark liner. "Just … pick off the stray ones before some stupid flipping human goes and gets themselves killed." He flicked his gaze away like he couldn't bear to look at me. Hopefully that was more because he *wanted* me than because he was disgusted with me, but I guessed romance matters were best left until *after* the zombies had been dealt with.

"Right. Got it. Pick off the stray ones." Holy fuck, I was *exhausted*. There was no way in hell that I was letting some reanimated fucks kill off my new husbands though. As much as I was loathe to admit it, they were seriously growing on me—and not just because they fucked like demons.

Digging deep into my elemental powers, I created basketballs of fire and lobbed them at some of the more slow-moving corpses, sending them up in flames. I figured since Billy was out of commission, fire was going to be the most beneficial here, and it definitely seemed to be slowing them down.

There had to be a better way though. The zombies were still clawing their way up from the sewer, and who knew how many more my bio dad had down there to come at us? Max—I mean *Warden*—was the only one of us at full strength and there was no possible way he could take on this many magically driven corpses alone.

What had Grams said about my bio dad's necromancer powers? He was a *spirit*, just like I was, so surely it must be possible for me to tap into the same power? Maybe if I could, it might be possible to stop this onslaught of rotting flesh before it got any further out of hand. As it was, bystanders had begun screaming in terror, and while I watched, a zombie grabbed hold of an unsuspecting civilian and bit a massive chunk right out of the man's neck. The blood spray traveled straight through my incorporeal body and I thanked *fuck* I was still in spirit form.

I needed to multi-task. Standing there like a plonker while my guys battled for their lives wasn't helping, so I split my focus in two. With one hand, I formed and threw fireballs while simultaneously digging deep into my mind and searching for the magic that was uniquely my own.

Wielding the other elements was coming easily to me, and I suspected it was because of my bond with the guys. Wielding my own didn't seem to come with an instruction manual though.

"Come on, come on, come on," I muttered under my breath, fighting the urge to shut my eyes as had become my habit when trying magic. Now was *not* the time to take my eyes off the road.

"Watch it!" Warden yelled, slamming a lightning bolt into the zombie that was a scarce foot from biting a chunk out of my calf muscle. "You need to pay more blinking attention, Smokey!"

"Sorry," I muttered, my heart thundering. Holy shit, that'd been close. I hadn't even noticed that I'd turned solid again! Unsurprising though, given how quickly my energy and magic were depleting. It might've been *easier* to use magic while in that form, but it sure as hell was difficult to *stay* in it.

Sucking in a deep breath, I hurled a couple more fireballs, then as quick as I could screwed my eyes shut to reach for my spirit magic with both mental hands.

The magic responded like an old lover, leaping into my grip and engulfing me in a rush of adrenaline and excitement, giving me a little boost to keep going.

My eyes flew open again and locked onto my target. The zombie I'd chosen was just crawling from the nearest manhole, and was still down on all fours when I turned the force of my magic on him … or her … It was really hard to tell with all the soupy decaying flesh dripping from the person's remains.

The moment my magic hit, I saw a reaction. The zombie froze, stiffened, then locked its gleaming eyes on me. Inside my head I could *feel* its consciousness, like an extension of my own that I could will to act as I pleased. Experimentally, I pushed another thread of magic into the corpse, and felt a satisfied grin slide over my face when the zombie obeyed my command and twirled in a circle like some sort of macabre ballerina.

"Guys, I think I've got this!" I tried to project my voice out to my lovers but it just squeaked out in a weak sounding whisper. Fucking hairy dingo balls, I was almost tapped out. This needed to end *now.*

In one massive sweep, I shot my spirit magic out to every corpse within a fifty yard radius and prayed it would be enough. The consciousness of the entire horde crammed into my head all at once and I screamed.

The pain was like nothing I'd ever experienced. It felt as though my brain was being shredded with a rusty cheese grater and deeper, toward the back of the swarm was something dark, evil, and *very* strong.

Bio Dad.

His malevolent presence tapped at my mind, like he was knocking on a door, but I shoved him aside. I barely had the strength to stand, let alone have a little mental chat with the evil being who had sired me and was currently trying to kill me. Disable the zombies. That was my *only* concern.

Sending out my will to some seventy reanimated corpses sent pain ripping through me like someone was scooping out my insides with a spoon, then pouring lighter fluid in the gaps and setting me alight. My knees buckled and I crashed to the concrete but didn't for a second let my focus waver.

STOP!

I was all I could think of. Thankfully, that one simple order was all that was required and as I watched, all seventy-three (I could count them in my brain) zombies paused, stared straight at me, then crumpled to the ground in lifeless sacks of bones and rotting flesh.

Seconds after they dropped, so too did I.

In my dream, I was back in college. Max, Britt, and I were all laying on the grass outside my dorm and laughing about something Britt had just said—something pervy, obviously. While she chattered, acting out a scene from her wild night, Max met my eyes and the world around us faded.

"You're so beautiful, Smokey," he whispered, tucking a stray curl behind my ear then trailing his fingers down my jaw.

"Max," I sighed, leaning into the warmth of his palm and embracing the rush of affection, lust, and even love as it coursed through me. Why had I run from this man? He was my soulmate. Or one of them at any rate.

"Baby doll, you need to wake up now. Everyone's flippin' worried about you." His hazel eyes were sad, and I could see bottomless depths of pain in them. Deep down, I knew I was the cause of all that hurt.

"What are you going on about?" I smiled at him and glanced over at Britt, still reenacting an argument she'd had with someone at a bar the night before. "I'm awake, here with you, where I should be. I never should've left you ..."

Max's beautiful eyes tightened a little as he flinched. The wound was obviously still as raw for him as it was for me.

"Well, you did. Unfortunately no supernatural has the power to turn back time, as far as we know, so we just need to deal with life as it is now." His tone was short and clipped, and he made to pull away from me.

Grabbing his hand, I forced his gaze back to my face.

"Max, please don't pull away. I've missed you like you couldn't possibly imagine."

"Trust me, Smokey," he said with a bitter smile, "I can imagine. And more. Now you need to wake up before your new husbands lose their ever loving minds."

"Will you be there when I do?" I asked in a small voice. All the hurt and regret I'd carried with me for so many years was as fresh as the day it'd all happened, and when Max shook his head, I swear I heard my heart crack in two.

"No. I won't. Just … don't get yourself killed and we'll all be fine." Max forcefully withdrew his hand from my tight grip and stood up. The sun was behind him, so I had to squint to try and make out his face. "Be seeing you, Smokey."

"Max!" I yelled as he turned and walked away from me. "Please, Max! Don't leave me! I'm sorry … I'm so fucking sorry!" Tears were streaming down my face as I watched him leave and knew he didn't hear me as I whispered, "Max, I love you …"

"Hey, Blossom." George's gentle voice reached my ears as the vision of Max's retreating form faded and was replaced by the pink and white roses of Gram's guest bedroom.

"George?" I murmured, blinking a couple of times to try and clear my double vision. Had that been a dream? Or something *else*? "Where's Max?"

"He's …" George grunted a noise that sounded pissed off. "He's sorting some things out."

"Oh." I sat up and swiped a hand over my face where I could feel tears still running down my cheeks. "Was I, um … did I talk in my sleep?"

George slid his hand into my hair, cupping my head and kissing away another stray tear that had just slipped from my eye. "Yeah, babe. You were."

"Oh," I said again, sucking in a deep breath to pull myself together. I was *not* the kind of girl that cried over a man. Not then, not now, not *ever*. What the hell was wrong with me? I blamed it on the zombies.

"Come on, let's go downstairs so the guys can see you're okay," George suggested, hopping off the bed and holding out a hand to me. "You've been out for almost three days, so we were all really worried about you. The healer said you'd be fine, but …"

"Three days?!" I exclaimed, gaping at him in shock. "Christ, no wonder I need to pee like a goddamn fucking waterfall." Swinging my legs out of the bed, I went to stand but wobbled like a little old lady and George caught me.

"Um … help me to the loo?" I asked and he grinned down at me, his teeth a gleaming white against the bronze of his skin. Fuck me, my husbands were sexy.

"It'll be my pleasure, Blossom," he chuckled and swept me up bridal style to carry me.

"I said *help* not *carry*, George," I muttered, but quietly loved how these men kept picking me up like a doll. I tried not to psychoanalyze the reasons behind that. In my own mind, I was still a badass bitch.

"I know, but I wanted to carry you. Is that okay?" He tilted his head to the side, actually checking my permission as he kicked open the door and started down the hallway to my bathroom.

"I suppose …" I murmured, not wanting to give in *too* easily. As we entered the main bathroom, the same one that had started out this whole mess back when my drains just needed cleaning, my jaw dropped.

"George, what the …"

"Oh yeah. We remodeled your bathroom while we were waiting for you to wake up." George looked *supremely* pleased with himself. "Charlie felt bad about the way everything had gone down, with the whole tree roots situation and whatnot, so he let us go a bit crazy on the fixtures. Do you like it?"

When George said they'd gone *a bit crazy,* he was grossly understating things. The bathroom looked like something out of a fucking palace!

"Is this … how is this even possible?" I gaped. My main bathroom was big, yes, but this was … enormous.

"We knocked out the wall into the next bedroom and expanded. You didn't need that many bedrooms anyway." George shrugged, placing me down carefully on the countertop beside the sink.

Jesus fuck. That was a *lot* of work to get done in three days. Guess using their supernatural powers for construction work *was* a smart idea. I supposed that was how Joan's men had managed to buy that massive fucking house, getting big jobs done in a fraction of the time like that. And the quality of the work, well it was *exceptional*. Holy hell.

"Right." I was a little at a loss for words. They'd installed a shower big enough for seven, with jets and rainfall roses all over the place, as well as a bench running down one side that I just *knew* I'd be fucking someone on sooner or later. Most impressive though was the tub—if it could even be called a tub.

It was more of a swimming pool or oversized hot tub with a legitimate waterfall cascading into the jasmine scented water.

"I thought maybe you might feel like taking a bath," Reg said, leaning in the doorway and running his eyes all over me. For once, his gaze wasn't predatory and lust filled, but instead full of concern.

"We felt you wake up, so I ran the bath …" he trailed off as a blush stained his cheeks. Evidently this caring, considerate Reg was new to him as well.

"That's the sweetest fucking thing …" I smiled and watched as his blush deepened. I'd let it go for now, the last thing I wanted to do was embarrass him into never being sweet again.

"I just need to pee and then want to hear everything that happened after I passed out, if that's okay?" I raised my eyebrows at the two elementals and they just nodded and stared back at me. "So … if I could have a moment?"

Yes, I was aware that I had recently let four men publicly fuck my brains out, but I was nowhere near ready to pee in front of them. Some things just needed to stay private.

Reg rolled his eyes and George chuckled, but they both left the bathroom so I could sort out my bursting bladder in peace.

They obviously didn't go far though because seconds after I'd pulled up my panties and flushed, they were right back in the massive bathroom with me. Someone must've cleaned me up and dressed me after the zombie attack because I was in just a pair of bat printed knickers and an oversized t-shirt that smelled distinctly of Billy. Not to mention there was no elemental semen crusted to my inner thighs, and considering the state I'd been in prior to passing out … *shudder.*

"So fill me in," I prompted as I washed my hands out of habit.

"Get in the bath first and we will," Reg growled, a tiny sliver of lust back in his voice as he leaned on the wall. Cocking a brow at him flirtatiously, I slowly dragged the t-shirt over my head, then dropped my bat panties.

"Not joining me?" I teased, turning my back on them to step into the steaming water. The tub was only raised a couple of steps off the ground, but then sunk much deeper, so I was fully submerged up to my neck as I sat on the little ledge inside.

"Don't tempt me," Reg muttered and George whacked him with the back of his hand.

"Leave her be, Reg, you horn-dog. Ari's been through a lot lately, without you trying to stick your dick in her every chance you get." George rolled his eyes, but the look he gave me said he was seriously considering joining me himself. Goddamn bloody sexy husbands were going to be the death of me, but luckily the water was deep enough to obscure my rock-hard nipples as I fantasized about fucking them all here in this tub.

"Really?" Billy asked with a voice so dry it could probably mop up the flood between my legs. Metaphorically of course, given I was in a tub full of water, but if I *wasn't* ... well let's just say my sink would be overflowing.

"You're just going to stand there and let our wife wash her own hair?"

Billy yanked his t-shirt off and threw it on top of my own discarded clothes, followed by his pants, before sliding into the hot water with me.

"Honestly, some elementals these days," he muttered under his breath as he glided through the water to assess all the options for bath products. There was a *huge* assortment of different bottles lined up on a low shelf at one end of the tub, and I was curious to see what he came back with.

"We were letting her have some time unmolested by all of our raging hard-ons," George sighed, rolling his eyes at Billy and folding his arms over his smooth bronze chest. We were no longer in public, so he obviously didn't need to wear a shirt anymore.

"Uh-huh," Billy muttered, clearly not really listening. "Sure."

"You were telling me what happened after the zombies?" I prompted, dipping my head back to wet my hair and sighing in pleasure at the warmth of the water. Billy glided back over to me and moved so he was behind me, his knees on either side of my waist as he squirted a pile of shampoo into one hand and began lathering up my hair.

"Ugh, yes. The fucking zombies." Reg grimaced. "They were fuckin' foul. That *smell*. After you hit them with your spirit whammy, they all just dropped like puppets with their strings cut. You and Billy were unconscious and there were half decomposed corpses fucking *everywhere* so ... we grabbed you both and ran."

He shrugged, nice and loose and easy, his Sailor Jerry tattoos rippling over the corded perfection of muscles in his arms and shoulders.

"You just *ran*?" I repeated, stunned.

"Billy, what the hell are you doing?" Shane snapped, also entering the bathroom and giving Billy a glare that could skin a cat. "That's not how you wash a woman's hair!"

Throwing his clothes off, Shane joined us in the tub and grasped me by the waist. He dipped me back to rinse the shampoo Billy had already applied, then turned me to straddle the fire elemental's waist while he applied a fresh dose of shampoo to my hair, rubbing and massaging my scalp like a fucking professional hairdresser.

"Yes," George replied to my question, after a bit of a pause watching me get my hair washed between two naked men. "We ran; we had no choice. The incubi and succubi were left to clean up the mess of rotting bodies, and COCS handled crowd control to erase the public's memories. It doesn't do the supernatural world any favors to have people knowing about us."

"Makes sense," I murmured, then groaned in pleasure as Shane's magical fingers massaged out the tension that I'd apparently been carrying in my scalp. Fuck me. Who knew getting your hair washed could be such a damn turn-on? I clearly wasn't the only one who thought so as Billy's pierced pipe was sitting firm between us, and Shane's was bumping my ass. "So, um, do we, uh …" Forming logical and coherent thoughts was not coming easily to me in that moment. "Do we know why the demons tried to drain us in the first place?"

"Considering they killed the entire COCS delegation that went over to pay Adonis and Rachel a visit, it's *hard* to say," Reg said as he leaned over and put his hands on the edge of the tub. I was pretty sure he'd emphasized the word *hard.*

"Where's Gram?" I managed to choke out, and yelped as she appeared in the doorway to the bathroom, scrambling away from the, uh, double copper pipes below the water. That just proved it right there—clearly I was magically drugged at the club if the sight of my dead grandmother hadn't shaken me out of my sexual reverie.

"Right here, Duckie," she said, covering her eyes with one wrinkled semi-see-through hand. "If you wanted to speak with me, perhaps you might've put some knickers on first?"

"Here she goes again," Billy murmured trying to drag me back onto his lap. "Talking to dead people."

"My skills with dead people seem to be working out pretty damn well," I said, remembering the horde of zombies dropping like flies. That and ... Max. Warden. Damn it. Who cared what his stupid name was?! I just wanted five minutes to talk to the man ... "Where were you during the fight?" I asked, letting Shane continue his ministrations on my hair. Billy rolled his eyes and dipped under the surface of the water as George took up a position on the outside of the tub and crossed his legs.

"I was staying well away from that .... that *sperm donor*," Gram sputtered, reaching up to pat at her coiffed English curls. "Did you see how you wielded the power of the dead against his own creations? Do you want to see me forcibly sent over to the other side?"

Um, was that a rhetorical question because the answer was, uh, yeah, kind of.

Anyway ...

"So I'm a necromancer, too?" I asked as Gram waltzed into the bathroom and gave the shiny new chrome fixtures, marble floors, and French baroque style mirrors a filthy look.

"All of this useless excess ..." she murmured with a sigh, coming ... uncomfortably close to Reg as he slipped off his pants and shirt and climbed into the tub, magicking the water that sloshed over the edge straight into the sink. "You do understand what's happening here, don't you, sweet bottom?"

"Not particularly—out of the loop, remember?" I said, trying not to shriek as I pointed at myself with a single finger. "Raised human, *remember?*" That second half was a tad accusatory, but ... well, Gram could get stuffed. Or ... ew, I'd just rather she didn't. "I *don't* actually happen to know what's going on."

"Your ... sperm donor," she said which was sort of a weird thought considering I had like, six moms. Which one birthed me? Were they all egg donors? The science of elementals was a wee bit out of my grasp. "He wants the power of the storm dweller without the sacrifice."

"He doesn't want to suck my egg donor moms dry?" I asked as Shane let go of my hair and Reg used his magic to rinse the soap from it, sliding warm water over my hair without getting a single drop into my eyes.

"These one-sided conversations are totally weird," Billy murmured from my left. I ignored him, the runes on my skin sparkling prettily in the water. Guess all that magic had killed my new glamour, huh? Fantastic. Couldn't wait to choke down another rat tail.

"That's why he raised cuntmuffin, right?" I asked, because shit, if I couldn't remember to call Max Warden then I sure as hell wasn't going to remember some ancient elemental word for *storm dweller.* I had enough new supernatural facts to memorize, thank you very much.

"He raised *kuntemopharn* because he wants to use *you* to get the magic he's not willing to trade his wives for. Do you understand?"

"He wants to unstop our pipes and drain us dry?" I asked, figuring a plumbing metaphor was most apt for the situation.

"You're not as dumb as I'd always thought," Gram said, rubbing at her small wrinkled chin. I didn't want to say anything, but even as a ghost, there were a few wiry hairs dotting the skin above and below her lips. Heh. Well, lesson learned—if I was going to die, I was going out *plucked.* "But yes, that's the gist of it."

Gram paused at the edge of the tub and looked through her spectacles at me, face drawn and tired and sad. I felt compelled to grab a pair of loofahs and drag them over my hardened nipples. Hopefully my hoo-ha—and by hoo-ha, I mean cunt—

was covered by the soapy film floating on the surface of the water.

"I'm sorry, sweetie," she said as I cocked a brow and watched Gram lift her face to the ceiling. "I'm so sorry."

As I followed her gaze up, I saw the ceiling sparkle with a pattern, much like the runes on my skin. They glimmered for a brief moment before going out ... one by one, sizzling away like they'd been burned.

"I'm so sorry, Duckie," Gram whimpered, putting her face in her wrinkled hands, see-through tears dripping down and dangling from her chin. "I had no choice ..."

"The wards!" George said, standing up suddenly, like he'd just *felt* what I'd seen. There was this snapping sensation in the air, as if that entire transition from fall to winter was happening in a single cold snap. The water in the tub around me literally *froze,* locking me into a thick block of ice.

A scream managed to scrape from my throat as Reg shifted into dragon form, hitting his tail against the surface of the solid ice, freeing me, Shane, and Billy in a rush of warm water.

"I'm so bloody sorry!" Gram was screaming as I rushed out of the tub and snatched up my bat undies and t-shirt—just in time, too, because a woman was stepping into the bathroom doorway, her face in a severe frown, fingers curled around the edges of the door frame.

As soon as she saw me though, her mouth twisted up to the side in a smile.

"My sweet little baby," she said mockingly, holding up a hand palm out when Reg snarled and bared his glimmering white shark's teeth at her. "If I were you, I'd hold off on the theatrics for a moment."

The woman swept her finger in a circle and cut the electricity.

Well.

Didn't have to guess which elemental *she* was.

"Outside—you'll want to see our bargaining chip."

She retreated slowly, long blonde hair cascading over her shoulders and falling almost to the floor. But that mouth, that hair, her nose … it all looked like … well, *me.*

"Bargaining chip?" I asked as Gram's wails echoed around the house like a proper ghost, my heartbeat thundering like a team of horses. "And what the fuck is wrong with Gram?"

"Blossom, all the wards on the house are down," George said, putting a hand on Reg's watery neck. This time, Reg was about the size of a small horse, a reminder that even though they *did* look like dragons, the boys were fluid, elemental—small enough to climb in a pipe or large enough to give me a ride, didn't matter. It was their choice. "They're all down," George repeated. The look he gave me said he was debating grabbing me around the waist and making a run for it. But bargaining chip? Dude, if the bad guys had Britt … or Siobhan, I couldn't let anything happen to them. "Your grandmother took down her protection spells."

Shit.

Well that explained the apologies …

"What the flipping fuck is going on?!" I growled, taking a page from Max/Warden's coloring book.

In my undies, I stormed out of the new bathroom and down the old staircase, heading straight for the open front door.

As soon as I emerged onto the sagging porch, I knew.

I *felt* it.

"Max," I whispered as I caught sight of my ex/supernatural soul mate lying in a crumpled ball near a man's feet.

"Hello Arizona," the man said, his blonde hair ruffling in a gentle breeze, a cluster of women surrounding him like a group of deranged Charlie's Angels. Knowing they were all somehow my biological moms was … really fucking weird.

"Stay sharp, Firebug," Billy said from my right side, narrowing his eyes and pursing his lips. He looked about ready to kill somebody—good thing, too because it looked like that might be where this was all headed.

The bio dad bad guy and the mom horde was bad enough, but add in Warden … and the giant undead *monster* floating behind them and this was basically my worst nightmare come true.

A quick glance over at the boys revealed that we also had an *audience.* Alberta O'Sullivan was on her porch smoking a pipe and glaring at us, her wings fluttering slightly as she narrowed her eyes on me and mouthed *fumblin' Dublin* under her breath.

I ignored her and flicked my attention back to the supernatural army on Gram's lawn.

"What do you want?" I asked as Gram's wailing echoed out through the open door and around the neighborhood. Guess it was one—Arizona and one—Bio Dad. I'd taken his zombies; he'd played my grandma.

"I'm not interested in standing here, cackling and rubbing my hands together," Bio Dad said, stepping over Warden's prone body and coming up to stand next to me. "I'm not into the villain routine."

"Really?" I asked with a healthy dose of sarcasm and a dollop of skepticism. "Because coming to my house in the middle of the night with my college sweetheart lying half-dead on the ground, magicking my Gram, and freezing my bathwater sure cast some suspicion your way."

The man tucked his hands into the stylish black jeans he was wearing. Honestly, like Charlie and Joan he looked *way* too fucking young to be my father. His eyes were the same color as my own, a pale mossy green with flecks of brown and gold. As soon as he met my gaze, I knew without a doubt that it was all true—this man was the source of at least part of my DNA.

"Daniel Troy," he said, holding out a hand for me to shake.

I stared at it like it was poisoned, my breath coming in long, harsh gasps. I just wanted to save Warden and finish bathing and put some clothes on. What the hell was *wrong* with these people?!

"Well, being raised by humans has certainly affected your manners," he said, lifting one curved blonde brow. Daniel dropped his hand. "Listen, Arizona, I'm not here to kill you and your husbands. In fact, I'm actually here to offer my *help*."

"Your help?" I asked, crossing my arms over my breasts and wishing I was wearing a bra. It just felt like maybe I'd be able to kick a little more ass and take a few more names if my headlights weren't on full blast. "Why do I find that so hard to believe, after what happened with the COCS delegation?"

Daniel waved his hand dismissively, like that was of no concern to him.

"Originally, yes, I considered taking what I wanted and leaving, but Arizona, it doesn't have to be like that." Daniel reached up to touch me, but Shane's hand lashed out and took hold of his wrist, shoving him back.

My bio dad just smiled.

"The thing is, there's a war coming, Arizona." He retreated a few steps and moved over to the fruit tree in the middle of Gram's front yard, plucking a honey crisp apple off the branch. I watched in increasingly frustrated disgust as he took a bite out of it. "And yes, I *could* take your energy and run. But ..." Daniel trailed off and cocked his head to the side, studying Alberta O'Sullivan like she was fascinating to him. After a moment, he glanced back at me. "I'd rather you keep making more."

"Pardon?" I asked, blinking stupidly in his direction.

"Like a faucet," George said from my other side, using yet *another* plumbing metaphor, "if he turns the tap on, he can have as much energy as he wants. As long as we're alive, we'll keep making more."

"You want to … drain us not once but over and over and over?"

Daniel smiled and crossed his arms over his chest as one of my er, moms, knelt down and rolled Warden onto his back, putting her palm flat over his chest. It was the blonde woman, the energy elemental. As I watched, she pushed magic into Warden's chest that I could *feel*. The hairs on my arms stood up at attention; my scalp prickled. I felt like I'd just stuck my finger in an electrical outlet.

My heartbeat started to pound in time with Warden's—she was messing with the electrical impulses in his body.

"Arizona," Daniel said, waving his hand and drawing the rotting, stinking snake of cuntmuffin's putrid flesh over to us. "This war, it'll benefit all of us, I promise. It's for a good cause." He shrugged his shoulders like he didn't much give a shit if I believed him or not.

"A good cause?" I snorted. "I find that hard to believe given your casual disregard for life this far. Thanks but no thanks, *Dad*."

I sneered at him, not trying to hide the disgust on my face or in my voice. As far as I was concerned, he was little more than a build up of toilet paper that needed breaking up and flushing away. Until he was, the shit would just keep piling up.

"You may want to reconsider that answer, *daughter*," he warned, walking back over to Max's lifeless form and placing a foot over his neck.

"Or what?" I bluffed, hoping to keep him talking long enough to think of a way out of this mess. As it was, my guys were slowly spreading out around the yard and preparing themselves for a fight while Kuntemopharn loomed closer. Red tinted drool dripped from his massive fangs and his wings looked like they'd been nibbled at by giant moths.

"Or I'll change my mind about your usefulness and take your life as a consolation prize instead. Don't think that just because I'd *prefer* to keep you alive as a renewable source of energy, I won't be plenty satisfied with the one time magic boost I can get by draining the lot of you right here, right now." His gaze held firm on mine, as unblinking as a sewer alligator, and I returned his stare with a stubborn tilt to my chin. Never negotiate with terrorists, right?

"So that's what you raised cuntmuffin from the dead for? To drain our magic for you to what? Take over the world?" I eyed the decaying mess of the undead dragon warily. We'd yet to see him in human form, if indeed he even had one, but I couldn't imagine it was very pretty.

"Actually no, I can do that all myself. We raised him to gain the knowledge of how to do so, but as I'm not *quite* prepared to sacrifice my own *sept* just yet, I'll need to settle for yours. Now, he's just *exceptional* backup, don't you think?" Daniel admired the festering sore of a reanimated elemental as though he were a prize poodle, and I shuddered. The *smell* of him alone was enough to curl my arm hairs.

"As charming as that offer is," I grimaced, "like I said, thanks but no thanks. If you want our magic you'll have to fucking take it."

For a moment, Daniel stood there considering my words then nodded and glanced at his wives. What a sexist pig, needing six wives to keep him happy.

"Kill them."

His command was spoken in such a casual tone of voice he might just have easily been asking to pass the salt, had his wives not all burst into their dragon forms with enviable synchronization.

As one, they launched at my husbands and my front yard exploded in a clash of elements and battling dragons. Everywhere I looked there were teeth and claws and scales. The elementals battled with everything they had, but I was left alone.

My focus was distracted for a moment, watching in terror as Kuntemopharn swooped toward Billy only to be knocked back by a wall of flame, and when I looked back to where Daniel had stood over Max's body, my bio dad was gone.

Seeing an opportunity, I rushed down my porch stairs with the intention of getting to Max and checking he was okay. I'd barely made it three steps off the porch when something hit me from the side with the force of a Mack Truck, knocking me down and sending me skidding across the now soaking grass.

Groaning, I held my side and gasped for breath. What the fuck was *that*? My wondering didn't last long though, as a huge aubergine elemental pounced on me, pinning me to the ground.

"Don't worry, *sweetie*," the dragon sneered—as much as a dragon could, really—as drool splattered my face, "Daddy's got you …"

Bracing myself for whatever was about to come, I gathered up some of my magic and used air to forcefully shove his scaly ass off me. Or, I intended to shove his scaly ass off me, but barely managed to halt the descent of his jaws from ripping out my throat. Oh well, small wins.

It had been enough to make him pause though, so I pressed my advantage and hit him with a ball of fire followed by some daggers of ice which forced him to release his grip on me and focus on defending himself.

Like some sort of overgrown crab, I scurried backwards on my butt to gain a bit of distance before hitting his with another hard gust of wind, this time tipping his balance and sending him crashing ass over tit farther down the lawn from me.

From my left, a flicker of light caught my attention. Lightning was raining down on the enemy elementals, striking them all repeatedly and tipping the scales back in our favor. The blonde energy elemental who, I guess, was also one of my mothers, tried to return fire but her bolts were weak and thin in comparison and Max knocked them aside with a wave of his hand.

"Max!" I gasped, the relief at seeing him alive almost knocking me on my ass. If I weren't already on my ass, that was.

"Sharpen up, Smokey," he growled at me, "these hectic bastards are as slippery as greased up piglets."

What the fuck *that* meant, I had no idea. But he was right that I needed to sharpen up. Daniel had shifted back into his human form and was picking himself up from the grass and glaring daggers at me. My eyes darted around the lawn, making a quick assessment of how we were fairing, but it was hard to judge. Bio parents had us on numbers, but even I could tell that my sext was stronger—both magically and physically.

"Take a good look at your lovers; it'll be the last time you ever see them," Daniel sneered, stalking closer to me before running smack into the wall of air I had erected in his path.

Obviously I knew it wasn't enough to hold him at bay forever, but it slowed him down and gave me a twisted thrill to see him bounce off the invisible barrier and land on his ass.

Not stupid enough to waste my time engaging this maniac in conversation, I kept my trap shut and prepared for him. As expected, he used his own magic to smash my wall of air down, then moved faster than I had thought possible, wrapping his hands around my throat as we flew through the air and landed on the grass some three or four yards away.

"Now, be a good girl for daddy and don't fight this." The sick fuck pinned my limbs with steel-like shackles of tree roots then sunk his fingertips deep enough into my neck that blood began trickling down my throat.

Fuck. I was screwed. How the hell was I getting out of this?

The moment Daniel began sucking out my magic was unmistakable. Similar to when I had returned the shop assistant's essence—when I accidentally stole it during my mind-blowing orgasm—the sensation was like that of a giant Band-aid being ripped off my soul. Only this time, while the Band-Aid was being ripped off, someone was pouring bleach all over the wound underneath it.

Suffice to say, it fucking hurt.

Screaming in agony, I gathered my magic to me and prepared to shove the leech off me. Just as I was about to hurl it at him with all my strength, my eye snagged on George. Or rather, on Kuntemopharn about to bite George's head off.

Without a second thought, I redirected the trajectory of my magic and slammed the undead elemental with it, bending him to my will. I forced so much of my will into stopping the zombified dragon, it felt as though I was wearing him like a sock puppet.

When I willed him to back the fuck up and sit politely, he did.

Gasping from the exertion of will, I mentally severed the ties that held Kuntemopharn's will to Daniel's and the second I did that, the putrid, rotting elemental slumped like someone had just hit his off switch.

Thank fuck for that. Hopefully it was permanent.

My bio dad's maniacal laughter brought my focus back to him. He was still gripping me by the neck, but the look on his face was pure glee. Too late I realized that by using my magic on Kuntemopharn, I had all but handed it to bio Dad on a silver fucking platter.

"Thank you, dear," he said with a sharp grin. "This would've taken forever without that little push from your end. I had no idea you were so willing to help our cause."

"Fuck you," I snarled, or ... tried to snarl. I was getting the shit choked out of me so it came out as more of a strangled squeak and croak. Stupid, Ari.

"It's a shame you didn't want to cooperate, you know," Daniel mused, easing the pressure a little on my throat as I sucked greedy gasps of air into my burning lungs. As if it weren't bad enough that he was tearing my magic from my soul, did he really have to strangle me to death with his bare hands too? Seemed a bit overkill.

From the level of pain I was experiencing from my magic being forcefully stolen, I doubted I would live through the process anyway. My whole body felt as though it had been dipped in acid. Every nerve ending was screaming and crying for mercy, but none came.

"It's not too late to change your mind, you know?" Daniel offered, his eyes gleaming with greed and power. Now that he had a taste for my magic, he was doubtless thinking of how he could keep it on tap to use again and again.

"Fuck yourself," I coughed, then mustered up what little saliva I had left and spat it in his face. Seriously though, I would rather die than let him do this to me on a regular basis, and god only knew what he planned to do to the human race with all this power at his disposal.

At my response, his face twisted in a snarl of rage and his fingers tightened once more around my throat, this time cutting off my air altogether. Fantastic. I had *maybe* a minute, max, before I passed out and another three after that before I'd be dead for good. Where the hell was my guardian ghost when I needed her? Or really, what fucking use was she anyway?

From the corner of my eye I could see my guys still deeply entrenched in battles of their own. Even without Kuntemopharn, they were still outnumbered.

Desperation clawed at me and panic rose from my gut. I couldn't let this deranged fuckface kill me like this! If I died, so too would they, and they didn't deserve that. Yes, they'd tricked me into this supernatural marriage, but they didn't force me to care for them. That was happening all of its own accord, whether I thought was a good idea or not.

Seeing Grams suddenly appear over Daniel's shoulder, a rush of hope speared through me. Had she come to help? What could she do though, as a ghost? No one else could see her or hear her, and it wasn't like she could pick up a frying pan and bash this wanker's head in with it. No, I was still screwed six ways to Sunday, and this time not in a fun way.

"Hold tight, Duckie," Grams whispered, "help is coming. Just a few more moments. Breathing is overrated anyway, right?" She chuckled at her own terrible joke and I wanted to fucking kill her. Bring her back from the dead, and kill her.

I so didn't feel sorry for her dying with a hairy chin; she *deserved* eternal chin hairs.

I dug deep and tried to find that spark inside of me that would let me go elemental, fade away from the world and crawl out of the sperm donor's clutches. But I had nothing left, and yet it *still* felt like Daniel was pulling energy from me.

The boys.

Daniel was draining them *through* me, his fingers tipped with dragon's claws.

As his nails dug into my neck, spilling blood, hot and metallic down the sides of my throat, I saw his green eyes widen, almost imperceptibly. Deep down, I felt an answering twinge, like the man was plucking each one of the metaphorical strings that tied me to my men: a rush of flame for Billy, cool air against my face for Shane, the soft kiss of green things for George, warm water for Billy, an electric charge for Warden.

And something else.

Daniel plucked at this thread, teased at it with his magic, digging so deeply into me that it felt like an assault. Screams tore from my throat, escaping in low, ragged, breathy squeaks. I couldn't even *yell* properly by that point.

"Blossom!" George shouted, and I felt the tree roots around my arms loosen, flowers blooming along the stalks and bursting open in bright sprays of color. Yellow pollen sifted from them with a little help from a supernatural breeze and went straight into Daniel's face, making him scream and retract his claws, nails gouging at his own face.

I had just enough slack to pull my arms free, rolling onto my belly and then struggling up to my knees.

"I've got you," Billy said, grabbing my hand and yanking me up and into his arms, enfolding me in his embrace and blocking this terrifying wave of silver, like a tsunami made of steel, with an answering wall of flame. The silver melted and splattered across the lawn in hot, round balls, glistening and reeking like a smithy's workshop. "Stay away from her," he warned me—although it was pretty obvious I didn't want to get too close, "if she touches you, she can leach metals from your body."

Hey, I was a barista, not a chemist, but that sounded like pretty bad news to me. Drain all the iron from a person's body —they'll pass out and then die.

My eyes locked onto the silver dragon, the one I'd seen at Charlie's house, before flicking back to Daniel. We might've been powerful overall, but we were tired, and I was new at this, and Daniel had seriously drained the hell out of me. I felt like I could barely stand. Beyond that, we were *still* outnumbered.

As I watched, Shane and Reg tag teamed—and not in a sexy way—one of the other women, the one I'd seen before with the bloody lips. Watching her wield flame like she was draping streamers at a children's party, it wasn't difficult to determine her element.

On the other side of the drive, George was huddled over Warden's body. Either he'd passed out from using too much energy or else … god, if he died I'd have a regret in my heart that would fester and putrefy. I'd never live down the mistakes I'd made with him.

"Watch out!" I shouted, feeling this sudden *pull* like I was yanking energy away from the earth itself. The shimmering pink dragon, the pretty one with all the flowers, had literally launched her *tongue* at George, wrapping it around his neck and yanking him away from Warden with a sharp snapping sound that frightened me to my core.

With a wave of my hand, I sent the strangely dried and shriveled fruit trees shooting out of the ground and crashing

344

into the earth elemental's side, pinning her to the ground with a shriek that echoed around the neighborhood and made my ears ring.

Before I could think too hard about what I'd just done—I think I'd literally *stolen* the life energy from the trees—Billy was throwing me to the side and just barely saving me from getting myself railroaded by Daniel, once again back in his dragon form.

He hit the ground on the other side of me, claws scrabbling desperately on the lawn as he made a whiplike turn with the aubergine sleekness of his body and came barreling straight back. Billy tried to cut him off by shifting and throwing the flaming heat of his body between us.

A navy blue dragon that shivered and glowed, the surface of its scaly hide like stars reflecting off the dark surface of the sea, swung its tail around and connected with Billy's side, sending a rush of white steam in the air as a snarl ripped from his throat. He took off after her with the force of a semi, but it didn't matter—water trumps fire, right? As soon as they connected, he *physically* had the advantage, but I could feel his pain as if it were my own.

Reg was right there by my side as I stood in front of Warden and tried to use my powers to shift, but then I saw the stricken look on Reg's face …

"You fucking son of a bitch!" he screamed, shaking Max/Warden by the shoulders. "You shouldn't have tried to help, you stupid asshole."

Tears were streaming down his face, big fat wet tears.

And Reg … he didn't exactly seem like the type to cry over nothing.

Time seemed to slow around me as I dropped to my knees, vaguely aware that Shane had just grabbed Daniel in silver-blue claws and chucked him against the side of the boys' van, knocking the entire thing over with a screech of metal on concrete.

"Maxi Pad?" I asked, sniffling as I reached out and touched the very still side of this throat. He was alive at that point, but fading fast. I could feel him, draining out of me like the blood still leaking from my throat. Daniel had started with Warden first—and I was losing him. I was going to *lose* him. "Come on, Maxi Pad," I whispered, hoping his college nickname would bring some sort of response, enough recognition for him to fight.

"Duckie," Gram said softly, appearing near the edge of the house, looking at me like she was starting the mourning process in my stead. "Just hold on a little longer ... Help is on the way."

I ignored her.

Help was on the way? Help would come too late for Warden.

I looked up at Reg, standing up and shifting back into his dragon form, getting ready to protect me ... and the comatose body at my feet. But it wasn't me that needed protecting—it was the people around me. Sure, they were weird pseudo nymphomaniac plumbers, but ... they were my weird pseudo nymphomaniac plumbers.

I had to save them. And I had to make things right with Warden.

The runes flared on my skin as I straddled his still warm body and put my hands on either side of his face, palms pressing into his cheeks. Digging deep, I looked for energy that wasn't really there anymore, that'd been drained right out of me, and then I went down, even further into this shimmering pool that I knew was *me*. That was my essence.

Looking at it like this, I could see the small ethereal strands that led to each of the guys.

There were ... more than fucking five of them.

Good lord, there were *six*.

Taking a deep breath, I pushed back *that* particular revelation for later and wondered if, like in a plumbing situation, I could cut the pipes and seal them off somehow. Cut my energy off the from the men so that Daniel couldn't get them ... and so I could save Warden.

All around me, I heard and felt the rise and fall of energy, the smattering of blood, a scream of rage, but I pushed it all back, ignored it, made myself concentrate.

Looking more closely at the sixth string attached to my aura, I saw that it was almost ... frozen. The way my mind perceived the connection showed me a piece of glimmering twine, its end dipped into a silver pool. But part of the twine was frozen solid and none of that glowing shifting energy was sliding up its length like it was with the other men.

That was it.

That's how I'd cut them off.

Starting with Shane, I mentally took hold of our connection ... and I shut it down. Pulling energy from what little I had left (that I'd stolen from the poor honey crisp apple trees—sorry!), I slicked that silver energy up the shaft (go ahead and make your sex jokes here) and then imagined it crystallizing, shutting down, freezing.

As soon as I did, I felt that loss of connection to Shane and it fucking *killed* me. I hadn't realized how much I wanted it until it was gone ...

But as I worked my way through the other men, I could see Warden slipping away from me, his connection fading, disappearing into the dark recesses of my mind.

I finished the rest of the boys as quick as I could and then stopped, holding an image of Max in my head, his face smiling down at me as his body thrust inside, that explosive burst of feeling toward him, that *love*. Grabbing every last drop I had in my pool, I pushed all of my energy up and into Warden's connection.

My eyes snapped open and my body slumped to the side like I'd been shot, crumpling to the lawn next to Warden. I had just enough energy left to reach out and touch the side of his throat, feel the hopping beat of his pulse.

Thank god, I thought as my lids felt heavy, blood pooling around my face, staining my mouth. *He'll be okay; he'll be alright.*

"Useless fumblin' Dublin," I heard muttered over one shoulder and then a gnarled hand was coming to rest on the side of my head. "Drink up, why don't you? I owe your gram *one* favor and this is it. Last time I ever bargain with a bloody witch."

As soon as those wrinkled old fingers touched my cheek, my body reacted on instinct, sucking spiritual energy from the old faerie woman like she was an endless well, filling up that empty pool and reviving me like I'd just been stabbed with a shot of adrenaline.

With a gasp, I sat up, shaking and panting, heart thundering so loud I felt like the whole neighborhood might be able to hear it.

"Bloody redcoats," Alberta O'Sullivan scowled, spreading her thin, webbed wings out behind her. "Never much liked them lobsterbacks anyway," she continued, giving my bio dad a look. I had no idea if he were English or not, but oh well—if old Mrs. O'Sullivan wanted to be a racist prick for a second and save my life, I guess I'd take it.

Drawing a sigil in the air, she created a rune that shimmered and then floated to the ground, sealing itself there like it'd been spray painted onto the lawn. As soon as Daniel touched it, tossing Shane aside and making a bee line for me, it activated and lit the entire neighborhood up with its glow.

A violent scream exploded from the dragon's throat as dark arms of energy shot up from the rune, gnarled hands the color of oil with grasping yellow claws tore at his flesh, shredding ribbons of skin and spattering the yard with blood.

My, er, moms didn't waste a second in abandoning their other fights and rushing to his aid. I took that split second to take inventory—Shane, Billy, Reg … and George. I breathed a sigh of relief as I saw him slump against the wall, rubbing at his neck with one hand and folding his other arm across his ribs. He might be hurt, but he was alive.

I stood up, glancing back down as Warden groaned and struggled into a sitting position.

"Shit on a motherfucking sunbeam," he whispered, looking up and watching with wide hazel eyes as whatever the fuck those creatures were tore literal *hunks* of flesh from the female dragons as they tried to save their mate. Sexist prick.

It only took a few moments, but they managed to get him out, oozing puddles of blood and stinking the air up with that awful copper scent that churned my stomach. As soon as they left the radius of the rune, it closed up, sinking into the ground like it'd never been.

But the damage had been done.

They were in no shape to keep fighting.

"Fucking teabaggers," Alberta said, wiping her hands on the front of her knitted shawl and then tottering down to the end of the yard to dig through the trash cans. Huh.

"I'm sorry about the wards, Duckie," Gram said from my

right, "but bargaining with the fae, it's not a good idea … unless you get the upper hand."

Staring openmouthed at the bleeding dragons, I had to hold up a hand to keep Billy from going after them.

"Don't," I said as one of the women picked up Daniel—hey, no sexism here!—and carried him to an SUV on the opposite side of the street. They were hurt, but I was also just *barely* recovered myself. Alberta had given me a boost of energy, but it was only enough to get me up and standing, not enough to really *fight*—my connections to the guys were frozen, Warden was still sitting on the ground, George looked like he needed serious medical attention …

No, we'd have to finish this fight another day.

Just before he climbed into the back of the SUV though, Daniel looked my way, meeting my eyes from across the street … and then he smirked at me.

My heart started to pound inside my chest and I felt this … twinge, like claws plucking at a string.

I touched my palm to the base of my throat, fingers smearing in the blood, and I tried not to have a panic attack.

"You okay, ST?" Reg asked, pausing to give the dumpster-diving old faerie a *look* before turning to me.

"Define okay," I said as I looked back and saw … that Warden was gone again. That motherfucker … I turned back to the dead trees on the lawn, the uprooted mounds of earth, the blood soaked grass … "There's another one," I said, feeling like I wanted to scream and laugh and cry … okay, maybe not cry because you know, that just wasn't my thing. "There's another one of us—a metal elemental."

The other boys slowly made their way over to me, the only sounds on the street their labored breathing and the clatter of Alberta digging through old tin cans and liquor bottles.

"Honeycomb?" Shane asked, looking a little green around the gills. Guess he wasn't so much into getting another husband either. I could barely even fathom Warden's existence let alone some mystery dude.

"There's another guy out there," I said, suddenly so scared for him that I couldn't breathe. I didn't know him, but I knew they'd be after him—bio dad and his polygamist cult, the incubi and succubi, and whoever else was planning on participating in this stupid war of his. "And Daniel's going after him."

"I might have an idea," I heard a voice say from behind me, whipping around to find Siobhan standing there with her orange curls in disarray, makeup smeared, holding an overnight bag in one hand and a pair of high heels in the other. The expression on her face said it all—something bad had happened to her, something that must be connected to me or else she wouldn't be standing here in upstate New York (she considered the countryside a useless waste of space unless it involved growing organic shit for her to buy at expensive NYC restaurants).

"Siobhan?" I asked, blinking away my surprise and trying not to hyperventilate from the sudden rush of adrenaline. She smiled at me and I could see that her white teeth were smeared with blood.

"I think I might know where Daniel's going," she said, and then the heels fell from her hand and she collapsed on the sidewalk—right next to the faerie digging through the trash.

My name is Arizona Smoke, wine aficionado, ex-barista, and wife to four … five … six supernatural plumbers.

I just can't decide if I'm lucky … or completely out of my fucking element.

Maybe a little bit of both.

COMING SOON!
HIJINKS HAREM BOOK #2

Arizona Smoke, supernatural badass, and wife to ... six husbands?!

ELEMENTS OF

RUIN

HIJINKS HAREM BOOK TWO

TATE JAMES
&
C.M. STUNICH

ELEMENTS OF RUIN

THE VIXEN'S LEAD

TATE JAMES

Flip the page for an excerpt of chapter one.

1

CHAPTER ONE

In the background, the shadowy outline of a naked woman haunted a painting of lilies. The rich imagery held me captive. Reportedly the work was worth a few hundred thousand dollars, but I couldn't decide if it was because of the image or the person who painted it. Maybe both. Whatever the reason, the Beverly Hills gallery had it on its walls, which meant it was without a doubt expensive.

"Nine minutes and thirty-four seconds until security systems are back online. Stop gawking at the paintings and hurry the fuck up!"

How the hell had Lucy known what I was doing? Our comms were audio only. Still, Lucy had a point. I left the painting and crept down the corridor on silent feet. At the end a large, open room held several ostentatious pieces of jewelry displayed in glass cases on pedestals. They were part of a colored diamond showcase in which the wealthy allowed their prized possessions to be displayed for the common folk to drool over. It was a clear night, and the full moon streamed light through the windows. The moonlight refracted against the jewels and created a rainbow of Christmas lights in the darkness.

Pausing at the entrance to the room, I fished my phone out of the pocket in my black jeans and ran an application labeled "You Never Know," which Lucy had designed to scan areas for hidden security features we might have missed in our mission planning. It took a minute to fully probe the room, and while waiting, I snaked a finger under the short, black wig I wore and scratched at my scalp. Using a disguise was just sensible thieving, but seriously, wigs itched something awful! Maybe next time I would try a hat. The image of myself pulling a job while wearing a top hat or a Stetson made me chuckle.

Seconds later, my screen flashed red with an alert and surprised the hell out of me. It was the first time the app had actually caught something.

"Are you seeing this?" It was a pointless question. She had a mirror image on her computer screen.

"Huh. That definitely wasn't there a week ago when I did a walk through," she muttered, and her furious tapping at her keyboard echoed over the comms. "Okay, it's a laser beam grid linked to a silent alarm that will trigger the security shutters on all external access points. I don't have time to hack into it and shut it down, so..."

I could picture her shrug and sighed. "So, don't trip the lasers, yes? Got it. Send me the map." An intricate web of red lines appeared on my phone, overlaying the camera's view of the room. If I watched the screen and not my feet, it would be possible to avoid the beams.

Conscious of the ticking clock, I carefully started stepping across the floor. All seemed to go well until I got within ten feet of my intended loot. Suddenly my nose started twitching with a sneeze. "Dammit," I hissed, then fought to hold my breath.

358

"What's going on in there, Kit?" Lucy asked, worry tight in her tone.

I wriggled my nose a few times to shake off the itch before replying, "You know how I often get pretty awesome hay fever in Autumn...?"

Lucy groaned like I was doing this to deliberately test her nerves, but I wasn't trying to tease her. I might actually sneeze.

"I think it's gone," I said, relaxing minutely, and raised my foot for the next step. Of course, Murphy's Law prevailed, and the second I shifted my weight, the urge to sneeze returned full force. I clamped my mouth and nose shut, but I lost my balance even as I tried to swallow my sneeze. My leg rocked into one of the laser beams.

"Shit!"

"Fucking hell, Kit! You have thirty seconds until you are trapped. Get the hell out, now!" Lucy yelled in my earpiece.

Already screwed, I lunged the remaining distance to the display case. The current tenant was a ring with an obnoxiously large, canary yellow diamond surrounded by smaller chartreuse colored diamonds, all inset in a band with pink sapphires. The overall effect was a bit sickening, but who was I to tell the wealthy how bad their tastes were? I often wondered how many of them deliberately wasted their money on tasteless items with obscene price tags simply because they could.

Aware of the ticking clock, I whipped my arm back and smashed my gloved fist straight through the toughened glass. It shattered under the force I exerted. After snatching up the ugly bauble, I dropped a little plastic fox—my signature calling card —in its place.

"Kit, quit dicking around and get out!" Lucy screeched over the line at me. "Twenty-two seconds remaining, don't you dare get caught, or I swear to God I won't let you live this down!"

Satisfied at having grabbed my target, I raced out of the room and down the corridor, not hesitating before crashing straight through a tall picture window and plummeting thirty-odd feet onto the rooftop of the next building. I tried to break my fall by rolling as I hit. Instead, landed awkwardly on my left shoulder. It popped out of its socket. Hissing with pain, I glanced up at the gallery just in time to see the steel shutters slam closed on all the windows simultaneously.

"Kit," Lucy snapped, barely masking the tension in her voice. "Give me an update; are you clear?"

The evil little devil on my shoulder wanted me to mess with her, but my conscience prevailed. "All clear," I said, then added with a laugh. "Plenty of time to spare; not sure why you were so worried!"

"Any injuries?" A growl underscored her words.

"Nope, I'm totally fine. I mean, if you don't include my shoulder, which is for sure dislocated, then all I have are a few scratches from the glass and a tiny bit of swelling in my knuckles. I got the God-awful ring, though!" I was rather proud of completing the job we had come there for.

"That was too close this time, Kit," Lucy admonished me. "You're bloody lucky you heal so fast, but it's still going to hurt like a bitch getting that shoulder back into place. Get sorted then drop the ring to the courier, and call me if anything goes wrong. Otherwise, I'll see you when you get back. Stay out of trouble."

My best friend occasionally cursed like an Australian ever since she developed a Heath Ledger movie crush. "You know, most people would say 'good luck.' You say, 'stay out of trouble.' Should I be offended?" Teasing her was fun, even if my track record wasn't the cleanest. In my defense, I always got myself out of trouble without too much hassle. Lucy didn't dignify me with a verbal response and left the dial tone as she hung up to serve as her answer.

Tucking my earpiece into a zippered pocket of my leather jacket, I headed over to the A/C unit on the far side of the roof. Using it to leverage my shoulder back into place, I kept my cursing to a minimum. It slid back in with a sickening pop, and the relief had me wavering on my feet. After catching my breath, I brushed some glass out of my wig then swung over the fire escape and descended to the street below. Stripping off my gloves, I blended into the crowd. Even though it was autumn, it was still nowhere near cold enough to be wearing gloves unless committing a crime. I nervously checked the time on my watch. I had a very long drive ahead of me to get back to school and still needed to drop the stolen ring off with our middleman.

SPIRITED

C. M. STUNICH

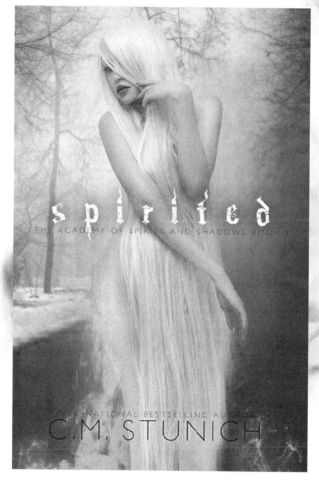

Flip the page for an excerpt of chapter one.

1

BRYNN

The instrument of my own destruction loomed above me, casting a long shadow in the bloodred rays of a dying sun. Its crumbling facade was decorated with a morbid metaphor of a face—soulless eyes, a gaping mouth, tangled green locks. Okay, so I was exaggerating the broken windows, the front entrance with its missing doors, and the cluster of wild blackberries that had morphed into a monster of their own making, but come on: the former Grandberg Manor was bust.

"This is the place?" I asked, hoisting my equipment up on one shoulder and eyeing the crumbling old house with a raised brow. "It looks half-ready to collapse. You know me—if there's an even the slightest opportunity that I might trip, I will. Just be honest: am I going to fall straight through the floor?"

"Probably," Jasinda said, moving around me and over the twisted, rusted remains of the front gate. Once upon a time, this place was crawling with nobility from around the world, and its gardens ... even the drawings were enough to make my mother's green thumb well, green with envy. "Air and I have a bet going on whether or not you'll make it out of here alive."

She thew a smirk over her shoulder at me and I pursed my lips.

Jasinda and Air were always making bets about me despite the fact that Air was the flubbing prince and shouldn't be making bets with anyone, let alone my handler. I had to admit though: if there was anyone around that was worth betting on, it was me.

First off, I was a half-angel which meant I could see spirits. And second, I was a half-human which meant those spirits actually deigned to communicate with me. A full-blooded angel was too haughty and highbrow to give any ghost the time of day, and a full-blooded human couldn't see one if they tried.

This special ability of mine did end up getting me into heaps of trouble. For example, there was that one time I followed a ghost straight into the queen's chambers and found her, um, indisposed with the head of the royal guard who, you know, also just happened to be my mother.

Then of course, there was the fact that I had the small, slight frame of my mother's desert dwelling ancestors but the wide, heavy span of wings from my father's side. Let's just be frank and say I toppled over a lot. Oh, and I ended up having long, in-depth conversations with people who weren't really people but were, in fact, very tricky ghosts. Even my first kiss had been with a spirit.

I took a deep breath of the cool, lavender scented air and followed after Jas, tripping and cursing in my own made up language.

"Go flub yourself," I growled at a thick tangle of blackberry that had gotten wrapped around my ankle. "You bleeding blatherer."

"Are you making words up again?" Jas said, parking her hands on her hips and sighing at me. "Can't you just say you bleeding bastard like everyone else? And don't even get me started on you using the work flub instead of fuc—"

"Hey!" I snapped, putting my palm over her lips with one hand and pointing at myself with the other. "Half-angel over here. Just hearing somebody use a word with an extreme negative connotation makes me lose a feather."

"Oh, please," Jas said, pushing my hand away from her full red lips and smirking at me as I tried to rub her makeup off on my breeches. "That's a myth and you know it. Air told me that when you were kids, he used to chase you around the castle saying damn and bastard and the like, just to see if you'd lose any feathers—you didn't."

I narrowed my eyes on her as she turned and headed up what was once an impressive flight of marble steps, now cracked and chipped like an old beggar's teeth. I shivered and followed after her, examining the red stain on my palm that stunk like copperberries. A lot of women painted their mouths with the stuff, but to me that fragrant floral scent was tinged with a metallic sting, like copper. Like blood. Thus, the name—copperberries.

As I hurried up the steps, I kept my eyes on the decaying black facade of the manor, all its intricate moldings and details stripped away by time and rain, the harsh winds that curled across this part of the kingdom in summer.

"Let's do a quick walkthrough and see if you can't sense any residual energies," Jas suggested as I set my black leather satchel on the floor and knelt beside it. The ground around me was littered with debris—leaves, twigs, bits of crumbling plaster, a dead mouse.

"Oh, that's flubbing sick," I whispered as I caught sight of the creature's spirit hovering nearby, its furred sides almost completely translucent as it took long, heaving breaths. Of course, the mouse didn't need to breathe anymore, but it didn't know that.

I pulled a dagger from the sheath on my belt—please Goddess, don't actually ask me to use this thing in combat—and prodded at the mouse's body with the jeweled hilt.

Fresh blood stained the white leather pommel and made me shiver.

"Jas," I started, because a long dead carcass was one thing, but a fresh one? Hell's bells—since Hell was an actual place it didn't count as a curse word so no lost feathers for me—but I hoped it was just a cat that had taken the rodent's life and not … something else.

"Brynn, you need to see this!" Jas shouted and I sighed, wiping the mouse's blood on the already dirty leg of my breeches and tucking it away. Before I stood up, I clasped the silver star hanging around my neck with one hand and reached out to touch the mouse's spirt with the other. The poor thing was too scared to even shy away, its soul becoming briefly corporeal as my fingers made contact with its fur.

"Goddess-speed and happy endings," I whispered as the image of the mouse morphed and shivered, turning as silver as a beam of moonlight and fading away until there was nothing there but the warped and rotted boards of the old floor.

I stood up, leaving my satchel where it was on the ground and rubbing my shoulder as I followed the sound of Jasinda's voice. The road up to the manor was riddled with broken cobblestones, weeds, and the skeletons of long abandoned carriages. It was too rough for any sort of pack animal to make the trek, so we'd had to carry ourselves on foot, lugging all the equipment that a spirit whisperer—that's me—might need to exorcise a ghost or two or ten.

"Jassy?" I asked as I moved past the formal foyer with its

double staircases, and down a long receiving hall that would've been used by servants in times past. The wallpaper was peeling like old skin, leaving behind water stained walls and flaky plaster. At some point, thieves had come in and stripped the old place of its wood moldings, sconces and chandeliers; they'd left nothing but a skeleton behind.

"In here!" she called out, drawing me through an empty archway where a swinging door might've once stood and into the kitchen. As I moved, I was conscious of keeping my wings tucked tightly against my back. My clumsiness was not limited to my feet. I was notorious among the castle staff for breaking things with the feathered black wings that graced my back. As a kid, they used to call me Pigeon Girl because I caused ten times as much damage to the royal halls as the flying rats that plagued the old stone building.

"What is it?" I asked as I leaned against the wall outside a small servant's room—a tiny square that would've belonged to the head cook. "Jas, there was a mouse—"

"Flub mice," she said, only she didn't actually say flub but I wouldn't lose a feather even thinking about the F-word that famously rhymes with duck. As a half-angel, my powers were bound to the light goddess and she was a serious stickler for avoiding words with negative connotations. I supposed I couldn't blame her; the very words I spoke held power. The more positivity and light I imbued those words with, the more powerful I was. "Look at this, Brynn. There's a distinct spiritual signature written all over this room."

The room itself was so small that with the collapsed remains of a small bed and a sagging dresser, there wasn't space for us both. I waited for Jas to step out, pushing her long dark hair over her shoulder, sapphire blue eyes sparkling with a scholar's excitement.

HIJINKS HAREM

"Brynn, this could be it," she said as I took a deep breath and stepped into the room. "Our big break."

Jas was always looking for that one case, that one unique spirit that we could exorcise that would prove our worth to the scholars at the Royal College. In just two weeks, I'd be turning twenty-one and that'd be it; that was the cut off date for acceptance into the prestigious training facility. It wasn't that Jas cared about the status of being a student there, or the potential for a high-ranking position after graduation, it was the library. Only students of the Royal College were permitted to use the vast, twisting hallways of the catacombs. There were books there that couldn't be found anywhere else—not to mention ancient artifacts, exemplary professors, and vast resources that could be used for research.

It was Jasinda's dream, even if it wasn't mine. I hoped she was right; I hoped this was it.

I stepped over a small hole in the floor and into the tiny windowless room.

As soon as I did, it hit me, the pressure of an angry spirit, bearing down on me with the cold burn of something long dead and waiting. Waves of icy winter chill tore across my skin like knives, despite the warm evening air that permeated the rest of the building. Whatever this was, it was powerful.

I grasped the silver star at my throat and closed my eyes.

"Haversey," I whispered, invoking the name of the light goddess.

If I were Jas, I knew what I'd be seeing: a girl shrouded in silver moonlight, her tanned skin pearlescent and shimmering, her hair as white as snow lifted in an unnatural breeze.

I opened my eyes slowly and bit back a gasp.

Every inch of the walls was covered in the word Hellim, the name of the dark god. What I had originally thought were decorative splotches on the wallpaper were actually his name, written in blood a thousand times over. It had been impossible to see in the dim half-light, but now that I had my second sight open, the letters glowed with a strong, angry spiritual signature.

I started to take a step back when my foot went through the hole in the floor, and the rotting boards around me creaked and toppled into a black pit below.

"Brynn!"

Jas screamed my name as I fell through cold shadow and frost, hitting the soggy wet earth with a grunt and a crack of pain in my shoulder that almost immediately went numb. That was bad, really bad. Pain was one thing, but numbness meant that what'd just happened to me could be really serious.

I tried to stand up, but my arm gave out and I found myself lying in a mound of decaying wet leaves and dirt, the scent of rot thick and cloying in the air.

As I blinked to try and orient myself to the darkness, I felt a cold hand on my shoulder and a gust of icy breath at my ear.

When I turned, I found myself looking into the face of a handsome—and very angry—spirit.

His lips curved up in a smile meant to disarm me.

"Boo," he whispered as he reached out and pushed my dislocated shoulder back into place.

White-hot pain crashed over my vision and I passed out.

SIGN UP FOR A
TATE JAMES *or* C.M. STUNICH

NEWSLETTER

Sign up for an exclusive first look at
the hottest new releases, contests,
and exclusives from the authors.

www.cmstunich.com
www.tatejamesauthor.com

SIGN UP FOR A
TATE JAMES *or* C.M. STUNICH

DISCUSSION
GROUP

Want to discuss what you've just read?
Get exclusive teasers or meet special guest authors?
Join C.M.'s and Tate's online book clubs on Facebook!

www.facebook.com/groups/thebookishbatcave
www.facebook.com/groups/tatejames.thefoxhole

BOOKS BY

C. M. STUNICH

Romance

HARD ROCK ROOTS SERIES
Real Ugly
Get Bent
Tough Luck
Bad Day
Born Wrong
Hard Rock Roots Box Set (1-5)
Dead Serious
Doll Face
Heart Broke
Get Hitched
Screw Up

TASTING NEVER SERIES
Tasting Never
Finding Never
Keeping Never
Tasting, Finding, Keeping: The Story of Never Box Set (1-3)
Never Can Tell
Never Let Go
Never Did Say
Never Have I

ROCK-HARD BEAUTIFUL
Groupie
Roadie
Moxie

THE BAD NANNY TRILOGY
Bad Nanny
Good Boyfriend
Great Husband

TRIPLE M SERIES
Losing Me, Finding You
Loving Me, Trusting You
Needing Me, Wanting You
Craving Me, Desiring You

A DUET
Paint Me Beautiful
Color Me Pretty

FIVE FORGOTTEN SOULS
Beautiful Survivors
Alluring Outcasts

MAFIA QUEEN
Lure
Lavish
Luxe

DEATH BY DAYBREAK MC
I Was Born Ruined

STAND-ALONE NOVELS
Blizzards and Bastards(originally featured in the Snow and Seduction Anthology)
Fuck Valentine's Day (A Short Story)
Broken Pasts
Crushing Summer
Taboo Unchained
Taming Her Boss
Kicked

Violet Blaze Novels

(My Pen Name)

BAD BOYS MC TRILOGY
Raw and Dirty
Risky and Wild
Savage and Racy

HERS TO KEEP TRILOGY
Biker Rockstar Billionaire CEO Alpha
Biker Rockstar Billionaire CEO Dom
Biker Rockstar Billionaire CEO Boss

STAND-ALONE
Football Dick
Stepbrother Thief
Stepbrother Inked
Glacier

BOOKS BY

C.M. STUNICH

Fantasy Novels

THE SEVEN MATES OF ZARA WOLF
Pack Ebon Red
Pack Violet Shadow
Pack Obsidian Gold
Pack Ivory Emerald
Pack Amber Ash
Pack Azure Frost
Pack Crimson Dusk

SIRENS OF A SINFUL SEA TRILOGY
Under the Wild Waves

THE SEVEN WICKED SERIES
Seven Wicked Creatures
Six Wicked Beasts
Five Wicked Monsters
Four Wicked Fiends

HOWLING HOLIDAYS SHORT STORIES
A Werewolf Christmas
A Werewolf New Year's
A Werewolf Valentine's
A Werewolf St. Patrick's Day
A Werewolf Spring Break
A Werewolf Mother's Day

ACADEMY OF SPIRITS AND SHADOWS
Spirited

OTHER FANTASY NOVELS
Gray and Graves
Indigo & Iris
She Lies Twisted
Hell Inc.
DeadBorn
Chryer's Crest

Co-Written
(With Tate James)

HIJINKS HAREM
Elements of Mischief
Elements of Ruin
Elements of Desire

THE WILD HUNT MOTORCYCLE CLUB
Dark Glitter

FOXFIRE BURNING
The Nine

BOOKS BY
TATE JAMES

Fantasy Novels

KIT DAVENPORT NOVELS
The Vixen's Lead
The Dragon's Wing
The Tiger's Ambush
The Viper's Nest
The Crow's Murder
The Alpha's Pack

Romance

STAND-ALONE
Slopes of Sin (originally featured
in the Snow and Seduction Anthology)

Co-Written

(With C.M. Stunich)

HIJINKS HAREM
Elements of Mischief
Elements of Ruin
Elements of Desire

THE WILD HUNT MOTORCYCLE CLUB
Dark Glitter

FOXFIRE BURNING
The Nine

STALKING

LINKS

KEEP UP WITH ALL
THE FUN ... AND EARN SOME FREE BOOKS!

TATE JAMES

Join my group! - www.facebook.com/groups/tatejames.thefoxhole.

Like my page! - www.facebook.com/tatejamesfans

Be my friend? - www.facebook.com/tatejamesauthor

Instagram me! - Instagram.com/tatejamesauthor

Tweet me! - twitter.com/tatejamesauthor

Sign up for my newsletter that I may or may not ever send! -
www.tatejamesauthor.com

Pin me! Or ya know ... whatever the correct term is for Pinterest: -
pinterest.com/tatejamesauthor

C.M. STUNICH

JOIN THE C.M. STUNICH NEWSLETTER – Get three free books just for signing up
http://eepurl.com/DEsEf

TWEET ME ON TWITTER, BABE – Come sing the social media song with me
https://twitter.com/CMStunich

SNAPCHAT WITH ME – Get exclusive behind the scenes looks at covers, blurbs, book signings
and more http://www.snapchat.com/add/cmstunich

LISTEN TO MY BOOK PLAYLISTS – Share your fave music with me and I'll give you my
playlists (I'm super active on here!) https://open.spotify.com/user/12101321503

FRIEND ME ON FACEBOOK – Okay, I'm actually at the 5,000 friend limit, but if you click the
"follow" button on my profile page, you'll see way more of my killer posts
https://facebook.com/cmstunich

LIKE ME ON FACEBOOK – Pretty please? I'll love you forever if you do! ;)
https://facebook.com/cmstunichauthor & https://facebook.com/violetblazeauthor

CHECK OUT THE NEW SITE – (under construction) but it looks kick-a$$ so far, right? You can
order signed books here! http://www.cmstunich.com

READ VIOLET BLAZE – Read the books from my hot as hellfire pen name, Violet Blaze
http://www.violetblazebooks.com

SUBSCRIBE TO MY RSS FEED – Press that little orange button in the corner and copy that RSS
feed so you can get all the latest updates http://www.cmstunich.com/blog

AMAZON, BABY – If you click the follow button here, you'll get an email each time I put out a
new book. Pretty sweet, huh? http://amazon.com/author/cmstunich
http://amazon.com/author/violetblaze

PINTEREST – Lots of hot half-naked men. Oh, and half-naked men. Plus, tattooed guys holding
babies (who are half-naked) http://pinterest.com/cmstunich

INSTAGRAM – Cute cat pictures. And half-naked guys. Yep, that again.
http://instagram.com/cmstunich

P.S. We heart the f*ck out of you! Thanks for reading! I love your faces.

<3 C.M. Stunich aka Violet Blaze & Tate James

ABOUT TATE JAMES

Oh, hello there! I see you would like to know more about me... Well here goes:

My illustrious literary career began in high school, with an epic tale about a kick ass heroine and her swoon worthy boyfriends, but was put on ice for a number of years while adult life happened. I moved across the ditch from my native New Zealand and met my now husband, we had a fur baby and then a real baby, we opened two bars and a restaurant, and then life came full circle and by a series of unfortunate events I uncovered a 'book' I had written as a fourteen year old. It was... atrocious. But it inspired me to begin again! And do it better this time... or at least I hope so...

With the skeptical support of my darling husband, our cherubic baby and a possessed cat, Kit Davenport came to life.

For more rambling, contact me directly!

Peace, love and mung beans.

Tate x

ABOUT C.M. STUNICH

C.M. Stunich is a self-admitted bibliophile with a love for exotic teas and a whole host of characters who live full time inside the strange, swirling vortex of her thoughts. Some folks might call this crazy, but Caitlin Morgan doesn't mind – especially considering she has to write biographies in the third person. Oh, and half the host of characters in her head are searing hot bad boys with dirty mouths and skillful hands (among other things). If being crazy means hanging out with them everyday, C.M. has decided to have herself committed.

She hates tapioca pudding, loves to binge on cheesy horror movies, and is a slave to many cats. When she's not vacuuming fur off of her couch, C.M. can be found with her nose buried in a book or her eyes glued to a computer screen. She's the author of over thirty novels – romance, new adult, fantasy, and young adult included. Please, come and join her inside her crazy. There's a heck of a lot to do there.

Oh, and Caitlin loves to chat (incessantly), so feel free to e-mail her, send her a Facebook message, or put up smoke signals. She's already looking forward to it.

44862803R00241

Made in the USA
Lexington, KY
12 July 2019